FLESH AND FRAUD

THE LIES WE TELL OURSELVES

David J. Brown

Published by David J. Brown Books, LLC

#2

Reader Praise and Reviews of

Flesh of a Fraud

"Brilliantly Masterful!"

David Brown, if I could compare your book to any other I'd compare your book to 'Angela's Ashes,' a comparison of high acclaim. Angela's Ashes is a memoir by Frank McCourt published in 1996 and won the Pulitzer Prize in 1997.

Ryan Logan New York State

"Beautiful heart, total class!"

This author has donated both of his books to the 'National Library Service for the Blind and Physically Handicapped.' People can listen to his book for free. Bless your heart David Brown!

Anonymous Duluth, Minnesota

"You did it again!"

Mr. Brown, you said you write to "Stir the soul, not with a mixing spoon but with a canoe paddle." You did that Sir, you most certainly did!

Kevin and Beverly Newton Joshua Tree, California

"Fourth wall down!"

David's skills are wickedly superior to most any author of the past or present. He didn't simply break the 'fourth wall,' he demolished it! The author brushes against his character's shoulders like a downhill ski racer.

Madeline Morehouse   California

Author of: "Code: 10-71 Victim to Victor"

"Rogue Genius!"

This author does not follow the rules of writing, he makes them!

He exposes the lies we tell ourselves and how we allow our fears to defeat us and kill our dreams. This is nourishment for the soul.

Deloris Getty   Kentwood Michigan

"Read this before you give up!"

The lessons of giving validation and receiving the same in-kind is life changing for me. There is never a time to give up but there is always time to restart. Thank you Mr. Brown for your amazing gifts.

Jacqueline Bjork   Pahrump Nevada

"Lessons in living."

This book as well as his last book, belong in every high school, college and public library in the country.

Bonnie Cannon   Director at Fraternal Order of Police Auxiliary DC Lodge #1, Washington DC Legislative Correspondent

"Soulfully honest, emotionally transparent."

Nothing is more attractive than a man who openly speaks of his own truths. This author is the sexiest man alive!

Gail Phillips   Retired Teacher

"Absolutely loved it!"

I have great respect and admiration for this writer.

Adam England   EMT shift supervisor, Marion County Kentucky

"Truthfully powerful!"

Most truthful and powerful book I have ever read, besides my 'Blue Book' and my Bible!

Penny O'Briant   Artist/Photographer Longmont Colorado

"Wisdom for the ages."

If you can't find life's answers in this book than you want to remain broken. This book set me free. Free to live, free to love, free to laugh.

I adore this author, he speaks to my heart.

Lisa McElveen Ramsing Firefighter/EMT

PUBLISHERS NOTE

'Flesh of a Fraud' is a companion novel to 'Daddy Had to Say Goodbye.'

It is suggested by the author that the reader first read 'Daddy Had to Say Goodbye.'

This story is a work of fiction. It is inspired, in part, by true life events. In certain cases, locations, incidents, characters and timelines have been changed for dramatic purposes. Certain characters may be composites, or entirely fictitious.

This book and Mr. Brown's other book, 'Daddy Had to Say Goodbye' are available in audio book, free of charge through, "The United States Library of Congress National Library Service for the Blind and Physically Handicapped."

FLESH OF A FRAUD
The Lies We Tell Ourselves

A novel by David J. Brown

Copyright © 2019

DJBROWNBOOKS LLC

www.davidjbrownbooks.com

Duluth Minnesota

A special thank you to my website and book design artist:

Angie Simonson of Main Idea Creative Marketing and Design

www.maincreativeidea.com

This novel is a companion book to the novel:

'DADDY HAD TO SAY GOODBYE' by David J. Brown

INTRODUCTION

The word fraud has several definitions. The most agreed definition has to do with wrongful or criminal deception intended to result in financial or personal gain. Another definition is the intentional concealment, omission or perversion of the truth. The word impostor is also sprinkled in several definitions of the word fraud.

You only know what I tell you of me. I am a fraud, I am an impostor. I pretend to be in love with life, yet each morning I awaken, I quietly ask myself, "Is this the day? Is this the day that I finally decide that the pain of living is far worse than the pain of dying?"

Seven years ago, I told only a few people that I was going to write a book and word got out quickly. Most all scoffed, some openly laughed. They would grin as they asked, "Hey, how you doing with that book you're writing?"

I too, had serious doubts of my ever finishing, let alone wanting to live long enough to having it published. I am a total nobody, no college, no writing classes. Just a desire, a dream and a promise to God.

In loving memory of my lifelong friend and cousin
ROLENE EHLENBACH ROGERS

Never let anyone tell you that you can't do it.
Never tell yourself that you can't do it.

Dreams are worth Dreaming
Dare to Dream
AND
Dream BIG My Friends!

DEDICATED TO:

Heather, the love of my life.

You believed in me during those times

I could not find the strength to believe in myself.

WITH SPECIAL THANKS TO:

Sean Carrigan & Tina Carrigan

My friends who have always been my family.

Within all fiction, lies a bit of the truth.

Within all truth, lies a bit of fiction.

Our perceptions are the deciding factors.

David J. Brown

CHAPTER 1   DATELINE: DULUTH MINNESOTA

If you have read my first novel, "Daddy Had to Say Goodbye," you are intimately familiar with the character Heather. As with all the characters of that book, Heather is a real person. I returned to Duluth (my Hometown) in June of 2016 to spend the rest of my life with my forbidden love, Heather. My friends in Colorado asked me before I left, why Minnesota and why Duluth of all places, isn't that the coldest part of the state? My answer to my Colorado pals was, "Yes damn cold. Weeks on end of low hanging oppressive clouds, bitter flesh biting cold. Snow up to a giraffe's ass and it takes five minutes of suiting up just to go outside for a cigarette for a mind numbing two minute smoke break, before your nose hair shatters and falls to the ground with 60° below zero wind-chill. You also get to lose 18 to 20 pounds| from shoveling snow if your heart doesn't blow out of your chest from the exertion. Your jacket sleeves and gloves glisten from wiping snot from your constantly running nose. If you've had your Bic lighter in your outside jacket pocket, you have to jump start it to have a smoke. Now that I have established the many benefits of living in tropical northern Minnesota, my true answer is; I'm going

1

for the love of a good woman."

I had made some good friendships in Duluth, with my neighbors and the folks of AA meetings, through my last two brief attempts to live in Duluth.

The Duluth people ask me why I have returned, my answer is, "It never quite gets cold enough in Colorado, but mostly for the love of a good woman and you darling folks!"

Duluth has always been a depressing place for me. It is a beautiful city, tourists come from all over the world to visit the area. My childhood and young adult year's memories won't allow me to enjoy what is directly in front of me. There are a few bright spots in each week. It seems that life begins each day when Heather brings Taylor, our most senior of our Papillion's and puts him on the bed to wake up daddy and her with a fresh cup of coffee. Taylor will put his nose just inches from my sleeping face and stare at me. Heather will pat me until I stir. The moment I open my eyes, Taylor goes in and gives his daddy a facial with doggy kisses. Taylor lays down and snuggles into me as I drink coffee and talk with Heather. Out of bed and it's time to visit the other 3 kids (Papillion's) and dish out copious amounts of pets and kisses. When Heather leaves for work, I feed the kids and put them in their kennels with a Charlie Bear and a kiss for each. That is when my world stops, until the kids tell me it's 11:40 am and it's time to get up and that mom will be home soon for lunch and they have to go out and do their business. Heather comes home to spend some time playing with the kids and then she goes back to work. I put the kids back in the kennel with a Charlie Bear and kisses and once again I'm left with my own thoughts and loneliness. At 4:15 I wake the kids for outside business and we have kisses, several pets and play fetch until the garage door opens and the kids go nuts and run for the top of the stairs to greet Mom with barks of joy. It's play and snuggle time until bedtime at 10:00 pm, other than that I've been pretty much a recluse.

2

I don't drive about or walk the city to enjoy its beauty and the many open air, free events during the summer. I sit on the deck on nice days and look down on the bay of Lake Superior and I just let my mind wander as I write my next book in my mind. I take only a few notes and lock paragraphs and chapters into my mind until I'm ready to put it all down on paper. I sit up each night until 2:00 am and just write in my head with the TV on for company. It is hard to pick up a pen and commit to finishing my new book 'Flesh of a Fraud' as sales of 'Daddy Had to Say Goodbye' (my 1st novel) are poor. I will probably never break even with the costs of publishing and book signing tours. I was told by a well-known and well-thought-of newspaper editor from the West Coast that I was the Boogeyman for adults. "You're writing makes people cry and at some point, we come to the realization that we are crying for ourselves!"

The people who have read it love it, but I had to give away more than 700 books to get them in the hands of the people that I wrote the book for. The book has never been about profit or fame, it's always been about helping people with similar lives as mine. To help them to heal and save the lives of those who suffer with depression, alcoholism and PTSD. I can only hope that I can someday reach those goals.

There have been some, 'saving grace' events each week that pull me out of myself. I go to enjoy my pals from drunks-R-us, every Monday night in Piedmont Heights and we do lunch at Bridgman's on Fridays. Bridgman's is a long time ice cream, dairy store and restaurant.

The fellowship is very enjoyable, they are all great guys. One of the fellows owns an 18 1/2 ft. boat that we go out on Lake Superior to fish when the winds are light. There are always three of us on board and we tell stories of back in the day, swill volumes of coffee from our thermoses and we unmercifully tease the shit out of each other, as we troll for lake trout and salmon. We will

3

usually catch a few on each trip but it is the camaraderie that makes the trip so enjoyable. I breakfast on most Saturday mornings with my lifelong pal, Bob Boynton who is the character 'Toby' in my first novel, "Daddy Had to Say Goodbye." Bobby is retired and is a crazy assed sailboat racer, he knows damn near everyone in this city of 68,000 people. Bobby is a somewhat junior historian and tells me of the many changes in the city and its people since my 40 year absence. We meet at Mike's Western Cafe which is located in a small part of the old Western Tavern which was once my Dad's daily watering hole. It's the place I wanted to tear apart after my brother died several years ago. Each time I walk in there, I look at the floor tiles and tell myself, "I am making new, good memories of a tragic and ugly past, in the very same place that stole my dad away from me so many years ago."

The best and most enjoyable event of each week was when I got to sit with my cousin Rolene Rogers. Rolene and I were pals at a very young age when she was only knee-high to a short duck. Her parents were usually at odds with each other and my Uncle would bring Rolene to stay with us for a few days until things settle down in the marriage.

I was even Rolene's very first official date! She was running for "Duluth Heights Winter Carnival Queen. "She was 13 years old and hated those "Stupid ole' icky boys." So my Aunt asked me to take her to the, "Snow Ball."

I was such a loving entrusted cousin to her, that one day she called when she was 14 years old and asked me to come to her house so I could teach her how to smoke cigarettes. I was honored!

Her mom was home when I got there so we walked back into the wooded lot behind the house. Rolene told me that she had been practicing in the mirror in her bedroom as how to hold a cigarette and look cool doing it. She used a small golf course like pencil to practice with. I did my best not to laugh but I failed miserably. I smoked camel non-filter cigarettes and the moment she put the cigarette into her mouth she was spitting loose tobacco and trying to pluck tobacco from her tongue. She had to put the cigarette out as she was choking and spitting from the tobacco smoke. She insisted that she have another one immediately, as with the first cigarette she had the end of the non-filter cigarette sopping wet like an infant's pacifier.

I had to step up alongside of her as she was getting dizzy and turning a bit green around the gills. She again demanded another cigarette and as she lit it, she started to stagger and then threw up, between coughs and gasps. She kept puffing as I helped her walk back to her house. She said she really enjoyed her first time smoking. I opened the side door of their home as she stepped in, I gave her a light shove and I ran like a rabbit. Sadly, I spoke of these two events while I was doing her eulogy last year.

Rolene and I lost track of each other over the years. When I came back to Duluth to visit my family, I would look her up and we would catch up over drinks and dinner. I hadn't seen her for three years when I came back home to attend my Mother's funeral in 2011. Rolene was at my Moms funeral. I was shocked to see her using a wheeled walker and she did not look well. I asked her what happened and she told me that she had a stroke and lost most of her hearing and vision and had trouble with balance and walking. I am three years older than her but she looked like she had ten years on me. Rolene was always on the go with a high level of energy. It was very sad to see her in that condition. The bright side of it all was that she was married to a very nice fellow that was tending to her comfort and needs.

A month after I returned to Colorado from my Moms funeral, Rolene's husband who was in good health, unexpectedly died at home. Rolene attempted to revive him but because of her condition, her CPR efforts were unsuccessful.

It was very sad to know that she lived in a rural area all alone. There was no one nearby to help her out or look after her, I felt guilty with not being there for my best lifetime buddy.

When I finished my book I sent her a copy in a three ring binder, as I was unsure of its value as a legitimate book to consider for publishing. Rolene was always brutally honest with everyone. If she didn't like it I was going to burn it in the fire pit. I trusted her that much.

Rolene called me the day it arrived, her only comment was, "If you really thought that much about me, you would have hand delivered it, asshole!"

Well, that was Rolene. I never told her at the time, that her sole opinion was the deciding factor of the value of my six years of work on the book.

Four days later Rolene called me and said, "You bastard, I have been crying since I opened that binder and have slept less than six hours during these last four days. I had no idea of your suffering and loneliness."

I matter-of-factly asked her if she would buy it for a friend. She said, "Yes but I'd rather steal it!" We called each other some bad names for a few minutes as we always do, exchanged 'I love yous' and hung up. I immediately called my publisher and told them to go to press.

When I returned to live in Duluth I spent a lot of time visiting with Rolene. I would visit her weekly during the open water months. I would bring her fresh caught trout that I caught that morning. Rolene loved to bake, I would call her the day before I went fishing and tell her, 'Babe, fire up the oven.' When I arrived the next afternoon with fresh trout, she would have a plate of chocolate chip cookies on the table and a gallon size freezer bag for me to take home.

I had to laugh every time I would come to her door, she would look through the screen and ask, "Are you here to eat my cookies or just to piss me off?" Rainbow and Brown trout were her favorite food. We would sit for an hour or so and drink two pots of coffee with cookies, smoke a ton of cigarette's and just giggle about all the things in our past and all the hell we raised. We also talked about how blessed we were to make it thru the many hard times and we both agreed that we are tougher today because of our past struggles.

Cookie day was the high point of both of our weeks. On one visit she told me she bought a mobility cart that had a cabin, a windshield with head and tail lights that she could drive on the street without a license. The next week as I pulled into her driveway for the cookie/fish exchange. There was a very cool, 'George Jetson' kind of a looking mobility cart, parked in front of her back door. She beamed as she showed me the windshield wipers, backup horn, storage compartment, sound system and a few other car-like amenities. She said she had driven to town the last three days in it (11 miles) and got the speedometer up to 40 miles an hour. I of course wanted to kick her ass for being so crazy but Rolene was very independent and she would just tell me to go reproduce myself. Nobody told Rolene what to do. That is one of her many quality's that I deeply respected. She said she only drove on wide paved shoulders but never on the roadway.

I didn't believe any part of that story but I let it slide. Rolene called me the next day and said she wanted to take me to lunch on Thursday. I said OK and asked her what time I should pick her up. She said, "I will drive my cart and meet you there."

You won damn few arguments with her. She would give you the 'death ray look' just before she told you to go to hell.

We were to meet at a country restaurant and bar, six miles from her house. As I pulled into the parking lot I saw her shinny little red cart and it gave me the shivers as I thought of her driving that damn thing for six miles from her home on the highway. I wanted to holler at her but it would not do any good and I was secretly proud of her for her independence in not just giving up like so many others would. I deeply admired her courage and

7

mental toughness. Few people could stand that measure, I don't think I could.

During lunch a fellow she knew stopped at our table to say that the old bar that had just been remodeled in their neighborhood would open on Saturday night.

The bar was four miles from Rolene's house, she told her friend that she would see him there. I wanted to protest about her being on the cart after dark but she had already told me that the cart had high and low beam headlights and tail lights. I knew I would not be able to win her over on that one and talk her out of that bar trip.

Heather and I were drinking coffee on our deck on Saturday evening about 9:10 pm. We had our police scanner on to enjoy the crazy shit that happens in every city on every weekend.

Police dispatch toned out police, fire and ambulance for a single vehicle rollover accident with a woman pinned under a 'golf type' mobility cart. The location was three blocks from the bar that Rolene was going to, on that Saturday night. I looked at Heather and said, that's Rolene and I started to cry. I somehow knew that she was already dead. The fire department radioed for a helicopter for an unconscious and unresponsive female with severe head trauma.

Heather and I sat in silence as we listened to the radio traffic of the 1st Responders and the helicopter crew. I waited for 15 very long minutes before I called the hospital after the chopper had landed. I asked if they had received a patient who arrived by helicopter named Rolene Rogers. The ER staff member said, "Yes the trauma team is working on her now." I hung up and we drove to the hospital. When I asked the unit clerk about Rolene she directed us to the family waiting room where the family would be briefed by the surgeon in the next ten minutes.

Rolene's children, their spouses and their children were in the waiting room. Rolene had told me and showed me many photos

8

of her children and grandchildren but I never met any one of them. I introduced Heather and myself to them. They all said that they had heard of me. Her daughter said, "You're the trout for cookie guy that writes books."

Two surgeons came into the room and said they are doing all they can for her but a part of her brain stem was disconnected. With my experience that meant only one thing, Rolene is dead. Her children asked if she was going to be ok. I kept my mouth shut as a doctor said that they could visit her but just two at a time and it would have to be brief. The surgeon cautioned that she would look much different than a few hours prior, due to her injuries. I did not go in to the see her. I wanted to remember her from our lunch, three days before.

The doctors pronounced her dead 12 hours from her arrival to the hospital. I shudder when I think of her lying on that dark highway all alone and dying. I cannot drive on that highway any longer. I've only been fishing in that area once, since we lost her. I didn't wet my line, I just sat there and all I did was cry.

I now only go out on Lake Superior with my pals but I can't bring myself to visit the inland lakes and streams that produced Rolene's 'trout for cookies' program, it is just too sad for me.

CHAPTER 2   FINDING MY WAY

My world was much larger in the Western States. Admittedly, I do miss the attention and recognition as a successful, published author.

Now living back in my hometown after a forty plus year's absence, I know no one and no one knows me. The few people that I've been reintroduced to, stand in shock after they ask where I have been and doing all these years? It's a bit of a blow to my ego to be just a regular Joe. I know I had to stop hiding in the house and become a part of this society. Since I don't drink or care for large crowds, I had to figure out a way to become part of the population. I contacted or attempted to contact the local newspaper features editor to no avail. After three phone calls, five days apart, with messages left as to my requesting she do a story on my book. That is what she is supposed to do with local authors. I figured that she and her paper were too good for the likes of me.

I went to the only locally owned legitimate bookstore in the area to pitch my book to place them on consignment. I met with a very gracious and sweet young lady named Tami. She was the manager of Walkers Book Store. The store owners, Seth and Mary Walker were out of the store at that moment. Ms. Tami happily

10

took three of my books and placed them in the 'Local Authors' section.

A few weeks later, I read in the Sunday, special sections local, 'fish wrap' (yup the same editor that ignored my phone calls) that there was going to be two local authors presenting their latest published books during a 'Meet and Greet the Author' event at the newly opened Walker's bookstore in two weeks. It was the same bookstore that I placed my books with a week ago. The article was a full section on the two local authors that are both photojournalists as well. They both had several publications to their credit and only did local work. On was a naturalist the other a historian, both did coffee table books and calendars. The six page section had a well done layout of all of their work. "So that's why the editor didn't have any time for the recently returned nobody, from Colorado!"

My thought was, "She can kiss a large portion of my ass if not my entire ass! I'm going to do an end-run and when I pull it off, she will be chasing me down to do a story."

I called the book store that Monday morning and made an appointment to meet with the owners, Seth and Mary on Wednesday afternoon of that week. When I arrived I couldn't help but notice (who I assumed was the store owner) and his manager, Ms. Tami were in a deep and troubled conversation.

I stood a ways back and eavesdropped on their conversation. I overheard them saying that the response from the last weekend's newspaper article and their social media posts had brought in so many reservations that they could not possibly fit all those people in their store. An undertaker could not have removed the grin on my face.

I approached the owner and introduced myself and told him I couldn't help but overhear their conversation and I may have a solution for him. Seth was looking pretty rattled as he asked what I had in mind.

I told Seth and Ms. Tami that I ran into an old acquaintance the other day who was in charge of special events and banquet services at the refurbished, former Seaway Hotel, now known as the, 'Corker Hotel.'

The Corker Hotel was named after the sailors life jackets (made of cork) in the late 1800's to early 1900's. Duluth is a seaport city, located at the far most west end of Lake Superior. The sailors wore their life vests when they left the ship as a prideful badge of courage. The locals called the sailors, 'Corkers.' The Corkers from the Mediterranean's were well received as they brought virgin olive oil for lamps for barter as virgin olive oil burnt much cleaner than whale or coal oil. The Corkers almost never paid for anything because their oil was more valuable than money.

My friend Vicki told me she was having a lot of trouble in booking any events to showcase their many improvements of the hotel. I went on to say that I would talk to her about using their ballroom for his event. I thought Seth was going to kiss me. I told Seth that if he would add me to his book signing, 'Meet and Greet' that I would speak with my old friend on the following morning.

The company that owned the Corker Hotel specialized in buying turn of the century hotels and getting them listed as historical sites then getting federal money for restoration. They buy those wrecking ball rescues, get free federal tax dollars and they use their own construction company to do the remodels.

They then sell them for a huge profit, so in essence her hotel corporation is in fact a construction company that flips hotels that they buy for parts of a penny and dump them for a fortune. They get it on both ends and with a very marginal investment. Well, for some reason the company could not get the federal government or any other governmental agency to accept their national registry applications so the company was on the hook for the very first time, for their own construction costs.

As I sat with Vicki the following morning she told me the company would not give her a dime for guest services or banquet advertising or promotions. The ship was tied to the dock and it was sinking! Her manager put her on final warning that if she didn't do something to immediately improve the ballroom and hotel room activities that she would be replaced shortly. That same 'undertaker grin' came to my face as I told her of the bookstore owner's dilemma. I told her that we could fill the 400 person plus

12

ballroom if she gave him the room for free on the weekend after next. She could set up a couple of wet bars in the ballroom, give room discounts to the out of town guests attending the 'Meet and Greet' and give discounts in the upscale restaurant to the attendees. Well this time I did get a kiss. Vicki had tears rolling down her face as she thanked me. I smiled as I told Vicki, "You have to rent a woman's white tuxedo" and I left her office. I called Seth and told him that he was buying me lunch in 30 minutes.

Seth sat in absolute disbelief before we ordered our meal. I grinned as I asked, "You are kind of new at this bookstore deal aren't you?" Seth said he opened the store seven months ago and he was terribly failing, making rent was frightening and he didn't know how much longer he could last. He had burned through most all of his and his wife's life savings. I told Seth that I had locked down the deal, that wine and liquor would be served that would help generate more sales (billfold lubricant) but the, 'Meet and Greet' had to run both Saturday and Sunday. There had to be three presentations on Saturday and two on Sunday. Seth blanched as he asked how much all that would cost. Back to my mortician grin as I said, "The total cost of this two day event in that hotel, in that gorgeous ballroom, is the price of this meal we have yet to order! The look of utter disbelief and the longest exhale I've ever heard, was priceless. His eyes welled up as he grabbed his cellphone off the table and said, "I gotta go call my wife, I'll be right back." Seth came back to the table with red eyes and he now had his own 'morticians grin'. During lunch I told him how the event should be handled and how many staff he would need to work it. Seth only had himself, his wife, his manager and three part time college kids.

I told Seth that he better make nice with family and friends as he needed twenty people each day and they all had to have 'Award-Winning' smiles and be willing to set up chairs, pour coffee, pass appetizers and do anything else his guests would want, to put them in a buying mood. The hotel would provide for parking valets but Seth would have to provide two door opening greeters and at least ten people who would be lined-up inside the interior doors to offer their arms, to personally escort the guests to the

13

'Grand Ballroom' and seat them. I told him that he must close the store because the event would demand his full attention. Him, his wife his manager and all three part timers would handle the sales in the ballroom. As we were parting the restaurant I said, "Oh yea, one more thing Buddy Boy, "You, your wife and your entire staff need to rent white tuxedos for the event. I'm not fucking kidding. Just do it."

Seth called me late that evening and was bubbling about a conversation he had with the naturalist author (who does a newspaper article and wildlife photography lay-out each month for free so as to keep his name out in front of his readers) named Kirk Meyer. Seth said he told Kirk of the change of venue location and schedule.

Kirk told him that he had to make another call but would get back to him in an hour or so. Kirk called Seth back in twenty minutes. Kirk had spoken with the managing editor of the newspaper, told him of both Seth's and Vicki's dilemma and their joint 'Hail Mary' attempts to salvage the store and Vicki's career. During that twenty minute phone conversation, the general manager said the newspaper will host a Friday night wine tasting kick off for the book signing weekend. Seth said that all of the events would save his business. Seth said that he would finally get to sleep tonight. I said, "Buddy Boy, I wasn't shitting you on those white tuxedos, you all must go in to the tux shop in the morning and be fitted. The women as well, the store is opening early at 8:00 am and they are expecting you guys at 8:00 am, no excuses!

Early that next morning I got a call from who other but the newspaper's special sections editor! Yup the same one that had no time for me just a few short weeks ago. She asked me if I would do an interview with her that day at the newspaper office. I said, "Nope" and waited for her response. She came back with a weak shaky voice as she tried to apologize for her not returning my calls. I said, "Missy, in the future you may want to use caution as to whom you blow off, there is a whole world of people out there much bigger than you." I paused for a bit to let that statement soak in. I told her to meet me at 11:00 am at the bookstore for the interview and to bring her top photographer, no photographer, no interview! With the tiniest of a surrendering of voices she said, "Yes Sir Mr. Brown I will be there, thank you so much Sir."

I got to the bookstore at 10:30 to talk to Seth and look at the tuxedos. The special sections editor was already there with her photographer.

Seth introduced us and I thought the poor little thing was going to pass out or turn to dust. As I expected, she was quite young and unsure of herself. She said her boss told her to do as I suggested. I told her "I know, I talked to him this morning and he gave me his personal cell number, if there were any problems." I thought she was going to melt into her shoes. I told her she could tag along as I directed Ricky (the photographer) as to what to shoot. I made sure that Seth and Mary (his wife) and Ms. Tami (his manager) had to be in each shot. There were not to be any photos taken of me. This was to be only about the bookstore and its key people.

After the photo shoot I said, 'Young Missy,' I will accept your apology but you are buying lunch. She said "I don't have any cash and my credit card is pretty much maxed out for lunch for everyone. I told Missy that I would buy lunch for her and her photographer as the store staff had a lot of work to do to get ready for the event.

After we were seated in the restaurant I told Missy to take her cellphone off the table, "You are in a business meeting and you will act accordingly." I gave her a moment to recover from her scolding as I told her I was not trying to destroy her, but I was going to help her grow up and I was going to hold her feet to the flames, as I had an assignment for her and Ricky. The shock on her face was priceless. I told Missy and Ricky that their general manager of the paper, gave me full authority to do as I wish with them to make this entire event a success.

I looked at Missy and said, "You are to be the hostess and coordinator for the Friday evening reception. You are to hire the Food Service and Beverage Departments, from the Corker Hotel. You are to select the Hors d'oeuvres from the hotel's banquet

15

department and you will order cocktail bar service with four bartenders and six waitresses for 400 people. There cannot be any self-service of any kind. We want to make every person in that room to feel as they are royalty. You also have a fitting appointment for 2 o'clock today for three evening gowns.

The staff of the clothing store will select the gowns, shoes and clutch purses. You have no say in the matter, they will pick out your outfits. Now reach into your purse and drag out your cellphone, you know, the one that you are to never have out on any table in a business meeting. She did as I told her. I had her call her hairdresser for an appointment for a formal hairstyle. I told her, "Go to the business office when you get back to work and they will have the money ready for you for your hair appointment."

As Missy was dialing the hair salon I turned to Ricky the photographer and said, "Now for you young man. You and three of the staff photogs will each have a photo booth set up at each author's table and one photographer will be doing roving candid shots of the crowd. Each author table will have an instant printer attended by a newspaper staff member to print author/guest photos so the authors can sign them.

"There can be no glitches Ricky, and I mean none! Am I clear?" Ricky nodded his head and said, "Yes Sir Mr. Brown, I will take care of it all and I won't let you down."

Missy hang up her phone and said she had her hair appointment the afternoon of the reception. She set her cellphone on the table as I gave her, 'the look', she snatched it off the table and threw it in her purse with an apologetic grimace. She actually looked much calmer than before we sat down for lunch. I then said, "Now you two listen to me and listen tight. I don't and I haven't given you suggestions for your consideration, I have given you orders, orders fully supported by your boss. Is that clear?"

Both said, "Yes sir," as they nodded their heads. I said to them, "Guys this is for all the marbles, for there are people's careers and livelihoods at stake, including your own. If you haven't figured it out yet, your weekend days and evenings off have been canceled. You will be paid overtime for your hours. This is your

16

one big shot to be noticed, people will be watching and this is your time to shine. If this makes you two a bit nervous, that's a good thing. The most successful people do their best work under extreme pressure.

Ricky, you and you're three associates have appointments to get fitted for two sport coats, slacks, shoes, shirts and ties. You lads will now have professional attire. Now you guys need to get back to work. I will see you all at 4:00 pm Friday afternoon." I grabbed the check and went to the cashier.

I phoned Seth and told him to have his other two authors to both bring a carload of books to the Friday reception as we don't want to lose any opportunity to sell our products. I told him to have everyone be in the ball room at precisely 4:00 o'clock Friday afternoon, for a final set up and to greet the early arrivals. I got there at 3:30 to look things over.

People were already sitting in the ballroom for the 6 o'clock event. For three days prior to the event, the newspaper placed a quarter page ad for the event with photos of the store and their staff. Seth and Vicki both said that their phone lines had been blowing up with reservation requests. Vicki had told me on the first day we met that the 68 room hotel was only at 40% occupancy and today they were booked at a 100% for all three nights and she received several phone calls from tour bus companies inquired about bus parking!

Missy entered the Ballroom and she looked like a princess, her hair and gown looked like a matching set. I could see her radiant eyes sparkle as she walked over to me with a comfortable stride and asked if she could have a few moments in private. We went into a side meeting room, she smiled and said, "Thank you for setting me straight on my attitude. I have thought a lot about my behaviors for the last several days. I know that you could have crushed me anytime you wanted to and if you tell my boss to fire me right now, I know that he would do that. Mr. Brown, I know I'm not very good at my job, the people I work with don't like me much because I'm bitchy. I know that I act arrogant and bitchy but I'm really, really not! Well sir, what I am is....is, I'm scared. I dread every payday because I know that there will be a pink slip in my paycheck envelope. Every time I get a page or phone call to come to the assignment editor's office, I want to vomit. I get so scared that she will tell me to turn in my keys." Poor sweet little Missy started to cry. We had been standing face-to-face during our conversation. I unfolded my arms and walked over to a chair, pulled it out and said, "Sweetheart have a seat." She sat down with a look of total surrender with her trembling hands in her lap.

I remained standing as I said, "Missy, I know I've been short and snappy with you the last several days. I intentionally talk hard-and-fast with you and I've been unmerciful in my demands and now I will tell you why. Missy I know you don't believe in yourself, I could smell your fear on the phone the first time you called. Your snootiness is as transparent as cellophane. I know what sadness and fear looks like. I too have a mirror at my home and I look at that same face every day, the same as you do.

I have been roughing you up because I believe in you, I pushed you far beyond what you thought your limits were, because you have been settling all of your young life, because you are terrified of failure. You have never challenged yourself. What you have done to put this event together has been exemplary. I'm proud of you, the work is now over. Now we will enjoy tonight and the next two days because we made this happen. This is your transition sweetheart, say goodbye to that scared little girl. She left when you put your gown on today and she is not ever coming back! By the way, how do you like your new dress? You better like it, because it's yours, this and the other two are yours to keep because you will need them for your new job.

Your boss, Mr. Eriksson wants you in his office on Monday morning at 7:00 am to tell you of your new position. You best not be late!

Now Missy, ah...... hell, I need to show you proper respect, the respect that you have earned and deserve. What IS your name?"

"Cathi with an 'i' sir." I told Missy, (now Cathi, with an

18

'i') that I will no longer use the condescending name of Missy, and I will use her proper name.

Missy, the now Cathi, jumped out of her chair and said, "Oh no, please don't stop calling me Missy. I like the sound of the name, it's like you gave me a pet name just for me. No one has ever given me a nickname. At first I called you Mr. Brown because I was afraid of you. You just look so powerful and it gave me the shivers, but now I call you Mr. Brown because of the huge respect I have for you. You have taught me so much about myself and I love watching you talking to people and how you are so respectful and make each person feel important. You are the coolest man I have ever met. I want you to call me Missy, please?"

I asked her if her parents were coming tonight she said no, they were not invited. I looked at her and said, "Missy, reach into your purse for that cellphone that never belongs on a table during a business meeting. Call your parents and give me the phone." Missy's dad answered the call, I introduced myself and extended my personal invitation for him and his wife to attend tonight's gathering.

Dad said, "We have heard all about you, (with a brief chuckle) as he said, Cathi lives with us and you are all she's talks about, nonstop for the last two weeks. We would love to meet you, we will be there at 6 o'clock Sir."

I gave Missy back her phone and she had a new set of tears running. "Thank you Mr. Brown that was so nice, I can't wait to introduce you to my Mom and Dad, thank you for believing in me and being so nice."

She gave me a hug, I kissed her on her forehead, held her at arm's length, dropped my voice to that of a scolding parent and said, "Young Lady, go freshen your make-up, we've got a show to put on." We both laughed as Missy skipped out of the room.

During our less than ten minute conversation, the lobby had become abuzz with semi-formal dressed guests. When I entered the ballroom, just inside the main doors Vicki was greeting the new arrivals and handing them off to the escorts for seating.

Vicki held up a finger as to signal me to wait for a moment. After she greeted an elderly couple and handed them off to the escorts she floated over and took my arm and guided me to the back corner of the room. She was beaming as she said, "This is so wonderful you are wonderful. I just can't believe that this is happening, my big boss from corporate just flew-in on his corporate jet, he wants to meet you and he can't believe that this is actually happening! The mayor is even here and she is going to give an opening welcoming speech and talk about the history of the hotel. I've never been so excited in my whole life!"

I complimented her on her slick move with having a banner ad for their "Re-Grand Opening," placed directly above the newspaper 'house-ad' for the event. Vicki said she didn't do that, she said a newspaper advertising sales rep came in with a proof of the ad with the banner. "I felt so badly for this 'ad guy', he comes in every week to sell me advertising but I have to tell him each week that I would like to buy an ad but I have no budget. But he still comes in every Tuesday and is always very pleasant, he always smiles and tries to cheer me up with a cute little joke.

I told Vicki that after this weekend with her boss getting a true read on the people of the city, he just might find a few bucks for her promotions. The 400 person capacity Ballroom was all but full in a half an hour before the official 6:00 pm starting time.

I noticed that 'Ole' Seth' had game too. He was helping his bookstore staff set up two large easels at each author's table, they then placed the metal framed 3'x5' photos of each author on one easel and their current book cover on the other easel at each author table. I approached Seth and said "Slick move Pal, how did you get my pictures?" He said with his largest mortician grin, "I went to your Facebook page and your website and borrowed them. I hope you don't mind."

I said, "Not at all, find a Sharpie and I will sign them and have your other two authors do the same, you have a lot of open wall space in your store and you should start a 'rogue's gallery' of local authors. This will not be a one-time shot at this hotel. I'm thinking you could do it every quarter and do in-store signings every two weeks." Seth was showing his entire mouth of teeth as he asked, "You want a job?" We both laughed as I told him, "I have a job. I'm a writer, an independent writer. I don't want to have a boss. I could probably sell my work to a publishing house but I don't want any editor giving me timelines and telling me to rewrite my work. I'll just stay hungry and ride on my own damn pony."

Seth introduced me to the other two authors, Kirk Meyer and Angie Thompson. Angie didn't look well, I asked her if she was OK, she said she felt like she was getting the flu. I suggest she sign her books now so if she had to leave, the store staff could still sell her author signed copies in her absence. We went to her table, Kirk opened her cases of books and stacked them so I could open each book to the signature page. Angie signed them and Seth and Kirk re-boxed the signed copies and in no time at all, the production crew had 200 signed copies boxed and sealed. It was actually fun to do as we had some light banter and laughs.

Seth and Kirk were members of most all of the local fraternal and service groups. They knew most every person in the city, they dragged me around for introductions and glad handing. When I was introduced to the newspaper GM he asked me if I wanted a job as a staff writer. I thanked him but said, "I already have a full time writing gig" and we both laughed.

What no one else knew is that the GM and I sat together three times in the last ten days and went over every plan for this event.

He did say Cathi has done a complete about face with her efforts and behavior, "I am of the thought that you had something to do with that?"

21

I looked around until I saw Cathi and pointed to her as I said to the GM, "You see that lovely young lady gliding through the room? Well, you did that, those gown outfits are a class act, and oh yah, she likes to be called by her nickname, Missy! "We smiled, shook hands and off I went to glad-hand more of the guests.

CHAPTER 3   THE CORKER HOTEL

At the 6 o'clock mark, the mayor took the stage and graciously gave welcoming comments. She gave a very well put together historical tour of the hotel from back in the day. She explained that even small hotels by today's standards had huge ballrooms for dances and banquets. She went on to say, "Your Great Grandparents, Grandparents and parents may have had their, 1st wedding dance on this very floor that we are standing on now! History is not just about buildings, history is also about people, the people we love.

At some point Missy came up to me and asked if she could bring her parents over to meet me. I said, "No you cannot. You take me to meet your parents, they out rank me and you should know that!" Her parents were very nice people and thanked me for giving their daughter some tough direction.

Vicki then came over to me with a well-dressed man. With her radiant smile she introduced me to her boss. He said he had spent a lot of time in this city with, 'The powers that be' but could not get any help with getting the hotel on the 'Historical Register' list.

The gentleman's name was Paul Roberts, he told me he was

amazed with the turn out and my efforts to put all this together. He thanked me for placing the newspaper ad directly above the newspaper house ad for the hotel event. I told Paul that, "Your newspaper advertising rep placed that add. I had nothing to do with it. It was placed at no charge."

I said to him, "If you can stay until tomorrow night I will show you the true power of advertising and maybe you could find a few bucks for an advertising and promotional budget, so Vicki could work her magic." He was all smiles as he said, "Vicki is a treasure!"

I did the author photo sessions for about two hours and called it a night. I was exhausted although I acted like I do this kind of stuff all the time, but I was beat.

Saturday morning I arrived at the Corker hotel one hour early. The valets were already parking cars. The two sport coated doorman greeted me with big wide smiles. I found out later that they were Seth's nephews. Just inside the hotel lobby doors stood a group of twelve to fifteen year old, girls and boys. The girls were all wearing pretty summer dresses, the boys had slacks, white shirts and ties, as they were the escorts. I later found out that those kids were relatives, neighbors and friends kids. As I entered the ballroom I saw Seth was talking to a small group of people in the back of the room. I waved a hello to Vicki, who was placing reserved banners on the chair backs in the first and second rows. The room was abuzz with chatter. As I walked by the stage and got to the center, I saw a couple sitting in the first row, directly in front of the podium. I heard them whisper, "I think that's him, he looks a lot like the guy in the picture on the back cover but his hair is a lot grayer and shorter than the guy in the picture. It could be him, the book came out three years ago he might have grayed up in that period of time. I think it's him!"

I wanted to stop and say, "Who's him?" But I wanted to say hello to Seth first. Seth looked at me and excused himself from the group he was speaking with and started towards me with a panicked look.

Seth came up to me and said, "We're screwed, Angie is too sick to come today, what are we going to do? Suddenly, Ms. Tami and Vicki were both standing with us with a look of apprehension, waiting for my answer.

I said, "Do you remember when we helped Angie sign 200 books last night as insurance? Well, file the insurance claim, Pal! Go ahead and introduce me and I'll make the announcement of her illness and advise her readers that her books are signed and will be for sale this weekend and if people would like to have a personalized copy you will schedule another book signing at your bookstore, as soon as she recovers. I could see the light come on in Seth's head. Seth was now sporting his own 'morticians grin' as he said, "Hell that will bring a couple of hundred people into the store. You are a genius!" Ms. Tami asked me, "How do you think so fast?" I answered, "Life's lessons sweetheart, there may be snow on the rooftop but I still got game." Vicki looked puzzled and asked, "What is snow on the rooftop mean?" Ms. Tami giggled and said, "I'll tell you later."

I told Seth that I would go first and take Angie's twenty minutes as well. It will give us time to fill the room for Kirk's presentation. "Hell, I can talk about myself all day and well into the night!" Seth let out the second longest sigh I've ever heard. The girls were all smiles.

Seth then nodded at the couple who were sitting in the front row, dead center of the podium, he said, "These people have been sitting there for almost an hour, they desperately want to meet you." I said, "Yeah, I kind of knew that, let's do it. You girls get back to work, you're on the clock." Seth led me to the very well-groomed couple who wore what looked to be, L.L. Bean, type casual but expensive clothing.

I inwardly grinned as I visualized him in an African Pith Helmet and her wearing a faded, but new olive drab pink lettered OP logo cap with her golden hair pulled through the back adjustment strap. With all their earthliness I was pretty sure that they were not here to see me. They sure didn't look to be star struck! The couple stood as we approached them, they each

25

introduced themselves as Forest Quinn and Madeline Quinn. I
smiled and said, "I like what you two just did." They had a
quizzical look as I said, "I could see that you two are a couple but
you each introduced yourselves. I like couples that realize that they
are also individuals."

With my experience as a police officer and a writer, I study
people's facial structures so I can better paint a clear picture as I
write. I'm guessing they are Norwegian.

Forest said, "We brought ten copies of your book along
with us, we bought them as Christmas gifts for our family. We
would also like to buy another twenty books for our friends. If you
have enough with you today and if you wouldn't mind signing
them all for us?" Seth said, "I will go and set aside twenty books
for you right now." As Seth scurried off, I thought, "What the hell,
I got time." I looked down at Forest's obviously very expensive
oversized leather laptop bag, sitting next to his chair.

I asked, "These your ten family books? He nodded his
head. I said, "Well grab your bag and follow me to a table. The
book bag hung heavy on his shoulder, as I sat down and looked at
him and said, "Set your bag down and unload it."

I quickly signed each with the header "A gift from………
(I thought I'd let them fill in the blanks) joyful reading." As I was
signing their books I thought, holy shit, they are star struck!

I excused myself as I wanted to check on the set-up of the
rest of the room. As I walked away I shook my head as I thought,
"Holy double shit, I have never sold thirty copies to any book store
at one time, let alone to one person. This could be a breakthrough
day!"

I saw Seth gathering up all of his employees along with
Missy and Vicki and leave the ballroom. In less than ten minutes
one of the bartenders who had already served me a full pot of
coffee, came up to me and said, "Seth needs to see you right away
out in the lobby, I think it's important!"
I didn't stop to think about what was going on, I just went there. At
the far wall of the lobby stood nine beaming, smiling faces, with
white tuxedos and four photographers wearing matching sport

coats, slacks, white shirts and ties. I walked up to Seth and said, "I don't do inspections." I went down the line and thanked each one of them for their being good sports. After all the handshakes and hugs, I stood back and marveled at all of their efforts and personal achievements in just ten short days. "I said, OK you bunch of slackers, you all have a job to do. It's show time!"

I had to step out to the garden for a smoke and a few prideful tears.

Seth introduced me as the first presenting author of the day. I had to chuckle a bit, as I am always the first, "Presenting Author," because I am the tag along, a nobody author that was invited only to warm up the crowd as the seats fill before the 'Main Acts.' I am the '*Filler.*'

I took the podium and echoed Seth's welcome and appreciation for their attendance. I informed the audience of the three cash bars at the back of the room, one in each corner and one in the center. There are two tables midway on each side of the room with complementary coffee tea, juice, donuts and muffins. "There is nothing in front of the podium in front of this room, other than me. Please don't walk in front of me when I am speaking as I have a fully loaded squirt gun and I am not afraid to use it.

People were still slowly filing in, when I announced that Ms. Angie Thompson, "Our local historian and published author, has taken ill and would not be able to attend this weekend's event. Ms. Thompson did sign several books last night and the staff from Walker's book store will be selling them on her behalf. If you would like a personalized, signed copy of Ms. Thompson's book, please take a business card from any of the tables and join, Walker's Books Store Facebook page and watch for e-mails as to when Ms. Thompson will be at the store to personalize your books. Please take note of the nine smartly attired people in white tuxedos who will assist you in your purchase of your books today. We will also be here tomorrow at 1:00pm and 5:00 pm presenting our work for purchase."

As I was giving out the dutiful information I couldn't help but notice the Norwegian's looking at me as though I was a deer in

27

a rifle scope. They were intently studying me. They didn't look left or right or shuffle their feet or cross their legs. I don't think they even blinked. I got the mental giggles thinking that they had X-ray vision and I was inwardly grinning at the thought that the Norwegian princess wishes she had come alone!
More about them later.

"Ladies and gentlemen, I would like to introduce myself. My name is David J. Brown. I'm the author of the published novel, "Daddy Had to Say Goodbye." My second novel, 'Flesh of a Fraud' is in final production and will be available in the next three weeks. Please watch your email from Walker's Book Store, when they arrive. Seth from Walker's books will schedule an in-store signing event. Well luckily for me and probably not for you, I am also a national motivational speaker. So to fill the forty minutes before the main act, I will speak about me! After all, who doesn't like to talk about themselves?

I would now like everyone to join me in a brief exercise by all of you raising your right hand. High into the air please. Our greeters today, have been using a hand click counter, as you came in today, so I expect to see 64 hands in the air. Thank you, put your hands down please. We have now established that we have 64 guests in the room who can all raise their right hands. Now I would like to see by show of hands of the people who have written a book. Please count them for us Ms. Tami. Six you say, please put your hands down. Now of you six that have raised your right hands, how many of you have published your book and currently have it for sale. I don't need your help this time, Ms. Tami. I can only see one hand in the air. So excluding these six writers, I would like to see the hands of those who have thought of writing a book, wanted to write a book, is or was, in process of writing a book, any kind of book? Please hold your hands up high, as I can see a few slightly off the lap hands. How many Ms. Tami? "Seventeen hands in the air Sir." "What is the headcount in the room now Ms. Tami?"

"83 in the room now and they're still coming in sir." "I can only speak to the original 64 who were here for the start of this exercise.

Excluding the 5 who are actively writing and the 17 who are kinda-sorta thinking about writing, I have to inform you that 41 of the original 64 people that started in the beginning of this exercise are all liars!

Yes, 41 of you are liars, but nice liars. Let me explain before you start throwing stuff at me and bear in mind that I do have a fully loaded squirt gun, filled with pure, cold, Lake Superior water!

The number one reason why we all lie is, fear! Let me tell you about fear. Fear is not a word! Fear is an acronym for: False....Evidence.... Appearing....Real.

Most often times we fear being judged. Most every one of us has had the thought (perhaps just fleeting) or still do think 'I should write a book,' we hear that statement often from friends, family and coworkers. We even might say it out loud, when we are sure that no one's in the room to overhear us. Your mere presence here this morning is indicative of your interest in reading and I have yet to meet an avid reader who has not at least had a passing thought of putting pen to paper. So now that we put that fear thing to bed, please show by hands in the air, how many of you would like to write a book? How many now Ms. Tami? "Looks to be about 30 hands in the air, Mr. Brown." "How many people in this room now Ms. Tami?"

"I have lost count sir, we have at least doubled in size from the beginning of our exercise, Sir."

"Ladies and Gentlemen I am in great hopes that you all would consider becoming writers, I hope in the next 45 minutes that number dramatically grows.

Karaoke has been around for some time. If you ever wanted to sing Karaoke but never have, you know the feeling you get when you go to the neighborhood bar with your pals on Karaoke Night. You want to sing but you're afraid they will make fun of you.

We ask ourselves.... What if my voice cracks?
What if I'm flat?
What if I screw up the lyrics?

29

What if I look stupid?

What if....

What if....

What if....

The 'What if's' are never ending. We all know of those feelings, whether we sing or not! Well it's like that for me of sorts. As I started to write my first novel I was stricken on two fronts, first was I capable, secondly will anyone believe me? Which of course takes us back to fear. As we now know, fear is not real and only has the power that we give it.

I will tell you about my ongoing fear but before I do I must ask you, Ms. Tami of the current headcount in the room. "My staff and I count 312 people in the room and people are still coming in Mr. Brown" Thank you Ms. Tami, and now I must give you all my heartfelt apology, especially to our first 64 people who participated in the original exercise. You see, I used this exercise to wait until the room was mostly filled. Now you know what it's like to be used as a *'filler.'* You are now all well on your way to becoming published authors!

So let's get started, first I'm going to take away this podium so we can have direct contact without any barriers.

I have a secret. I don't think I belong here. I have no business to present this book. I sure enough did write it and I also published it independently. You can see my picture is on the easels and on the back cover of my books, over on those tables. It is hard for me to look back and see that little boy who seriously considered suicide at the age of 7 and to be here now, as a grown man, without thanking God.

I never wanted to write anything in my entire life, well except tickets for traffic violations when I was a police officer. So how did I become the published author standing in front of you today? And at what point in my life, did I ever dream that my signature would someday become known as an autograph?

In 2011 my mother passed away. She lived here in Duluth and I lived in Colorado. I drove from Colorado to Minnesota for my Mom's funeral, when I drove back to Colorado (ten days later)

I had a spiritual experience. I am by no means a religious man but I do live a very simple, spiritual based life which is pretty much just about decency and kindness. During that spiritual event I heard a voice say, "Write the book." Was that God's voice or the voice deep inside of me? It's not for me to know, but I did hear that voice. That first day I sat down to write, I had a full pot of coffee, a gut full of doubtful anxiety and with only a promise to God.

I twirled my pen and stared at my basic inventory of writing supplies. A five pack of Uni-ball #207 gel pens and four 5 packs of office depot 8-1/2 X 11 yellow legal pads. I was heavily armed with severe doubt and all but paralyzing fear. Much like wanting or thinking about wanting to sing Karaoke. I have no skills in this area. The only true skills I have are, I know how to save your life and the know how to take your life. Shivers anyone? Here is the deal behind my fear. I was held back and repeated the 1st and 2nd grades. I never earned a passing grade from kindergarten to high school graduation. I attended summer school each year of junior and senior high school. At the end of the 2nd grade for the 2nd time, the school district deemed me to be mildly retarded. I was every bit convinced as the teachers, that I was stupid. I knew that I was not smart enough to go to college. Now I'm going to write a book? I felt that God was trying to bully me. I didn't know how to type, when I go anywhere near a keyboard my fingers instantly turn into hoofs. My computer skills are poor and I can barely navigate through Facebook. For the first five hours of my new writing career I developed blisters from my pen spinning in my fingers and stomach acid after my fourth pot of coffee. I still had a blank legal pad and even more reasons to know I would fail. If I did start to write I certainly would not finish and publication is not even a thought. Without any college or writing classes, never googling any how to stuff, I plowed into writing. For five long years I wrote and wrote and I wrote.

After several 'walk-a-ways,' multiple tantrums, and 68 legal pads later I had this book. Yes, I hand wrote this entire book. I found a typist it put it on paper, she was a speed typist.

She did not correct any of the many misspellings or punctuation errors, she simply typed. I could not afford the cost of a professional editor. There are errors in the 1st edition of this book. It stands to reason that if a flawed man writes about a flawed man than the book itself will also be flawed. Since publication, several readers have contacted me to offer their editing services as they are so taken by its contents. The books I brought along today are the second edition books.

Well enough about me, it is customary at a book signing that the author reads a few paragraphs and at times even a full chapter. This morning I'm just going to read the introduction to my novel, 'Daddy Had to Say Goodbye.'

"The small bodied 8 year old boy sat at the edge of his bed, waiting for God to come, to kill him. With his small hands in his lap, his chin on his tiny chest he prays that the end will come soon. Staring down at his black, 'poor box' shoes from Saint Helens Catholic Church. He was determined not to cry. 'If God doesn't come to get me soon, then Daddy will kill me and Daddy will kill me even more-harder and even more-worser.' With morbid resignation he smiles and finds comfort in knowing that either way, today would be the end. 'Nobody can never hurt me again. I will never have to wonder why Daddy beats me up so bad and why God hates me so bad.' Little Clinton Flanagan was ready for God to come and to put him in hell.

No child should ever know and understand fear. Not the fear of monsters under the bed or something bad happening, but the paralyzing fear of what has already happened will happen again and it will happen soon. This is the true life story of a beaten child who becomes a bully and that bully becomes a batterer."

I have read this introduction at all of my book signings. I have never been able to get through it without my voice breaking, my lip quivering and a brief tear or two.

While I paused, to gather myself, I saw the effects on the audience's faces. I went on with; "I write to stir your soul, not with a mixing spoon but with a Canoe paddle." Another pause. "If you remember nothing else of our time together this morning, please remember these three short sentences. These are the sentences I use to sign each of my books.

Dreams are worth Dreaming
Dare to Dream
AND
Dream BIG my friends!

Thank you all for your time."

After a rather surprisingly lengthy applause, I announce that, "I am going to be at my tables to sign my books for you after Mr. Myers presentation. I want to shake each of your hands, hugs and photos are welcome. Please call, email and tweet your friends of our next appearances at 2 o'clock and 6 o'clock this evening, as well as on Sunday at one o'clock and 4 o'clock. The bookstore staff in the white tuxedos will be asking you how to spell your first name. Please don't take offense, the only name I dare spell without asking is the name Bob. They will also ask you if you if you would like a personalized message in your book from the author, so you may want to think about that message. You don't need to buy a book to stop by and say hello. If any of you would like to read the book and don't currently have the money with you, I will gift you a copy if you promise to buy a copy in the near future and gift your family or friend that may benefit from reading it."

I was shocked and a bit embarrassed with a thunderous applause when I left the stage to go have a smoke and catch my breath. That and to switch gears from speaker to signing author. I couldn't help but notice the Norwegian's bolt from their chairs with 'reporter style' notebooks and ink pens and disappear into the crowd the moment I left the stage.

When I got to the garden I lit my cigarette. As I blew out my first drag I couldn't help but smile at the fact that all of those nearly 300 people came early only to get a good seat, to hear Angie's and Kirk's presentations.

33

I was met by a grinning and giggling Ms. Tami as I reentered the building. She was bubbling as she reported, "Mr. Brown sir, over half the people in the room are buying your book and are waiting for you to sign them! For the sixth or seventh time, I asked Ms. Tami to please call me Dave. She just beamed as she said, "Sir I have so much respect for you as a person, yes I respect you as being a novelist and all that but the way you spoke to all of us in those few minutes just now was just so personal and we really do feel you do believe in all of us, that was such a beautiful gift. I will always call you Mr. Brown and Sir could I have a hug please?"

I told Ms. Tami that I had tons of respect for her because of her warmth, her energy and her commitment to the book store and their readers. "Ms. Tami, I think we will always be Pal's." We shook on it.

As Ms. Tami started down the hall to return to the ballroom, Kirk Meyer came rushing past her and came up to me with bugged-out eyes.

Before I let him say anything I started for the patio garden door, and said, "Come on, I need another smoke." Kirk was certainly no kid (mid 40's I guess) but he was acting like he just had his first kiss and wanted to tell the world. I thought he was going to explode as he said, "Dude, you are a fricking rock star! I have published 17 books in 22 years, three of them are novels. I have done more than 160 book signings at multiple author venues. Never in any of my experiences have I heard such lengthy and thunderous applause at a book signing! (I lit another cigarette) You frigging killed it when you read you're introduction to your book. There was not a dry eye in the entire room. Even the bartenders and waitresses stopped what they were doing, to listen. People are going nuts right now, asking who you are and where did you come from. You owned everyone in that room, including me! You have such a smooth easy voice that you sound like a top actor. Kind of like a Charlton Hesston type. You look so comfortable and confident that people can't believe you introduce yourself as "A *filler*, nobody author." I have to ask you why in the hell do you live here in Duluth?"

With my very best 'morticians grin' I answered, "For the love of a good woman." I waived Kirk off as I said, "We better get inside. People are waiting for your presentation. I complimented Kirk on his well-trimmed red hair and beard (I'm guessing Scottish) that he did not have last night. I smiled as I said, "You clean up good old son." He said, "After last night I realized that this is a much bigger deal than I thought it was going to be. I want to look as good as everyone else, so I called my friend who owns a beauty shop. She opened her shop at 7 o'clock this morning for me! I brought her and her husband with me today. I hope you don't mind."

As we walked into the ballroom together, Seth pulled me aside and said, "I want to apologize, I was embarrassed for you during your presentation. You said you were there as a filler guy. He went on to say, "I have never heard such an empowering speaker. You gave such validation to everyone in the room, we most certainly got our money's worth. I will tell Kirk to go first for the rest of the weekend."

Kirk came up to us and said, "Guys, I am going first as the presenting author. I will only take 10 minutes. I would like to introduce you Dave to the audience, hell, I can sign any time, 'old son,' as he grinned, Seth is my cousin!" Kirk and Seth both laughed. "I got to tell you Dave, not only were you charming and engaging with the audience but never in my life have I heard any author tell his audience that if they don't have the money to buy his book that he would give them a free copy with their promise to buy a copy at a later date! That sir, was an absolute class act!"

I of course, was greatly honored and a bit embarrassed by Kirk's compliments as I thanked Kirk for his time. I realized my 10 minute break had become 20 minutes and sweet Ms. Tami had disappeared as I hustled past the of book buyers line. I than saw Ms. Tami talking to an elderly lady in a mobility cart. Ms. Tami motioned to me to come to her. She introduce me to Mrs. Johnson. Mrs. Johnson said that she had three sons that each had three sons.

One son had a daughter also. Mrs. Johnson went on to say that each of the family boys were involved in public safety.

"I cooked at the county jail, some of the frequent flyers said they kept coming back for my meals! One of my grandsons is a deputy sheriff, three are police officers, one is border patrol, and four are firefighters, (three city and one wild land)."

Mrs. Johnson's face was beaming with Grandmotherly pride. She tapped my hand and said, "Young man, my granddaughter is also a city firefighter and you know what? She's only 5' 2" and she drives a great big red fire department 'Heavy Rescue' Truck!"

I thought sweet little Mrs. Johnson was going to bust with pride. As she was telling me these things I counted ten books in the front basket of her mobility cart. I nodded to Ms. Tami towards my signing table and back at Ms. Johnson. Ms. Tami was way ahead of me, she said quite loudly, "Mrs. Johnson, all the people here in this line would like you to go first, because you are such a nice grandma!"

The people around her, started clapping as Mrs. Johnson's eyes begin to tear. I walked ahead to take my chair at the table. So here comes sweet old Mrs. Johnson with her frilly edged, pink flowered handkerchief dabbing her eyes and waving to everyone. I signed all ten books for her with each of her grandchildren's names.

I paused for a moment and asked, "Sweetheart where's the book for you to be signed?" She said, "I can't see well enough to read anymore, my Mr. Johnson used to read to me every day but we were in a terrible car accident three months ago that took my Mr. Johnson's life, and put me in this cart. The people at the nursing home don't see any better than I do, so I don't need a book." I glanced at Ms. Tami and nodded at the purchase tables across the room and she was at a full sprint in seconds. I asked Mrs. Johnson what made her come today, she said, "I heard two nurses say that there was an author who loves all First Responders and he was one himself and he wrote a book to save their lives. I just had to come!" I told Mrs. Johnson that she did not have to read, to own a book.

I signed the book to: "Mr. and Mrs. Johnson, the parents of three fine men and ten remarkable grandchildren." As I was signing her book Ms. Tami asked her for her cell phone to take pictures to send to her family. Mrs. Johnson said she only had a phone with a cord on it in her room at the nursing home. Ms. Tami took several photos of myself and Mrs. Johnson together and her stack of books and the special book that I signed to her and Mr. Johnson.

Ms. Tami asked her for her son's phone numbers. Mrs. Johnson rattled off those phone numbers in parts of a second. Mrs. Johnson asked how much she owed me for the book Ms. Tami brought me.

I said, "Mrs. Johnson, I had a really nice grandma named Esther, my grandma passed away several years ago, but I am sure that she would like to give you this book, kind of a gift from one grandma to another grandma. Would you mind if I collect a kiss on the cheek from you Mrs. Johnson?"

As she drove away with her ten books in her basket and pumping her arm in the air with the book I signed to her and her husband, I had to turn my back to the room, to gather myself for a moment.

At some point I heard Seth at the microphone apologizing for letting things get out of control. "I should have announced that the authors would be signing their work at the conclusion of both of their presentations. I must ask you all, to please take your seats." Most everyone did take their seats. Seth was introducing Kirk as he briefly spoke of Kirk's world travels and award-winning photos and books.

Kirk took the podium and stood silently for a moment, before he said, "A number you were here earlier for the opening presentation and saw David play the hands in the air game. Now I would like to see the hands in the air of the people who were as surprised as I was with David's brilliant performance." Kirk said that in his twenty-two years of doing book signing appearances he had never had his trolley leave the track is it had today. Kirk went on to say that he read my book and just finished it yesterday morning.

"Folks, I never heard of David J. Brown or his novel, 'Daddy Had to Say Goodbye,' before last week when Seth told me of a third presenting author. I secretly thought, 'I hope this guy isn't any good, he could cut into my book sales.' I thought I had better scan through the book to see what this guy's all about. I didn't get past five minutes of scanning when I knew I had to read the entire book from cover to cover. When I met David at the newspaper reception party last night, he told me he was a first time, independent, nobody author. I beg to differ with you David, you may not be well known at this time, although I think you were exercising great humility with your 'nobody statement.' David, what you have done with your book is astonishing. I will compare it to the final game of the World Series.

It's the final inning, bases loaded, two outs and your team is down by three runs. Here comes the rookie walk-on, a total unknown who has rode the bench most all of the season. As he strolls to the plate, he steps into the batter's Box and stands there like he's waiting for the bus.

The very 1st pitch and you sent someone a very valuable World Series winning, Grand Slam baseball!

That is what you did David, both with your book and with your presentation. When word gets out about you, I'm sure the big publishing houses and movie studios will be in a very active bidding war!"

I was honored with Kirk's praise and embarrassed at the same time. I've seen used car salesman over-sell a used car before, but Jesus Christ even I am impressed!

Kirk said, "You all know me, you all know my work, most of you have been into my camera shop and many of you have taken my six-day Wilderness camp-out photography classes. I'm not going to waste any time with my presentation. I usually do a 'Q and A' session. Which mostly has to do with lens settings, lighting etc. etc. I have all that info at my tables that I'll be happy to hand out. Let's all take a 15 minute break and we can watch David work his magic at the signing tables."

I sold more books that morning then my last eight book signings combined! When I was finished I broke for the door to have some me time, a smoke and to bring my ego back into check. I walked the two blocks to the beach of Lake Superior and skipped a few rocks. I also had a chat with God before I returned to the Corker Hotel. The doorman told me, "Your people are waiting for you in the lounge, nobody has eaten yet."

I entered the dining room and found the only seat that was left was next to Seth's wife Mary. I asked her, "Do you mind if I sit next to you?" Mary gave me a big smile, patted the seat cushion and said, "I saved this seat for you. I want to talk with you." I was shocked to hear such a proper and dignified lady say, "You saved our ass, we were going to close the store next month. You didn't just save our business, I think you've also saved our marriage. We took out a Mortgage against our home that we had paid-off nine years ago, to start the business. Six months ago, we had to take out a second mortgage and we are about to default on both loans. Seth has had terrible bouts with insomnia and depression. I'm very worried that he may take his own life."

Mary began to cry as she said, "We now have honest hope for our future and you saved our business, our home and our marriage. I will always love you!" I took Mary's hand and held it for a few moments before I said, "So.......what's for lunch?" Mary kissed the back of my hand and started laughing. We all had a nice lunch, as we were eating I asked about the baby roses on everyone's tuxedos and sport coat lapels. Mary said, "Mr. Roberts bought them for us isn't he nice? The girls are so proud of the way they look with their tuxes and roses." As we finished lunch, Mr. Roberts asked if I could give him a few moments. We went to the hotel manager's office. Mr. Roberts told me he had the wrong read on the local people he met last night and this morning, they showed him an entirely different side of the city. He said, "I'm staying here through Monday, I'm thinking of keeping this hotel for a profitable venture and also use it as a corporate retreat and for a 'Dog and Pony Show' for other interested cities. I'll make my decision after tomorrow night. The comments on the hotel and the ballroom have been very favorable. You have showed me the errors of my ways! By my withholding a promotional budget, I have dug a hole, you have taught this old dog a few new lessons. If you ever want to move to Chicago I'll make room for you as a corporate executive, interested?"

I smiled as I said, "Naw, I have a job, I'm a writer." Mr. Roberts said, "I will be at both signings today and tomorrow, this has been a great test of the likability of our property, numbers are not the only unit of measure. To be here to witness the flow of people is a much better yardstick. I wish I had the time to visit all of our properties and do what you are doing here." I said, "So my corporate job offer is for me to travel and do all the cities were you own properties and put on book signing events?"

Paul looked at me in mimic of the 'morticians grin' as he said, "You're crew said you had a quick mind but damn that was quick!" With a complementary grin I said, "Well, Mr. Roberts, it's like this, $100,000 and I will work for you for five months a year. I don't want to be bothered by you or anyone from your company for the other seven months. You pay all my expenses up front with a corporate credit card and cash for incidentals. I'll sell my books and all sales will belong to me."

Another grin from Mr. Roberts as he said, "You obviously know your worth, I will give that some serious thought. I will shake your hand for $70,000 right now!"

"Nope, nobody lowballs me, the price is now at $110,000!" We both laughed and left the office.

The afternoon presentation and signings went well, with standing room only, and who do you suppose were sitting against the opposite walls across from each other, with their backs to me, facing the audiences while madly scribbling? Well of course, it was none other than the 'Norwegians!'
I don't think they ever looked at me as I was speaking.

I didn't do the 'show of hands' deal that I did in the morning. I opened the floor for Q & A and I was surprised at the hands in the air of several people who had attended the morning presentation. When I finished I went out for a smoke and who was standing in the garden? No one other than the Norwegians!

The Norwegian's and I said hello and they drifted off. I had two cigarettes and I returned to the ballroom to sign the books from the afternoon presentation. As I was signing Missy came behind the table and asked me for a moment of my time. She said, "Mr. Brown I really do like wearing this lady's tuxedo but would it be ok if I came to the 6 o'clock show in one of my other new gowns, they are so beautiful!" I gave her a look of fatherly disdain and held it for a few moments. Missy lowered her head as if to surrender.

I said, "Missy it all depends on how fast you can bring me a cup of hot coffee." Missy sprinted across the room and returned with a steaming cup of coffee along with an assortment of all of the different creamers and packaged sweeteners. I thanked her for the coffee as she stood still waiting for my answer. I asked her if she had grandparents, she said yes. I asked if they lived in a city and were they in relatively good health. She said yes. My patented grin overtook me as I said, "Call your parents and both sets of grandparents. Tell them all to be here, in the lobby at 5:00 p.m. sharp. The Corker Hotel would like them to be their honored guests for dinner. It's not every day that your grandparents get to see their granddaughter wearing an evening gown and looking like a Princess." Missy smiled a big toothy grin as she skipped off to make those phone calls.

CHAPTER 4   THE VIEW FROM THE TOP

I found Vicki at the hotel front desk where she was taking a room reservation over the phone. I stood at the counter and waited until she hang up the phone and finished the reservation on the computer. The phone rang again and I deeply lowered my voice and said, "Don't answer that, there are two other people here to take that call, come with me." Poor little Vicki was obviously torn between her duties and my demand. She knew that I was the boss at the moment and I carried Mr. Roberts's full blessings. She came from behind the counter with a dreadful look as she feared she was about to get hollered at. I hooked her arm and led her out the front entrance. I hailed the first cab in line at the taxi stand. She asked, "Where are we going, what's going on?"

I said, "Get in, we are not going to speak until we arrive at our destination. Enjoy the ride and catch your breath." I had the cab driver take us to the Radisson Hotel. It is a round, sixteen story hotel with an all glass, top floor restaurant that revolved were you could see the entire city in sixty-six minutes without turning your head. I had made the reservation that morning, the guest hostess took us to our table. I thanked her and said we are ready to see our server now. The hostess nodded with a bright smile. The waitress came with a satin cloth covered silver serving tray. The hostess

42

came along with her, the waitress looked at me and asked, "Now sir?" I said, "Yes, now." The waitress remove the satin cloth cover.

On that tray were three different colored corsages and a large, jewelry store box. Vicki just sat and stared. I told her to pick one, she just stared as I said, "Pick one or I will pick one for you." Vicki picked a beautiful blue corsage. I told her to stand up so the Hostess could pin it on her. As she did, the Waitress said, "I don't ever remember seeing a woman in a white tuxedo, but you make it a smart looking outfit!" Vicki blushed as she was being pinned. I told Vicki to stay on her feet as I told the two restaurant workers to each pick one. "Vicki would be honored to pin these on you Ladies." Suddenly, there stood three little giggling girls at a sleepover with moist eyes. When everyone was properly pinned, I took the jewelry box from the serving tray and thanked the ladies as Vicki and I sat down. Vicki smiled and said, "I don't know what to say."

"I don't want you to say anything, I want you to listen to me. What do you see out the window directly in front of us?" Vicki said, Enger Tower. I said, "In sixty-six minutes we will see that very same view after a full revolution of the city. You are to listen and enjoy the view. You are now looking at your future, pay attention. I'm going to give you a life lesson that I hope you carry throughout your lifetime. I trust that you will share it with many others along your journey, so listen up.

What you just witnessed was an exercise in validation. When you pined those corsages on the wait staff, you transformed them to people. People that matter, people that now know they are not just restaurant workers. They have been shown that they are valued human beings. You did that for them. Who knows what kind of battles they face in their everyday lives. They most definitely will have a better day today. Validation is a rare gift that very few receive. We don't look at each other anymore, it's just a mechanical 'thank you and have a nice day' and we're off to the next thing. You just now made a difference in two people's lives. We will get back to this lesson in a few minutes.

Now I need to admonish you. Your heart gets in front of

43

your head and you put yourself at risk. You lose focus on what is in front of you, as you try to do it all, trying to be all things for all people. You were not hired to do it all. You were hired to promote and book events.

You have all but appointed yourself as the hotel GM. The hotel has a GM and you are not her! Your coworkers have told me that you even vacuum and dust the lobby at 6:00 am each morning. That is not your job. Stop it, stop all of that and stop it now! You want so badly to make this hotel a success that you are destroying yourself. Yes, you have done the admirable thing but not the smart thing. Now that crummy ole' mean Mr. Roberts has witnessed first-hand what the problems actually are, he is bringing your GM to corporate for more training for ten days. He is going to hire seven additional staff that should have been hired from the very beginning. You will have a viable budget to work with.

Now for lesson number two. Corporate exec's only see numbers and act on the 'Bean Counters' advice. On paper, you have been a miserable failure. Again, all corporate sees is numbers. They can't see you dusting and vacuuming the lobby at 6:00 am. Nobody knows that you cover shifts of employees who have to pick up their sick kids from daycare or school, or that you cover for employees Doctor's appointments, clean guest rooms when a maid calls in sick, or the dozen other things you do, that are not in your job description. Numbers don't show effort or heart, numbers only show profit and loss. Numbers don't show a perky young lady with an electrifying smile with a kind voice, who is willing to do anything for anyone. You young lady, went out of your way to tell them that they should fire you! Do your job, stay focused and help out when you can but protect the company and yourself, by staying the course.

Now go dry your eyes, come back here and we are going to have a meal together. I have been told by several staff members that you have hardly left the hotel in the last week and nobody has seen you eat anything. Go freshen up, I'm hungry!"

I forced her to order a large meal and said, "You may now

speak." During the meal (that she gobbled down) I asked her about her family. Vicki said the entire family are all devout Christians and attend church services three times a week. She admitted that she has missed several church services due to her job. As we finished lunch, I asked her how she got along with Kathi from the newspaper. Vicki hesitated for a moment and giggled, "Oh you mean Missy? She asked me to call her Missy. She is so nice that I'm sure that we will be friends forever! She told me how you hard-assed her. I kinda knew that this was coming for me as well. I just didn't know how or when. Can I ask you a question?"

I leaned back in my chair and said, "Go ahead ask away." Vicki cleared her throat as she asked, "Why do you do so much for all of us when you don't get anything for it?" I looked at her and smiled. "Sweetheart, I have failed many people most all of my life, my family, my former wives and employers. I also failed myself greatly, today I do what I do for others as a living amends to those I have wronged. I have been blessed with this second chance to be a decent man. Keep in mind that I am also doing this, in-part to sell my books also. And like everyone else, I need to prove my worth….to myself. Now back to you, young lady. Did Missy tell you about the three evening gowns her company gave her?" "Oh yes, she tells me everything! I smiled and said, "No she hasn't told you everything. Missy said you two are the same size and wear the same size shoes, she would like to loan you her other evening gown that she has yet to wear, for the 6 o'clock show tonight." Here came the tears again. I said, "Stop that, wipe your eyes we are not done here and you are still on the clock." I asked, "What do you think is in this jewelry store box that you have been eyeing for the last hour?" She of course said she didn't know. I said, "Well it's for you young lady and it's not from me." I turned my back to her and pulled out the sharply folded note from inside the jewelry box and snapped it closed. I handed her the note and said, "Read it to me."

Dear Vicki,

I wish to extend my most sincere apologies for the way I have been treating you. I knew nothing of your many colossal efforts. You have taught me about my jumping to conclusions without seeing the total picture.

Please accept this gift as a token of my appreciation for your many efforts.

With admiration and respect

Paul E. Roberts

I handed her the box. Inside the box was a gold necklace with a pretty gold filigree pennant with a cross in the center. There was also a matching bracelet with a cross in it. Once again here comes the tears.

"So now young lady, you get another lesson in validation. That nasty mean ole' Mr. Roberts said you WILL attend church with your family tomorrow morning and come directly to the hotel afterwards. You and your family, grandparents included, will join Mr. Roberts as his special guests for a private Sunday brunch.

Keep this last hour and your gifts from Mr. Roberts as a secret. You may only tell your grandchildren someday, as you explain the importance of kindness and validation. Now, look out the window and tell me what you see directly in front of us." Vicki said, "Oh my Gosh, its Enger Tower again, it's directly in front of us! I did not even realize we were rotating all around the city." "That's right young lady, you are 6 minutes passed your one hour lunch break and you have to get back to work!"

The taxi cab dropped us off at the front door of the hotel. I went to the lounge and saw Missy sitting with her family. I called Mr. Roberts cellphone and told him that he was buying lunch for the party of eight who are currently seated in the dining room and he had a brunch date of which he will personally host, with ten in the lounge for tomorrow. I said, "It's all on your dime, Buddy Boy.

46

He said, "Bullshit, it's coming out of your $110,000 salary!" I said, "Every time you talk-back to me, my salary increases by $10,000 increments." Mr. Roberts chuckled as he said, "Yes Sir, so sorry Sir!" and hung up. I went home for a quick nap.

The afternoon presentation went well. We were at about 80% capacity. I couldn't help but notice the Norwegian's were seated half way down the room, one on each side of the room. This time their chair backs were flat up against the wall. They were still scribbling like mad as they constantly were scanning the room.

I was ten minutes into signing books and doing photographs when I looked up to see Forrest and Madeline were next in line with their stack of 20 books to be signed. We were lightly chatting as I was signing their books.

Madeline said, "We would like to take you for a meal and conversation anytime in the next two days," Forrest jumped in with "We have a proposition for you that we hope you will enjoy." I'm thinking, "I bet these guys must be swingers." "Morning would work best for me besides my first presentation wasn't until 1 o'clock." We agreed to meet at 8:00 am the following morning at Perkins Restaurant.

CHAPTER 5   THE GREAT AMERICAN FARMER

I did have one remarkable experience with a mid-60's year old woman (I'm guessing Finnish). I noticed that she was in line to have her book signed but she kept going to the back of the line when a few people got behind her as though she wanted to be last. I leaned over to Ms. Tami who was opening each book for me to the 'author signing page.' "Tami, do you see that short gray haired lady in the pink and blue striped blouse at near the end of the line?" Ms. Tami said, yes. I said, "Go get her and bring her to the far end of the tables and wait with her, until I get there in a few minutes. I told Mary (who had given the newspaper employee a smoke break and was manning the photo printer) to go down-the-line and to tell the fourth person in line and on back that I am going to take a fifteen minute break." I could see that the Norwegians were intently watching and continued to take notes at a respectable distance. When I finished signing for the final forth person with a handshake and photo, I walked over to Ms. Tami and the lady in the blue and pink striped blouse. I introduced myself and she said her name is 'Marge.' I told Marge that I've been watching her and plainly saw her playing, "Leap Frog" in the line. "What is it that you want to say to me in private, Marge?" Marge started to tear up as she said, "I read your book and I realized that I

48

know your character, 'Flanagan' better than I do my own husband of thirty years. We never talk we just watch TV and eat, but we never talk. I honestly don't know what his childhood was like. I don't know what he is thinking about himself or me. We don't argue or fight or anything like that, we just don't talk about ourselves. I feel like he doesn't care about our marriage or maybe he doesn't like me, it just makes me so sad.

Then I read your book and Flanagan puts it all out there about why he never told his wife's about himself. I'm so ashamed about failing my husband."

Then came the real waterworks, I told Ms. Tami to take her to the ladies room and I will meet them in 10 minutes in Vicki's office. I went to Vicki's office. She had her door open and was seated behind her desk. Vicki had a mini conference table in her office that sat eight people. I said, "Vicki I need your office for twenty minutes or so." She sprang to her feet and said, "Yes Sir, I'll be in the lobby." I said, "No you won't, Ms. Tami will be bringing a lady in, in a few minutes. The four of us are going to have some girl talk, you sit the lady in the center chair facing the wall, and you girls sit on each side of her and remove that picture from the wall. I don't want any distractions when I'm speaking. I'm going out for a smoke. You girls chat it up until I return."

As I entered the office Marge started to stand up. I motioned for her to sit back down. I said, "Marge these young ladies are my dearly trusted confidants and they will hold our conversations in the strictest of confidence. Do you understand Marge? A slight nod of her head as she still wasn't sure why we were sitting there.

"Marge, I want to tell you about Clinton Flanagan. Yes, Flanagan is a cool guy and has most things about life, himself and others figured out. Yes, he also takes responsibility for his behavior and tries to never blame any of the women in his life for his failings. Yes, Flanagan emotionally fillets himself in his quest for his truths. But Marge, Flanagan is not real! You must understand that Marge. Clinton Flanagan is a fictitious character in a book that is a work of fiction, it's a novel, Marge.

49

No man or woman would ever dare to gut themselves for the entire world to see!" Marge had a small smile as she said, "But you did, everyone that heard you read from your book is sure that you are him. You are Clinton Flanagan and your book is actually an autobiography. I know that you are him, just by the way you've been talking to me. You sent Ms. Tami and told her to tend to me just like Flanagan would do. You knew I was troubled before I even spoke. You saw it when I was way back in the line, besides everyone knows that you were Flanagan when your eyes started to mist and your voice started the crack. Everyone was teary eyed and when you left the stage, everyone was talking about that poor little boy, it just broke our hearts!"

Missy and Vicki looked at each other in shock as they realized that Marge was right. They put their hands to their faces and cried. I stood up, reached over on Vicki's desk, grabbed the box of Kleenex and slid it across the table and said, "Nobody move, you girls gather yourselves up. I'll be back in 5 minutes." I left the room and hotfooted it out, to the safety of the garden for a quiet smoke. I returned to the room and the girls were all holding hands and wiping their eyes."

I said ladies, "I must tell you and I emphasize the word, '*must*,' tell you, that I am not Clinton Flanagan. I don't want to hear another word of it, do you all understand?" I paused for a moment and asked Marge what her last name was. She said, 'Kivi.' I asked what her husband's name was, she answered, Axel.

"Well Mrs. Kivi, here is what you do. You go home, I don't know if you and your Mr. drink coffee and snack on cookies or drink beer and chew pretzels. You go home, layout cookies our pretzels with the corresponding drinks. You call your Mr. into the kitchen tell him to sit down and you remain standing and say, 'Mr. Axel Kivi, I find you to be quite attractive and you look to be a very interesting man, my name is Mrs. Marge Kivi and I would like to get to know you. Shake his hand firmly and you sit down. You look him squarely in the eye and say, Mr. Axel Kivi tell me all about yourself, I've got all night!' I think that it is at least a starting point." I stood up and said, "Ladies I have to go back to work and you two youngsters have to change clothes for the six o'clock show."

Marge said, "Mr. Brown, I am going to do exactly as you said, can I ask you for one small favor?" I said sure Marge. She said, "I forgot to have you sign my book." She handed me the book from her purse. I signed it, "To my friend Marge, a lady with remarkable courage. Being someone is easy, knowing yourself is a lifelong challenge. Be brave my friend. Your pal, Dave."

The girls lined up for hugs, as I said, "Go easy on my sport coat with all that running mascara and teary stuff. I only own two sport coats." We all chuckled and hugged. I collected cheek kisses and went to go find some coffee and quiet.

As I left the room I said, "Marge, you might want to invite your new boyfriend, Mr. Axel Kivi to a, 'Meet and Greet the Author' event tomorrow at 1 o'clock in the ballroom of this very hotel. Girls go and get dressed, Marge you head for home and do the deal, see ya all later."

As I left the office I saw the Norwegians standing behind a tall potted plant pretending to be having a conversation. When I left the office earlier to go out for a quick smoke and to get away from the 'tear-fest', they were in almost the same spot.

I went back to my tables to finish my book signings. I started to laugh as I thought, "These fuckers are Russian spies! They are like Boris and Natasha from the Bullwinkle Show!" I sat drinking coffee and giggling about the, not so secret Russian spies."

The evening performance went well with nothing of importance to report. The girls looked stunning in their gowns. I signed about a 130 books and the Russian spies took even more notes than they did all day.

They reached out and engaged with most all of the people in the room, they took notes as they were acting like they were reporters, doing interviews.

CHAPTER 6   THE RUSSIAN SPY REPORTERS

I went home bone tired. My last thought was about having breakfast with Boris and Natasha, the undercover Russian newspaper reporters as a giggled myself to sleep.

I woke up early and after my shower, I'm in the mirror shaving and the thought came to me. "Hey maybe these guys aren't Russian spies, maybe they're just like, rookie reporters or court room artists and are in training and have to do facial drawings and stuff like that."

I arrived 15 minutes early at Perkins, they were seated on a couch in the lobby. They both gracefully stood with bright smiles. Forest put his hand out, we clasped hands and he put his other hand on my forearm as a gesture of approval like an elder may do. "Elder my ass, I have at least ten years on these two." I put my hand out to Madeline to shake and she grinned and said. Oh, hell no, I want a hug! Her embrace was a heartfelt welcome, kind of like a grandmother my do. The thought came to me, "These two fuckers want to adopt me!" We sat in a booth.

I said to them, "This is my time, I will run this show, let's forgo the pleasantries and how well we slept last night and how we look so rested bullshit, you're going to pay for breakfast because I don't work for free.

So, what gives with you two?" They looked at each other and begin laughing Forest said, "God I love you, and my wife is absolutely *in love* with you! We won't try to stroke you with our observations of you or of your book. We think Kirk Meyer said it all. But first we have to get our names straight. Please call me Woody rather than Forest, I only answer to Woody. I am a Forest Jr. I grew tired of people trying to distinguish me from my dad. When I was a kid, people thought they were funny by calling me stump, brush, twig, branch, and all that other bullshit the goes along with it.

Please call me Woody. I glanced at Madeline and said, "Do you have any special requests for your name?" Madeline said, "Madeline is my Great Grandmother's name. It's a beautiful name but terribly outdated. I'm not an old lady, please call me, Maddie."

I sat back in the booth and had a laugh and then said, "As we sat down I told you both that this was my show and my time. The very first thing you two do is give me instructions on how to address you guys." I smiled and said, "I think we're going to get along just fine. Now you better get to it because I don't talk when I eat, I eat when I eat". That set them back a bit as they glanced at each other with a cautionary look. Maddie said, "We would like to tell you who we are and then what we want.

I have a PhD, in psychology and I specialize in forensic case studies of the criminally insane. I work for the state of Minnesota and teach classes for two universities with a course study on Alcoholism, depression, domestic abuse survivors, and abusers and suicide. I also give court recommendations for treatment for abusers." My thought was, "Well fuckkkkk me."

Then came Woody, "I'm a retired high school principal. I have a double master's degree in English Literature and Social Work. We're both EMT's, we are volunteer ambulance crew members at Meadowlands Ambulance Service." Maddie then said. "We found your book on a desk at the Meadowlands fire hall, it's where we headquarter our ambulances.

We both read it, we are greatly taken by the story and you. We planned out this meeting for the last several days. We had a

53

well-organized list of questions but all that went out the window when we first saw you walk into the room, yesterday morning.

Your first paragraph of the first chapter described you to an absolute, T! You do carry yourself like a Diplomat and you do have the stoic posture of a Marine. Your eyes broadcast a deep kindness like a Priest. As far as Flanagan's good looks, you have him beat by a country mile!

When you were introduced and took the stage I heard a smooth, controlled voice of firm conviction and humility. When you read the introduction to your book you threw us both back into our seats. As your eyes started tearing and your voice broke, I wanted to jump from my chair and hold you forever. The entire room suddenly knew that the highly skilled novelist and motivational speaker in front of us was in fact, Clinton Flanagan! We all knew that we were looking into the soul of a true survivor, and I was ashamed!"

Maddie reached across the table and took my hand. She grasped Woody's hand and Woody took my other hand. We three, bowed our heads for a brief few moments, to regain our composer.

"OK you guys, you both told me who you are in these last few moments and I saw who you are. Now let's get to why you are here." Woody had a sheepish look on his face when he said, "We want to study you, I have always wanted to get my PhD, but never could settle on a strong topic to base it on. I have found that topic in your book. I want to explore the effects of trauma and suicide of First Responders." Woody ended with a sheepish, soft pleading look and said, "Would you please help me?"

Maddie then said "Your book told me that I had it all wrong for all these years. I've written many papers and publications in journals and I taught all these classes, examined hundreds if not thousands of clients, made recommendations to the courts that change the course of their lives and I never understood the extreme depths of a broken man. David I am so sorry and now, with your help I will right my wrongs. I am asking you to mentor me to make amends. I will rewrite everything I've ever done.

54

I will change every future presentation. I have done a terrible disservice to you and my many students. I wish to rewrite those books and contact each of my former students and gift them my new books, to set them straight. I want to dedicate my new books to you and invite you to be a paid, guest speaker at all of my presentations."

Luckily, our breakfast was served, we sat in silence and ate. Woody and Maddie constantly glanced at each other, I could see it was killing them to not speak during the meal. I had the giggles inside. I finished my meal first and went out for a smoke. When I came back in the restaurant they were both beaming like little kids, like when the teacher left the room and now they can talk again.

I sat and said, "I only have a few rules, if you break any one of them, we are done.
Rule #1 is.... don't bullshit me.
Rule #2 is....don't speak or write bullshit about me.
Rule #3 is....don't violate my 'safe word' policy.
Rule #4 is....your safe word is 'PASS.' When you ask me a question and I say, 'Pass,' that means I'm not going to answer that question. My reasons are my own. If you try to back door me by asking the same question in another way we will be done at that moment. No 'do-overs.' I will be done with you both.
Now, let's talk about rule #1.

I could see by your cautionary back-and-forth glances that you were asking each other, "Should we tell him now?" I don't read minds but I do read people. I can tell that you both come from money and a lot of it. More money than you two could have earned in your what, 40 years of life?"

Maddie said, "We are ashamed and embarrassed to admit that we both grew up with extreme wealth. We both lived in large mansions in the same neighborhood. We belonged to the same country clubs and still do today. We grew up with everything that you didn't have. We only got cold when we were outside ice skating or building snowmen with our nanny's or parents. We walked away from meals prepared by our live-in house cook or the

55

Country Club Chef. We had more food on our plate then you probably ate in a week's time. We were the kids whose ice skates you wanted to grind into dust. We were spoiled and obnoxious little shits. We cared about nothing but ourselves. We hated and made fun of poor kids. We both attended the most prestigious Ivy League schools in the country. In collage, we owned high-end sports cars and had a very large monthly allowance.

Our parents were best friends and both sets of our parents decided that they were going to give us the bulk of our inheritance when we turned 30 years old. We both have a great passion for literature. We own homes in London, Madrid, and Athens. In the U.S. we have homes in New York City, Palm Beach, Aspen, and of course, here in Duluth.

We've read most all of the greats, the greatest of the greats. We have a very nice collection of signed first editions."

I waved her off on going any further. I said, "So now you two decided to go slumming?"

The look of sheer horror on their faces was absolutely priceless! Woody cleared his throat and said, "It's even worse than you know.

We have traveled the world, to every city of the literary greats, to visit their homes. We did this for five years, neither of us worked. For five full years we blew through millions of dollars without a care. About ten months ago we came to the realization that we had become so self-absorbed and self-indulgent that we became sick of ourselves and each other.

We met a man named, Don Prince in Boynton Beach, Florida. He was putting on a public seminar about the true value of life. Mr. Prince helped us to understand the most basic of life skills, of which we knew little about. We engaged Mr. Prince in conversation after the seminar and asked if we could join his group. Mr. Prince gave us an appointment the next afternoon in his office. That afternoon we were shown into his office but we had to wait for twenty minutes as his other appointment was running a bit over. We were standing in front of his bookcase's looking over his collection when he came into the room. He walked over to the far wall, pulled out a book and said, 'This book was written by a personal friend of mine, who I deeply admire. He lives in Duluth Minnesota, the same city you live in. I suggest you read this book and contact him. You can't have this copy, it is a personalized and signed copy, to me. Go on Amazon and get it.' David, it was your book!

We attended three more of Mr. Prince's seminars and came back to Duluth. I have to admit that we did not buy your book. Because of our brief time with Don Prince who works with a lot of First responders with depression, alcoholism and PTSD, we decide to take classes to become volunteer EMT's in our community.

We saw your book on the EMS desk in the fire hall. We told the EMS director, Troy Maly, that we saw that same book in Boynton Beach, Florida a few weeks ago. Troy smiled and said, 'David is a dear friend of mine, he was here just last week for the EMS Appreciation Week. We had a community barbecue for EMS and Fire Volunteers. David came to thank our people for what they do, he donated two books to our free raffle and gave away another three books. One, to our longest, (now retired) EMS volunteer. Another book went to a neighboring Fire Chief for his firehouse as a loner, and the flight paramedic who gives us much of our training was the third recipient."

I gave them the wave off as I said, "OK enough of this, we have to move on. Yes, Don Prince and Troy Maly are greatly respected friends of mine. Now I've been watching you two, watching you interviewing people.

So now I have an idea of what you guys are up to. I'm your next project, I get it. I'm not so sure I want to be your lab rat. I will let you guys know after the one o'clock presentation, assuming you going to be there lurking around and scribbling notes, right?"

They both nodded their heads and we walked out of the restaurant together. Their 2018 Lincoln Navigator was parked directly behind me. As I put my key in in the door lock of my truck, Maddie said, "That's a pretty truck, do you collect old trucks?" I said, "No Hun, it's a 1998 GMC, it's 20 years old with 205,000 miles on it, it's paid for and all I can afford." Maddie and

Woody's faces turned a bit red with embarrassment. I said, "See you guys at the hotel."

I drove to, 'Canal Park' and strolled the pier to clear my mind.

When I got back to the hotel I went to the lounge to get a cup of coffee and a check in with the crew. Vicki and her family were seated at a banquet table with Paul Roberts, at the head of the table. I noticed corsages on the women and boutonniere's on the men. I caught Paul's attention and I gave him a nod and a wink. He stood from the table at the same time Vicki did and they walked over to me. Paul shook my hand and grinned as he said, "I see you slept in this morning." I said, "Nice touch with the flowers." Paul said, "Those flowers and the meal are coming out of your $120,000, Buddy Boy."

My turn to grin, "Buddy Boy, it's coming out of my $130,000, can you dig it?" We both laughed as Vicki grabbed my arm and said, "Please come to the table and meet my Aunts and Grandparents."

After introductions I went to find Seth and the crew. There were about 30 people in the ballroom sipping coffee, tea and bar drinks.

The first crew member I saw was Ricky, the photographer. I went to him and asked him how he was holding up. He smiled at me and said, "The four of us have never taken so many pictures, in this short period of time. I did family photos for everyone on the team."

I grinned as I said, "Yup, and I saw you doing 'family shots' last night for the audience members and the slick way you palmed and pocketed those green 'appreciation' gifts as you handed them their instant photos from the company printer. Well done Sport, don't get caught."

I told Ricky that I suspected we would have a small crowd at the one o'clock show due to church and family stuff on Sundays. "The six o'clock has been sold out. 410 tickets have been sold, you guys have to step up your game. In the meantime, I want a shit load a promo shots of the hotel lobby, exterior, ballroom and two different size master suites. Go to the front desk and ask for the bellhop, he knows the drill. At three o'clock you and your crew will be having a, 'whatever you want' dinner on Paul Roberts and the Corker Hotel. Order from the top of the menu, I want pictures of the food." Ricky grinned as he asked, "Before or after?" I really did like this guy. He was one hell of a good fellow and had a great sense of humor. He worked his guts out. I started to walk away and turned with an afterthought. "Ricky, do you and your guy's have any special woman in your lives?" Ricky said, "Two of us here are married, the other two have serious girlfriends." I said, "Good deal, everybody call your ladies and tell them dinner is at the Corker Hotel, at 3:00 pm sharp! You cats have been putting in some long hours, it's my small way of saying thank you." Ricky smiled and said, "Way cool, thank you sir!"

I saw Paul Roberts talking with Ms. Tami and Missy. I called his cell and said, "Pauly Boy, eight for dinner at 3:00 pm, and four long stem red roses. He laughed and said, "Why is it that every time you call me, it costs me money?" I said, "Put your phone on speaker, I want to girls to hear this. I could see he put it on speaker and I said, "Ladies, those dozen long stem red roses you'll be receiving this afternoon are from my friend, Mr. Paul Roberts." I saw Paul shake his head as he took his phone off of speaker. He dropped his head and said, "Well played Mr. Brown, well played."

I said, "Now Buddy Boy that's a total of eight dozen, long stemmed, red roses and you're pushing it to $140,000."All this time, I was standing only thirty feet behind him. I walked up to Paul and the girls, slightly brushed past Paul and said, "Hi kids!" without breaking stride. I went on to visit with Seth and Marry.

The 1 o'clock show went smooth and as I expected the crowd was less than 200 people. The highlight of that presentation was when sweet ole' Marge, brought (who I could only assume was Mr. Axel Kivi) a gentleman over for introductions. Mr. Kivi was about 5'6", 160 pounds. He was wearing a faded green John Deere ball cap, a twenty year old or older brown, shapeless, hounds-tooth sport coat, blue shirt with a blue and cream striped

59

tie. He had a weathered forehead but his face was pale. It's the look of a man that had worn a full beard for a very long time.

Mr. Kivi's face was smooth and shiny with razor cuts from an obviously dull razor blade. I don't think the Kivi's were poor, just damn frugal due to the many hard times the American Farmers constantly have to face. I fully knew, exactly what I was looking at. Before me stood, "The True American Farmer!"

Mr. Kivi shook my hand with his, dry old saddle leathered hand and a toothy grin as he leaned over and with a quiet voice and said, "After my Mrs. had her talk with me last night, we had some kissin and other stuff!" As he nudged me with his elbow. He had the slyest wink that I have ever seen. Marge was cool all by herself but throw sly ole' Axel in the mix and these were two beautiful people that I could not help but fall in love with!

When the photos and signings were over, I took Woody and Maddie into the private dining room, where Missy and I had our, 'come to Jesus meeting' the day before. I said, "OK guys, I will go along with you but understand that I call the ball. Let me ask you two, a rhetorical question, rhetorical because I don't believe either of you know the answer and I'm not going to piss away any more of my time playing games.

So I will give you the answer, that answer is, 'TIME'. Time is the only correct answer. Now for the question. What's the most valuable thing on earth that we don't ever get back or get more of? Again, that answer is time. Time is the only answer, if you doubt me, go to a hospice, or better yet, go to a trauma unit and watch a person fight for their final breath. They have no time left. Now, am I clear on the value of time?" They both nodded and said, "Yes Sir," with very sober faces. "So, about time, my time is very precious to me. I might be sitting on my couch gorging myself on doughnut holes or potato chips, watching westerns but it is my time, and my time belongs to me! Is that clear?" Again with the head nods in unison.

"Here's the deal kids, you two will be here, in these chairs tomorrow at 7:00 am, every day this coming week and the next week, Monday through Friday. I don't give a rat's ass of what you

60

have appointments for, change them! I will give you five hours a day to ask any questions you want to. At precisely twelve noon of each day, I will walk out of this door.

Now, since neither of you have asked what's in it for me, I will tell you.

I am giving my most precious time because I'm going to use this weekend's events and the next two weeks to finish my second book. Seth told me that you belong to three book clubs and your group's burn through an entire book in just six weeks. How many total members of your book clubs including yourselves?" Woody answered, "thirty-four."

"When you leave tonight, take thirty-two books with you and deliver them to your book club members. I'll go the cost on them. Tell them to set down whatever is in their lap or on their nightstand. They have two weeks to read the book.

I want your members and yourselves in the ballroom the Saturday after next for a 'Q& A meeting with the author, with coffee tea and cookies at 9:00 am sharp. Tell your people about the value of time. They and you, are on the clock, my clock. When you come here at 7:00 am tomorrow I want to see two tape recorders on the table. You can take brief notes but I don't want to see the tops of your heads with you playing 'ink-pen wiggle worm' when I'm talking. Got that, good, enjoy the six o'clock show. I'm going home to a quick nap."

I walked through the dining room and saw Ricky's photo crew sitting with four lovely young ladies, who each had a vase of a dozen long stem red roses in front of them. I stepped up to the table and thanked the ladies for giving up their men for the last 3 days. I walked over to the bar and ordered four glasses of champagne, for the ladies and I went home for that nap.

61

CHAPTER 7   THE DEADLY AGENDA

The 6 o'clock show was a sellout. Angie was there and looked much better but was still quite weak. She did not give her presentation but it was announced by Seth, that Angie was there to autograph her books. She had a sizable line at her tables. I was happy for her. She came up to me after my presentation. She told me she was almost glad that she had become ill, she said, "I could not have followed after you, now I know why everyone was talking about you. What the hell are you doing living here in Duluth, Minnesota with all of your talent?" I said, "Ask Kirk" and I just smiled.

Paul came over with his own rendition of the 'morticians grin' as he said, "Our beverage sales for the last three days are better than any three wedding receptions. I'm becoming quite fond of you writing and reading types. My Corporation is much larger than we let on, we don't speak of our 31 South Sea Island resorts or 16 casinos throughout the world. Rehabbing historical site hotels is a very small part of our overall operations. Got a minute, let's go to my office I need to speak with you in private? "We went to Paul's office, he had coffee brought in.

Paul said, "I'm going to level with you, the world is my playground and has been for many years. I have enough money to fund the next five or six generations of the Robert's clan. I work my ass off, I work too much. My wife has told me that we will never have a happy marriage if I continued my affair with my mistress. My mistress is of course money, money and financial power.

The city of Duluth was the first city to ever tell me no on this venture. David, they spanked me. I fell into a bit of depression over that. I now realize that I needed that spanking, it humbled me.

It made me look at myself, my attitude and my lifestyle. In a moment I'm going to tell you why I asked you in here, but first I have to confess that I have had you watched since I first heard your name. This corporation has a sizable staff of investigators that travel the world. These people's abilities would rival the FBI and Interpol and even the KGB. Many are retired FBI and Secret Service agents. I have never met any of them because they won't allow that. There have been two agents on you since you came to this hotel three weeks ago. They have run a full background on you. They sat in on every one of your presentations. They have followed you everywhere you have gone, identified everyone you have talked to. They and a few of their associates have gleaned your school records, from kindergarten to high school graduation. They have reviewed all of your medical records from birth, your paramedic reports and police calls and arrest reports. I received their reports late last night. Everything you said about you on stage and in your book has been 100% authenticated. The only thing you left out were the many awards you received for the lives you have saved and the countless honors that have been bestowed upon you for your service. You are one of the very few or perhaps the only one who I have met, that, 'walks the talk.' I came here to investigate you for myself for two reasons.

Number one; I've never met anyone, who had absolutely no resources, walk into a failing Mom and Pop, hole in a wall bookstore, offer up three of his books for a consignment and three weeks later to be sitting across from me, as every bit my equal. The way you gained the confidence of these many strangers and rally them to the point where we are at this moment, is incredibly mind numbing. I can't even imagine where you would be today if you had the position and financial backing I've had. I'm most certain that you could have given us a run for our money. I came here to see how your mind works, all I have learned is that your mind does work and I believe your soul is what drives you.

Number two; from the minute I left Chicago on Thursday afternoon, I have gone dark, other than with my wife and our investigators and of course the hotel staff here. No one from corporate knows that I'm here, I've locked all my electronic devices so nobody can ping or track me. I needed this time alone to make this decision. My decision now, is to level with you. I dare not trust anyone else, so here it is.

I didn't plan on returning to Chicago. I was going to rent a small pleasure boat, go out in Lake Superior and jump overboard at full speed, into two-hundred feet of water, after dark tonight.

I have no or very little hope for myself. I am an incurable drunk. I have gone to eight different treatment centers, under assumed names and even a few of those treatment centers I was in disguise. I have read every bit of the AA literature including the Big Book and all the other hardcovers along with several 'Self Help' books. Again, so very much like you were, I am without faith. I have sat with all different kinds of shrink's. I have come to no other conclusion other than I'm a hopeless drunk. And I, much like you, know it will work for others, but I too am convinced it won't work for me. Your book put it straight for me. The last chapter of, 'Daddy Had To Say Goodbye,' took away all my excuses. I am now asking you if you would help me get and stay sober. David I don't want to die. I know you are busy and.....''

I held my Palm up and said, "Buddy Boy, shut the fuck up and listen to me. I'm not a cheerleader, I'm really just a generalist. I know a little bit about a lot of things but I don't know a lot about any one thing. Lucky for you, the one thing that I do know a lot about is, living sober. The greatest thing I know about living sober is that anyone can do it, even the likes of you, Buddy Boy!

It's simple, stop your chicken-shit hiding from your own truths. Get honest, go to meetings like any other alcoholic does, don't drink between meetings and go to lots of meetings. Get a Chicago sponsor, don't look for your equal because anyone in that meeting room is smarter than you, if they have at least one week of sobriety. Do what you are told and you can do this deal the same as me and the millions of other sober alcoholics. I will pick you up for a meeting at 6:00 am tomorrow. Now we have business to attend to in the ballroom." We stood, had a hug and as I turned to walk out of the office, Paul said, one more thing, as he reached inside of his suit pocket and drew out a thick, # 10 white envelope. And said, "This is $10,000 to help you out with your book business." I smiled and said, "Can't take it Skippy, I am your AA sponsor and we are not allowed to accept bribes. I'm planning to have my feet deep up your ass for many years to come. I'm not going to allow you to side-slip anything, you're just another common, garden variety drunk.

Get sober, get grateful and most importantly get humble. Sit back down, call your wife and tell her about you. You have caused your wife enough worry, leave out the pleasure craft and the late night swim plan. Actually leave that out for a very long time."

I went to the ballroom to press some flesh and pose for photos. I first found Boris and Natasha and told them that tomorrow's meeting would go from 10:00 am to 3:00 pm. I grinned as I said, "I'm the boss and I get the change the rules at any time." Maddie sweetly smiled as she said, "Of course you do." She leaned over and gave me a peck on the cheek.

At 8 o'clock things started to slow down and more than half of people had left the ballroom. All the crew were still acting like it was the first night of 'Mardi Gras' they were all still smiling and full of energy.

Paul came over to me and looked 50 pounds lighter. You couldn't have not noticed that he had been crying. Paul asked if I would gather everyone up and have them come to the private dining room, right away. He leaned close and said, "My wife said thank you and she wanted me to tell you that she loves you."

The entire crew was assembled in the dining room entry. It was Seth, Mary, Ms. Tami, their three part time college students, Missy, Vicki, Kirk, Angie, Ricky and his three photographers. I somewhat expected to see the Norwegians, as they had come to become embedded with, 'The Crew.'

Paul asked for everyone's attention and said, "The Randall Corporation and I, can never thank you enough for what you have all done, in the course of this last month. I can only offer you a small token of my gratitude and our corporation's appreciation. Please find your name on the place cards on the tables." On the tables stood several, 6" by 9" two inch thick clear plastic slabs that looked like they were made of crystal. They were mounted on a polished piece of stone that looked like a piece of cork. The crystal had an etching of the Corker Hotel with each person's name etched in 18 point type. It had today's date, and read, '2018 Champions of All Things Good.'

There was also a #10 white envelope at each place setting, with each person's name on it. I found out a few minutes later that there was a $1,000 in each of those envelopes.

Vicki screeched, "David come here!" Vicki had big tears as she said, "Look at this!" She held up a Cordova, Kid Leather, briefcase with her name embossed in 24 point, gold leaf. Paul walked up to us and asked Vicki if the briefcase would work for her. Vicki dropped her head as she said, "It is beautiful, it will work just fine and I will work for you forever!"
Paul brushed up against me as I did him earlier in the day and said, "I had a plaque for you too but I took it away because I was informed by a very wise man that you can't bribe you're AA sponsor."

The next morning, Paul was standing on the curb as I pulled up at 5:00 am. He was wearing jeans and a knit sport shirt. It was the first time I saw him in anything other than a $2,000 + suit. He had two, to-go cups of coffee in his hands and a very large smile. Before and after the AA meeting Paul introduced himself as, Paul Roberts. After the meeting we went to breakfast with a bunch of the guys from the morning meeting. As we left the restaurant he said, "My luggage is already out on the plane, would you mind taking me to the airport?"

"Sure Buddy Boy, I just have to make a brief stop and deliver a final lesson to the visiting dignitary from Chicago. I pulled up in the front of Larson's Bakery. "Paul, this is lesson #47, pay attention!

Larson's Bakery has been a family owned 'made from scratch' operation since 1943. That's more than 75 years at the same location and is solely owned by the family, with the third generation driving the bus. Some of their employees have served time, the Larson family believes in second chances. At the end of each day they donate and deliver their unsold bakery goods to the many shelters and charity groups in the city.

Your operation is all about, 'best deal pricing.' Best deal pricing, does not draw or hold loyalty. You own gazillion dollar properties and you offer your guests frozen donuts and packaged muffins for the continental breakfast? You want people in Duluth to play ball with you when you bring in goods from other states and countries? If you want to sell local, you buy local. Larson's Bakery will now be delivering at 4:30 am each morning, starting on Thursday!" We went inside and I made him buy me a donut, a very fresh donut!

During the ride Paul said that he was in love with Minnesota people. "Never seen so many hardy but kind people. That whole 'Minnesota Nice,' slogan is absolutely true! I am going to make several improvements on the Corker Hotel. The Corker will be our company's flagship. I will bring every city's prospective client to visit our, Vista Queen!
I also want to frequently visit the wise man who, *can't be bought.'*

As Paul started to walk up the steps of the jet he looked back and said, "I gotta get the hell out of here, I can't afford the way you like to spend my money!"

As I was about to pull away from the executive side of the airport my cell phone rang. It was the flight attendant from the airplane. She said, "Please come back, Mr. Roberts left something in your truck."

I pulled up to the stairway of the jet and the flight attendant came down the stairs with the identical briefcases that Vicki had received. My name was embossed in gold leaf.

She said with a toothy smile, "Mr. Roberts never takes no for an answer, you are going to have to learn that about him."

Before I could find any words, she spun, ran up the stairs and closed the door of the aircraft. I pulled away and parked on the tarmac next to the FBO office to process it all. I felt the heft of the weight and had a pretty good idea of what was in the briefcase. Inside was the etched crystal plaque with my name on it. I sat and had a few tears of gratitude, looked up and said, "Thanks God, what's next?"

CHAPTER 8   THE INTERROGATION

I arrived at the Corker at 9:30 for my 10 o'clock with 'Boris and Natasha.' I wanted to check on Vicki first. She was in her office with the door open, she had several large stacks of note cards piled all over her desk. Her head was down as she was writing. I taped my knuckles on her door, she looked up with a partial smile as she said, "This is all you're and my Grandma's fault!" I smiled and said, "Please continue." She said, "Gramma told me that I had to hand write a 'bread-and-butter' thank you note to everyone who registered online. David there are more than 900 online registrants, you're getting the bill for my surgery for my Carpal Tunnel Syndrome. Gramma told Mr. Roberts what she told me, Mr. Roberts had these printed yesterday." She handed me a card. It had the identical picture of the front of the hotel that was embossed on the front of the crystal, 'Champion' plaques.

She asked, "How do you find a print shop to open on Sunday and print these?" I looked at her and smiled, "Ever watched the Wizard of Oz? The 'Great and all-powerful Oz', can do anything! Mr. Roberts is the wizard of modern times." Vicki said, "Guess so, and yeah, Mary and Ms. Tami are pissed at you too!" I said "How so?" "I found out that Mr. Roberts, had Ricky show him all of his pictures that you made him take at the bookstore when you first met Ricky and Missy. Mr. Roberts had the outside front of the book store imprinted on their 900 'bread-and-butter' note cards. The only good part is that Mr. Robert's had the courier deliver the cards along with $500 to each of us to pay for the postage.

Mr. and Mrs. Quinn are waiting for you in the private dining room. Coffee, tea, milk, juice, muffins, and a fruit basket are in their also. Call room service if you need anything else. They will deliver lunch when you ask for it." "How did you know about my meeting and what's up with all the food stuff?" Vicki stood up, stepped around her desk and stood in front of me and said, "Guess it's like everything else that's happened this weekend. The 'Great and all-powerful Oz,' you prick!"

Vicki gave me a hug and said, "Now, get your ass out of my office, I've got work to do!" As she dramatically flung her arms towards the stacks of bread-and-butter note cards. "Get, I got work to do, you prick!"

Woody and Maddie both rose as I came into the room with big smiles. Woody shook my hand and Maddie stepped around the table and gave me a hug and a kiss on the cheek. She smiled as she said, "I'm going to hug and kiss you each time we see you and when we leave you. I hope you don't mind Mr. Brown, if you do mind I will hug and kiss you twice as much Mr. Brown." Woody rolled his eyes and said, "I can't do anything with her, she is a free spirit!" I smiled as we sat down and said, "If we're going to be pals I want you two to knock off that Mr. Brown and Sir, shit. My name is Dave." Maddie grinned as she said, "I'm more inclined to call you Flanagan but Missy and Vicki have cautioned me against it. I get that Flanagan is a fictional character, you sly dog." I sat back and said, "Let's get a few more things straight, you two are far too worldly and far too old to be star struck and I'm sure as hell no star. So let's get started, I'm going to eat a muffin and pour myself a cup of coffee and yes I'm going to talk with my mouth full, so ask away."

Maddie: We along with many others just can't understand why your book is not a 'best of the best' top sellers. The TV talk shows should be fighting to have you on their shows. If it wasn't for Don Prince and Troy Maly we would never had known of you or your book and that would have been a tragic loss for us and your readers. Why aren't you famous?

Me: Every writer, performer and inventor hopes that the right person comes along to discover them and their craft. Only in the rarest of the rarest cases does that happen. Nobody comes to you, if you don't go to them than you go nowhere. I am a youthful 70 years old but I don't have the juice to chase rainbows.

Woody: Dave we want you to know that we have a ton of respect for you as do all the other people we have spoken with this last weekend. You have made yourself accessible to everyone, what you have done for the principles of this event is astonishing but most of all, you have set our trolley off the same track as you did Kirk Meyer. Maddie and I are quite anal. We always have to have everything lined out, we plan and we plan and then we plan even some more. We try to wrap a plan around the simplest of things, even going to the grocery store. We look and listen to you and you are so relaxed, everything just seems to flow for you. We hope to learn how you do that, we don't want to be rigid and calculating in everything we do. We hope you could help us with that in the next two weeks.

I held my Palm up to quiet Woody.

Me: Kids it's like this, at a very young age I realized that everyone poops. In my early adult years, I learned that we are all going into the same size hole when we die. A few years after that, during my EMT training while sitting through several autopsies, I learned that our guts all look pretty much the same. I don't do hero worship, we're all just human beings.

During my years as a paramedic and years later as a police officer I learned that planning what you're going to do enroute to a call was a waste of time and I developed tunnel vision rather than look at the things as they are right there in front of me. I had to learn to relax and let my training and experience take over. I am as a guilty as you, as well as the rest of the world. We are so fearful of being wrong that we never get to enjoy the ride. It takes us back to the whole fear thing. False-Evidence-Appearing-Real. Stop believing your own lie, the lies that we tell ourselves. Those lies are the same for all of us. Our number one lie is, 'I'm not good enough, people will find out about the real me and they won't like me.'

We're burning daylight, get to your questions. I did see that you two had your recorders on when I came into the room and you have damn near a ream of paper between the two of you. If you're going to talk with me, your script will not work.
Get the fuck out of your heads and come out from your gut." They glanced at each other as if to say, 'see I told you so.'

Maddie: We have been so foolish, you are so right about our fear, hell, you've been right about everything from the first moment we saw you! You are dead right about our fear, we worry about everything, we plan and plan but rarely do our plans work out, we become frustrated and we take it out on each other.

Up went my Palm again.

Me: Maddie, do you have a question in all this bullshit or are you using me for a life coach? Talk to my pal in Boynton Beach, Don Prince. That's what he does. Let's move on, I know you were embarrassed that you can't keep up with me and I certainly don't want to challenge you or your intelligence but educated does not always mean intelligent or smart. We come from different worlds. Now, I'm into 36 minutes with you two and you have yet to ask me one question.
Stop fucken around with explaining yourselves, I'm not a rabid Wolf that's ready to spring on you.

Woody: We are afraid that you will get bored with us or mad at us. We're afraid to ask the wrong question, we're afraid of losing contact with you, or you just getting up and walking away, and yes David you are right, we do live in fear, fear owns us and you taught us that."

"Good deal I said, I hope you are both willing to change that, now shut up and give me a fucken question."

Maddie: How did you know that the elderly lady in the mobility cart was so special, everyone loved her!

Me: First of all, Ms. Tami spotted her and waved me over. I could see the pain of loneliness in her eyes. I could feel her love and pride as well.

Maddie: Will you tell us about the little old lady that was crying at the end of your tables that you took to the office with Missy and Vicki?

Me: That, 'little old lady' is not as old as she looks. She is several years my junior. She's a farm woman, she has worked her guts out all of her life. She grew up on a farm and she married a farmer, she had 6 kids and has never been on a vacation, or left the county in her entire life. She's not old, she's just damn tired! She has worked, worried about; whether, crops, insects, livestock, well water, and every other thing that all the other farmers age from so quickly. As far as her tears and our conversation, that is not your business. I think you two have your own shit to deal with.
 I'm going out for a smoke, 'alone.' You guys should have brought coloring books and crayons.
When I came back in the room they had their heads down and we're drawing farm animals, at an 8 year old level.

Maddie: You know us better than we know our own selves or each other!

Me: That's not a question, but yeah, I heard almost that very same thing just the other day. (God-bless you Mrs. Kevi)

73

Woody: We have been all over the board with where to start with this. We want to know about you. We want to learn everything we can. Can I ask you where we should start?

Me: Woody, you have a cagey way of backing out but I will help you, the both of you. Both of you, listen to me and listen tight! The back cover of my book states that the author's past, runs many close parallels to that of his main character, Clinton Flanagan. Hear me now, when I tell you that I am not Clinton Flanagan! I 'must' say that I'm not Clinton Flanagan. I emphasize the word *must*. I don't want to be asked if I am, him anymore. Am I clear? You both are highly educated, and successful adults, stop jerking me off!

I will start with the beginning of my writing, but first I'm calling room service for lunch. We had a quick light lunch, Maddie got out her credit card to pay the waiter as I told her that the snacks and meals are comped, tip included by Mr. Roberts. I said, "I love getting into that man's pockets, let's get back to work. You first Maddie."

Maddie: We heard you talk about your first day writing, sitting at a table with your supplies twirling your pen, what about the first day you actually put your pen to paper and the days that followed?

Me: My first day of writing on paper, I was sitting in my truck, the same truck that I still drive today. When I returned from my Moms funeral in Minnesota, Steph asked me to leave. I had very little cash and a very limited credit card balance. I did not have enough money to get an apartment. I couch-surfed at four different homes for three months. I left their homes early each morning before they did. I sat in my truck and wrote all day long. I would park in a parking lot of a big box store so I had access to a bathroom and coffee. I was living solely off my social security which was only $20 above poverty level. My two dearest friends invited me to move in with them in Fort Collins, Colorado.

74

Without the loving hearts of Sean Carrigan and Tina Telson-Carrigan there would have never been a first book. More about them later.

Woody: Jesus Christ Dave, nothing has ever come easy for you has it? I have to tell you that we were both sure that either the Author or Flanagan were writing this story from a, Maximum Security Prison or a well secured Mental Hospital. We had a conversation with Paul Roberts about what parts of your book were true or fiction. Paul told us that the only parts in that entire book that are fiction, are the names of locations and the names of the characters.
He said, "Trust me, I had everything checked out!"

Maddie: We owe you an apology, several apologies in fact. We checked you out in all of the social media sites, we ran credit and job histories, birth and death records before we even met you. Since Friday night we have tried to interview everyone that showed up with the slightest of interest in you. Another few days of your book signings and we would have nearly as many note pads that would rival your sixty-eight legal pads. We both have swollen wrists and aching fingers. What we have found out from our countless interviews, was that most every one of these people believe you, they trust you and they love you! You are the Pied Piper of all living souls! We all want to be just like you, 'I daresay, none of us would want your past', but we would kill to have your life today.
I held my palm up for silence. I dialed a number, when she answered I said, "Bring them in and hurry!" In less than thirty seconds there was a soft tap on the door. I said enter, Vicki came flouncing in with a box of crayons and handed them to Maddie. As she turned to leave she brushed her hand on my shoulder and said, "I still hate you." As she laughed going down the hall. The Quinn's looked puzzled as I said, "There is a back story to every story. These crayons are for you farm art, I gotta pee and have a smoke."

When I returned from having my smoke, the gang was looking more puzzled than ever, I looked at them and asked, "What now?"

Maddie: How-do-you-do this, how-do-you-do this, this thing you do? Everybody, does love you! We just watched Vicki come in, walking hard throwing down a pack of crayons, punching you on the shoulder, looking at you and telling you she still hates you, and she walks out of the door laughing. You have that effect on everyone, people are just so drawn to you and they trust you and your so accessible. You are just so real. We have watched you since Friday afternoon and we've sat through what, five of your speeches and none of those five were the same. The message was different each time but each was powerful, in the way you gave validation to everyone. How-do-you-do that?

Me: There is more, please continue.

Woody: Your charm, your likeability, your brilliance and your wisdom has us upside down. We just have to tell you David, that our trolley has again left the track. We don't know which way to turn. We have so many questions, we feel like we know you so intimately, yet we know there is something so different about you and so welcoming, that we just can't figure it out.

Me: Well guys, here's the deal. If your trolley leaves the track one more time, I'm going to remove its wheels. Understood? Let's stay on point and let me focus so I can answer your questions. Your question was about the process of how I wrote the book. So let's get back to that.

I wrote in my truck for a couple of reasons. One, I needed privacy, living with Tina, Sean, Scott and two large Labradoodles was a beautiful experience but all the barking, phone calls, movement back-and-forth, ringing telephones, TV and music, I needed privacy to concentrate. So that's one of the reasons. The other reason is, I could smoke as I was writing rather than sitting in

76

the house and going out to take a break, it was just too time consuming.

I think my best writing experience was when I got a job working as a security guard for one of the top microbreweries in the nation. My job was to check in-and-out, semi-trucks. I had to inspect the trucks for cleanliness and equipment safety and refrigeration functions, so as to carry our product. The truckers had prearranged schedules. We had to run the schedules because of the custom packing on each pallet, so on average we got about 70 to 75 trucks a day. I had a lot of down time between trucks so I would sit in my truck and write.

When I first started the job I was looked down upon by the truckers and the employees of the brewery warehouse. People look at security guards as just some loser, wanna-be cop. I know when I was a cop, I looked at security guards in that very same way. I discounted them as non-people. It was a humbling experience.

During the course of my duty's I had to interact with eight principle warehouse personal, several times each day. In the beginning, these people were rudely dismissive. My thought was, "I will find a way to make them respect me." I got to turn them around by first watching the process, looking for ways to improve loading times and to make the warehouse employees jobs easier. It took me only a few days to see where I could improve the process. There was a two hour, 'sweet spot' where first and second shift overlapped. There was always a few loading dock bays open, but thirty or more trucks were waiting to load who had a later dock time appointments. I visited with the crew leader of the packaging department that does the custom pallets (mixed product in the same pallet). They were building the mixed pallets from a schedule that came from the order desk. I suggested they build the custom pallets by dock time schedules, rather than just going down the order desk list. From that day on, there was never an empty dock door. Most all trucks that came to load had just dropped off a load. Oftentimes they would miss our dock time because they were still off-loading at another warehouse. If they were late, I would bring up the next appointment early, to avoid an empty dock door. I would only allow 'straight loads' (non-mixed pallets) during the 'sweet spot' hours. It took a lot of pressure off of both shifts, got the truckers on the road much quicker and employees got to take their breaks without interruption. There were five different employees who would come out into the lot, to seal the, "Bonded" loads with federal tax tags and to have the drivers sign for the loads, and do a final check on the refrigeration units for proper temperature settings. They would stop by my truck to BS for a few minutes. I was always writing and they would ask about how the book was coming. At first, they would show a sly grin as if to say, "Bullshit, a security guard, is sitting in a truck, writing a book?"

When the warehouse crew saw I had a strong work ethic and a brain, the respect came quickly and I still have friendships with a number of those folks today.

The day after I received my first shipment of two-hundred books, I brought a case of them to work. The look on their faces when I showed them the book, set it down on the desk, personalized and signed the book and got to say, "This is for you," well, the look in their faces had its own rewards.

They couldn't believe it and they would say things like, "I watched you sit and write this and now I have the finished product, an actual book in my hand! Why the hell are you working as a security guard?" I would just smile and say, "It's just my lot in life. We all gotta eat!" After several days of their reading, the guys would come up to me and say things like, "I love your book!" or "Holy shit, what a life you have lived."

I made some great friends with many of the independent truck drivers. Three fellows come to mind. They built their own trucks, did all of their own repairs and maintenance. Their rigs were spotless inside and out. I was always amazed with the many thousands of miles they drive each week, in all kinds of weather and their trucks were always glistening. They were prideful and humble people, and they were all perfect gentleman. They saw me as a person, rather than as a loser security guard, they valued me and I learned from those men how to value other people. So it was a great lesson for me. It was a very humbling experience and the transition of being some goofball to a legitimate guy that people really liked and enjoyed being around was really a blessing for me.

The many nights I couldn't sleep I would get up at 1:00 o'clock in the morning and sit at the dining room table and write. Sean and Tina would come into the kitchen between five and six o'clock in the morning and I would still be there writing. They would just say, 'good morning' and go about their business. They never asked me if I was OK because they knew what I was facing and that was really endearing to me. They knew my heart and they knew my strength and they also knew my sorrow. They never challenged me in any way, as to my writing or my writing abilities, for that I'll always be grateful. We are still very dear friends today, as a matter of fact I was going officiate at their wedding and at the last minute, I had something come up where I couldn't make the trip back to Colorado. We have visited several times since I've moved here to Minnesota and it's always great to see them. I'm looking forward to our next visit. That's pretty much about the physicality of writing my book, as to the where and how of it.

Woody: What inspired you to get out of bed in the middle of the night and to sit in your truck all day and write for countless hours?

Me: There are people that still are asking what the major inspiration was that drove me to write the book. For some reason when I tell them I had a spiritual experience, it seems not to be enough, they need to know more.
Well, in part I start most every day by watching YouTube videos of a few of the singers on the 'X-Factor' and 'America's Got Talent, in their very first audition appearances. People like, 19 year olds, Will Jones, and Simone Torres. 50 year olds like Susan Boyle and Mary Berms, Christina Ramos and Rachel Potter. That may sound hokey to you and others, but I draw strength and hope. There is a certain beauty in seeing people realizing their dreams. Of course, these people have had voice lessons, coaches, and countless hours of rehearsal. But they still made it happen. To

79

watch them and their family's reactions to the judges input is magical. To witness the joy and pride of their years of efforts, is intoxicating. Sadly, the hair, makeup, wardrobe, voice and song selection coaches work them over and the next week they are no where's near who they were the week prior. I like raw not polished.

I realized there may be a day when someone might wish that they were me, so I have to keep close to what inspires me. I watch others struggle to achieve their goals, to achieve their dreams and to be who they want to be. I think that is one of the true beauties in life.

I certainly wouldn't be on this journey with you today, if it wasn't for the support of my sweetheart. I know you guys are dying to ask me her name. She is a very private person, I respect that. She has a profession that she's very good at. She allows me the privilege to sit and write all day. She asks nothing of me. I do help around the house. She respects my work, doesn't give me chore demands or a honey do list. She understands the importance of my writing to me and she further understands the importance my writing for others. I am blessed with having this relationship, she's a wonderful girl and no I'm not going to tell you her name, but I can tell you this, in my book 'Daddy Had to Say Goodbye,' her name is 'Heather.'

It's funny, I was just now flashing back, on before I came to be with Heather, in Minnesota. I dated a gal for a brief period of time, (less than a month) she was a really nice gal. We would go out often and run into people who were friends of mine. I have a lot of friends in the Western States and whether we were having coffee or a meal or just walking down the street or whatever we were doing, we ran into someone that knew me or knew of my book. I'm a rather social guy with many friends and even some fans. People would stop to chat and ask me how things were and asked me about the book and my next book. They would tell me about their experience with reading the book. I could see early on that she was miffed by this and finally she had a bit of a tantrum and she snidely asked, "Can we not go anywhere, without you having your fans hanging around us, we never get to have a private conversation. Your fans are always stopping to say hello and engage in conversation and I don't like it!" All I could do was smile and say, "Babe this is my life, and no, you cannot be a part of it. I wish you well," and that's the last time I spoke to her.

Me: Well kids where next?

Woody: Glanced over at Maddie and said, we don't even know at this point. Can we call it a day so we can go home and recover from all this data? It is absolutely wonderful being with you and listening but our minds are just so…. I don't even have a description. We don't even have a comparison that we can come up with. We are absolutely overwhelmed and we're still very excited and we hope we can continue this for the next 2 weeks!"

I held up my palm as I said, "Kids, as I think of it, we're going to need more than 2 weeks. Let's schedule for three weeks. Monday through Friday 7:00 am to 1:00 pm. If you have an appointment that is an absolute must, let me know well in advance. We're going to get through this, in the meantime, I'm going to email you the first fifty pages of my new book, 'Flesh of a Fraud.' That will give you a more in-depth view into both of these books. 'Flesh of a Fraud' is a companion book. The sub-title is, 'The Lies We Tell Ourselves.' I'm tired too, it's been a long morning. I will see you cats at 7:00 am tomorrow. Be here on time!"

CHAPTER 9   DANCE WITH WHO BRUNG YA

Well Tuesday morning came early. I didn't sleep much the night before, I had just too many words bouncing in my head. On the other hand, the Quinn's looked quite rested and once again, big smiles and happy faces. I just wanted to smack them! My God, those people are always up. Maddie wanted to get right to business which was quite refreshing.

Maddie: Who was your greatest cheerleader? That one person who helped you push through?

Me: I have already mentioned, Sean Carrigan and Tina Telson-Carrigan. I would have to say that Rodney Desizlets was the first true friend that was my driving force. When my roommate (former wife) asked me to move out, I had coffee the following day with Rod. Rod has been a friend of mine for some years and I made mention that I was looking for a place to stay. Rod mentioned that he had a friend (who is also a mutual friend of mine) that worked out of state and is looking for someone to look after his house when he was gone. Well it all worked out just fine, and Rod would come over every day after work (he was retired and he drove a school bus for golf fees. He would stop over after school bussing) and we would sit and smoke on the back deck of this gorgeous home that was located on the fairway of a golf course. We would just shoot the shit.

82

One day, as I was writing when Rod came over and he said, "Is that your book?" I handed him the first eight pages, hand written on a legal pad. My handwriting is rather poor, as he struggled through it (Rod is a tough guy and is also a very kind gentleman) with tears running down his face. Rod said, "I don't know how you found this talent, but my God, you've already touched me." I said, "Well that equals about a page and a half of printed work." He said, "You've got to keep going, people need this book!" Rod came over every day to read the latest pages. Rod was always encouraging from the very beginning.

I also have three, independent over-the-road truck driver buddies who were also very instrumental in my completing my book. One of those of those fellows was Marc Lombardo, from the Denver area. Marc came to the warehouse every Friday. Percy Thompson from Wisconsin came every Monday and Ryan Smith from Kansas came every Wednesday. These three guys were real standouts and they were the absolute gentleman of the road, they truly were the old school truckers of day's gone bye. Each of these guys would come in about three hours before their appointment. Only because they've just finished elsewhere and didn't want to hang out at some truckstop. The three of us became pals. Just after my book came out I tried to give Marc a copy but he would only take it if he could pay for it. He insisted that he pay for it. Marc told me that as soon as he got home his wife took it from him. I would see Marc every Friday and ask, "Where's your wife with reading the book?" He would say, "Well she's having a little trouble with it."

I told him, "If she had a troubled childhood or knew someone with a similar life experience she would have some trouble with this book." Seven weeks went by and every Friday I would ask him, "Where is your wife with the book?" On the seventh Friday I asked, "Where's Lydia with the book?" Marc had a shit-eating grin when he said, "We were just talking about you last night as he pulled out of his shirt pocket a business card with his wife's name on it and he said, "Lydia would like you to call her this afternoon. She wants to talk to you about your book." I thought, "Oh crap,

83

maybe I triggered something in her or maybe she doesn't like the book." I called Lydia that afternoon, she was a very gracious lady.

She said, "David, I absolutely love your book, but I'm not in love with your spelling and punctuation." I said, "Oh" as she said, "David, you are in love with commas, you have far too many commas along with a number of other errors. Would you mind so much if I were to do some corrections for you? I said, "Jesus Lydia, I'd love to have it edited but I checked into it and I can't afford the $45 an hour rate the editors charge for only three pages!" Lydia said, "Don't worry about the cost, I'll just be happy to do it for you as a friend, Marc thinks the world of you!"

Three weeks later Marc drove into the lot and I could see he had a passenger, it was his wife Lydia. She hopped out of the truck, approached me and threw her arms around me. She gave me a lengthily, warm hug and a kiss on the neck as she reached into her pants pocket and pulled out a Flash Drive. "Here is your corrected book. When I asked her what I owed her, she just smiled as she shook her head. We went to dinner later that evening and at dinner I said, "Lydia, I have to make this right with you. What can I pay you?" She just smiled as she said, "I would like 1/2 of 1% after your first million book sales." And that's how the book went into a second production.

Percy Thompson and I would spend a couple hours every week just chatting as he was waiting to load. Percy is very much a family man. He speaks highly of his wife, 'Roxy,' and their children and he adores his grandchildren. This guy is a straight up family man, he is a no nonsense fellow.

Ryan Smith who is out of Kansas is another quality guy. He would be in every week to load. During the summer months he would bring his son Bodhi along. Bodhi was every bit as tall as I was and was only twelve years old. Ryan also brought his wife Nikki, along on several trips and we enjoyed dinner meals together.

These 'Gentleman Truckers,' were very nice, quality people that loved life, loved trucking and were in love with their families.

84

My third wife 'Sandy' has been a powerful influence as to my completing both my books. She would bust my ass every time I wanted to quit. I will always love her for that.

My greatest cheerleaders, without question, would be Sean Carrigan and Tina Telson-Carrigan. They rented me a room for almost free in a very large, very nice home in Fort Collins. I had never met Sean before and I've known Tina for almost 20 years. Sean turned out to be much like a brother, if not a son. They both helped me a great deal in formatting and structure in my book. I don't have any computer skills, as a matter of fact, Tina took me to buy my first laptop. She knew what I needed, I had no idea and she walked me through it all. We brought it home and she set it all up, she set up all the printer programs for it and off I went. I would realize that I needed this paragraph moved to another location or this changed and I don't know how to do any of that stuff. I did not know how to copy or paste. I still don't. Tina would do those things for me. Sean would do things for me as far as the layout and the technical aspect of the computer. Sean was without question, my greatest cheerleader. Sean and I worked for the same company, he worked nights. He would take reading material to work every night, as his only job was to watch a locked gate, sitting in a patrol car and making sure that that locked gate remain locked, for twelve hours every night.

When I finished the book and put it in a three ring binder, I gave Sean a copy to take to work. Every morning I'd be at the table writing when he came home. He would just shake his head as he said, "I finished a couple more chapters and at the end of each chapter I thought, Man it's got to get better for this guy in these next few chapters. But no, it was the same if not worse. There is just no relief from the suffering of your character."
Sean is retired military, he was an M.P. He is a gentle soul but I saw a tough guy, both emotionally and physically (if need be). Sean had been in many different armed conflicts throughout the world. One morning he came home from work with a waxy look about him as he said, "I finished your book, you've got to get this published, you just absolutely have to!" Before me stood a big and

powerful man who looked heartbroken as his tears started to come down his cheeks.

I thought well, I've got one more person to push this past, to be sure. That of course was my cousin Rolene, who I have told you about earlier. So those were the people that carried me to and thru pre-production, if you will.

I think that one of the biggest thrills of my life, was the day that UPS pulled up and had my author's exclusive copies. The very first ten copies off the press. That was a very big day for me, to hold a dream which was so far from any level of reality. To actually hold my dream in my hands was very humbling. I smiled and cried for several days. Enough about that, where do you kids want to go now?

Maddie: Tell us about the actual publishing process, How did you go from handwritten, to printed, to published?

Me: Well again, I never dreamed this book would ever become a published book. That was so far away from any kind of a dream I ever dared to have. Again, I sent a three-ring binder of printed pages to my cousin for review and if she would have said, "No it's garbage." (Rolene was that honest) I would have put it the fire pit, without any remorse. I started researching publishers online and of course, my being a 'complete nobody', my only option was to use a 'vanity press.' I just don't go for all that fancy kiss ass bullshit to get noticed. Some authors send their work to hundreds of publishing houses and beg them to publish their book. I am not that guy, so I knew I had to pay to have it published and no vanity press will print anything for free. They offer extensive, a la carte menu options for printing, distribution and marketing enhancements. I had an acquaintance with a woman, who claimed to be a literary agent but I found out later (after several thousands of dollars) that all she was doing was lining her pockets by her having me pay a slime ball, publishing house that she got a kick-back from as well as my paying her a monthly retainer. We met for lunch (that I paid for) every Tuesday. She was acting as an editor and told me I needed to make several changes every week we met. She was mighty slippery, the way she had me paying for her rent, her groceries and utilities for several months. When I was done with her scamming me, I fired her and told her, "If you have any questions or want to claim 'breach of contract,' I will be happy to explain it in depth, via a felony criminal complaint. You will look great in an orange jail-house jumpsuit!"

I found a publisher that looked to be forthright. Well, they did give me what they promised (and I paid for) but they were quite sly. They, like most all vanity printing houses, don't care about content. All they care about is you paying them a great deal of money. They had an extremely large, off the menu order system, where they will sell you all kinds of promotional things.

All I wanted was the book and I supplied the cover text and art work but they still screwed me out of $500 for artist work. I'm not an artist, I can't draw. I can't even draw a stick man, he would look like a dying weed. I just downloaded a bunch of clip art and taped it all together on a storyboard. I photographed it with my cellphone and sent it along with all the colors and descriptions of where to be placed. They somehow ended up sending me back some kind of a European type of police riot helmet and a firefighter's helmet. That told me something about their operation but nonetheless I got a published copy. They got very deep into my pockets, the price they charged me for a copy my own book was just mind numbing, but I paid the price to have the book.

Maddie: What was your marketing strategy and do you have an agent?

Me: I started developing my marketing strategy, into my second year of writing. I took me seven years to write this damn thing. I walked away from it many times, just thinking it was garbage and it wouldn't go anywhere, so why even bother. And then something would always pull me back to it. I lost faith in myself quite often.

My marketing strategy? I had no money for that. So what I did was, I friend requested people on Facebook who were either in the EMS, Police or Fire service along with mental health workers and teachers. People who I thought would best benefit from reading the book. It took over three years to develop 5,000 Facebook friends and a few hundred followers. That was my entire marketing strategy. No, I don't have an agent. A true professional agent will take their 10 to 15% off the back end. I'll be happy to give 10 to 15% of nothing all day long. But that's not how it works. The first question of any professional agent is, "What is your budget?" The reason they ask that, is because the agent must guarantee the book store buyers that the author will visit each store for a book signing, in order for them to purchase the books. They wanted me in their stores with my book, which is now 'their product' and they want me to be available to sign my books. Well if I sold into a big box corporation I would have to guarantee the sale and buy back all unsold copy's as well as pay the return freight. Returned books are most often time's shelf worn and not resalable. I would be traveling all over the country and I simply don't have the credit availability to support that. The risk is huge for an independent author in distributing their books into bookstores. The other part is they buy at a discount and take 40% of the retail price. My publishing house takes another 40%, then there were some incidentals along the way down-the-line, well-hidden. The author doesn't get paid for 180 days from the sale. Amazon takes a pretty good bite at the end of the day on a $17.95 book. I get paid a $1.82 per book and I wrote the damn thing! And I paid $7,800 to have the damn thing published! So the numbers have never worked out. I will be in a hole for my entire lifetime. I've gifted over seven hundred books (that I had to buy and paid the postage) as part of my strategy to these professional people, so they in turn would tell their coworkers about the book and encourage them to buy the book. Now if I had the money, I would give the book away to everyone in the world. Since I'm not that guy, I have to sell the book to be able to afford to keep printing the book.

The worst thing I could ever hear is, (and I hear it often, too damn often),"I just loved your book, it's wonderful, I'm so excited about it, that I shared it with a friend and I have three other friends in line that want read it! It's just so wonderful that all my friends can read your book."

All I can do is just drop my head and be grateful that people are reading my book. Sharing a gifted book does not sell books and I am so upside down financially that I will never come close to breaking even, let alone ever profiting. I do want the message to get out but I have to pay for every one of these books I send to people and I even pay the postage so I have $11.86 into every book that I give away. That's not counting all my production costs. So yah, I guess I just did a good thing and will just call it that. I don't play all the cute games that many other writers do. People say, "Well you need to Blog and you need to do Quara and you need to Tweet, do this, you need to do that and you need to join a local writing group." You know that, that's just not me.

I did as a matter of fact, go to one of those, 'Nano' writing groups. I sat through two sessions, everyone in the room went around and introduce themselves and talked about all their pedigrees and education and they were all quite impressed with themselves.

When they got to me I said, "I've got a high school diploma that I did not earn," and they all looked down their noses at me. In this particular group you would bring 3 or 4 pages of your written work, with copies for every one of the eight to ten people and then they would critique your writing. Well the 1st week I didn't have anything of course and the way they didn't acknowledge me as a viable writer, pissed me off! The following week what I brought was my publishing contract and I just brought one copy.

When it came my turn I said, "I can't afford to swing copies for everyone, so I'll just throw this the middle of the table for whoever would like to grab it and read it. Go ahead and pass it around. That my friends, is what's called a publishing contract." Several eyes opened wide and some people leaned back in their chairs. I reached into my briefcase and brought out a copy of my

89

book and threw it on the center of the table as I said, "This is what a published book looks like!"

I never went back to that group but it was pure pleasure to spank those phony little bitches! I have no interest in that bullshit. So that should finish with your question of my marketing strategy.

I do walk into independent bookstores and asked them to take my book on consignment, knowing they will email me in thirty to sixty days to come in and pick up my unsold books. Most times, I pick up all of the three books I had originally left them.

I never approached any newspaper editors as I knew the book was rough with a lot of errors. I knew libraries and newspapers only want to work with established and professional writers. There are also plenty of supposed review agencies that promote author's books with monthly magazines they claim to distribute to library, book store buyers and retail stores. You better have some large bucks for that program.

Than you have a fistful of writer magazines that tell you who is accepting manuscripts, for the price of a decent lunch. Next is the regional and national book fairs where you can spend a fortune on travel, lodging and meals where you can rent a table to display your books and pay an additional fee to sit and pitch your work for ten minutes, with a publishing house rep or a literary agent, for the cost of raising three kids for their first five years of life.

Then there are the, 'Awards Agency's' who promote dozens of competitions throughout the country, several times a year. You send them three copies of your signed book and for a hefty fee, they will judge your work and you may win a plaque or a certificate of honorable mention. You can even enter your book in several different categories, for additional fees in each category. You can also attend the 'Awards Banquet' for an additional fee and receive your certificate (suitable for framing), in person and for an additional fee you can get a picture of yourself accepting your certificate from the event promoter! Additional photos can be purchased for an additional fee, of course. I'm pretty sure that most of those 'author sent signed books,' find their way to eBay long before the awards are issued. There are all the many Independent publishers (often times called, 'Vanity Presses') who prey on their customers with awards programs of their own. Understand that there are 800,000 plus, books published each year. Kids write books for Grandma and Grampa and other relatives and school friends. Most all independent published books go to the Amazon cemetery (including my own) in a very short period of time.

I also do signing events. My first three signing events were a complete bust. Only one person came to, 'Meet the Author' at these three different bookstores. That one person was the same person at each store. It of course, was my best buddy, Sean Carrigan. He drove 40 to 80 miles one way, just to walk in and say, "How you doing?" Because he knew in his heart, that I would be sitting alone. Sean always brought coffee and donuts for that two or three hour period. What a friend he is, what a great guy! I never made a sale at those first three book signings.

I have attended a couple of, 'Author Book Signing Fairs', which were just absolutely ridiculous! I did one book fair where it was just prior to Christmas, on a Saturday. The weather just turned to total shit, snowing and blowing with close to zero visibility. It was held at a county fairground complex and there were several events in the fairgrounds but we were in a separate building far removed from the main buildings. No one showed up other that the eighteen local authors. Most all sat and just chatted with each other, all day long. It was a total freak show. I guess I'm just not of this era.

The guy next to me, wrote Sherlock Holmes stuff. He wore a Sherlock Holmes type, hounds-tooth wool hat with a bill on each end, whatever the hell that's called. He had a fake Sherlock Holmes pipe, a tartan vest and a long billowing wool, floor-length coat. The guy next to him was a superhero comic writer and he had on a skin suit with some kind of bullshit cape and mask.

The gal next to him wrote Robin Hood stuff, she should have been dressed as Little John as big as she was, but she had a Robin Hood costume on and she had an assistant that had on a Little John costume and I'm guessing she weighed less than a buck

91

ten. It just continued all around the room. People that wrote fantasy were wearing fairy costumes, mystery writers had floppy hats like you see at the Kentucky Derby.

There was a 'Leather couple' with leashes on each other and with plenty of flesh showing, who did S&M porn. They had sex act, coloring books!

There was a clown with a cute little clown car that he drove around the room like you would see at the circus. He had an oversized framed certificate that attested to his graduation with honors from some clown college. He had pocket size books that were popular in the 1940s. Then a fully garbed cowboy with spurs, who had a long and tall saw-horse with wheels, a tooled leather saddle with a real stuffed horse's head mounted to it and of course a horse's tail on the back. He had western 'coffee table' books on saddles, spurs, hats and barbwire collections.

Many had very expensive booth set-ups that cost thousands of dollars with six and eight tables, with live plants, flowers and carpet. I had one table, a maroon table cloth that I bought at Walmart, a wooden easel that I bought from Hobby Lobby that was damaged, (that I paid $7 for) that held a framed 3x5 foot poster of the cover of my book that, Tina Telson and Sean Carrigan, gifted me before the book even came out. I wore a white dress shirt under a crew neck sweater and grey slacks. I kept to myself for the first few hours, thinking, "What in the hell is this shit? None of this is me, none of it!"

At some point, they all seemed to be bored with their own conversations and decided to do a traveling, 'courtesy critique' on each author table and their work. The group went to each table, when they got to my table this one woman who thought a great deal of herself, pointed out quite loudly, "It is, such a beautiful cover but the title tells such a dark story. It scares me, who would want to read something like that, around the holidays, it looks awful depressing." She nodded her head as she looked around the group as if she was looking for votes with agreeing head nods.

I just looked at her and I said, "Ya know hun, life can be awful depressing, even around the holidays." She just turned up her snooty little nose and charged off to the next table.

Those weren't my people. I'm not that kind of a writer. I'm not a joiner. I can be a part of a lot of things but I don't like clicks. I don't like clubs for the sake of being a club member and I don't kiss anyone's ass for their approval.

I had some other interesting experiences in book promotions. I was a guest author on a national podcast show, twice about a year apart. It is a survivors group of adults who are survivors of a battered childhood. The host was very nice man, they're a very nice group of people and they truly do all they possibly can to help battered and endangered children. I was the sole guest for the entire hour and a half show. At that time I had never done a live radio or podcaster interview, of any kind. So I was apprehensive but I calmed myself with making faces at the dogs. It was funny as Tina and Sean were upstairs listening on the radio when I was downstairs doing this interview over my phone. There was a panel of three plus the moderator. They were asking me questions about how it was growing up as an abused, battered and beaten child. I pretty much just stayed with the contents of the book because the book is what it was all about. When they got to the part of the book about my being nine and ten years old, having sexual relations with women in their mid to late twenties, the ladies on the panel went nuts. They all were trying to convince me that I was sexually abused. "You were molested and damaged by these sexual predators!" I had to tell these well-meaning ladies that, "I understand what you're saying, I get that, but I have to tell you, that in my particular case those women saved my life. I was on the cusp, I was teetering on the very edge of jumping over the cliff and these women gave me a reason to keep living. Yes, although negative, they still gave me validation. Did it screw me up in my future years? Well of course it did. How could it not. These women used me and when I finally got it figured out as to how they used me, I developed a plan to use them. It taught me how to think, it taught me how to think like an adult and it taught me how to win.

It taught me to fight back and how to win. These were invaluable lessons in regards of checking adult's motives when they were nice to me."

The female panelists were very gracious during the whole show but they didn't buy any part of what I had to say. They all had their own agendas.

Well that's pretty much where my marketing is today. What happened here with these last three days, was a God thing. I just happened to walk in at the right time, at the right place and what it took for me to get pissed off. I was going to make some action happen, I think I've always operated my very best under duress. If I can turn my anger into energy I can always win. I will always win but I have to learn to process those things.

CHAPTER 10   THANKS FOR DOUBTING ME

Maddie: What was it like for you when you were able to show those doubting people, those people that didn't believe you had the ability to write and publish your book? What was their reaction to see that you actually had a viable book?

Me: Well a lot of them said nothing, they just thought, 'well I guess this one time he wasn't full of shit.' That was the read I got on a lot of people I actually know. I gifted a number of books to non-first responder people. Many of who I thought to be a good acquaintances or even friends. I give them a copy of the book but very few have read it. The few that have read it seemed to be indifferent and I think where that comes from is, there are a lot of people who lived some good life's and when they're faced with the reality of other people's lives, they become embarrassed and perhaps even a bit ashamed. We will get deeper into that as we take the book apart chapter by chapter. But it disappoints me greatly, the number of people who I gifted copies to can't even take a few minutes out of their day to tell me how they felt about reading the book. Many want to critique or give me advice on how I should have written the book. I easily tell them, "I don't give a shit about what you think of the structure, or the spelling, or the punctuation. You can go pound sand up your ass. I want to know what your experience was as you read the book. That's what I want to hear about, I don't need you to pat me on the back or blow smoke up my ass. I also won't listen about my laziness or lack of education. Just tell me what your experience was, what your emotional and psychological experience was, as you were going through the book."

It amazes me how few people have the courage to go there, to go to their gut. They all want their own comfort, in their own way, and you know people don't read like the used to. We all take our information in snippets. I am as guilty as everyone else. We want the world info in 60 seconds so we can go play and do whatever else we like to do. So people don't read like they used to. Reading used to be a form of entertainment, now its television and videos and whatever else people do, but reading is not a priority in many people's lives. Do you know that the #1 selling books worldwide are children's books and sadly the #2 selling are either, horror smut or porn, which I find repulsive and it disgusts the hell out of me. I've had a lot of a different experiences and different comments but here's a few that really strikes home for me. Mind you that I paid for these books and gave them for free.

I had four people who (were given free books) responded and complained that because I personalized it and put their names on it, that now I have ruined it for resale on eBay. Can you believe that shit? That's the kind of ungrateful people I get to enjoy every day.

For me to mail a copy of my book to Canada it costs me $15 just in postage. I had a Canadian woman send me a picture of a book that I gifted her, (she is a member of one of the associations that I'm a member of) she didn't have the funds to buy the book, so like a dumb cluck, I sent her a copy of the book at no charge. So I get this picture a few weeks later of the book, laying shredded on the floor and her dog with the binding in its mouth. Her note asked if I could please send her another book because it is no longer legible and she wanted to know how soon she could expect to receive it. I was quite proud of myself for not telling her to go romance a Moose!

Probably the best asshole deal, was when I gifted my neighbor a copy, who is a retired firefighter. We spoke every week. He raved about the book, he claimed that he had told all his fire dept. buddies to buy the book. He claimed that several had bought the book and were in the process of reading it. I knew that was bullshit because I have access to, up to the minute sales reports and the cities and states where the books were purchased along with the shipping addresses.

This neighbor clown was moving and had a garage sale. He invited me to his three day sale. His driveway, lawn and garage were full of tables and the tables were stacked high with stuff. Much to my displeasure I found the book I signed and gifted him, on his $5 dollar table. I acted like I didn't see it as we chatted for a few minutes. The next day I went back and found my book on the $1 table. I again didn't mention seeing it, during our brief conversation. The following day I again returned to the neighbor's yard sale and found the book on his 25cent table. I picked up the book and waited until I had his and his wife's attention and said, "Can't go wrong buying a 25 cent book but it's probably a piece of crap anyway, so I'll just save my money," as I flipped it back on the table.

At this point in my life I only gift people a copy of the book that I personally know. I have and will continue to send books to First Responder, fund raising events to assist sick or injured sisters and brothers.

Since moving back to Duluth, I've met some great people with the local police depts. fire depts. and EMS that I've gifted copies to, which leads me to the most remarkable and rewarding chain of events that I've enjoyed since publishing the book.

CHAPTER 11   GOD'S GRACE / CARL'S LEGECY

Two years ago, I happened to be messing around on
Facebook and I saw this person's last name, which is not a
common name, even for this part of the country. That last name
was the name of the fellow I had worked for and worked with for
many years. In the book, 'Daddy Had to Say Goodbye' his
character name is, 'Jack.' His name was actually Carl Bergl. I
thought, "My God, I wonder if this was Carl's daughter?" I knew
he had been killed in an industrial accident several years ago. I
remember he had a daughter, she was a tiny little thing, maybe
three or four years old. She was most certainly daddy's little girl.
    I remember her mom bringing her to headquarters to visit
Daddy on long 72 hour weekend shifts. It was common to have
crew family's come to visit on long weekend shifts. So I contacted
this person via email and asked, "Are you the daughter of my old
friend, Carl Bergl?" The woman wrote back saying, "No I am his
niece, his daughter's name is, Corrina Maly."
    I sent Ms. Corrina Maly an email explaining myself to her
and told her of my working with her father and that I had written a
book and her father is a character in my book. I asked her if I could
gift her a copy in her Fathers memory.
    She said, "Gosh yes, I know so little about my father, he
was killed when I was only fifteen years old, so I know very little
about him." I offered to mail a copy to her or meet in person for a
cup of coffee. She chose to meet for coffee. I arrived at the coffee

shop early and as I started walking toward the coffee shop I saw this high energy woman exit her car and I recognized her from her Facebook page. My first thought was, "High School Cheerleader that has aged remarkably well!"

I called her name, she stopped and smiled with tears in her eyes as we shook hands and introduced ourselves. We sat at a small table as she told me that she really knew very little of her father, other than he worked a lot at the ambulance company. She didn't get to see him often. Mom and Dad had a difficult and painful divorce and of course children hear things (either real or imagined) at that young tender age that perhaps they shouldn't. I think she was six years old when they divorced. I sat with her as she told me of not knowing her Father other than his was kind of moody and selfish. She went on telling me that she didn't like her Dad as she didn't think he liked her. She said she has always been mad at him and had developed a distrust in all men because of him. I let her keep talking until she started to wind down before I said, "Now you listen to me young lady. I'm going to tell you exactly who your Dad was."

I told her of the many times that her Dad and I did CPR for more than an hour together drenched in sweat. About the many times we were side by side, shoulder to shoulder with our hands in someone's guts trying to stop the bleeding. How we carried patients for several blocks to the hospitals due to the streets being blocked by abandoned cars during snow storms. The times we laid in overturned, wrecked cars treating severely injured patients, waiting for fire rescue to cut the car open for extraction with gasoline, motor oil and hot antifreeze dripping and saturating our hair, our skin and our clothing. The times he wept when we lost a patient. How I watched him comfort and soothe an injured or frightened child in a car accident. About the times he lived at headquarters because he couldn't afford to rent an apartment and had no money for food, as he tried to get the company on its feet. How he never went 'out-on-the-town' or dated because his only focus was on delivering a superb product to his customers and taking care of his employees.

99

In conjunction with the Ambulance service we also supplied medical oxygen tanks and refill services. Back in the day there was no such thing as in home oxygen making machines. Many people were on a 'Keep Fill' program where we delivered the large 'H' oxygen tanks on a schedule. Carl studied the schedule every morning and if there was a major snow storm coming he would have his delivery guys deliver a few days early for his customers comfort and safety. There were times that customers would call and claim they didn't need a delivery as they had cut back on their usage of oxygen. Carl knew that that wasn't true, he instinctively knew that these people had to choose between, food, utilities and rent. Carl had the delivery crew bring them fresh tanks and tell the customers that some civic organization gave a grant to supply free oxygen for the next ninety days.

I told her of her Dad setting up a secret code of grading a patients living conditions and their ability to pay. We simply used an A-B-C-D grading system and wrote one of those letters on the upper right hand corner of the call report. If the patient did not have insurance, Medicare or Medicaid and was graded to be a C or D he never sent them a bill. Carl stood firm on the principle that, "Many people who are down on their luck have little left other than their dignity. I will never challenge a person's dignity with their ability to pay and I don't ever want them to avoid calling for help just because they are broke or poor!"

That brought on the water works as she said, "I never knew these things about my Father. I have spent my entire adult life thinking he was a selfish jerk. I would have never known these things about him if not for you."

During our conversation she told me that she had a relative through marriage that was the director of the ambulance service in Meadowlands Minnesota, where she lived. I asked his name as I reached into my briefcase for a book to sign for him. I signed his book, "To: Troy Maly, A gift; for the selfless things that you do, for the so very many, whose name's you don't even know. With respect and admiration." We left the coffee shop with Corrina tightly grasping her two books. We had a warm hug and I watched

100

her glide if not levitate across the parking lot to her car. I sat in my truck and lit a cigarette, I drove to the far end of the parking lot where there were no other cars.

I knew that I had just witnessed a young woman in transition. She found her answers and the peace she has prayed for, all of her life.

I found my own tears as I reflected on Carl's character and kind heart. My memory flashed back to my first days working as a ride-a-long with only a twelve-hour CPR certification and a forty-hour, Advanced First-Aid card. I rode with six different crews, one week with each crew. I was not allowed to treat any patients, I was just allowed to observe and assist the crews. At the start of my third week, I rode along with Carl and his partner, Vern Sievers, for a 72 hour weekend shift. Those guys were incredibly smooth in everything they did. The hardly spoke to one another, as they acted so matter-of-factly, on some very difficult calls. We were toned-out to a head-on traffic accident near Island Lake. When we arrived we found all three victims of the accident were dead. Carl showed me each injury on each victim and told me how we would have treated their injuries if they were still alive. I helped to remove the bodies from the cars and place them in the Ambulance.

Carl nodded to Vern as he closed the loading door. Carl looked at me and said, "We are going for a smoke and a little walk, Vern will stay with the bodies."

I pride myself as being, 'read-less' when it comes to my showing emotions. Somehow, Carl saw what was in my gut. As we walked he said, "For a Rookie you are damn good, you don't panic, you don't over-react, you are good with talking with the patients. All the crews like you, but I need to tell you that not everyone is cut out for this kind of work. Something tells me that you are internally unsettled with the job. After we drop-off the bodies at the Morgue, I will take you home and Vern will follow, driving your car. You will be paid for the rest of the shift, I just want to give you some time to think about the job, and if it's really meant for you. If you don't come back everyone will understand and no one will think anything less of you."

That was the Carl Bergl I knew. I wish the rest of the world knew him that way.

CHAPTER 12   THE HUMAN LEATHERMAN

Several days later I got an email from Troy Maly thanking me for the book and saying he was feeling a little cautious about going beyond the part where it gives a cautionary warning. I wrote back that the cautionary statement was meant for non-first responders. "It won't be as painful because of your experience, so you should not have much trouble with it." Troy read the book in just a few days. He really liked the book and he spoke to other people that he worked with, about the book. We met for coffee to shake hands and say hello. I gave him a few copies to leave around the firehouse.

Troy and I met a few other times for coffee just to visit. I have been a guest in his and his wife's home for a meal and he and his wife along with Corrina and her husband have met with Heather and me for meals around town a few times since.

Me: Guys I am spent. Let's call it a day. See you in the morning.

The next morning.

Me: As I told you earlier, Troy invited me to their Meadowlands Ambulance BBQ in honor of National E.M.S. appreciation week. I was invited to participate in their barbecue as his guest, I got to meet a lot of the local people, nice folks. I was introduced to the very first EMT they ever had on their ambulance service, she is a very nice woman. It was an honor to give her a copy of the book. Troy allowed me to donate two books to their raffle. Troy took me around to meet most all of the attendees. It was also an honor to gift a copy of the book to two neighboring fire department Chiefs, for their fire stations.

Troy is a man for all seasons. He is like a universal tool belt for humans. He is the all but elected 'Godfather of Meadowlands' area. He does tons of stuff for the Ambulance Service. He sponsored a 'Honor Flight' trip for two local, Viet Nam Veterans and he was a 'Medical Needs' attendant on that flight.

Troy's wife, Carrie and he are true partners. They designed and built a stunningly beautiful home with help from just a few family members and friends. They cut the trees and milled and dried their own lumber! Troy and Carrie along with their eight year old Grandson plant a ginormous garden each spring and give away most all of the vegetables. His grandson's specialty is pumpkins. Early every morning he waters and talks with his pumpkins in his pajamas, the entire summer and has a pumpkin pre-order sales operation. Troy and his grandson load up the pick-up truck and visit the areas 'Shut-in' population to deliver the very best pumpkins to them, free of charge.

Troy coaches T-ball, little league, football and I'm sure many other things that he is too humble to talk about. He also works a full time, demanding, long hour job. He, like the rest of the Meadowlands Ambulance Team, rolls out of bed to run rescue calls, regardless of weather or time of night. Now that my friends, is a true Renaissance man! The aforementioned information did not come from Troy or Carrie as they are both far too humble to speak of their extreme kindnesses.

How can anyone not absolutely be in love with all of our volunteer First Responders? Those are my people, those are my Heroes!

I will always maintain a friendship with the, "Miles for Medics" people that I met in Michigan. Those kind of friendships are invaluable to me, they just don't come by every day!

So back to my gifting a book to Troy Maly for the EMS desk at the Meadowlands Fire Hall.

I received an email from a woman named Angie Simonson. She is a Volunteer Fire Fighter for Meadowlands and was reading the book. It just so happens her husband is the Fire Chief of the Meadowlands Volunteer Fire Department. She was just starting her EMS training for the Ambulance Service. She wanted to thank me for writing the book and giving her insights as what she was about to enter into. I emailed her back and asked her how she felt about reading it. Angie told me it gave her a lot to think about. Angie, along with her husband raise four children and she operates a small regional community type newspaper, along with her being the President of the local county fair. As I was thinking that this gal hardly has any time to breathe she said. "I also develop websites. Do you have a website?" My answer was, "No I can't afford a website, I've looked into it and for me to have a website is not affordable. From what I looked at, the websites run somewhere between $8,000 and $10,000 for an interactive, online hosted website and I just don't have that type of money." She said, "Well let me look and play with it for a bit." It was not even a week later and she sent me a suggested website. It was beautiful and she all but gave it away to me. This is a gorgeous website that anyone would be proud to own. It should have cost me a tremendous amount of money but out of the kindness of her own heart and her experience in life, she felt that I could best reach my audience with this website. I can now interact with people, and they can contact me to purchase signed copies and to book speaking engagements. This was a huge boost for me.

I told Angie that I had two different business cards, neither of which were very professional looking and now that I have a website to advertise, I needed new business cards with my website address. I asked her if she knew anyone that could design a new business card for me. She said, "Let me throw something together for you." Two days later I get an email with her idea for my new business card. It was a stunning design, an absolutely beautiful business card with all the information. I'm very proud of both the website and business cards.

Me: Before we take a break, I want to wrap this up with a bit of truth for your ears only. Turn off your recorders. Frankly, I am embarrassed with the book. Not by the story line or its contents but by the sloppy grammatical and spelling errors. I rushed to publication because I was having returning symptoms of my last bout of illness. I was thinking that this time, it was going to take me. Since the book came to print I have secretly wanted to reprint it so I could sell it into libraries and the big retail stores.

That's where Lydia Lombardo came in. She put a fire in my belly to republish but I could not afford my publishers fees. I looked into Createspace, KDP and a few others. Again, I have very few skills with a computer and I could not understand the publishing jargon, or how to set up an account to publish with them, but I know someone that does! Yup, back to sweet and overworked Angie Simonson. Angie said that it was an uncharted territory for her but she would give it a shot.

I had also wanted to change the graphics and add a subtitle. That arrogant nasty ole' bitch at the pre-Christmas, "Meet the Author" event was right! The title did scare people away from the book. I wanted to add the subtitle, "A Story of Hope."

My Pal, Don Prince suggested over a phone conversation one fine bright and sunny day, that I add something to the front cover that speaks of PTSD and include something that acknowledges, volunteer first responders. "You experienced PTSD and have lived with it all these years even before it ever had a name. Your book screams of it all throughout. You may be missing your target audience!" Don, was also dead nuts on. I downloaded several fire helmets and sent them to Angie with my wanting the top front rocker to read 'Volunteer' the bottom rocker to read 'Firefighter' with the center to read P.T.S.D.

I also wanted the side of the wagon to read, "Volunteer First Responder." Angie worked her magic and my book has been reprinted by Createspace, with a stone killer cover!

The things that have happened for me cannot be about me and is not always about money. Sometimes the rewards come from other people's hearts, I have been blessed with so many loving people in my life.

Who would have thought that me finding this woman's last name on Facebook, would lead to all these beautiful things?

Carl Bergl's memory will live on forever. His Legacy will sit within this book and alongside my first book, 'Daddy Had to Say Goodbye' on the shelves of, The United States Library of Congress. I can only hope that I have done God's Grace and Carl's memories justice.

I'm going out for a smoke, why don't you guys order lunch. I'm not hungry. Oh yah, go buy a god damn coloring book would ya. Your art skills suck and it is an abomination to all farm animals!

After a few smokes I went back to the room to find the Quinn's enjoying a salad. I went to the front desk and got a guest coloring book and a pack of crayons. I sat and colored as those two giggled thru their lunch.

Me: Now that lunch is over and you have sat flat-assed for nearly four hours, I want you two to go for a twenty minute brisk walk. When you get back, I'm going to drop a bomb in your lap! Enjoy your stroll.

One hour later

Me: You kids look way fresher now, let's get started. I can only guess that you two had a conversation about what bomb is about to be dropped in your lap this afternoon. You might even have a question as to why I have cut each of these sessions a bit short, well here is the short of it. I have to stop when I start to lose my vision. I've been having a problem with my vision.

107

I had been told six weeks ago, that I may have developed Glaucoma. I've tried to stay quiet about it to friends and family but at some point the doctor says I may lose my vision entirely. It could happen tomorrow morning upon awakening. I don't know and neither do they, so here is the deal. You cats think that you are going to get me to almost write a book for you, and you get to atone for all of your many sins? Well Kids, it's just not that easy, here is the deal.

I reached into my briefcase and pulled out two separate double spaced contracts. I handed one to each of them as I said these are agreements, legal and binding contracts, that state if I were to lose my vision during the process of writing or publishing my book, 'Flesh Of A Fraud,' that you two will complete my book. In my presence of course because it's just that important to me. This book must be released, there are a lot of people depending upon it being published. I'm done for today. You kids take these home, read them over and come back tomorrow morning. If you're not willing to sign these contracts tomorrow morning, then we will be done. Vicki is a notary and she will notarize your signatures. This is to be kept strictly confidential and no one is to know about this, absolutely no one! Now, it's time for my nap, I hope to see you in the morning, if not I will understand.

I walked into the meeting room at exactly 7:00 am. There sat the Quinn's with big smiles. There was a large box of, 'Larson's Bakery' donuts, (the best donuts you can find anywhere in this part of the country) and a gift wrapped item which was the size of a shoebox. Maddi said this is for you. I opened the shoe box and inside was a, 120 count box of Crayola Crayons. Maddie said, "I don't like the pastries here so we went to 'Larson's Bakery' and the complementary crayons this hotel gives out to little kids, absolutely suck!"

Me: Let's get down to business. Your presence here this morning tells me you both are in agreement with the contract. I want both of you guys on your feet, it's time for some hugs. I went and got Vicki to come in to notarize both contracts. Vicki had a brief look of confusion but was too mature and experienced to question what she was witnessing. I couldn't help but smile when she said, "I will need to see a driver's license or two legal forms of identification from each of you." As I signed all three copy's I put my thumb in the chocolate donut on my plate and made my mark next to my signature. Vicki gave each of us a hug and closed the door behind her. I said, 'Kids I'm sure with my rambling for the last almost 10 hours we've gotten a bit off the track, so let's get back to what are your next questions, thank you for allowing me to continue on with my answers."

Maddie: Can I ask you a difficult question?

Me: Yea Babe go ahead, what it is?

Maddie: Are you going to allow us to continue with our meetings? We both have concerns about your wellness, can we talk about this? You do have a history of not telling people with what's going on with you. Are you doing that now with Heather and the rest of your family?

Me: Maddie, that's a fair question. Heather and her brother are the only two that know of my situation. I told my friends Tina and Sean as well but I haven't taken them to the depths of my concerns. I just stated the facts that I have a situation that may not be remedied and it could not go down well, other than that, I just don't want to be a burden on anyone, with what my fears are. I know that I have a great deal of history of withholding my emotional truths but that's just the way I operate. I don't see that changing any time soon.

Maddie: What are you doing to prepare yourself for hopefully not the inevitable but in all appearances, perhaps the inevitable?

109

Me: Well I first want to tell you that I didn't really tell anyone about my vision problem for the first three months. I pretty much knew what it was before I had medical confirmation. I wasn't going to say anything until it was confirmed, I'm not an alarmist and there's no need for worry when there is no information to worry over, it's just a waste of time.

Maddie: Last night, Woody and I talked about your emotional condition and we have to tell you of our personal fears because you act so cavalier and unaffected. You've been sober for more than twenty-seven years, do you think you'll find alcohol as a relieving agent, do you see yourself going back to drinking and where do you think you will end up?

Me: Well it's like this. I remember many years ago when my oldest brother Donnie died at age twenty-eight. My dad had been sober about ten years at that time. My dad was greatly shaken with his loss. Donnie was sober for one year when he died. My Dad did everything any loving parent would do to help their child to find sobriety. Dad carried a great deal of shame with his inability to reach Donnie, when he was such a great influence on total stranger's lives, but he couldn't help his own son. With my knowing and sensing his perceived guilt I looked at my dad and asked him just before my brother's funeral, "Dad is this going to cause you to drink again?" My dad had the most perfect answer of any answer that I've ever heard. He looked back at me and said, "No I will not dishonor you're brothers sobriety with my drinking!"

Now that's my answer to you two and the rest of the world. I have a number of great friends that don't necessarily look up to me but they do respect me and I have a responsibility to show all people, that nothing has to change our life's. It's just a situation that needs to be dealt with and we as alcoholics must remember that we've been up against the worst of the worst. If it comes to where I'm actually blind, I'm still not dead! I will figure a way, just like the millions of other people have. I will figure a way to continue to prosper and enjoy life.

Woody: Have you done anything to prepare yourself for the potential of the inevitable?

Me: What I've been doing is, I have been taking visual snapshots and downloaded them into my brain of what things look like. I have done dozens of visual floor plans in my house, the location of every item on every counter, the distance between one thing to the next, of the number of steps it takes to go from point A to point B. We have four Papillion dogs who I will love forever, who I have petted for several years but now it's different. I try to feel them as I look at them. I feel the texture of their fur. I feel their body shape, their form, their muscular structure and their skeletal structure. I want to put to memory each of these dogs so I will know which one I am touching and petting. I'm listening to their voices and breathing patterns. I pay a lot more attention to their kisses to better identify who's given me kisses. We have a couple that are heavy duty face kissers, so that will help. I just want to know what is going to be near me wherever I am in the house. I have studied our home continuously, I count the number of stairs, I mentally and physically measure the width of our doorways by stretching my hands out and believe it or not I can tell different doorways because no two of them are exactly the same width. I study the location of the bed, how to get around the dressers, I memorize the dresser drawers, what's in each drawer, what's left, what's center and what's right. So yes, I have been doing some preparation work. I don't feel a bit foolish about doing this. I think this is just a smart thing to do. I don't want to be a burden on Heather and I'll be damned if I'm going to sit in one place all day, fearing that I will break something or hurt myself. I've got to remember that there are people who don't get a chance to prepare, there are people that lose their sight instantly. So I'm way ahead of the game in that area. As to my writing, yes there's a bit of fear and I'm trying not to panic about completing this book. I don't want to let this be unfinished, so I've been writing twelve to fourteen hours every day for weeks on end. I just feel this burning passion with knowing that the message is not complete. There's more to be done and there is no one else better to do it than me. This book again, is about my life and I'm not done living it! What's next?

Maddie: Where do you draw your strengths to have this calm, rational response? As we look at you say these things, we both understand that you're not bullshitting us, you are just telling us how it is. We know there's no fabrication here, there are no exaggerations and you're not downplaying anything. How do you find that inner strength?

Me: I decided a number years ago that I was no longer going to be afraid of myself. In the past, I was always afraid of how I may look to others and I was always afraid that people would see me for having a weakness. When I meet a person for the very first time I glance them over, even passing strangers. I size them up and look for their vulnerabilities, in case I had to fight with them. I study their height, build and the way they carry themselves. In parts of a second I visualize my attack and gauge their response. That's just the survivor in me and that's of course the barbaric caveman type mentality, but that's how I have survived many attacks thru the years. At the same time I look for people's sensitivities so I don't accidentally harm them or say the wrong thing. If I do lose my vision I will mostly miss visual contact with people. As you both know, what I see in people is what people are. That's a God-given ability, it's not a talent that can be developed and it is dead nuts accurate. So again if that were to happen, that would be my greatest loss.

I have studied the furniture on our deck which of course we remove before the snow months. I've studied the trees, I study the lawn, and everything I look at, and I try to memorize shape, form and definition. I even do it with the neighbor's houses and the neighborhood sounds. I'm locking the sound of vehicles into my brain as to know what neighbors are moving around. I'm trying to build comfort in a very uncomfortable situation and be better prepared. I'm not anyone that needs any level of sympathy, I don't need any understanding, it is just what happens in life and remember we have to go back to everyone poops and everyone goes into the same size hole when our time is up. The upside of all that, is when I die, when we all die, we won't even know it. It's no different for the rest of the world. So what's next kids?

Maddie: Can I have a hug?

Me: Sure babes, but before that, I need to clear something up. You two show me a great deal of respect and admiration that makes me a bit uneasy. So please understand this. Don't be in awe of me, be in awe of the world's largest fellowship that I am blessed to be a member of. That is where I draw my strength from. Alcoholics Anonymous was founded in 1935 by two men with a dream and a passion of helping others. Then, as today, there are no dues or fees for membership. AA is worldwide, at last count, AA is in 180 countries. AA literature is printed in 67 different languages. There is no mystery in following, good orderly direction, (G.O.D.).Now let's have those hugs.

OK, before we go on, I have something a little more to say. I haven't finished up with my many blessings since the book has been published. I want to tell you about my sister-in-law and her husband, Bonny and Tinker (he goes by Tink) Fender. Bonnie was married to my oldest brother Donnie. Early in his life Donnie became an abusive, violent and vicious drunk. They had 2 children together, Donny was most often times not present, he was either drunk, hanging out with his pals, or in jail. He spent a great deal of time in jail and the county work farm before he sobered up. Donny did little to ever financially support his family. My dad and I would take trips to their house and bring them groceries and oftentimes dad helped pay the rent, Bonnie never forgot that. You would think that a woman that has been so badly mistreated would be angry with her in-laws and with extended family but that wasn't Bonnie. Not by a long shot.

113

My mother never learned how to drive. After my father's death she attended two different driving schools and was kicked out of both because of her extreme nervousness.

Bonnie would bring the boys when they were just youngsters to visit Gramma on a very regular basis. She always brought the kids for holidays and for special events. The kids were always very clean and well-cared-for. Bonnie has always been a friend to me. The three different times I moved back to Minnesota I reconnected with Bonnie on Facebook. Bonnie has always treated me as family. Bonnie and Tink do a real cool thing during the Christmas season. They rent a large hotels pool area and a medium sized adjoining banquet room (approx. 100 people) for the kids to use on Christmas day and do potluck. Everyone brings a great amount food, the kids get to swim and play all day long and the adults get to visit. There is a schedule for each adult to play lifeguard at all times. I have been invited to that event every year. I've been to their cabin on a lake on a number of occasions. Their doors are always open. My nephews are always respectful and engaging. There's not many people like Bonnie and Tinker Fender in this world. I am blessed with their friendship and affections.

Then there is my almost sister-in-law Dianne Johnson Agustsson. Dianne was engaged to my brother Petey. Petey called off the wedding when he realized that he was terminal. Petey was an honorable man, he didn't want to drag her and her daughter thru the financial ruin of being married to a dying man and the several hundreds of thousands of dollars of medical bills.

Dianne had always been crazy about Petey and would do anything in the world for him. You could see the pain in her eyes when she realized that she could not help him live. She could only help him die. Yet Dianne held herself together for Petey's and my mother's sake. She spent all the time she possibly could at the hospital (160 miles from home) with Petey and my mom. Dianne had a seven year old daughter named Katie that adored Petey and he deeply loved that precious little girl. It tore him up in his thoughts of Dianne having to tell her baby when he died.

114

After Petey passed, Dianne kept in close contact with my mom. She came to my mom's house weekly and always brought Katie with her. My mom loved them both dearly. As Bonnie Fender did, Dianne always came by to visit for holidays.

I wish I could have been there when Dianne brought John Agustsson to mom's house to introduce him as her fiancé. Dianne had become a daughter and my mother was a Momma Bear. I'm sure poor John got the once-over, several times. A few years later Dianne and John were going to have a baby. My mom lost her mind with baby supply shopping. Mother insisted that Dianne come to the house each week for my mom's visual inspection as to how the baby was developing. Dianne being the sweet and dutiful gal she is, showed up each week so mom could inspect and give her approval with the baby's development and Dianne's rest and eating patterns. When the baby (Paige) was born my mother lost her mind. She finally had the granddaughter she always wanted. One of the hospital baby photos was a superimposed picture of newborn Paige in a peapod. That picture went up on mom's refrigerator and stayed there for many, many years. Every time I came to visit, there was that picture on the refrigerator. My Mom and Pops were both chain smokers, the picture had yellowed and curled but it remained there until after my Moms and Pops deaths.

Dianne and John brought the girls to visit often. Their kindness brought a great deal of joy to my mom's otherwise, mundane and lonely life of guilt and shame. If not for the warm hearts and loving attentions of the Fender and Agustsson families my mother would have let herself go, many years earlier. They gave her the gift of purpose.

There's another person who I have reconnected with because of Corrina Maly and the book.

When I worked for the ambulance service and long after Carl's divorce, he met a woman that most of us already knew from a local hospital. Carl worked in the office during the day and was always armpit deep in insurance forms. The only time Carl ran emergency calls during the day was if all the crews were out, so he rarely saw day-shift emergency room personnel.

115

Kathy Bomey, was a single mom raising two young children. She was a nurse at a local hospital emergency room and she applied for part-time work in our road-trip division. She would come down to our headquarters every day when she got off work, gather up all of our laundry (pillowcases, towels, sheets, and blankets) we went through a lot of laundry every day. Kathy would bring all of that home with her, do all that laundry and bring it back before she went to work each morning. Everything was wrinkle free and perfectly folded.

CHAPTER 13   THE INSURANCE FIXERS

Insurance billing was an absolute nightmare. I tried to help Carl with the billing between slow times and the nights I worked dispatch. More than half of our insurance claims were mailed back due to miscoding. This was pre-internet so mail was slow and we could go up to six months without being paid on many claims. During a Rochester Minnesota, one-way road trip with Kathy, I filled her in on the struggles with billing and cash flow on our return trip of six hours. She said two of her old high school buddies worked in the insurance claims offices at different hospitals. She said she would talk to them about billing practices. The next day Kathy called and said she was going to have breakfast with those two woman on the following Saturday. After their meal the three of them would come to the station and try to help us with submitting insurance claims.

We had stacks and stacks of denied and yet to be filed claims. When they saw our mess they both shook their heads. They told Carl and me to go wash something as they plowed thru our paper disasters. We washed and waxed three rigs before they came out of the office.

The older woman with premature graying temples said, "If you treated your patients like these insurance forms they would all be dead! We want a Sammy's pizza and Pepsis, if we are going to work all night!" Carl and I ran to our rig and we were out the door with lights flashing and sirens blaring in just a few seconds! This

117

hot call was about Sammy's pizza and saving our financial ass! Carl's eyes welled up with the realization that these two woman who we have never met were doing this for us. We double parked the rig with the emergency lights on and dashed into the pizza shop. As we approached the counter we realized at almost the same moment that we had not asked them what kind of pizza they wanted. Carl went back out to the rig and radioed dispatch for the pizza order. As we waited for the pizza Carl asked if I had any money. Between the two of us, we were able to pay for two pizzas and a 6-pack of Pepsi. I could read Carl's grim look as to say, "How am I going to pay them for their work?"

We got toned out to a traffic accident when we were only two blocks from headquarters with fresh hot pizza. Carl's toothy grin was the same as mine as we slid to a stop in front of headquarters and I jumped out of the rig with hot pizza. Kathy met me at the door and I shoved the pizzas and Pepsis into her arms. I hoped back into the rig as Carl said, "If you are thru screwing around, I would like to invite you to a multi-vehicle car accident, with injuries. That is if you have the time." We hauled ass to the traffic accident where all four patients refused transport.

We returned to quarters and could not help but hear the laughter of three woman coming from the kitchen as we were backing into our stall.

Carl and I were trying to slink away to the TV room, when Kathy stepped out of the kitchen with a scowl as she said, "You two boys come in here."

The women were happily munching their pizza. The younger one looked at Carl and said, "I don't expect you to remember me, but you took care of me in a car accident four years ago. All the Doctors said I shouldn't have lived. I have had five surgeries since then. This scar is the only thing I have left to get fixed (she had a deep and wide purple scar that ran from her left lower jaw bone up thru her lips and to her right eye) you saved my life that day. I never had the nerve to bother you with saying, thank you."

The older women looked at me and asked, "Do you remember the man who was mowing his lawn last summer and a rock killed his little boy and three months later he took his own life? That man was my brother. I heard about you from the neighbor's and I have seen you on TV several times. I remember you from my brother's funeral. When you knelt at my brother's coffin, it somehow made it all right for me. Than when I saw so many people hugging you and shaking your hand in the church, I thanked God for you and the love you showed my family.

We will work for another hour or so tonight and we will be back in the morning to finish up. We are teaching Kathy how to do the coding as we go along, you two keep your mitts off those forms. Do what you do best because you guys are horse-shit at billing!" With a warm smile they said, "No charge for our services and you don't have to feed us tomorrow."

Kathy became our billing clerk as well. She also became our den mother. Kathy gave all the guys free haircuts, she knew everyone's birthdays and always made a cake for everyone's birthdays. She was also our go to gal if the guys had a problem in a relationship with a woman.

Kathy always had her ears ready to listen. She rarely told anyone what they should do, she would just quietly listen with her soft caring eyes. She was a quiet girl, unassuming and attentive to everyone. She treated everyone the same and never showed any kind of favoritism. Kathy really was, our Mom, even to the guys older than her. If a crew was out for several hours on back-to-back calls, Kathy would have a piping hot Pyrex pan of Lasagna waiting for them. She made pies and chocolate cake almost every day. She made complete dinners for holidays and invited the crew's families to join us. I ran several road trips with her on my days off. Kathie's level of patient care and bedside manor was a beautiful thing to witness.

The day I first met Corrina I asked her if she had a relationship with Kathy, she said periodically but not often enough. So I signed a book for Kathy and asked her to forward it to her, which she did. A few weeks later Corrina invited me to join her and Kathy for coffee. It had been more than forty years since I last spoke with or saw Kathy. I was hoping the ladies arrived together and before me, because I was afraid I may not recognize Kathy after all these years. Yes she has aged as we all have, but I couldn't miss those soft, understanding eyes from twenty feet away. It was so nice to see her and she still is that same sweet gal. Kathy is a remarkable woman, who I respect greatly.

CHAPTER 14   MINNESOTA NICE

Lastly, there is Bill Stovern and Ronda Hughes. I met this couple at a pistol shooting range thru Heather. Heather saw them pull into the parking area and get out of their car. She said, "Those two are old friends of mine, I used to work with Ronda, she is one classy lady and Bill is a super nice guy. You will like them!"

Heather made the introductions and from our first handshake and eye contact, I sensed that these two were quality people. The kind of people that anyone would want to be friends with.

Ronda looked a bit timid, maybe even frightened to be around guns. We had several high quality hand guns laid out on our shooting mat. Bill let out a low whistle as he looked them over. I told them they could try anyone of them as they were all new and we were there to break them in and we had plenty of ammunition. The grin on Bills face was like a little kid getting to open his first birthday present from the stack of gifts.

Bill took Ronda down to the end of the shooting tables for the obvious gun safety talk. Heather and I went back to shooting. When we emptied all the guns and magazines we returned to the shooting table behind the firing line to reload. Bill took Ronda to the 15 foot mark where he handed her a small, lady size hand gun. She was so nervous that she almost dropped it. On her first shot she got a jam as she limp wristed the weapon. You could see the

121

embarrassment and frustration on her face, as if to say, 'go ahead babe, I'll wait in the car.'

Heather read that the same as I did. Heather walked up to Ronda to sooth her. Between Bill and Heather giving Ronda calm encouragements, fifteen minutes later Ronda found her comfort and was smiling as she blasted the shit out of the targets. Bill had yet to shoot. We all returned to the loading tables behind the firing line.

Bill said he wanted to shoot from the ten foot line. I nodded and said, we will wait here. Bill walked casually to the line and in one fluid motion, drew his weapon and began rapid firing as he moved backwards and to his right than to his left and back right. I thought, 'Jesus Christ, he is slicing the pie! He is either a Cop or military.'

'Slicing the pie' is a taught and a well-practiced maneuver used in urban close combat encounters when the officer is in the open and needs to return fire while going for cover. Bills quick draw, quick fire and footwork screamed badass! The technique looks simple enough but to do it right you have to point shoot, you don't use your rear or front sights, you constantly look over your shoulder for civilians and debris or curbs that you might trip over while still firing your weapon. Few police departments give you the range time or ammunition to become proficient in this life saving exercise. Bill had obviously spent a great deal of his own time and money to be that proficient.

Now I was grinning like a birthday boy. I looked back at the girls with a, W.T.F. look and Ronda smiled sweetly as she said, "Yes, he's a Cop." Well, that did it for me, we are gonna be Pals.

Bill and Ronda shot several of our guns and we all had a good time. During our time together I told Bill that I was a former police officer and I am currently a novelist and continuing author. Bill said he saw by the way I handled my guns and my shooting stance that I was very familiar with guns but the eye contact and posture gave me away. "You still look and walk like a cop! I don't get the author thing unless it's about slamming heads together, which you still look plenty capable of doing, yet today."

As we parted company that afternoon we agreed that we will have to get together in the next few weeks for lunch and maybe another round of shooting. It was a great experience to meet two genuine, straight up people. There was no phony posturing or airs of stature. Just solid folks, who are my kind of people.

On our way home, Heather told me that she had worked with Ronda a few years ago for a large company. Heather didn't receive the proper training to do the job, so she had to hit the ground running and learn as she went. Ronda befriended Heather and taught her the proper ways, shortcuts and systems to do her job. They traveled the country in their jobs and became personal friends. Heather knew both of Ronda's daughters when they were little kids and watched them grow into successful young ladies. One daughter is a Broadway actress and singer who has had several television appearances. The other daughter has equal talents as an artist, whose work is highly praised by the art world. Yup, Ronda's got game. Children don't grow up with that kind of talent without strong parental guidance and praise. When a parent openly shows approval and belief in their child the child will learn to believe in themselves. Nice job Mom!

I didn't know Ronda's last name until Heather mentioned it on the way home that day. I wondered if she might be the daughter of a kid I grew up with. I text Ronda and asked her. She was not. Ronda and Bill and I became Facebook friends. I had just received a new shipment of books so I asked them if they would be interested in reading my book. I gifted and mailed them a copy. Two weeks later I emailed Ronda and asked if she had a chance to read the book. She said no, "Bill won't give it up but he talks about it every day. I am out of town for three days during the work week." I signed another book and mailed it to Ronda.

I told them both that the actual city where I grew up was in fact, Duluth but I had to make up names of people and places to avoid legal complications from the potential 'offended.' Bill text me every few days to confirm his guess as to the actual locations and their names. He was 70% right. It was a fun game. Bill being a twenty plus year Duluth Police Officer, got it and said he

123

encouraged all of his pals on the department to buy and read the book. Ronda was crushed to know of children that could be so poorly mistreated.

A few weeks later Ronda sent Heather and me an invitation to Bills retirement party. We were flattered with the invitation. Heather had been battling a nasty head and chest cold, so the day of Bills retirement party I had to go alone. Ronda did a beautiful job with decorating the entire bar area and made several displays of Bills uniforms, badges, hats and there were four, 3-ring binders, of his achievement awards along with Mayor and Police Chief letters of accommodations and proclamations. There could be no confusion of Bill Stovern, being a cops, Cop!

Understand that I had only seen Bill and Ronda once before and that was at the shooting range. The extremely large, bar parking lot was overflowing for the closed and private invitation only party. The huge, standing room only bar was difficult to navigate as I moved sideways thru the crowd to find the gift table to drop off our envelope with a gift card for Dunkin' Donuts. I also brought two copies of my book as Bill told me in an email that he wanted to reread my book but his daughter, (who also works for the Duluth Police Department) took it to read after Bill talked about it so much.

Ronda was easy to spot as she has an elegance and posture that is unforgettable and is yet, totally approachable.

She of course was chatting with a group of people. I stood patiently amongst the two hundred plus people (none of who I knew) waiting to say hello. When Ronda saw me she broke away from the group and came up to me with a brilliant smile and gave me a warm hug. She looked around and asked where Heather was. When I told Ronda that Heather was sick, Ronda had a genuine look of disappoint and concern on her face. Ronda hooked my elbow and said, "Come on, Bill is going to be thrilled to see you, he talks about you and your book daily, to me and all of our friends. He is very proud to call you his friend. I'm afraid that you have a fan for life!" Ronda stood with me in the reception line to greet and congratulate Bill on his retirement.

When Bill became available he threw his arms around me for a bear hug with a wide smile. He thanked me for coming and said, "I have a lot of friends here that want to meet you. I still can't believe that a guy I met at the shooting range could write a book like that and live right here in Duluth! 'Brownie' I read a lot, but never in my life have I ever had the pleasure of reading such a deep and honest account of a person's life. I feel as thou I have known you all my life. I know you better than my own brothers. You are a brave man the way you left nothing on the table. You must have been one hell of a cop. I would have partnered with you anytime!"

I gave Bill the two books in my hand as I told him, "These are loaners for your friends so you can protect your personalized copy and not have it disappear or get glazed or jelly donut smears all over it, damn cops!" I opened the book to the author signing page and told Bill to read the inscription out loud.
He and Ronda laughed heartily when Bill read, "This book is the sole property of Bill Stovern, if you don't return it he will hunt you down and make you cry!"

I started to feel uneasy with taking up so much of Bills time with such a lengthy line behind me to see him. Bill sensed my uneasiness and read my mind as he said, "Give me a few minutes to greet these folks and I will find you. There are a lot of people here that want to meet you. I can't believe that a famous author came to my retirement party!"

It wasn't twenty minutes later that Bill was guiding me thru the crowded bar to introduce me to his many friends. I was a bit embarrassed with the accolades that Bill was showering me with when introducing me.

As I drove home I couldn't help but marvel at the perfect relationship that Bill and Ronda shared. They equally complement each other with an open fondness and respect. Those are two quality people.

A few months later, Ronda posted on Facebook that there was an upcoming benefit for a local music celebrity who played for several benefits over the years and now he needed help. There was a spaghetti dinner and silent auction at a large local bar. I emailed Ronda and asked if she thought my donating two of my books for the event would be welcomed. Ronda thought that that would be a wonderful idea.

Ronda gave me the contact information of the person who was accepting the donated items for the silent auction. I contacted her and she gave me the drop-off location. The benefit promoter did a daily broadcast on Facebook as to needing volunteers and listed current donations along with a brief mention of the donators. She wrote a lengthy and flattering description of me and my book.

Since we have never met or had any phone conversations, I knew that that information had to have come from my pal Ronda.

The day of the event, I arrived thirty minutes early and the place was already jammed to the rafters with people. Because of my many years of absence from the area and being a homebody, I had become accustomed with not looking for familiar faces. I know that this is of my own making but the loneliness washed over me like a Lake Superior white cap crashing against the tall cliffs. I tried to shake it off but as the many of hundreds of past similar experiences, I did my best not to show it. I still carry my painful little secret that, "I am lonely and I don't belong here, I don't belong anywhere."

I went to a large area where the silent auction items were displayed. If you were to judge people's love for this man by the items for auction, the most casual observer would see a great deal of affections. I found my two books in two different locations. They were each paired up with a bottle of some kind of wine, so it was a two-for-one item. Wine and a good book was a winning combination. Or so I thought. Each of the many auction items had bid sheets of course. I noticed most all of them already had multiple bids on them and the event hadn't even started yet.

My books and their partnered wines were blank sheets other than the descriptions. I had never been in this building before. There were multiple bars and several sizable side rooms. I decided to take myself for a tour. I found myself in the Spaghetti dining room that probably seated seventy-five people or more comfortably. There were only a few seats open so I bought a ticket and went to the serving tables. I got a plate of spaghetti and sat with the masses. The meal was better than I expected.

As in each room I visited, there were large groups of people visiting, with one or two acoustical guitar players and singers. As I was finishing my meal I saw Bill and Ronda take a seat a few rows in front of me. I went over to say hello.

As the times before, they were both very engaging and they insisted I join them. I got a fresh cup of coffee and we chatted as they tried to eat their meal. I say tried to eat, because of their genuine warmth and popularity, many people stopped by to say hello. Bill and Ronda introduced me to each person. One couple was obviously quite close to them. As Bill introduced me they both had wide eyes when Bill said, "This is the guy that wrote the book I've been telling you guys about." Bill said to me, "Tom here is also a recently retired Police Officer but he was a ranked command officer." Tom's wife, Patti said, "You don't look like how I would visualize an author would look. You look more like an actor that would be in an organized crime movie or TV show." Ronda smiled sweetly as she said, "Yes, as a hit man for the mob, you don't want to mess with him. He still may be on the job!" We all had a good laugh as I told them that I had been told that many times over the years. Bill said, "I think he has all of our backs, and I'm guessing that he is rattlesnake fast. Yup, I'll go with Ronda on this one."

Tom asked where he could buy my book. I gave him my business card with my website on it, as well as told him about the on-line availability at: Amazon, Barnes and Noble, and Walmart. I told him that I had two books in the silent auction and a few out in the truck so he would not have to leave without a signed copy. I excused myself to go check on the auction and to let them chat and maybe even allow Bill and Ronda to finish their meals.

Much to my dismay I found both of my book/wine items to have zero bids. With less than twenty minutes left of the auction, I bid on my own books. I bid $11.99 (my cost) on each book. I went outside for a smoke and to walk off my disappointment.

I couldn't help but find a laugh when I flashed back on the last two years that I donated my books to my shooting club for their annual banquet and silent auction fund raisers. The first year I donated two hard cover and two soft cover books. The hardcovers (retail $27.95) sold for $3.25 each. I bid $2.00 each on the soft covers and won them both. The next year I donated two soft covers and I bought them each for a dollar. Reading in this part of the country is trumped by the many outdoor sports and recreations, damn those 10,000 lakes!

I was also aware that the book title frightened some people. I had thought of changing the title on several occasions but I didn't have the money for the art work and reprinting. It reminds me of the current TV commercial for 'Life Alert' where the announcer gives a brief disclaimer of, "This is a reality commercial some viewers may find this commercial offensive," as they show an elderly person laying on the floor who can't get up. More evidence that reality is treated as if it is a horror show. Sadly, our society is severely broken.

I went back into the bar, checked on the ended auction and not to my surprise, I won both of my books and the bottles of wine. I paid for my items and struck out to find Tom and Patti to gift them a copy of my book. They were at one of the three bars in the building. They were still with Bill and Ronda. I told Ronda to pick a bottle of wine and offered the other bottle to Patti, which she accepted.

As I was signing the book for them, Tom and I had words, as he insisted on paying for the book. I won the argument when I threatened to T.P. and egg his house. Tom and Patti jumped deep into their interest of the book. They asked several, well thought out questions. But the one question that caused me to all but brain freeze and lose consciousness, prompted me to send Bill this email:

Hello Bill

It is Tuesday morning and I am still overwhelmed with our time together at the benefit on Sunday. I believe that everything

128

happens for a reason. You and Ronda shook me to my core that day, when you introduced me to Tom and Patti and from that, my world changed. I don't remember if it was him or her that asked the question of what drove me to write this new book. As I was explaining my spiritual experience and inspiration that brought the first book to life. They both leaned close to me and with hushed voices asking, "Did God speak to you? What did his voice sound like? What did he say? Did you actually have a shared conversation with him?"

Those questions threw me into a mental vapor-lock and my brain shut down. When I was next asked by Patti what the name of the city was where the early part of the book is based on I couldn't remember. I was so deeply affected with the God questions that I had to leave the building and go home. I had never asked myself those God questions. From Sunday, right up to this moment I have not been able to think of anything else.

Was it God?
Was it my Mother who passed away twelve days prior to my experience?
Was she giving me permission to tell the truth to help others like me?
Was it my deceased baby girl telling daddy to dare to dream again?
Was it God telling me that I could be a better man and live a decent life of meaning and joy?

From my experience at the benefit I have decided to add two chapters to my new book, 'Flesh of a Fraud.' I am asking you and Ronda for your permission to use your names, please advise. I will leave you with this. So….was it dumb luck, divine intervention or serendipity that placed us at the pistol range on that warm fall day?

End of email

Bill wrote back the next day that they would both be honored with their names in my book but he did admonish me with, "Ronda does not have an 'H' in her name. It's Ronda." I had been using the "Rhonda" spelling. A few weeks later, Heather and I joined Ronda and Bill for a Sammy's pizza. I assured Ronda that I would never misspell her name again, as "I smashed and burnt the 'R' key on my laptop."

Every time I see a Facebook post from Bill or Ronda I can only smile at the thought that someday there will be billboards on every roadway entering the state with their smiling faces, titled:

MINNESOTA NICE!

CHAPTER 15   GETTING TO KNOW ME

There are so many other people who should be mentioned that I would have to write 2 more volumes, but the they know who they are and that's one of the blessings about growing up is that I could look at a person today and say thank you without shame or without a grudge. It just feels nice to be nice and that's my big reward in life today. I get to be the man today that I've always wanted to be.

Me: Ok, where do you want to go now?

Maddie: This is just so embarrassing but I have to tell you, we were and still are so taken by you, that you have overwhelmed us like no other person ever has in either of our life experiences! We forgot to even ask you the very first basic question that we would ask of anyone, especially a writer. So let me ask you the first question. Who do you read, do you have a favorite author?

Me: I don't read like I used to, only because I'm so busy with writing.
I haven't read anything other than what I call, 'Trash Westerns' since I started writing back in 2011. I don't want anyone's writing to infiltrate my head and to find myself blending my thoughts with

another writer.

Trash westerns are stories of Frontier Justice that always have a plot but without all of that cutesy bullshit where it takes the author three pages to describe the landscape.

With trash westerns there is nothing heavy, there's nothing mysterious, they all have story lines about the old days of the west, when if people weren't given respect, they would take respect at the end of a smoking barrel. I fantasize about living in those days. If I could live at any time period, it would be the mid to late 1800s. That's where my soul comes from, I believe in riding for the brand, you take a man's money you do what the man says, a day's work for a day's pay. I also believe that some horses 'can't be rode.' There is an old cowboy saying, 'step down from that Mare old son, she can't be rode.' That carries on into my life today. I am fiercely loyal, if you wrong me, you will answer to me. Since we are in modern day times, I can't out-draw you and put your dead ass up on boot hill, so I just walk away. I read most all of the trash western series books, I refuse to read any author's releases after their deaths. Their family somehow miraculously found a number of his unfinished writings up in their attic. The family claims they are releasing them for the public's enjoyment, well that is pure unadulterated bullshit. The minute I start to read these newly found books that the family published after the author's death, you could see it was a completely different writer and so I just lost my taste for those type of books. Also of note, many of the westerns from the long series of the hundreds and hundreds of books, that certain chapters are written by certain writers. It's not all one writer, writing the entire book. The tempo and the flow of the writing is grossly apparent. I usually put that book down and never pick it back up again. I'll take it to a used bookstore and trade it for something I want to read.

OK, what's next?

Woody: Dave, with all this and with what we've been speaking about this morning, about your medical condition, I have to ask you, where do you draw your strength and do you pray?

Me: Well I have learned (I had to be taught) to pray. I hedged on that God stuff for about the first four years in my sobriety. I was miserable as hell and it was my only hope. But today, yes I do pray but I don't pray like most others. Not that I'm unique but I'm a realist. I don't pray for the outcome of anything for me or for the outcome for anyone else. What I pray for is my ability and their ability to best deal with what the situation is. I've never prayed to win the lottery but I sure as hell would like to! I don't pray that someday I can afford a new truck or a bunch of stuff, that's just the ridiculous side of the selfish, self-centered, self-seeking human endeavor. I'm cautious with my prayer and I have to tell you this is kind of funny when I do public speaking. I will tell people about the often heard statement that 'God never gives us more than we can handle.' Well I turn it around and it snaps a lot a heads up, when I say, "I never give God, more than he can handle! The reason I say this is that by my very nature along with my contemptuous and distrusting belief in God, I closely examine his results. It's like God is a probationary worker in my employment and I try to look for his weaknesses, try to help him find ways to improve and develop a better delivery system." That's where my mind goes, so I like to test God which is a foolish waste of my energy and time. What I do today is I allow there to be a God in my life. I don't try to give him form, shape, or definition. I just allow there to be a God in my life. I ask God for maturity, I ask him for peace, I ask him for humility. Those are the things that I constantly struggle with and pray for. In the past, I've always viewed humility as a weakness. Today I realize that humility is an extreme strength. So yes I do pray, I pray cautiously, and I pray often. I don't clasp my hands or go to my knees, I just sit and talk to God. I call him God, he calls me Dave.
We get along just fine.

OK, what's next for the second, third, and fourth things that you should have asked me from day one?

Maddie: What has been the response from your ex-wives and the people of your past, in reference to your book? Would you talk to us about that?

Me: My first wife; passed before the book ever came out. We hadn't seen or spoken to each other for more than 40 years.

My second wife; I haven't spoken with since our divorce. I do know where she is but I don't feel any kind of need to reach-out to her. My third wife is still one of my very best friends and is an actual fan of mine. We text weekly, usually brief and we are Facebook friends. She's married to a wonderful guy who I've known for a number of years. On my last visit to Las Vegas for a book signing, I rented a car and drove to their home and spent the day with the two of them. They're very gracious, loving people and I couldn't be happier for the both of them.

My fourth and fifth wives each received the copy's I sent them. I have no further comments about them. Let's move beyond this, what's next.

Woody: What were some of the reactions of the people you gifted your books to?

Me: You may find this interesting as I had many people who were very excited about receiving the book, when I offered them a free copy and I paid the postage. I asked only one thing from them. To post a picture of them with the book in their hands on Facebook to help get the word out about the book. Of the probably 550 books I gave away to people on Facebook, I got only eight people that did photographs of themselves with the book. It's not that I need to learn about people, I understand people quite well but even I was taken back and I was frustrated. I was angry, I felt betrayed but that's just the way I felt. It's not their fault, it is just what life is and the way most people are. But I carried a grudge for a period of time.

I checked with each person I sent books to, three days after the post office projected delivery date to insure that they received their copy. Only a hand-full responded or even sent a thank you. I sent free books to help in fundraisers for fallen or injured First Responders. I rarely received an acknowledgement of receipt, let alone a simple thank you. I told you before of the assholes that bitched because they couldn't sell them because of the personalized messages.

Heather's father Tom, is a neat guy and has been a friend of mine for many, many years. He decided that he wanted to help promote my book and he asked me to give him several copies, which I did. I first gave him four copies of the book and he started his own little library system. We met for lunch each week. He would be so excited to tell me about his giving a copy of the book to this person or that person. He would tell me that he was having trouble with picking up a book after the reader finished it because they gave it to someone else. Suddenly all the books seemed to grow legs. He asked for more and I gave him two books with a stern admonishment to keep track of who had the books and to tell them you want them back and they were not to loan them out.

Tom called me the morning of our standing lunch date and asked me to bring more books to the restaurant. When I approached the booth that Tom was sitting in, he asked me where my briefcase was and "Did you bring my books," before I even sat down! I did not bring him any books as we were about to have a bit of a 'come-to-Jesus meeting.'

Tom is a well-meaning guy but he doesn't always understand the ways of the world. Tom is also very sensitive and I didn't want to hurt his feelings. But it was time. I tried to come in soft, but early-on I saw he wasn't getting it. I stepped up my game when I said, "Tommy, there will be no more free books. It's all good and well that you're trying to get the word out about my book but I can't afford to pay for all these free books and for you to be playing librarian. It doesn't help me sell books, the best way to get the word out, is to sell the book. The best way for me to recover my expenses is to, sell the book. I am not in the library business." I could see by his facial expressions and body language that he hadn't heard a word. It didn't fit his agenda. I than told him that, "At last count, you had let fourteen people read the books but you have not said a word about any reader response. What are your friends saying about the book?" Tom had a sheepish grin as he lowered his head and softly said, "They liked it." I let him have it. "Are you fuckin telling me that fourteen people, all had the same response? Jesus Christ Tommy, a 6x9 novel, 334 pages, 125,000 words that took me seven years to write, publish and market at the cost greater than my and your annual social security income and all you can tell me is that, 'They liked it'? Are you using those fucking books to level your couch?"

After the waitress took our order Tom said, "I will buy four of your books at your cost." I gave Tom my, "You are near death" look as I gave him a hard grin and I said, "I'm damn glad that I don't own a new car dealership!" I didn't and won't continue to play that game with him.

Some people show anger towards me when I do a, 'Meet & Greet the Author' event. Some people say, "You open scars, old wounds are now fresh again, I wish I would never read your book." My responses is always the same, "We can all deal with what was in our past, if we want to have a better future." I don't take it beyond that. I had a local church lady who seemed very sweet, as she said, "I felt like you had your way with me because I would never read a book with such filthy words but I never saw the filthy words because the story just kept bringing me into it and bringing me into it. A friend of mine asked me after I shared the book with her, "How could I read such filthy trash with all those terrible words?" I said, I didn't know that there were terrible words, somehow they got right past me." She said that while smiling, I hoped that that was not a death ray look instead of a smile. People's comments run the gamut as I'm sure you two have heard as you were playing 'Junior Reporters' two weeks ago! By the way, when are you two going to share those responses you recorded?

Woody: We thought we would do that as we take the book chapter by chapter next week, if that's ok with you?

Me: Yes, that will be fine. Let's finish this up right after I have a smoke. We have an hour left when I get back.

Me: The reprint of 'Daddy Had to Say Goodbye' of course has an enhanced cover, title and author identification on the header and I now have readers' comments and those comments had been wonderful. There were a lot more comments that I was unable to print because that would just get boring and appear to be self-serving. I'm still just a regular guy and I'm luckily that people see me as just a regular guy, who just so happened to have written a book. So I enjoy that very much, I never wrote for fame or fortune obviously, you've seen my truck.

Maddie: (as she jumped to her feet) Bullshit! There is nothing regular or average about you! (as she threw her wrinkled muffin wrapper at me). I am sorry David, but that just pisses me off the way you downplay your blessings! If not to us at least admit to yourself, that you carry a gift from God that very few, and I mean damn few, if any at all possess. I'm going to the bathroom!
    I looked at Woody and asked "What the fuck was that?" Woody leaned back in his chair with his hands clasped behind his neck as he grinned and said, "You just stepped in it, don't put any of that on me!"
    I broke for the garden and a cigarette. I made a brief phone call and as I lit my second cigarette. Vicki came hurriedly out to the garden and I held up a finger as to say 'one minute'. I finished the phone call as Vickie nervously said, "Mr. Roberts is on the phone for you, please hurry!" I went into Vicki's office and she closed the door behind me. I picked up the phone and said hello. A female voice said, "I am Mr. Robert's personal assistant, please

hold for Mr. Roberts. When Paul answered he apologized for disturbing me.

I said, "What's up Mr. Bigshot?" After a few minutes of conversation I said, "I will be there." I called Heather and asked her to pack a bag for me as I had a flight in three hours.

As I entered the meeting room I saw Maddie was crying. I bent down and picked up the muffin wrapper that she threw at me and rolled it across the table to her as I said, "I think you dropped this." She called me a fucker and began laughing. Woody said, "I wish I was a smoker so I could get away from you two crazy fuckers." We all laughed as we hugged and dried our eyes. I knew exactly why Maddie called bullshit on me, we all knew. Maddie started to apologize but I waved her off. I asked her, "What's in your gut that you just have to get out? Most of this in not about me, so let's have it."

Maddie: I have lived my entire life in a very tidy box. I have lied to myself for my own comforts. I have lied to my patients, my clients and my students. I have lied to the entire world. I pretended to have all the answers when I have never truly understood the questions. I don't ask my patients what's wrong with them, I tell them what's wrong with them.

I am the fraud that you write about! I teach my students about mental illness like I'm a shop teacher rebuilding a carburetor! Then you come along and you trap me. I have learned more about people and life in the last three weeks that I've studied you, than at any time of my life. I apologize for my arrogance. I thought I would study you and figure you out. As I have thousands of times before, I would complete my masterful observations of you, roll it up tight and tuck it in the proper pigeon hole. You have punched me in the guts so many times that I can't even eat a full meal.

I can't sleep, I can't even do a load of laundry without thinking of what a failure I am. If it wasn't for Woody I would have pulled the bed covers up to my neck and never left the house. Every morning Woody brings me a Latte at wake up. He reminds me that if we are late to meet you, we could lose it all. When we get into the car to head to the hotel Woody looks over with a grin as he asks, 'Well Hun, you ready to go pet the Alligator?'

You are a complete enigma! Your eyes are so loving, your voice is so soothing that people become mesmerized with your charms and nobody can ever remotely guess of your past pains and suffering. When I see this I just want to hug you but at the same time, I see a vicious warrior that would unmercifully destroy any adversary. How the hell do I come to terms with my love and deep respect for a potential killer? Looking and listening to you and sensing the undertones of extreme violence is like watching a scary thriller movie and waiting for all hell to break lose. But you are not a thriller movie actor. I find you both seductive and revolting. It is very unnerving.

Me: Maddie you need to stop this shit. You are the very first person that I know of that has come to terms with their failings as a professional healer. There is that old saying that goes something like, "Those that can't do....teach." Sweetheart, you can't do! Settle down and listen to me. There are two reasons why you 'can't do.'

First: You go too deep with your relating to your patients and you lose your ability to help them. Do you want to play back your recorder and listen to what you have been saying for the last ten minutes?

Second: Now that you have come to terms with your teaching failures and are developing a true and viable teaching platform, you must teach!

Now you two ready for a pivot? We are quitting for the rest of the week. I have a plane to catch, you two are going home to pack for the next four days. You guys will go to the airport and meet a Ft. Lauderdale flight at 4:10 this afternoon. Our pal Don Prince will be riding in on his white stallion to save us all. You guys and Don will be staying at this hotel. Your room keys are at the registration desk now. Your rooms and meals are comped so please tip the staff accordingly. Vicki has a full itinerary with prepaid tickets for several events. You three are going to take a break and learn to breathe again. No therapy sessions allowed! I'm going to Chicago to play patty-cake with our benefactor of this four day respite. You kids play nice and I'll see you cats, Monday morning.

As I was driving down the street to the house, I saw a limo in front of the house with a chauffeur standing in front of the car in full attire, right down to his cap. As I pulled into the driveway I thought, 'Paul Roberts, you got class but you are also a total prick. What the hell are the neighbors going to think? Just for that, this limo guy just earned a hundred dollar tip, or should I make it two hundred?'

CHAPTER 16   007 REVISITED

Heather looked her usual stunning self. She had my bags ready just inside the door. A hug with kisses, two sets of misty eyes with joint I love you's and I was out the door with a steaming fresh cup of coffee in my travel mug. God, I love that woman!

The Limo driver pulled up to the Executive Terminal, spoke to the guard at the gate and a minute later a white pick-up truck with a flashing amber light-bar and a large, "Follow Me" sign on the tail gate pulled in front of us. He escorted us to a large private jet. I signed for the ride and added a $250 tip. As I got out of the limo the very first thing I saw was the tail section of the plane had a large, 'Randall' corporate logo on it. I made a mental note to tell 'Pauly Boy' about his security problem.

The limo drove off and standing in front of the stairs was the same flight attendant that gave me the briefcase from the last time I was there.

This time she looked more polished in a smart looking executive suit. Former beauty queen, I'm guessing. On either side of the stairs were a matching set of two male, human bookends. Huge guys, same suits, ties, shoes and sun glasses. The very same bulges under their suit coats also. The woman turned to the two men and said, "Gentlemen this is your charge, Mr. Brown." She turned back to me and said, "Mr. Brown, please follow me, sir." It was a pleasure to follow her up those stairs.

We walked briskly to the rear of the plane where she swiped a card and a door automatically slid open. This office was

141

bigger than I thought would fit in a plane this size. As the rest of the plane we walked thru, it was identical in the furnishings of plush burgundy carpet, highly polished Burl wood and gleaming brass trim with white leather overstuffed chairs and mini couches. She pushed a button on the wall and a closet door opened, she took off her suit coat and hung it up and closed the closet door with the same wall button. She said, "Mr. Brown please have a seat," as she went around the desk and sat down. I saw her reach under the desk and the main door closed with a vacuum sucking sound followed with a hard latching sound. She said with a smile, "We are now in a fire and bullet proof pod. This pod is also sound proof and we have independent oxygen and ventilation. If we rapidly lose altitude the pod will break away from the aircraft and we will float to the ground with two fireproof parachutes." I smiled and came hard with, "Who the fuck are you with all this James Bond shit?" She smiled sweetly with, "What I am about to tell you can never be repeated, my name is Mrs. Amanda Christopher. You, like most men, are thinking that I am Mr. Robert's 'side-piece' that he likes to dress up. Well I am not!

Yes, I may have slept with him, when I was a little girl when I got scared at night, all little girls want to sleep with their daddy when they are scared at night. Mr. Roberts is my father. I want your word that our conversations will be held in total confidence."

"You have my word Mrs. Christopher, if that's your real name." Another smile from her as she said, "Call me Amanda, Dad said you were quick and a bit smart assed. Yes, I use my dad's middle name as my last name. I don't use my married name for safety reasons in business or public, to protect my children and my husband and his family. I am the Chief Financial Officer of the corporation. I control billions, yes billions, of dollars with a 'B'. The only time I ever speak of Mr. Roberts as my father or call him daddy is in complete privacy. No one in the company knows that he is my father." "Ok, I know why I'm going to Chicago, but why are we having this chat?" Amanda put out her open hand and said, I need your cell phone. I handed her my phone, she handed me a

142

similar phone to mine and said, "This is a secure phone. We have downloaded your phone numbers to this phone the moment you broke the threshold of this aircraft. You cannot be tracked with this phone. We will return your phone Sunday afternoon as you deplane at your home airport. Our personal guests are always at risk for kidnapping as our enemies know we would pay dearly to have you back. The payment they are after, is control of our properties along with money. We own several islands."

She then picked up a desk phone as she asked, "Do you want to stay at the house or a hotel?" I said hotel. She said into the phone, "The executive suit with smoking vents" and hung up the phone. She reached into a desk drawer and pulled out an ash tray and slid it to the center of the desk as she said feel free, as she lit her own cigarette. I was amazed to see the smoke disappear the moment it left my lips. I smiled as I said, "Still waiting to hear the why of our little visit in this bubble, let's have it."

"I have been trying to size you up, I have read the dossier on you, it all fits, but I've been looking for a weakness that I can exploit. I want you to come and work for the corporation. I will pay you any salary you want. I will give you a $100,000, oh hell make it $200,000 as a signing bonus. We will go to the bank the moment we land, you want cash or certified funds? Anything you want if you can help keep my daddy alive." Amanda kept her composure as her tears flowed. I reached across the desk to take her hand but she shook her head, as she wiped her tears she said, "Nothing personal but I must maintain my professional composure. Daddy said I wouldn't be able to get to you. You really are your own man aren't you? My dad highly respects you, he tells me about your daily talks with him. He laughs every time you call him 'Buddy Boy.' No one would dare call him anything other than Mr. Roberts, I can see why he gives you a pass. As a side note, I don't approve of the cute way you have about spending our money. Dad thinks that's funny but you tipping the limo driver $250 was not funny!(I was startled to know that she caught that from just a few minutes ago, this chick is wicked fast!) My mother adores you and she can't wait to finally meet you. My parents are the happiest they

143

have ever been with my dad not drinking. Are you sure that you don't want to live in Chicago?"

"Amanda, I truly do wish I had the magic that you and your folks think I have, but I don't. The best way I can explain it to you is to borrow a few lines from my dear and trusted friend Don Prince of Boynton Beach, Florida. Don is a former firefighter and fire chief. He is currently a certified recovery coach and peer support specialist. Don specializes in recovery from all forms of addictions in addition to PTSD and trauma. In short, Don will help you find the will to live when all you want to do is die. He helps you lessen the demons that come to visit and shortens their length of stay. Don posted this on Facebook and gave me permission to use it at any time I feel it will help a struggling soul."

From Don Prince:
"Recently I was asked..." 'It would be great if you could give me something I could say to this person I care about that would get them to change so that I could have a better relationship with them."

My response was...

"I know of absolutely nothing you could say that would or could cause such change but I do have something for you that I think is way better then what you are asking for and that is to seriously consider detaching from your need to change them before and most importantly, consider giving up this whole idea that your love for this person is actually powerful enough to change them.
Why? Because to believe that is to live in frustration and disappointment. The only power we have is to change ourselves and in doing so become a vision of what's possible to others."

Amanda showed that she clearly understood but she didn't like it. She shifted in her chair as to take back control of the conversation as she said, "I have read your book and you took me into worlds that I never knew existed. I suffered a few moments of

144

shame for my privileged and protected life. More people need to be brought up short with their entitled bullshit.

Would you mind if I looked into making your book into a movie?" I told her that I have always wanted that but it was only a dream. "But you still can't buy me."

Amanda laughed as she said, do you remember the first time we met when I handed you the briefcase and told you that Mr. Roberts never takes no for an answer and you are going to have to learn that about him? Well 'Buddy Boy', I am his daughter and the same goes for me." I heard the muffled high pitched whining of jet engines starting.

Amanda said, "You need to leave now, we are about to take off. Remember that I am the C.F.O. of the Randall Corporation and not related to anyone in the company. I have work to do so I won't see you again until Saturday night. Your security escorts will give you your briefing when we land. You will see two familiar faces as you reenter the cabin and the flight hostess will serve you lunch. One more final thing, if this fucker crashes don't worry about me, I'll be just fine, enjoy your flight, Skippy!"

The vacuum sliding door whooshed open and I stepped into the main cabin. I paused to let my eyes adjust to the soft light of the main cabin. I think Amanda had her office lights on full bright as a control and power maneuver to intimidate me. The 'art of the deal' has just as much to do with the setting as the words do. I couldn't help but think of the old days of police work, when we sawed the front feet of a wooden chair two inches shorter to make the suspect you were interviewing uncomfortable.

I saw Ricky the newspaper photographer and his wife Sharon, staring at me in disbelief as I approached the seating area. Ricky sprung to his feet and grabbed my hand like an arm-wrestler. He was beaming as he said, "Thank you so much for recommending me to Mr. Roberts. We are so excited, I never dreamed that a job like this ever even existed! I won't let you down sir, you have my word!"

I acted like I knew what he was talking about as I excused myself saying, I just need to grab my briefcase up front and I will join you guys for the flight. I sat up front and dialed the new phone. Amanda didn't even say hello, she just started laughing. She said, "You now have two new worshipers, to add to your fan club. We have an ad agency that does all of our photography work. After I saw the photos you had Ricky shoot at the bookstore and hotel I have hired them as our corporate photographers. They are coming for new employee orientation then immediately after, they will be visiting each of our properties doing photo shoots for new magazine ads, brochures and menus. They have a career that pays three times their last salary and they will be constantly traveling the world with all expenses paid, maybe you could be their assistant!" This time I hung up on her as she was laughing her ass off. So, I guess I just got the both of them high dollar dream jobs, aren't I a swell guy!

I picked up my briefcase with my name embossed on it in gold leaf and went back to join Ricky and Sharon. Sharon gasped as she saw my briefcase as she asked, do you work for Mr. Roberts too? I said no, "I am a friend of Mr. Roberts, I don't work for him. I'm a writer, I work for me." The flight attendant (who looked a bit more like an aristocrat than a flight attendant) came over and asked us to fasten our seat belts for take-off saying, once we reached cruising altitude she would be back with lunch and take our drink orders.

It was more than obvious that these two early thirty somethings had little if any travel or large corporate experience. Babes in the woods to be sure. I liked them both and felt obligated to enlighten them. Before I could start, Ricky excitedly said they had all new camera cases with the Randall Corporation logo on them and matching briefcases but without their names on them. He said when they were hired last week, they were sent to Kirk Meyer's camera shop and Kirk laid out all the cameras and lenses the company had ordered. Kirk told us that he could never afford that kind of equipment for himself. He said it is all the best, of the very best. "We just can't thank you enough Mr. Brown."

The plane started to taxi and I could see them both sit back deep into their seats and flex. I smiled as I asked, first time flying?

146

They both nodded but apparently had lost their voices. I changed seats for fear of what was about to come as we powered up for takeoff. Before we even got to rotation they were making deposits in there tightly clasped air sickness bags. To comfort them I said, "You guys will be flying commercial flights for your work and they won't go nearly as fast and climb as steep as we are about to. You should be fine."

Once we reached altitude the flight attendant (who had an air of bitchiness about her) and one of the 'book-end' brothers named Bill, came back with warm moist towels and escorted them to the lavatories. They returned to their seats looking surprisingly calm but obviously embarrassed.

"Alright you two, time for some speed council. First, stop thanking me. I had nothing with you guys being hired. You did this by doing your jobs and it just so happened Mr. Roberts was there to see it. You two won the lottery without even buying a ticket.

Now listen to me and listen hard! Don't make the mistake of thinking that Mr. Roberts is your buddy. He liked your work, he had you hired and that's the end of it. If you work for this company for the next thirty years you may never see him again. So don't either of you think you hold a special attention or consideration card. You don't. Your boss is your boss, not Mr. Roberts.

I assume that you will stay at the properties where you will be doing your work. Do not ever think that you deserve special attentions or hold the 'Golden Ticket.' Don't drink anywhere on the property. Not on the beach, not in the bar and not in your rooms. If you want to party, take a taxi and go to town. Never use a hotels car or ride in hotel courtesy vehicles. Those are for guests and you are not guests. You hold no rank over anyone, you are just employees, no different than any other property employee. Ricky, you try to pull that, 'Family photo' gig with your palm open bullshit, they will dump your ass and you will be left to find your own way home. Be smart, be courteous, be kind and you two will have a kick-ass work life together. Your orientation will probably echo what I just told you. Major corporations all have confidentially policies, break the slightest rule and you will be history."

The flight attendant came to take our drink orders. Ricky and Sharon asked for a soda as they glanced at me for obvious approval. I didn't have to give it as the flight attendant smiled at them with saying, "Smart choice kids, trust Mr. Brown's advice." I could only smile as I said, "Be careful with how you perceive people and their rolls. Our flight attendant is actually one of Mr. Robert's personal assistants, she is here to observe and report on your behaviors. Yes, this plane is bugged, welcome to Corporate America."

CHAPTER 17   THE HUSTLE

The latest new hires sat quietly for the rest of the trip. I am sure that those two fresh faced, wide eyed cuties that first boarded the plane, would step off on the tarmac as a bit more mature.

I wished them well with handshakes as they deplaned. I returned to my seat for my security team briefing. The flight attendant and the two book-ends stood in front of me. The flight attendant smiled as she introduced herself as Edna as she brushed back her now open coat to show her shoulder holstered, 3 inch barrel, 9mm. semi-automatic pistol.

"I removed your Kimber Micro 9mm from your briefcase when you first boarded the plane. I watched you pause as you picked it up and the weight loss of your missing gun, registered in your mind. You didn't even flinch or break stride. You are one cool customer. You will get it back when we land back in Duluth in three days, along with your double barrel 38 caliber Derringer from your sneakers in your suitcase, you pack a bag well.

I will be your dinner date and interior-ring security for the next three days. These two gentleman are named Bill. They are identical twins. They will be with us when we drive, or walk. They will be in every room you are in but will give you plenty of freedom of movement.

There have been no threats and because of your low profile we don't expect any. This is all just S.O.P."

Edna nodded at the Bills as she took two steps back, and the vacant space was quickly filled by the Bills standing shoulder to shoulder in front of me.

Bill #1 to my left spoke first. "We are here as your first line of protection, we apologize if we have intimated you or have made you feel uncomfortable." Bill #2 grinned as he said, "That's our canned speech that we give everyone that we are assigned to. We read your file and your book, and we all know that you can handle yourself. But we have orders, so it's our ball field and we call the plays. We never use revolving doors, one of us will go into any door first, than you, than the other one follows, that is a must. We never enter or exit a vehicle from street side. If you feel our hands on your body pushing down on you, go down to the floor quickly. We will be over the top of you, don't try to go to cover unless we pull you or in the unlikely event of gunfire and one of us is hit. We both carry 9mm double stack, Sig Sauer's in our left waistband, we use open top holsters. We have the same weapon in 3 inch, on our outside left ankles. We are both southpaws. If we go down, you have our permission to use our weapons without prejudice, our spare magazines are on our right hip sides."

Edna suddenly split the sea as the brother's side stepped to let her in the middle like a well-rehearsed dance troupe. Edna smiled as she said, "I carry two Kimber's identical to yours but with super tuned action by 'Wilson Combat.' All of our weapons feed ramps are polished and chromed. We never have a jam or feed problem. We all carry the identical rounds of Hornady 124-grain XTP with 1,106 fps velocity. I have one weapon in my bra and one on my inner left thigh. If you touch either one of them and I'm not dead, you will be, I will kill you!

We ride in bullet-proof Limos and our drivers have all trained with the F.B.I. at Quantico in evasive driving escape techniques. You will always sit in the middle of the most rear seat. By the way, the limo driver that picked you up at your house, is one of us. That $250 tip you gave him was fucking hilarious!" We all laughed and shook hands. The Bill on the right said, "We would like to ask you about your book later in a different setting, if you don't mind. It was a real gut punch alright! But now we have a job to do and word has it that you could be our boss whenever you want to be. So we better look sharp!" Edna said, "Our car is ready at plane-side, Mr. and Mrs. Roberts will be waiting for you in their suite. You have a tight schedule these next three days, you will be plenty tired of our pretty faces before you leave. Tonight we will be joining the Roberts for dinner at The Oriole. It's a Five Star exclusive big dollar, small portions joint. We can grab a pizza later. I apologize for not serving you lunch but I didn't dare bring food around those two barfing kids. There is a full bar and pantry of snacks in your suite."

As we were about to deplane, the Bill's rolled their shoulders in perfect unison to enter the big game. It was all business and those two large fellows moved like cats. During the ride to the Ritz Carlton Hotel the three super heroes were on point. Not a word was spoken.

As we rode the elevator to the top floor, Bill left said, "Mr. and Mrs. Roberts keep a suite on the top floor of the hotel in case they are too tired to travel to their home in the suburbs or the weather is bad." The elevator stopped but the door did not open.

Edna checked her cell phone as the phone in the elevator rang, Edna answered and gave a code number from her cell phone. The elevator door opened and down the hall two doors opened in perfect unison and out stepped two more identical Bill's, dressed exactly as the original Bill's. A third door which was between the two new Bill's, opened and a butler stepped out and said, "Mr. Brown, you are expected, please enter sir."

As I started to step thru the doorway Edna nudged me and said, "Ladies first, and remember the rules of doorways." I thought that she would vaporize like the two original Bill's did as we stepped from the elevator.

I entered the massive (small ballroom size) fancy receiving area or formal living room or whatever the fuck this was. Standing in the center of the room was a stunningly beautiful 50's something woman with a smile that said, welcome in capital letters!

151

Edna was shoulder to shoulder and stride for stride with me. I inwardly smiled as I saw her smoothly switch sides, she was now protecting Mrs. Roberts and could give a shit less about me. Edna nudged me and stepped in front of me as she said, "Hi Mom!" As they hugged and exchanged cheek kisses. This was another of the many WTF moments in the last three hours and I could feel a massive headache building. Mrs. Roberts extended her open palm to shake hands as she said, "I finally get to meet this man of extreme greatness. My God you are handsome!" She gave me a polite hug as she motioned for us to have a seat.

She told me to call her Jane. She then said with a full smile, "Can I guess that Edna told you where she carries her guns and that she will kill you if you try to touch them? You needn't worry yourself with that silliness. Her husband will kill you first. He is the section chief and agent in-charge of the Chicago office of the F.B.I., he is also my son! All of our security staff comes from his office, he trains them and we hire them away. He doesn't seem to mind too much. You will meet him at dinner tonight.

Paul is in his office with his AA sponsor, they should be finished shortly. What you have done for my Paul is the most wonderful thing I have ever witnessed. After all the treatment centers, the shrinks and all the AA meetings, he finally found someone he believes. He trusts you and that is something he just doesn't do, with anyone. I can feel your magic in your handshake. You are the real deal. Paul is very excited that you are here.

Now, I would like to steal you from him tomorrow afternoon when you boys return from your fishing trip. You can of course say no but you better watch your ass, Edna doesn't like to see her Mommy disappointed!"

"Yes ma'am, I fully understand Mrs. Roberts."
We all had a good laugh. I smiled as I said, "Anything you need Jane, as long as your son is not named Bill. I just can't stand to meet another Bill!" She howled and almost spilled her coffee as she said, "Paul's sponsor is named Bill!"

"David I need your help with something else, which is very dear and important to me, my friends and our city. We are seen as the go to people to support every charity within the entire state. We don't mind that as we are blessed with the success of our companies. We are invited to some sort of fundraising, 'Gala Event' every week. We always make generous contributions but attend very few of those events. My personal interests however, are with helping children. I founded a non-profit designed to assist 'at-risk' children. Your book showed us how to do it right.

We thought that loading back-packs with school supplies and outfitting several hundred children with athletic shoes and socks would be of help and some kind of an answer. I was devastated to have several of our sixty plus members find these new back-packs and tennis shoes in second-hand shops. I suspect that these poor children's junkie parents sold them for a fix. It sickens me to no end. How do we get the teen gang members to stay in school and to help our city and the disadvantaged children who have nothing? Paul said that if anyone has a viable answer it would be you. I begged Paul to invite and bring you here. I know you can't be bought so I need to appeal to your heart. Will you please help me….please?"
Jane started to cry.

"David, you are a fighter, please teach me how to fight like you do. You rescued a falling down building from a wrecking ball. You developed a vision and you took action. What you did for and with those Jr. High School kids was simply genius, you will probably never know how many people you inspired with that project. You identified a problem (the shed), you identified and fixed another problem with the first problem (the at risk kids) you further found another problem and fixed that problem using the last two problems (children who had no winter clothing) I believe in you and I know you can come up with something. I so desperately need your help." Jane stood and said "I will be right back" and left the room. I looked over at Edna and she just held her arms up in surrender saying, "I got nothing."

So now I am sitting with two women who have everything money can buy and yet can't find a way to give it away. I was pretty damn sure that sweet sister Jane, very rarely if ever before, asked for help like that, with anyone. Jane came back into the room and said Paul would be out in a few minutes as she took her seat on the sofa next to Edna and held hands, with moist eyes.

"Jane, how do I not say yes? I don't have anything on the top of my mind at the moment, but let me sleep on it. Fair enough?"

The double doors opened and Paul and the guy who must be another damn Bill entered the room. Paul introduced us, Bill said "I've been looking forward to meeting you, I have to run for now but I'll see you guys at the dock at 5:15 am. Don't be late" as he quickly left.

Paul looked at me with his own version of the 'Morticians grin' and said, "Sorry about bush-whacking you, but my sweetheart asked and I never say no to her. You got it figured out yet?"

We all laughed as Paul put his hand to shake and said welcome to Chicago as he gave me an awkward hug. I looked at him and the ladies as I said, "Bush-wacked you say, Buddy Boy, you are much too refined to lower yourself to use such amateur tactics. No pal, you had a sniper at two thousand yards. Cute, lucky for you I like Jane more than I like you. At least she knows how to hug. And as long as I'm at it, I would like to point out some of your other failings. Your security program is going to get you all killed. Pull your corporate logo off the tail sections of all your aircraft. Lose all the embroidered logo and gold leaf bullshit off your briefcases and luggage. Jesus Christ, anybody looking to do harm just needs to look for the 'blue light special' in isle # dead! Not to mention that you just bought your new photo kids, tens of thousands of dollars of photo gear and top dollar carrying cases with your company logo that screams, "Steal me, I'm worth a fortune!" Jane piped-up with, "Gregory our son, has been telling him those very same things for years but our accounting firm insists we do all that for tax purposes."

"Buddy Boy, dump your bean counters and hire someone that understands that they work for you and they need to stay the hell out of your security business.

With that in mind, tell your security manager to grow some balls and not let anyone interfere with your safety for any reason." All three of them broke out in laughter, I quickly realized that I had just shit the bed. The beaming grin on Edna's face told the entire story. Paul said, "Our son would not like it, if we were to put balls on his wife. Our precious daughter-in-law here is former Secret Service, she was assigned to the Presidential Security Team. That's how Gregory and Edna met, you want to buck that tiger?"

"Well shit, kids. At least dress down the 'Bill Brigade', those matching head-to-toe outfits shout, 'take me out first, I'm the real threat.' Besides that, they all look like a church choir from the dark side of hell. At least put them in different color sport coats and ties. Do those lapel things you guys do in professional security as identifiers." Edna stood and filled my coffee cup from the gleaming silver carafe as she said, "If you weren't a guest and mother didn't so desperately need your help, I would tell you to go shit in your hat! You are right about everything but daddy rarely listens to us. It might bruise his cute, tiny little ego" (as she fainted a kick at his leg).

Paul put his hands up in surrender as thou he was being held at gun point. "Ok, Ok, all corporate logos are gone and we will re-dress our Bill's. You have been in town for less than two hours and you are already taking over my company! In Minnesota you spend my money like it was your first time in a whore-house and then you try to tip my employee two hundred and fifty dollars and for your 'Grand Finale', you amass my own troops to pull a coupe against me. I just may as well retire. I can't wait until we get on the boat tomorrow so the engines will drown out your voice!"

Jane and Edna could not stop giggling as Jane said, "Don't forget that I need David back in plenty of time for him to clean-up and sign his books for our 3:00 pm charity meeting which is halfway across town and we need to let him rest for a bit before his speaking engagement tomorrow night. Let's remember to show our honored guest the proper respect he deserves."

"Wow, what is all this schedule stuff, starting with the fishing and signing books and the charity meeting and now I am to

155

understand that I'm speaking tomorrow night, at some kind of meeting, somewhere? Spit it out Pal, I do have enough money for bus fare to get back home, just so you know!"

Jane said, "I am sending you boy's fishing for lake trout for some 'man time,' because I saw pictures of you holding several big lake trout on Facebook. Some of the books are for my charity members, some are for our friends as Christmas gifts and some are for Paul's employees and business associates."

"How many books need to be signed, dear Jane?" Jane brought up her award winning sweetest of sweet smiles as she sweetly said, "I only bought five hundred dear. The charity meeting is for a brain storming session and our members are anxious to hear how your project was such a success. They also will want to know your plan for our success that you come up with while you are on the boat tomorrow. Don't worry dear, Paul is quite boring and those boat motors will drown out his voice too, so you have plenty of time to create your strategy for the meeting. Paul dearest, please tell our honored guest of your plans for him tomorrow night."

The girls were gasping for air between giggles and laughter. Paul lowered his head and feinted like a little kid who was kicking rocks as he was saying, 'Aw shucks'. "Well, tomorrow night, just so happens to be that the Greater Chicago Area of AA, is celebrating our annual Founder's Day, with a small banquet and speaker meeting. My sponsor, Bill was to be the evening's speaker but has stepped aside to give his time to what he calls the, 'Minnesota Miracle-Worker.' That of course would be you!"

"Well, well, well, and where is this small, intimate affair to take place?" Paul dropped his head as a scolded child would as he said, "The McCormick Place Convention Center, but we are not taking up the whole place! We tried for Navy Pier but it was already booked. I'm sure that you will do just fine. Bill and I listened to a few of your speaker tapes from a few years back. Bill thinks that you have a stronger message with a lot more flair. So, Buddy Boy, once again, welcome to Chicago!"

156

"Do I have time for a nap before dinner, and I hate that 'Slow Food Movement' bullshit with bird food and greens."

Jane jumped to her feet and hooked my elbow saying, "Of course dear, we will phone your room one hour before the town car arrives, and we will go to any restaurant you choose, a steak house perhaps?"

Edna came to my other side and said, "I will show David to his room." She reached for the flapper door handle and a blinking red light came on above the handle. She said, "It's a layered security system, it double locks the elevator door so even the security code can't over-ride it. It also locks all doors on this floor so no one can exit a room for 90 seconds after this door opens and closes again. The security teams get an alert the moment we touch the door handle, they exit their rooms immediately and sweep the hallway and check all doors. We own all the rooms on this floor and that may sound to be a bit much, along with the security measures but keep in mind that we do business with many of the world's wealthiest people. We lodge them here for their visits. In many cases our customer's security forces demand it. They send advance teams to insure their charges are going to be as safe as possible. All of the exterior windows are bullet proof and all exterior walls have blast shields in case of air or missile attack."

The door unlatched with two green lights. As we left the room there was a Bill on each side of the door, a Bill in front of the elevator and a Bill at each end of the hallway. I was told by a Bill that there was a Bill in each adjoining room with two pass ways. He assured me that I would not be disturbed.

When Amanda confiscated my cell phone (which seemed like weeks ago) and gave me the untraceable phone, she had all my phone numbers downloaded along with all her families phone numbers. I called Amanda.

She answered with a curt, "What is it." I fully expected that response and I brought it hard.

"Amanda, it's your Mother." I paused for the desired effect. After I heard her suck in her breath and she asked, "What's wrong with my Mother" (in a panicked and helpless voice) I moved in for the kill. "Amanda, your Mother is about to destroy herself. She thinks her kind heart and her faith in God will help her make a difference in this shit-hole city of corruption and murder. Your Mom is about to get her ass stomped, she needs your help. Your entire family needs your help. Let's knock off the bullshit. You are the power in this family. You have been running this entire company for years from the back of that airplane and wherever else you roost. Your Dad is the face and the figure-head but you have the control. Your Dad has far too much free time to schmooze and bullshit, hell him and I talk on the phone two and three times a day! Young lady, I have friends too, and my friends in the secret world of corporate structurers tells me that you, and not your Dad pen all of these deals. You hold the power! Amanda, I understand, in part, the depths of your father's alcoholism. He would have destroyed the entire company and lost it all, if not for you. Only you and him, and now me, know of how bad things were. That truth is safe with me. Before you admit it (which doesn't matter to me) listen hard. Now I got the ball and I'm calling the plays.

Your mom is having a steering committee meeting for her charity tomorrow at 3:00 pm. It's at some community center. I will leave it to you to find out where. She wants me to bring my experience which is greatly limited. You need to not just invite the shakers and movers of the 'Windy City' but you better damn well make sure they are there. I don't want the mayor or his crew or the chief of any departments, I want the actual workers. I want precinct, church, party and union leaders. I want neighborhood leaders from the Cub Scouts, Brownies, Boy Scouts, and the PAL gym. I want people from the probation depts., school counselors, mental health, hospitals and anyone else that can help pull your mothers naive bacon from the flames. You got that baby-girl? She is expecting 30 people, I want five times that many! Remember, I don't want 'Sayers', I only want 'Doers.' One more thing sweetheart, if word of any part of this conversation ever gets out, I will tell the entire world that you never change your underwear! You better get busy, Tick-Tock, Tick-Tock"

I hung up on her as I stretched out on the bed with my mind whirling with how she keeps it all together with the business and the crazy security measures and the incredible expense of it all. I guess I greatly underestimated their wealth but then again, they buy and sell entire islands, and communities.

My room phone rang with a strange ringing sound, an unfamiliar female voice advised me that my hosts would be at the elevator door in preciously one hour. The voice asked if I would need a second call. I no thanked her and rolled off the bed to catch a shower and dress.

I didn't have the time delay as on the other doors but it did take fifteen seconds for the door to unlatch once I turned the handle. No green lights came on, just the sound of the latching mechanism releasing, guess my level of security is more like my sitting in the, 'cheap seats.'

Everyone was standing near the elevator. There was one additional person who I instantly knew by the way his mother held his arm. Paul was gleaming with pride as he approached me with the pride and joy of the family. Paul introduced me to his first born, Gregory. Gregory had a soft hand but a powerful grip. He grinned as he said, "I hear that you don't much care for Feds, 'spooks' you like to call us?" I grinned back as I said, "If you are sixty percent cop and forty percent bureaucrat or less, than I think we will get along just fine." Gregory smiled as he said, "We will get along just fine. I need a minute of your time as he nodded to the end of the hall." We went to the end of the hall where a Bill was standing with a briefcase. Bill handed Gregory the brief case and excused himself and walked twenty feet away where he reposted with his back to us. Gregory said, "I apologize for my little sister Amanda and her anal ways, she had no business taking your weapon. We can't have you running around Chicago naked." He unzipped the briefcase and held it open for me to retrieve my gun and holster. As I was putting the paddle holster on he said, "We took the liberty to run it over to our jeweler and had your feed ramp polished. We only use Wilson Combat to super tune all of our weapons. Wilson is the best in the world but they are just a

159

fancy machine shop. We leave our ramp polishing to our family jeweler. We also replaced your bushing spring with a Wilson Combat spring. We also replaced your hollow points in the weapon and your spare magazine with our custom made Hornaday, 124 grain XTP bullets. They are the highest velocity, that put you quickly back on target and with the best grouping. What is your preference in weapons and calibers?"

Me: For hand guns, I'm a 1911 frame guy. I carried a 45cal Colt for years. I went to Kimber when they first came out because of their superior quality but that was three of four owners ago. Now I think Colt has caught up and surpassed Kimber with Colt quality, I think it's a better gun now. I will go back to Colts when I can afford it. At my age they just got to be too heavy to drag around so I moved to 9mm a few years ago. I like all lengths of barrels but my Kimber Micro 9mm with a 3in barrel is the best for my body frame for concealed carry. I won't have anything to do with those 'Tupperware' guns the rest of the world gets so silly about. I like the grip, the balance, and the heft of steel. For a long gun, I like the Sig Sauer MPX 9mm. I shoot the shit out of it and have never had a failure.

Gregory: Well you sure seem to know your stuff about guns, do you practice with hollow points?

Me: No, I can't afford that, I always run 500 rounds of round nose for break-in on a new gun, than 50 rounds of hollow point thru it to check feed and extraction.

Gregory: That's a good way to do it but you should only practice with hollow points. You do know you are betting your life on your weapon and ammunition, right? I will send you home with some of our ammo, the same rounds that we replaced in your weapon. One more thing, my dad and my entire family think the world of you. My dad is not easily won over, by anyone! I think he would trade-me-in for you if mother would allow it. Please allow

160

my father to gift you as a sign of your two's friendship. As a
gentleman I am asking you to honor our family with your gracious
acceptance, of whatever dad sees fit to give. Can we shake on it?"
We shook on it. He then said, "You go back on our hand shake and
I'll call the cops, you are now carrying a concealed weapon in
Chicago. Illinois doesn't have reciprocity with Minnesota, and you
are only a phone call away from going to jail!"

Me: And you wonder why I hate Feds? Gregory slapped
me on the back, we walked back to the group as Jane said, "I've
been watching you two, and you boy's better play nice." We both
smiled as we said, "Yes Ma'am!"

We went to a high-end steak house. As we were waiting to
be seated, Edna whispered, "Thank you for not making us go to
that dreaded shit-hole European dining experience. Pizza gives me
heartburn but by the time we sit thru damn near three hours of that
slow dining bullshit, we are all starving and flat assed. All the
other decent restaurants are closed for the night so it's Pizza and
heartburn."

Jane had it set up that I sat between her and Paul. I was
already tired of the wait staff (two men and a water girl) flittering
with their productions of graciousness. Just to take them off stride,
when they came to me for my order I said, "I will order after you
take the orders or our other party members who are sitting two to a
table at the two tables on either side of us. You can't miss them in
their dapper black suits with matching ties."

The table exploded with laughter as the waiter was trying
not to swallow his own face. For the rest of the evening we were
like a drunken bowling team just coming off the bus. I'm surprised
that we weren't told to quiet down. It was obvious that this poor
family doesn't get to play together much.

My room phone rang at 4:00 am with another different
ringer sound and a female voice telling me that breakfast will be
served in forty minutes and my escorts would accompany me to
the dining area. Thirty-five minutes later, there was a knock at my
front door and two Bill's entered my room. They did not wait to be

161

let in. A quick breakfast with Paul and we were on our way to the marina. As we were let out of the town car two additional Bills were there to meet us. We rode a golf cart to an almost too big of a boat to use for sport fishing. The boat's name, "THE HAPPY HOOKER" was on the back and each side. AA sponsor Bill was already on board. Sponsor Bill told me that this boat owner and captain is his Nephew. There was the Captain, four mates, Bill, Paul and myself. As we backed out of the slip I saw two identical large power boats idling side by side ahead of us as thou they were waiting for us, and they were. One took the lead the other fell back and followed until we were clear of the harbor. When we got out onto Lake Michigan the two power boats were on each side of us about 80 yards away, I smiled at Paul as I asked, "Your boys I suspect. Do they have life preservers over their pretty black suits with matching ties?" Paul about spit his coffee on me. He said, "You bring smart-ass to a whole new level. We will see how you do with the 3:00 pm 'Do-Gooder'. I'm sure that most of them are good people trying to do good, but all the positioning and back-biting makes me dizzy. You better clamp down hard on them from the beginning, tell them it's a take it or leave it. Don't give them a chance to ask any questions or open it to a debate. My Jane will control them but they may try to out-flank her. Everyone wants to be in charge but nobody wants the responsibility, the little bitches they are, and that includes the men! I suggest that you do your presentation and leave. Don't make the mistake of socializing as they will try to capture you and tell you how great they all are. We have to be at the convention center at 7:00 pm.

About a mile out into the lake we slowed to approx. 2.8 mph (according to sponsor Bill) as the crew started to rig the lines. You get two lines per licensed fisherman. The boat holds six 'guest for a day' temporary licenses.

Sponsor Bill and his captain nephew came down from the bridge and sat alongside of us as their crew was readying the rods. Duane (the nephew-captain) offered us each a high-end Cuban cigar as he said, "Auto-Pilot, my wife will be up to take your drink orders and snacks in a few minutes."

162

I don't smoke cigars, I looked over at the two escort boats and asked Paul if his guys are going to fish too, with my very best, 'Mortician grin'. Paul said, "Oh yeah they got some real nice lures, as he picked up a pair of field glasses and said, check out their hardware. The bow of each boat had two men with who looked to be holding 308 caliber AR-15's and there were two gentleman on the aft end of each boat who had a tri-pod mounted, 50 caliber machine gun with a belt feed. Yeah they were sure going to do some bad-assed fishin! We all had some great espresso coffee with scones. Sponsor Bill and Captain Duane excused themselves as Bill said, "I will leave you two girls to chat. My nephew is much more fun than you two."

Paul told me that he had never felt so good. His employees seem to not walk as softly and even a few are starting to make eye contact with him now. Paul asked one of the crew members for a big book and a twelve by twelve. I looked at him as if he was crazy to ask for that kind of literature on a fishing boat. Paul laughed as he explained, "This boat is a sober house that supports itself with charter fishing from early spring until late fall. The crew members and the Captain are all in recovery. They all live on the boat. All of the fishing clients are in recovery and they hold morning, noon, afternoon and evening AA meetings, right here on-board." I couldn't help but to show my amazement. I have never heard of that. A crew member brought us two of each books. I asked Paul how far along he was in the twelve by twelve. He said he had read it several times but he could never connect with it. "This time it is different, I am different, because I want to be. You and Bill have given me the faith that I could never accept or trust before. I want to thank you for our daily phone conversations, you have done for me what I couldn't do for myself. I will always be in your debt."

"Ok Pal, I got it. Let's talk about staying that way. Step Ten is my favorite step. I see it as the 'Cliffs Notes' on how not to be a continuing asshole. Page 91 is very clear on how we must practice self-restraint of both tongue and pen. The entire chapter is about, since we found our way we must never back-slide. So again, we have set a solid foundation to rebuild the trust we once enjoyed and perhaps took for granted before we became drunks. We are rebuilding but the construction has not been completed. There is yet more to be done. Much more. So we move on to step eleven with the full and understood knowledge that we never complete any of the steps. We must revisit these steps all throughout our lifetime. We never graduate. Step eleven is the gateway to comfort thru meditation."

Suddenly we heard Captain Duane's voice booming over the loudspeaker system. "You girls want to land that fish that is about to break my fishing pole or do you need me to send down a guitar player so you can join hands in singing Kumbaya?"

I told Paul that was his fish, as he pulled the rod from the rod holder the poles on his left and right both folded over. Now we have three fish on!

These were all salmon and they were jumping all over. The fishing lines all got tangled and we had a mega cluster fuck, like I've never seen in my many trips out on Lake Superior. We started laughing as we realized the futility of hoping to land any one of those fish. I looked at Paul as we both struggled with fishing poles that were trying to destroy themselves. "Pauly Boy, this is just like an alkie trying to live sober without AA." Paul looked up at the bridge and hollered, "Get your people down here and cut these damn lines off. We are trying to rest!" We sat in the deck chairs and laughed our heads off as we both realized the insanity of such chaos, the same way we both lived our lives for so many years. We were fish on a string and no one could land us but we couldn't get off the hook either. That was a day of surrender for sure, for the both of us.

Somehow we caught four fish and it was a lot of fun. The guys on the crew were nice fellows. I watched Paul tip them in what appeared to be fistfuls of $100 bills as we stepped on the dock. We went back to the hotel for a brief nap and lunch. I took my shower and signed approximately forty books to take along with us to the presentation with the, 'Do-Gooders.'

CHAPTER 18   THE ASSAULT ON CHICAGO

As we went to climb into the limo to head out for the community center there wasn't just two Bill's waiting for us, no there were now four Bills along with the four Bill's from the penthouse floor. Obviously Amanda got word to their security team that there would be a larger crowd than first anticipated. I couldn't help but giggle to think of the surprise about to hit sweet old sister Jane. As we pulled off the eight lane highway to pull into the side street for the community center, there were police officers directing traffic and there were cars everywhere. Jane had a shocked look on her face and asked if were at the right place. The driver assured her that we were at the right place. The limo drove around to the back of a building and the Bills guided us thru the corridors into the center of the Hall. The crowd was massive, there were every bit of the 150 people that I asked Amanda for, that and a lot more.

After Jane got over the initial shock of the crowd size, she introduced me to Father James Martin, her family priest and her tireless co-sponsor in all of her charity work with "Boys Town," in Nebraska. He is the younger brother to Father Joseph Martin, a recovering alcoholic, author and a world renowned public speaker who died in 2009.

Jane introduced me to the group as the published author of the novel, 'Daddy Had to Say Goodbye' and the founder and executive director of the 'Heart Warming Foundation.' She told the crowd that she was presenting me today, in hopes that I could help them find a solution to some of their many community problems.

I started with telling those people what a beautiful city Chicago was. Like any other bullshit artist, I spoke about all of their professional sports teams that were known worldwide and how proud the residents of Chicago must be to hold so many championship trophies. I further complimented Chicago on having the greatest communications and financial districts in the world. (I was taught by the last presidential election speeches that the more times you mentation the current city's name the more applause and the more they appear to love you) I got a lot of smiles and applause even before I started to get to the point and purpose of my being there. I slobbered about the beauty of the 'Windy City, the Second City and the half a dozen other flattering nicknames for Chicago.

I paused for a moment and looked hard as I said, "Some of you may want to leave in the next few minutes. I hope you keep your seats and listen, please hear me out. Chicago is also known on a national and world wide level, as the city of
...............*DEATH!*

Strap into your seats, this ride is about to get bumpy. It's time to get honest, it's time to get nasty!

Chicago has a terrible reputation! Several of your people are being murdered in the streets daily. Not just gang-bangers killing each other but the murdering of infants, toddlers, children and even unborn children still in the womb of their mothers. They're being murdered on a daily basis and it seems that there is no way to stop it. But there is a way. I believe that there is a solution. If you're desperate enough to hear me out.

I don't have to travel through your city and your gang infested neighborhoods to see all of the poor areas. It's not about what happens, it is about what we allow to happen! You have the strength to change all that, dig your feet into every blighted community and make the difference. The greatest commonality in all cities with gang and drug problems are the grocery store deserts. It's understandable, what grocery store chain wants to plunk down millions of dollars to build a store only to have the shelves and cash registers emptied by, robbers, shoplifters and looters along with their customers being accosted and mugged in the parking lot? The good people of these forgotten communities that don't have cars have to take a bus or taxi out of their own neighborhood just to feel safe, to buy food. They have to spend part of their food money on transportation! This could not be more wrong! This is where it must start. Start here and nowhere else. The first challenge that is an absolute must is for you people sitting here today will be to leave your ego at the door. You, and I mean none of you, have a better idea, if you did than what in the hell am I and you doing standing here?

The problem, your problem, is gangs. Many of you think gang members are simply misunderstood and misdirected young teens. You couldn't be more wrong. Many gang members are third generation. Many babies in these neighborhoods are born drug addicted. The grandparents the aunts and uncles, the parents and their siblings are most often times active gang bangers or at least gang sympathetic. Whether it be a homicide, a rape, a burglary or a laundry list of other crimes, nobody sees anything. Some of those non-witnesses to a homicide have blood splatters all over their clothing but nobody saw nothing. Children are taught that 'snitches get stiches' before they learn their A-B-C's as they are using syringe plungers as teething rings!

If anyone finds that funny, leave this building NOW! You are part of the problem!

Young children are taught by observation and example. They are seduced by the flashy jewelry, the fancy clothes, fist sized rolls of cash and the custom and exotic cars. They are mesmerized with all the guns and chatter of people begging for their lives. They see criminal activities in their homes and on the streets. The also see that there are no consequences. They witness people on the street and in their homes celebrate criminal activities. It is their norm, it is also their future. Let me be clear that when I say 'homes' I am not talking about your kind of homes, I am talking about the shit-hole, rat infested, bullet ridden projects that you never want to admit exist.

You all get a pass for today because your mere presence here, is indicative of your desire to bring and to be that change. You don't get a pass for tomorrow however, tomorrows pass will come from your actions today and the many tomorrow's to come.

So here it is in a nut shell. I used a dilapidated tin shed as the core of the charity I started. Sadly this city is overrun with tin sheds so that won't fly.

Do this; build a grocery store. You have every necessary resource currently sitting in this room. Hire grocery store professionals to manage it.

Bring the neighborhood children in, and pay them to set shelves and product. Pay the children to carry people's groceries. Buy several little red wagons with side boards. Give these children mental and emotional ownership. Allow them to build their own sense of pride. You can't give anyone pride, only they can. Let them earn their own pride. Teach them how to earn their own self sense of purpose and pride and you will be amazed at the results. If you bring hope they will develop faith.

You of course are going to have some problems as you go along the way and that's to be expected. I'm sure that you all put your heads together and get that figured out. You won't have to worry about crime because the neighborhood has gone without any kind of a store for so long that they will protect their own. Once the grocery store is up and running and showing a profit other neighborhoods will want the same thing. Other business will see your success and will want to build there too, if you use the media properly. Romance the chain grocery stores to buy your stores.

If you remember nothing else from today, remember this. Your city is dying, the number of flight, hotel, sporting events and convention cancelations is at an all-time high because your people are killing each other. You people in this very room could just as easily, as anyone else, have your names in tomorrow's newspaper as a homicide victim.

I'm not an answer man, I'm a thinking man. I look at the problem and I speak of it. I am now done speaking."

I stepped back from the podium as the Bills swept both Jane and I up very effectively and got us the hell out of the building. We were well down the road with a police escort before Jane took her first full breath. She was just beside herself as she sat there and cried and cried and cried. She looked at me and she said,

168

"Young man you do give me hope. I very much enjoyed the way you stomped those snooty asses into the ground. You were brilliant!" I took Janes hand as I said, "Young lady, I am many years your senior but I appreciate your compliments."

As we were driving back to the hotel my assigned cell phone rang. It was Paul, he was laughing. He started with, "Son-of-a-bitch, you do bring it hard! I was sitting with the rest of the family and a few friends in the back of the room. One of my friends sitting with us is the owner of the Chicago Bears. He wants to hire you to teach his coaches to give locker room pre-game pep talks." Paul asked me if I could give his people a few minutes when we got back to the hotel, just to sit and talk about the book. I told him it would be my pleasure. He said, "We will meet in the conference room, the Bills know where it is, see you in travel time."

I sat with the Bills, all nine of them! They had several questions about the book. I was quite amazed. Yea, I guess we all make judgments and I just figured the Bills were just a bunch of knuckleheads that only had security on their minds and had no other life, other than the company. These fellows were quite well-rounded, well-educated and of course actually had a personality. Their stoic, unemotional appearance was just them taking their jobs seriously. We didn't get to speak before because it's not their job to entertain their assigned subjects. They were very professional that evening when we got to the convention center. They threw a human net over Paul, Jane and me as they rushed us from the limo into the loading docks and through the back of the building. They took us down all the hallways where you could see the scar marks on the walls from all of the serving carts, table and chair carts and all the other equipment to set up for conventions, that didn't require forklifts. We finally got through the hallway maze and came out behind the stage. The room was massive, there was a huge crowd there. I could not even guess the capacity of, or the crowd size.

We climbed the stairs and went on to the stage where they had the banquet tables set for the primary sponsors and local dignitaries. If there was any one person who I didn't expect to see there, there sat the lovely Amanda, dirty underwear and all!

I took my seat beside Paul with Jane next to him. We had a nice dinner and light conversation with the people around us. Amanda was about five chairs down and next to the podium, so I didn't get a chance to talk with her. When dinner was complete, Sponsor Bill walked to the podium, introduced himself and thanked everyone for coming. He then said he would like to introduce the people that made all this possible, and who do you think the chairman of this committee was, well of course, it was sweet ole', dirty underwear Amanda, who spearheaded this founder's day extravaganza. If this family does nothing else, they throw you a lot of curve balls. Amanda stood for a moment at the podium and thanked the committee members by first name and took her seat. Bill got back up and introduced the local priest, Father Martin (who I met just a few hours ago) who led the group in prayer. After the prayer Bill introduced me as the evening speaker. As I neared the podium Amanda's arm shot out and grabbed my arm. She pulled me down so she could whisper in my ear as she said, "Knockoff that dirty panties stuff, I don't wear any panties, go get em stud" as she gave me a smile and a playful shove. I had to step back from the podium twice because I had the giggles. When I finally got it together I thanked the committee for inviting me and their excellent dinner choice of beef over chicken. For the next sixty-five minutes I told my story as I have many times throughout the country. I told the identical story that is the final chapter of the novel, 'Daddy Had to Say Goodbye.' It is my life story, it is also my book. I wrote it, because I lived it.

I thanked everyone for their attention, left the podium and stood alongside Amanda, she grabbed and squeezed my hand hard, as the priest led us in the closing prayer. Amanda was crying.

Paul and Jane rushed over and we stood holding hands, I looked over at Sponsor Bill and mouthed the words, "Join us" and he did.

Amanda said, "I have been sober for twenty-two years, I have been to the AA World Conference several times and have been to AA annual roundups in this country and abroad. I have heard all of the top speakers but never in my life, have I felt a speaker in my belly. I have read your book twice, I have read your final chapter eight or nine times, it inspires me and touches me deeply. I know your book is your life story but to sit here, to look at you giving your printed words life, was not just amazing but I felt God's presence in you. You are certainly no Saint but I bet you hang out with a few! I will do everything in my power to put your book into a movie, only if you promise me and us that you will play Clinton Flanagan in the final chapter and you speak each word as it is in the book, just the way you wrote it and spoke it just now." I said, "Yes of course, I will be happy to make that promise."

Sponsor Bill said, "Look at all the people in line waiting to meet the guy that had everyone in this room in tears a few minutes ago. They are looking at you like you're a rock star." As we left the stage I told the Roberts crew to stand next to me in the receiving line. It is customary to greet every person that wants to simply shake hands, say hello or thank you. I wanted Paul to realize what his future holds, I wanted Jane to see, first-hand how good sobriety looks in all these people. I wanted to give Amanda hope for her father's future sobriety. I shook lots of hands and had several hugs. Suddenly I felt it hit me. The impact startled me as I looked straight up. The entire world went on pause for just for a moment. My mind flashed and I saw starbursts that took me back to sixty years ago, when my father stood in receiving lines and people thanked him for his speaking and how he impacted them.

I found myself saying softly, "Thanks Dad, thanks for being here with me tonight, I love you."

After a few more glad-handing's we finally got the hell out of the building. I excused myself and told them to go on without me as I needed to have a few smokes and a stroll and I will take a taxi back to the hotel. Jane said, "Absolutely not, we will wait right here for you, take all the time you need." I walked the sidewalk around the McCormick Square Convention Center. I hadn't gone more than thirty yards and I felt it. I quickly turned back and there

171

was a Bill half that distance behind me and another Bill ten yards parallel to him. I thought, what the hell and sat on the curb and lit another cigarette. I hadn't finished half of that cigarette when I heard the unmistakable sound of hard pounding, power walking, spike heels that I didn't even have to look up to recognize that it was Amanda. She said, "Slide over."

I had to laugh as there was a thousand feet on either side of me to sit down. Amanda said, "I need to feel your arm around me, I want you to bless me. Father Martin told me to come to you just now. He said that you needed to be comforted and the only way I can comfort you is to allow you to comfort me. Father Martin told us that you carry a shared soul. You have the soul of a fierce Crusader from the Christian Wars and you have lived the life of King David of Israel. Father believes as I do, that you are not of this era. We believe that you carry a power beyond that of mortal man. Father believes that you were ordained by a power beyond that of the church."

My only come-back was, "Get the fuck off of my curb with that bullshit. I am so common that even my dogs pee on my leg when they get excited! I am just a man who lived his life so poorly, that today I feel good about just making the bed. You cats got the wrong guy. Get your blessings from the guys in the black robes with a crucifix hanging around their necks. We better get back to the hotel. No more of that mystery stuff of the ancient times!"

When we got back to the hotel I was exhausted, we met in Paul's Room for a brief refreshment before we all called it a night. Paul told me that I had an early flight in the morning and I couldn't be late. The phone rang in my Room at 5:30 am and again it was a different ringtone. The caller advised me that breakfast would be at 7:00 pm and I would be escorted to the dining room. I got to the dining room and the whole family was there. Jane said, "We don't want you to leave, we would like to keep you. What will it take?" I said, "All I want from any of you guys is your respect and your love and nothing more." I did ask Paul about that nonsense with the different phone rings every time the phone rang. Amanda started to laugh and she said, "We deal with world leaders and

172

some of the biggest financial people on earth. We want them to have their own comfort so we have copied all different phone rings for every district of every country so there are comfortable with hearing their familiar phone ring tones. I know it's something very small but to some people it brings comfort, which to us is very large."

I just had to shake my head with thinking, "Man you guys don't miss a trick. That explains your success."

I found it hard to say goodbye, somehow in just three short days, I felt like I had a family. It was hugs all around. Jane insisted that I return soon and said, "You must bring Heather with you next time, I want to meet the woman that can keep you in check." I smiled as I told her that they would hit it off well, "Because you are both the same age!" Jane hugged me with a peck on the cheek as she said, "I knew you were a dirty old man!"

Gregory thanked me for being a mentor for his dad and reminded me of our deal and how he was a Fed, with a very long arm.

Edna thanked me for not trying to attach balls on her, as she gave me a long cheek kiss.

Amanda told me that if I was thirty years younger and twenty pounds lighter that I might have a chance with her. She gave me a light belly punch as she said, "See ya around, Skippy!"

Paul rode with me to the airport. I nudged him with my elbow as I said, "By the way Buddy Boy, I have to go back to Duluth and make nice with the nice man who you sole two of his employees from. I'm not sure if I like you for doing that. Is that how you operate?" Paul grinned as he said, "David, I am not a smart man but I am just smart enough to hire very smart people. I don't have the time or patience to bring someone along to their full potential. It's just not good business. Let me give you an example; my entire security team are either retired or former federal agents. I don't pick from the B team. I want the best and I pay them very well to stay with me."

173

Me: But Paul, you hired two small town kids from a minor league newspaper to cast them to the world. Is this one of your quirky social experiments? Word has it that you do some weird shit like that.

Paul: David that's on you, don't lay your crap on me!

Me: Enlighten me ole' wise one, how is that my fault?

Paul: I watched you run Ricky thru his paces. I saw you work him over several times and he never even knew it. Every time you got what you wanted and a bit more from him, you threw him a bone. You having him and his crew bring their ladies for dinner and insisting they only order from the top of the menus with price being of no concern was brilliant. You had him take pictures of the meals as they were set in front of the ladies. Ricky had no idea that he was doing a photo shoot. He thought he was taking pictures and showing-off his camera skills for his friends and coworkers. When he was actually shooting a hotel brochure and menu. You my friend are one sly dog! Keep in mind that Rickey's wife is an ad design artist. So I get a full ad team that can publish my brochures and do trade ads. I never told you that I can't see potential. I also saw his loyalty to you, he likes you and he wanted to show you that. I am drawn to loyalty and I reward that type of character. So what's the going price on you today, $800,000, maybe a $1,000,000?

Me: How about an airplane ride home today? And just so you know, you've been out bid, you cheap prick!

Paul: Speaking of loyalty, how is Vicki doing? I know that you are meeting with that husband and wife team you call Boris and Natasha but when I ask Vickie about it she dummies-up with saying, Mr. Brown is as polite and charming as ever. It's like she works for you, rather than me! How is she doing?

Me: She is struggling with repaying her student loans, her car is a piece of shit and she has to live with her parents because she can't afford an apartment. Other than that, she is fine.

Paul turned his head away for a few moments and stared out the window in silence. When he looked back, he had tears in his eyes.

Paul: I almost never visit any of my properties in the U.S., hell I have very successful property managers who have worked for me for years that I have never met! I came to Duluth to kill myself, so I was in a lousy mood and I almost destroyed that sweet little girl. I have to make it right with her! I am going to pay-off her student loans, buy her a new car and give her the money to buy her own house. David, she and some other asshole from Duluth saved my life!

Me: Buddy Boy, it's not nice to call God an asshole and I don't think he is from Duluth.

Paul dialed a number from the car phone. He said, "Sweetheart, "I am going to Duluth with David. I have some amends to make and that time is now. I will have three Bills with me so we will kidnap Heather and I will bring her back with me so this dummy sitting next to me will have to move here! Yes dear, I will tell him."

Paul hung up the phone. With a smile he said, "Jane wants you to keep me away from the water and for you to never stop writing. Why didn't I get to meet Heather during your weekend, 'Revival'?"

Me: Heather is her own person, she has excellent social skills and is brilliant in her job and she works her guts out. When she is done working for the day, she is also done with people. She fully supports my efforts as a writer and speaker but she demands

175

her independence and privacy. She might make an exception for you if you are nice to her and buy her a Steak-Cheese-French sandwich at Grandma's Saloon and Deli up over the hill. Do you want to stay at the house?

Paul: No thanks, I think I know of a joint that I can get into without a reservation.

We pulled up to the Jet. As a Bill opened the door for us, I stepped out and exclaimed, "Holy shit Paul, the Randall Corporation logo blew off the tail section of this fucker. Do you think this bird is safe to fly?"

Paul grinned as he gave me the finger. He turned back to the limo driver and the other two Bills and asked, "Any of you guys ever been to Duluth, Minnesota? They all shook their heads no. Paul said, "Call your family's and let them know that you are going to be in Duluth for the next couple of days to investigate what this Grandma's Saloon and Deli and their Steak-Cheese-French is all about! Stand down, you are now on two days of vacation, right after you do a bit of bull work after we land." Smiles all around as we were greeted by two new Bills and the flight attendant. Paul asked if the all the cargo was on board and a new Bill said, "Yes sir, the cargo is loaded and secured."

We boarded the inconspicuous aircraft with only 'N' numbers.

CHAPTER 19   BRING IN THE CLOWNS

The flight attendant introduced herself as Kris, she was quite shapely and obviously right handed according to the bulge under her left arm pit.

Paul said, "I'm going back to what you like to call, 'The Bubble' for a nap, enjoy your flight." So it was just me, Kris and the five Bills, they were all very personable. Kris served us drinks and snacks as we lounged in the white 'Kidskin' overstuffed lounge chairs. Kris brought over a small table and placed it in front of me. She walked away and was back in a few seconds with a large, expensive looking leather satchel. She put it on the table as she said, "I have been instructed by Mr. Gregory Roberts to remind you of your agreement with him and the long arm of the law, if that makes any sense to you. This is a gift from the Roberts family." I unzipped the bag. There was a purple drawstring bag much like a Crown Royal whisky bag but much larger. Whatever was inside had to weigh damn near ten pounds. I reached into the bag and felt a highly polished wooden box. The wood was so smooth that it was actually slippery and hard to grip. I was very careful not to drop the box as I took it out of the bag.

The moment I saw the box I was stunned. I saw a box like that only one other time in my life. It was in an alarmed, bullet proof showcase in the world famous, "Premiere Gun Store," in Las Vegas. This box was twice the size as the one I saw in Las Vegas but there was no mistaking the wood and if true to the one I saw, I also knew what was inside it. The wood was worth a small fortune. It is made from an African hardwood named Pink Ivory or Red Ivory wood. It is one of the rarest woods in the world. There was a built-in rolling combination lock where a handle should be. I looked at Kris with a pleading look, she smiled and handed me a card with the combination on it. My hands were trembling so bad that I told her, "You do it." She unlocked it but just barely lifted the lid as she said, "This is yours to open if you don't have a heart attack first."

All this time the five Bills sitting across from me were smiling their asses off. I lifted the lid and got the distinct smell of fresh gun oil. There was a white silk cloth over the contents. The box was lined with well padded, purple velour. Before I pulled back the white silk cloth, I lowered my head, squeezed my eyes shut for a brief moment and pushed all the air out of my lungs. I pulled the cloth and there was not just one, but two of the words finest handguns finished in brushed steel. They were engraved with, "Wilson Combat Arms 'Presidents Edition,'" on one side and the other side read, "To my Lifeguard, David J. Brown," with Paul E. Roberts, in an etched signature. They both were full size semi-automatic 1911 framed pistols. One was a 9mm the other a 45auto. The serial numbers were the same on each gun P/E-D.J.B. 1-of-1. The grips were made from the same wood as the presentation box. Instead of the Wilson Combat logo in the center of the grips, there was that damn 'Randall Corporation' logo! There was also two sets of Pachmayr pressure sensitive laser grips. The value of the box and its contents would easily put you into a shiny new luxury car.

The five Bills were looking at me as if to ask permission to come and look at my treasures. My turn to smile my ass off as I said, "Hey guys, check this out!" They all sprung from their chairs and in two strides were saying, "Holy shit." I grinned as I said, "You can pick them up but remember that I am a graduate of the 'Dunwoody School of Badassery' in Minneapolis, Minnesota. These are mine and I am still armed."

After Kris wiped the guns down with a silicone cloth she closed the box and put it on the seat to my left. She reached into her coat pocket and brought out my cell phone saying, "You've probably been missing this old Dinosaur. You desperately need an upgrade!" She smiled as she said, "I will be right back."

The five Bills all stood as Kris laid a heavily padded Kevlar rifle case on the table. She sat next to me and said, "This is from all of the Bill's from the Chicago office." I was overwhelmed and a bit embarrassed by their giving me a gift and I hardly knew them. The driver Bill said, "This is in our deep appreciation for your giving and signing us all a copy of your book, that and we will all have new suits and sport coats of our own choosing, both color and styles. No more look-alike Penguin suits, thanks buddy!"

I lifted the case to open it and felt its heft. It was a two compartment case with a rifle in each zipped compartment. One gun was a Sig Sauer MPX 9mm carbine that looked identical to the one I already own except this was a second generation with several system upgrades. The other was a Sig Sauer SIG516 Patrol FDE 55.6mm. I just sat there for a few minutes to gather myself. I stood up and shook their hands with my gratitude and thanks. I said, "I would fuckin kill right now for a cigarette." Kris smiled as she looked at the Bills and asked, "Should I tell him boys?" They all smiled and nodded their heads. Kris said, "Come over here." I looked back at the Bills and said not to anyone in particular, "Don't fuck with my shit while I'm gone, and remember where I went to ass kickin school!"

Kris took me to an area with a false wall but it wasn't a false wall at all. It was a suction area that would suck the smoke damn near out of your lungs! Kris joined me for a smoke. She said she wished she could stay in Duluth but because, "Pappa Bear" threw these spare Bills on board she had to reset several schedules for several upcoming events. She said she was a logistics coordinator for special ops teams for several years after she was wounded in action. I'm thinking fuck! Everyone in this unit is a bad ass, I better shut the fuck up and go sit down!"

We started to descend when Kris came back and said, "Time to buckle up, we are on final approach. Good news everyone, we have a light on the instrument panel in the cockpit, we all get to spend the day and night in Duluth! The aircraft security team will be on the ground in one hour, so we can all have lunch together."

Just then Paul emerged from the "Bubble" and sat down next to me. He asked me if Kris had taken good care of me during the flight. He then asked if it would be ok to ask her to join us for dinner at that Granny's place that has Heathers favorite sandwich. "Besides it will be nice to dine with two attractive young ladies rather than have to look at that ole' geezer mug of yours."

We deplaned as a pick-up truck was backing up to the cargo hold. Four of the Bills unloaded five 5000 round crates of 9mm bullets. Then came eighteen (25 count) cartons of my books. I looked at Paul with a question in my eyes. He smiled as he said, "The bullets are from the kids and the books are from Jane. She wants you to sign a few more for gifts and then you sell the rest on your website. She decided that those uppity assholes that she initially bought the books for can buy their own books. They will never read it but will keep them because they are signed so they can brag about owning it to their friends. "Fuck em!" Sorry, but I stole that cute phrase from your book."

I called Heather and told her I would be home in twenty minutes, with a bunch of unruly barbarians. It took three town cars to get everyone out of the airport. I didn't realize that there were three people in the cockpit. I asked Paul about that and he told me, "We fly with two full-fledged captains and one navigator. All of our pilots are former fighter pilots. We fly special cargo, such as yourself! So two pilots are our norm."

As we pulled into our driveway Heather came outside and I introduced Paul and Kris to her as the pickup truck backed to one of the garage doors. She gave me a puzzled look as the Bills unloaded the crates of bullets and the cartons of books as I just smiled and said, "I will tell you later, babe please go open the gun safe so I can get rid of this junk," as I looked down at the long gun case in my left hand and the leather satchel in my right hand. Heather shot me another WTF glance and the crew started laughing.

Paul asked if we would ride to the hotel with him. Heather said that she would like that as she had never been to the Corker. We pulled up to the front entrance of the Corker in the black three car caravan with black suits exiting each car. The doorman who was approaching the first car to open the door, quickly jumped back when he saw the crew of black suits surround the car and looking more than just a bit menacing.

He dashed up the three steps to open the hotel entrance doors for the entourage. The doorman did not recognize Paul, until Paul said, "Hello Tim, you look well." Tim was red faced as he said, "Hello sir." When we got to the front desk, Vicki was standing there and was nothing but smiles. She almost curtseyed when she saw Paul as she said, "It is nice to see you again sir." Paul smiled back and bowed like an English stage performer.

He then said, "Young lady, this is Sunday, may I enquire as to why you are not in church?" Vicki said, "Mr. Roberts, my family all goes to church on Saturday night and I go to 6:00 am high mass with my Grandparents on Sunday, I hope that meets with your approval sir." They had a brief stare down and both broke out laughing. Paul asked her, "Is everything ready for inspection by Mr. Brown?" She smiled, "Yes sir, as requested." Vicki looked at me and said, "Oh, hello Mr. Brown Sir, I'm so sorry Sir, I didn't see you standing there."

Vicki and Paul high-fived each other while laughing like children.

Heather looked like she thought everyone was either nuts or stoned. I think she was about to bolt for the door and run right over the top of poor Tim at the door, to make good her escape!

Vicki than looked at me and said, "I will get the keys for you sir, it's nice to see you brought your daughter along for lunch today," as she introduced herself to Heather. I looked at Paul as he said, "You created this monster this is now her show. I'm just a tourist along for the ride." He looked at the Pilots, the Bills and Kris as he said, "You guys go ahead and whoever would like lunch, we will be back in twenty minutes and meet you in the lounge."

181

Vicki came out of her office with a set of keys and said, "Please join me, as she pressed the up button on the elevator. We rode to the 8th floor, the top floor. Vicki put a key into the panel that read 'electrical room'. The elevator went up another floor. As the elevator door opened she stepped out and said, "This way please." We walked past three doors marked HVAC, Utility and Electrical. The last door in the hallway was marked Elevator Maintenance. I noticed that it had two dead bolt locks when the other three doors only had one each. Vicki unlocked both locks and stepped back as she said, "Mr. Brown you first please."

I took Heathers hand as I stepped into the room. We both sucked in our breath as we looked at what was before us. It was the most beautiful hotel suite I had ever seen. We were standing in a living room where the carpet was so thick and plush that you could barely see your shoes. Vicki said, "Please follow me," she opened a door that was the bedroom, it was just as beautiful as the living room. Next was a full kitchen and lastly was a ginormous open space with an open horseshoe desk with four very large monitors. There were keyboards and chairs at each monitor.

Paul said, "We will send in our I.T. people on Wednesday to set up any kind of system you want. The drapes close with the press of a button and you can make this room as dark as the inside of a cows stomach, if you wish. That printer over there, the one the size of a small car, will print an entire book with the color cover and bind it. You will have to put paper in the loading tray, however. I think it holds six reams. Paul opened a double door to a 10x12 room with boxes stacked floor to ceiling and several rows deep. He said this is Jane's touch. There are 5,000 copies of your book in here. The next room will house 5,000 copies of your new book that have already been prepaid. You can use our mail center in the lobby so you don't have to go to the post office any more. The mail center will ship your books anywhere to your book signings and speaking engagements. This is your exclusive office. This floor belongs to you. Even if I were to sell this property this entire floor will still belong to you. You actually own a clear title of this floor. There is another set of keys in our safe. This floor is alarmed, those other three doors are dummy's and are part of the full steel wall. If you want maid service you will have to let them in, the same for maintenance needs. You have the only elevator and door keys. All this makes me hungry, who wants lunch?"

We got to the lobby and I told Paul, "Dial up your wife and my girlfriend. You guys go ahead, I need a few minutes. When Jane answered Paul said, "Good afternoon Mrs. Roberts please hold for his Excellency and most worldly renowned Novelist, Mr. David J. Brown. He handed me his phone, took Heathers arm as he escorted her into the lounge. I walked into the private conference room and closed the door.

I said, "Hello Jane, I don't how to begin with thanking you. Tell me about all this."

Jane said, "We have been working on your office for the last three weeks. I have a close friend that is a world renowned author. She has a very similar life background as you and she likes your style. She told me how to set up your office. You have the identical equipment and layout that she has. It will be her I.T. people that will set up your computer systems. They will customize the system to your liking. You will also be using her editing staff as well." I had to stop her because of my laughing. "Jane, sweetheart, stop! Look, I have a $400 Asus laptop that has more programs than I could ever learn. My editing staff consists of spellcheck and Google. You somehow have me confused with a legitimate author and I ain't him. I'm just a regular guy that wrote a book." Jane interrupted with her own laughter, "David, you are full of shit. So I will talk, you will listen. I didn't think the time was right to tell you before we left the hotel to the convention center for your AA speech but I will tell you now. My phone was on silent vibrate when we were at the community center and before we got back to the hotel my phone was dancing in my pocket. I was a bit late for the car for the convention center because I was talking to the mayor of Chicago for several minutes. He heard of your, "City of Death" statement and asked what he could do to help us. I came straight out of your play-book when I told him, that the best help from him and his office would be not to help! "I don't

183

want to get sucked into the quagmire and cesspool of city power players. I need the end user department heads and their staff." He promised his unwavering support.

David, I sat with a calm and quiet man just a few moments before he went to war with the entire city of Chicago and beat them with their own truths. Four hours later I had the greatest pleasure of my lifetime, watching and listening to the very same man telling his truths of winning his battle. You gave everyone involved in your life credit for your win and took none for yourself. Your speaking is so soothing with the way you reach out and hold everyone's hand and yet they don't even know it. The way you bring your story to life is memorizing. Your brilliance is in the way you measure and deliver every word for its desired effect in your delivery and nobody catches it until they can no longer hold back their own tears. Nobody expected you to be that good, you took us all over. When I saw our Bills, who are tough seasoned warriors, with tear streaks and runny noses, I knew that we were in the presence of a spiritual awakening. My Paul will never be the same man. Hope can only be given and received if the giver has the trust of the recipient. You held the trust of every person in that room in the palm of your hand. They fell in love with you because you made them feel safe, so safe to bring out their denied and hidden tears. You didn't make them cry, you helped them cry. Now I finally understand why you write.

You lost me at first as I could not understand how you could write so well and yet be the worst businessman on earth. You are in the business of hearts, not book sales! You give your books away to bring comfort and change in people.

The office is for your comfort, you must finish your next book. I want to make it comfortable for you. I will go all of your production costs as well as a marketing plan a little stronger than book giveaways! Those books in the closet are for you to give away or sell. The second closet is anxiously awaiting the delivery of 5,000 books of, 'Flesh of a Fraud. 'Don't be surprised with emails or phone calls from TV and movie producers. You can use our legal department for negotiating the contracts for you. Your speech was taped, Amanda has a company that is already editing out some background noise. Those tapes will go to her contacts in the entertainment business as soon as tomorrow. David, this world is so ready for you and we are going to bring you to them! Amanda doesn't bullshit anyone on anything. She will make a movie on your book. I love you, now go enjoy your lunch. Give Heather a big hug for me."

I sat for a few moments after hanging up with Jane, just to let my mind settle. Everything she said about the book promotions were the very things I secretly dreamed of but I had to push out of my mind. I learned some time back that when I dream, nothing gets done.

I left the conference room and went to join the rest of the crew for lunch. It was a pleasant surprise to see the flight crew members sitting there across the table. I'd never actually met them so I introduced myself, each of them stood and introduced themselves. One pilot was named Bill, the other pilot was named Bill and the third person, a female and the navigator, well her name was Bill too! We all shook hands and I took my seat on the other side of Heather. Paul, who is on the other side of Heather looked over at me and said, "Well, you and Jane get all that TV show guest appearance and movie stuff squared away." Heather snapped her head around and said in a questioning way, "Movie and TV deals? You better get that grin of your face before you say, 'I'll tell you later,' because you damn well better." The rest of the table had a hardy laugh.

Everyone had already ordered their meals and Heather said, "I've ordered for you and yours will come with the rest of our meals." We sat and just lightly chatted for a bit of time. The meals came to the table, the waiter brought a covered tray and put the sterling silver covered plate in front of me and said, "With our compliments Mr. Brown." He lifted the lid and there was a large crystal bowl with a 'Dinty Moore Beef Stew' wrapper taped to the bowl and my favorite sandwich of Elliott's 'UP NORTH' Braunschweiger on two pieces of my favorite 12 grain bread and a can of Pepsi. Paul let out a low whistle as he said, "You must be

185

some kind of special, I understand thru a very reliable source that soda cans or any other kind of cans are not allowed at any time in the restaurants at these property's. Are you a rock star or something?"

I said to the waiter, "Is all of this just for little ole' me?" Yes sir he said, "One of the bellhops had to go to the grocery store and had it double bagged so no one would see him bring it into the building, he said he felt like a drug smuggler. The head chef said if it was anyone other than you who ordered this, he would have walked off the job and would have never come back. And to be perfectly honest Sir, it was hard to keep my breakfast down from the smell of it!" We all had a good laugh over that, and I thoroughly enjoyed my Dinty Moore Beef Stew and sandwich while the rest had their meals.

After we finished our meals, Paul told the waiter to go and get the head chef and the bellhop and bring them to the table and wait here for him. Paul did a head nod to signal me to follow him as he got up from his chair. I looked at Heather and said, "I guess I'll be right back." We went to the bank next door. Paul got a large envelope of hundred dollar bills. Paul gave me three, one hundred dollar bills as he said, "We don't want everyone to know what a broke joker you are, you are going to tip those three guys for you being such an ass-hole!"

When we got back to the lounge the effected three were standing in line and almost as rigid as thou they were at attention. They had a look of pure dread, thinking that they were in for a serious ass chewing if not being fired.

Paul said, "Gentleman, Mr. Brown and I would like to extend our deepest apology to you for the unbearable hardship that you suffered in the procurement and preparation of Mr. Brown's meal. I assure you that if it ever happens again, that you have my blessing to dump that shit directly into his lap!"

Everyone started to laugh and clap as I gave them each a hundred dollar bill and a hand shake. Those three collectively took their first breaths since we walked back into the room. The chef had a huge grin as he said, "Mr. Roberts, I am afraid Sir, that we will be working overtime tonight to disinfect the entire kitchen. I will need your approval for the overtime pay." Paul shook his head as he reached into his briefcase and fished out three one hundred dollar bills with a smile for the three effected souls. After his generous matching tip to his employees he looked to the flight crew and said, "Get that damn plane fixed and get me the hell away from this guy, every time I come here he spends my money like a drunken sailor!" Paul spun around to the two Bills who had been sitting at another table all thru our lunch, acting like they didn't know anybody in the room. He said with a smile, "Everyone here has a carry permit and is strapped. You two are on vacation, get the hell out of here and take off those damn black suits. I don't want to see your faces or another black suit until we board the plane tomorrow, and tell the others the same, you all look like a bunch of clowns!"

We had a few cups of coffee and I said, You know what guys, it's time for a nap." Heather said, "Yes dear, it's time for a nap and you've got a lot of things to explain to me, a lot of things!"

I never got that nap. I showed Heather the gift guns from the Roberts family and the Bills, as I told her of the last few days events. She acted as though she wasn't even in the same zip code as she was handling the twin Wilson Combat pistols. It was so distracting that I said, "I am trying to tell you about my trip. That is annoying, what are you doing?"

Heather had the sweetest smile as she said, "I am petting them, and I'm thinking up nice names for them."

How could anyone not love that gal? I lightly skimmed over the TV and movie potential stuff so as not to get either of our hopes up to high. Another sweet smile from Heather as she said, "Good, when are we moving? Somewhere warm with beaches and dolphins is my vote!"

Well babe, if the Roberts clan had their way we would be living in Chicago right now. "Oh honey that would be nice, you could fly down and visit me and the dolphins anytime you like!"

We drove our car to the restaurant and waited in the parking lot for Paul and Kris. The Corker Hotel car pulled in the parking lot and up to the entrance. Heather and I started to the door to meet them. I was surprised to see Vicki get out of car along with Paul and Kris. Vicki saw me and came at me in a dead run. She threw herself at me and about took me off my feet. She curled her arms around my neck like a python. Paul walked up smiling as I looked over Vicki's shoulder and said, "I guess you told her?" At that same time Vicki was rattling car keys in her hand saying, "I got a new car, I got a new car!" Heather smiled kindly as she looked at me and asked, "A friend of yours, perhaps another fan?"

We entered Grandma's Saloon and Deli. We were seated at a large round table with linen napkin tents. Heather and I have been going there on average of three times a month for several years. This is a sandwich and pasta joint with paper napkins. There were two, empty four place tables on either side of us. The tables had reserved signs on them. We have never seen cloth napkins or reserved signs in our many, many visits. And then it happened! Here comes eight, fully dressed clowns (full face paint, floppy shoes, wigs, red noses and white gloves included) that were seated at the reserved tables. Paul just dropped his head and laughed. It was the five Bills and the three member flight crew. The first Captain looked over and said, "We got an email telling us not to wear black suits. It said we should wear clown suits instead!" From that moment on it was the Chicago steak house with the Roberts family all over again. The drunkest bowling team in the state would bow to our rowdiness, yet nobody in the group had a drink. The waitress took Heathers meal order first and it was her standard, 'Steak-Cheese-French.' The other eleven in our party said in unison, "We will have what she is having," as thou they had been rehearsing that all day! The waitress walked away in hysterics.

Three wait staff members delivered our food, I was the last to be served. I smelled it before it got to the table. Yup, it was a steaming bowl of Dinty Moore Beef Stew with a Braunschweiger sandwich. Paul was laughing so hard that he could barely speak as he said, "Guess I'm with the clowns on this one!" Vicki spent almost the entire time telling Heather what wonderful men Mr.

Roberts and Mr. Brown were, and how lucky Heather was to have me. I'm sure that if I were sitting directly across from Heather that my shins would be bruised and bleeding, if not hemorrhaging. During the dinner Paul asked if I could meet him for breakfast at the hotel at 7:00 am.

Paul paid for everyone's meal as he thanked them for one of most relaxing and fun filled days in many years. As we were leaving Paul fanned out what I would guess to be seven or eight one hundred dollar bills as he apologized to the restaurant manager for our rowdiness and said, "This is for our servers and yourself."

CHAPTER 20   CHRISTMAS IN JULY

I walked into the Corker at 6:45 am for breakfast with Paul. As I was walking down the hall towards the lounge, I heard Paul's voice in the conference room. He was laughing and then I heard the unmistakable voices of the Quinn's. I stepped in and said, "Hi kids, how's everyone?" Paul said, "I was just getting to know the Quinn's a little better, you remember these two people Dave, I believe you refer to them as, Boris and Natasha?" They both looked at Paul and then me. Paul said, "It's kind of an inside joke, maybe Dave will enlighten you two a bit later." Paul said that he had won the coin toss with the Quinn's, so he gets to pay off the first and second home mortgage for Seth and Mary Walker. The Quinn's were going to buy the Zenith book store building from the landlord and deed it over to the Walkers if they were willing to take on Ms. Tami as an equal partner. The three of them were also going to retire all debt and give the store $75,000 for additional inventory, and fixtures. They were also going to collectively buy Ms. Tami a new, full size SUV.

I stood leaning against the wall and smiled as I said, "That's nice, there's ten minutes out of my life that I will never get back." Maddie jumped up and came to give me a hug with Woody right behind her. I told them that they looked refreshed and they said, "We can't wait to tell you of our time with Don Prince." I said great, see you guys tomorrow in the am but right now I have to meet some kind of bigshot in the lounge for breakfast.

Paul and I just had coffee. He said he wanted to get to the plane early because he had to get some things together to be ready for a Hawaii trip on Tuesday. I said, "Not before we talk about the last three days. Here it is Buddy Boy, I think you are back into the fold. You have earned another chance to build trust in your family, not just the business but also in their hearts. No one had to tell me and no one did, about your many broken promises, the deep disappointments, heartache and embarrassments you brought to them. Not to mention the fear and worries that you would kill yourself, either accidently or purposely. You are no different than any other alcoholic, we cause damage. I saw a family that is ready to go, all-in with you. No more raised eyebrows or smirks that scream bullshit. The other day you made some kind of sideways comment about how your security staff were doing their jobs just for the money. You saw what these people were about these last few days. For me it was when I went outside for a smoke after I spoke at the Founders Day Banquet. None of your Bills knew or gave a shit about me. But they shadowed me to protect me. Not for my sake but for yours. They knew that I was important to you. No one directed them to follow me, they took it upon themselves. That my friend is not just someone doing their jobs. That is called loyalty!

Let's visit yesterday's lunch. We all had a ball. Those same people that you scared the shit out of a month ago and were terrified they would lose their jobs because of the raging asshole owner that doesn't know his ass from a hole in the ground, who was looking for blood because he couldn't stand himself, suddenly changed. Low waged does not mean small hearts. They gave you a chance and you earned their trust. But it goes deeper than that, you taught them that forgiveness has its own rewards. You gave laughter, laughter means trust, laughter means safety, and laughter means love.

Last night's dinner. You gave everyone the day and night off with pay. Do you really think those two Bills were in the lounge yesterday to enjoy their lunch or were they looking after you on your day off? That whole clown suit thing last night? Jesus

191

Christ Paul, they all had a night off and yet they were there to show you the respect they have for you. If these were just folks doing their jobs they would not be anywhere around you on their day off!

The stuff you do for the people who are not able to do for themselves, comes from your big heart, not just your fat bank account. At some point you are going to have to accept the fact that you are a kind and decent man. You're ok Buddy Boy, you're ok! You have work to do and I have new guns to break-in. Let's call it a day, until we meet again my friend."

We stood, we hugged, we got teary eyed but neither of us shed those tears, we savored them.

I left the Corker and drove to Park Point. I walked in the morning cool sand, the lake was calm with gentle waves lightly washing to shore. I thought I needed to talk to God, I thought I needed to thank him. This was the perfect place. Suddenly a Seagull silently drifted overhead and cast his shadow on me. There it is.....It wasn't that I needed to talk with God, I needed to hear God, as he was saying, "You are welcome."

I drove home to find Heather sitting on the living room floor, surrounded by our four Papillion's and reading the Sunday paper. A kiss hello and with pets all around for our furry kids. I told Heather to finish up the article she was reading because she needed to get dressed, "We're goin shootin!" She gave me a hard and scolding look as she said, "You are not going to shoot those pistols! These are collector items, they are one-of-one's, are you fucking crazy? Nobody in the world has guns like these! I smiled at her as I said, "I only have one of those guns. The 9mm is yours!"

Heather is rarely swayed with gifts, beyond a mild smile and a thank you. She came up off the floor like a Jack-in-the-box and brushed by me, I asked her where she was going. She didn't even look back as she said, "I'm getting dressed, I'm going to shoot my new gun, and her name is, Muffy Ann!"

CHAPTER 21   BACK TO THE WORLD

Monday morning came with a mix of excitement and dread but I couldn't figure out why. I shoved the dread part into the back of mind for later review and in the hope that some level of clarity will come during the course of the day.

Today I must focus on the Quinn couple. It was obvious that they were trying to hold back the dam from bursting yesterday, while Paul was present. They had more than a bit to say, Don Prince must have really worked them over. I will give them all the time they need. I am certainly no therapist but I do know when and how to listen.

I entered the Corker to see Vicki sitting in a lobby high back chair, right out of the 1930's. She was sitting very straight and had a sweet looking mature look about herself. I started to wonder if my dread feeling was about to come to fruition. Nope, Vicki said she was waiting for her Grandpa to pick her up and take her to his friend's reality office. I smiled and said, "You should be driving your grandpa to your appointment in your new car. You didn't wrap it around a tree did you?" She smiled and said, "No sir, the weather forecast said it might rain today and I don't want my new car to get wet. The Quinn's are waiting for you in your conference room, there is a telegram on the table for you. I'm just going to sit here to wait for my Grandpa."

Telegram? I haven't seen or even heard of people sending telegrams for many years. Is the dread in the Telegram? I did not go down that hallway that leads to the private conference room. I

193

went the long way around, grabbed a cup of coffee from the lounge and went out to the garden for a smoke and to settle my nerves. The question kept pounding in my head, who the fuck sends telegrams? I called the Quinn's to tell them that I would be a little late, as I lit another cigarette.

I walked into the conference room. The Quinn's did not do their standard jump up, with handshakes and hugs, morning greeting, (Well, here comes the dread that has been bugging me all morning.)I got a polite soft smile and a simple good morning from both. I picked up the telegram and sat down as I opened it, without a word to the Quinn's. The three page telegram read. "David, there is an envelope in your top desk drawer, up in your office. It is for a new wardrobe. You cannot go on national television wearing you're off the rack, $60.00 sport coat from J.C. Penny. Go to the best men's clothing store in the city and buy at least six vested suits and six sport coats. Buy all new accessories including shoes for each suit. French cuffs and cuff links are a must. Put a rush on the tailoring and offer a large tip for 24hour service. Your incoming phone call for fame and fortune could come at any moment and you must be ready. Let me know when you get the call, one of my planes will pick you up. If the $25,000 is not enough, give Amanda a call. You are her new pet project and she never fails. Her mother and I won't allow it!

Remember to; shoot your cuffs!
Good luck, Skippy!
Keep Grinnin
Paul

I folded the telegram back into the envelope and dropped it into my briefcase. I looked at the Quinn's and said, "Guys, I need a few more moments, are you ok with that? Maddie smiled at me as she said, "We are practicing 'Less Living,' we are here for you today. Take all the time you need, we will be right here. We are getting pretty good at this coloring business."

I took the elevator to the top floor and put the key in for the, "Maintenance Floor." I unlocked the office door and all the lights came on. I lit a cigarette and watched the smoke disappear like in the jet and went to, what I guess is my desk. In the center top drawer was a large thick manila envelope with a white #6 envelope taped to it. The small envelope had two corporate credit cards, one was a Chase Sapphire the other a Capital one. There was a stickie note on each. "The Sapphire is unlimited funds, it will give you cash at any bank. The Capital One card is for flights and hotels." I didn't bother to count the stacks of hundred dollar bills but I'm pretty damn sure that they would fill a salad mixing bowl! I called the best men's clothing store in the city and told the owner that I would be there at 1:00 pm and I needed two tailors present for immediate alterations when I arrived. He started to balk and I interrupted with, "Unless you don't need the $25,000 in cash I will be bringing." I left the office as the door automatically locked and the lights went to dim. The elevator ride was not long enough as I was desperately trying to shake off this Alice in Wonderland story along with Maddie's, 'Less Living' statement. What the fuck is, 'Less Living?'

I started with asking them how their visit with Don Prince went. Woody said that he and Maddie wanted to hear about the TV and movie stuff. I said, "Later, what did you two do to him, where did you hide the body?"

Maddie: We went on the Vista tour boats three times each day for all three days and it was wonderful! We love practicing less!

Me: Did you two smoke your breakfast or did the, 'All powerful Don Prince' slowly swing his gold pocket watch in front of you? What gives with this 'less' bullshit?

Woody: Don did not come as a therapist to help us, he came to be with us. He told us all about how we are polluted from all the distractions that take us from our center. Our vision, and our

195

minds distort what is directly in front of us. He compares our senses with a sink drain. After years and years of pouring grease and all the other nasty stuff that we put down the sink, the pipes get clogged and stop to drain. Our minds are much the same. Our minds get clogged with trash and the "garbage-in-garbage out" stops to function. We become mentally and emotionally stopped up. Nothing drains and things develop a virus that spreads thru our entire being. We become polluted and toxic as our spirit dies.

Maddie: Don taught us that we need to practice less to find our way to empty. Empty is when we are detoxed and can start to rebuild our perceptions and get our spirit back. The reason we kept going on the tour boat was not to look but to see. To see without thinking, to see what is there rather than think about what we see. Each boat trip we went on was the very same tour. But each experience was measurably different. We saw things that we should have seen on the first trip. Even the sound of the boat engines was noticeably different on each trip. Our hearing improved and sounds took on a different sound, if that makes any sense. I actually heard the rhythm of the boat motors. The waves meeting the bow of the boat had a beautiful beat. I stood and wondered if the boat was pushing the water or if the water was pushing the boat.

These last three days have become life changing. We must slow down to go faster. Seeking less will bring us more. Don also taught us about expectations and perceptions. We went to an Alabama Concert and on the next day to see the classic movie.

We, along with Don are huge Alabama fans. We have all their albums on wax and cd's. And we have seen the classic movie before, as well as read the book. What Don showed us is how our expectations rob us of our experiences. We went into the concert expecting them to sound exactly as their records. Don pointed out that recorded studio music never sounds like a live concert. There are far too many distractions and variables. He showed us that it's the same as comparing a book to a movie made from the book. We start to judge and compare rather than to simply enjoy the experience.

Me: Sounds like you two got what you needed, did Don get what he came for?

Maddie: Don came to catch his breath from all his private counseling sessions and the traveling to all the seminars. He deals with first responders who are on the very brink of going over the cliff! He knows their pain and they trust him. I think you said it best a few months ago on a Facebook post where you said, "Don will sit next to you, side by side, shoulder to shoulder and bleed along with you." There is only one other person that I know of with that kind of ability and I am looking at him!
Enough about us, Paul told us how you kicked the shit out of the entire city of Chicago in the afternoon and held 8,000 people in the palm of your hand four hours later. And this TV talk shows and movie, about you and your book. We want to hear all about it. Give it to us, all of it!

Me: Slow your roll, kids. I have to tell you that I lost sight of your wealth. Yes, you did tell me of your inheritances and briefly of your successful investments but you are both so common and unassuming, I forget of your financial status. What you guys are doing for Seth and Mary, with their home and business financially, along with the stipulation of they must bring Ms. Tami on as an equal partner is a thing of heart and beauty. I love you guys for that.

Woody leaned back in his chair as he said, "You slow your roll!" Did you not hear us when we told you that we are avid if not rabid first edition book collectors? Before you propose us for Canonization you should know that we, like most all other people are opportunists. You can either earn loyalty or you can buy loyalty. We are doing booth with the Walker book store. We have several books on our want list to complete our collections. In all actuality, what we did was, we hired three search agents. They will work tirelessly to assist in our search. We are tired of traveling the world to attend book sales and auctions. Those three are well versed in the identification and quality ratings of rare books. We will send them to do our inspections and bidding. They get all expense paid trips around the world, to places they dared not to dream about but could only read about. We get to play book store employees when they are gone and get to go home and sleep in our own beds every night. Do you think ill of us? Are we evil? Guess you better withdraw your proposal, cause we ain't no Saints!"

Me: Not evil, cunning yes, but not evil. You two are also full of shit. You guys have more in common with the Roberts crew than you realize. You mask, just as they do, your kind intentions. You try to play off your kind hearts as some kind of, "Good business deal or good business sense." Go sell that shit elsewhere, I ain't buying! You don't help people to feel good about yourselves, you help people to help them feel good about themselves. Any more crap you two want to try to lay down?

Maddie: Don Prince has you figured out better than anyone, he told us that you don't just look at people. You look into them. And people seem to welcome it, we know we do.

With that, I went for a smoke. When I came back in, Maddie had a sad look on her face. I said, ok I'll bite, what's wrong sweetheart?

Maddie: I have a sinking feeling, oh hell, we have a sinking feeling that you are not going to tell us about the TV and movie deals. We are afraid that you will be whisked away and we will lose you. I know that I sound selfish and I am being selfish but we need you. Not for our studies or entertainment but you have taught us so much and we are hungry for your knowledge even more importantly your wisdom. I mean really, who doesn't look up to you?

Me: I don't need anyone to look up to me, please just look at me and I will be happy. Now for the TV and movie stuff. Yes there is some stuff in the works, I know no more about it than you do. Honestly, I don't want to know until it's in ink. I can even better answer your question by telling you both a bit about Heather and me. Heather and I are not just on the same page, we are on the same paragraph. Our life experiences are vastly different. Our core values, our beliefs, our political and social outlook is much the same. Hell I wouldn't be a bit surprised if our DNA was a match. We came together with our own ideals, neither of us tried to sway the other, it is just who we are. The only exception to that is this. Although we are both realists, Heather is more cautious than I am. I am a bit more of a believer, maybe a hoper would be a better word. When I tell Heather of a possible opportunity (mostly about the book marketing) she will always respond with the same phrase that pisses me off to no end. She always says, "Never get too happy." That fries my ass every damn time! Because I know she is right. Her life's disappoints are no greater or no less than mine. We just process them in different ways. She tells me to never get too happy to protect me. She understands that I go deep with disappoint and I take it very personal. So until the ink is dry and the money is in the bank, I can only tell you guys that I am hopeful. As for the losing me part, you can't lose a family member and I consider you two as family. Family, in very good standing. Let's have some hugs and Maddie you look like you could use a Mimosa. The bar doesn't open for another half hour but I think I may have an in with the bar manager.

They both laughed as Woody said, "Who are you trying to shit, everyone here already thinks you own the joint and they seem pretty happy about it! We understand that you even have a penthouse office. We would love to see it but even loved family members need to know their limits."

Me: Well said my friend, let's get you're sweetheart that drink.

We walked into the bar area of the lounge where the bartender was still setting up the bar for the day. I said, I know you're not supposed to be open yet, (state liquor Law) as I asked him for two Mimosas. He grinned as he said, "I've been around long enough that I know not to say no to the boss." We all had a good laugh as he made the Quinn's their drinks. The bartender put the drinks on the bar. Maddie picked hers up and lightly sipped it. She smacked her lips and said, "You boys go on without me. I think I just found my new most favorite bartender." We again had a laugh as Woody put a fifty dollar bill on the bar.

The bartender smiled as he slid the bill back to Woody saying, "There is no charge for your drinks." Woody said, "Yes, I know that Mr. Brown doesn't pay for anything around here, you would almost think he owns the joint!" We again had a good laugh as Woody slid the fifty back across the bar saying, "This is your tip." Maddie asked the bartender if she could take her drink back to the conference room. The bartender pointed to the sign over the doorway of the bar that read; "Absolutely no alcoholic beverages beyond this point." With a sly smile he said, "You folks can take your drinks anywhere you would like." We went back to the conference room.

Woody: Now that you are back from knocking the ass off of the entire city of Chicago, what is next for you.

Me: I have a book to finish, I have a woman to love and fur baby's to pet. I have the life I want. That other stuff would certainly be a bonus but I'm plenty comfortable at the moment. Now I have to call it an early day, I have an appointment to go to.

Being the ass I am, I tucked several hundred dollar bills in my shirt pocket like some would do with a scarf, before I walked into the clothing store. The store owner rushed over to me along with his two tailors. He said he saw my picture in the newspaper and that he had never had a famous author in all of his twenty-three years of owning the store. He was so gushy that I wanted to leave. I grinned as I took off my jacket exposing the hundred dollar bills that looked like a flower arrangement. I told him I wanted six vested suits, six sport coats, and all the accessories including a dozen pair of cuff-links and the same number of shoes. Price is of no matter, I want only your very best!

I think he was about to clutch his chest as I said, I want everything ready to be picked up no later than this time tomorrow, not a minute later. Can you fellas handle this or do I need to go elsewhere? The beehive exploded with activity, all I could do was grin with knowing that if they saw my bank balance they would call the cops to drag me out of the store.

Amanda called as I was about to lay down for a nap. She said, "I just have a moment, did you receive the package I sent you yet?" I said no. "Dad wants you to only wear those ties and no other. Those are 'Mors de Rire' ties, they are 100% silk and at three hundred dollars each, those dozen ties should take you places you never dreamed! Every time Daddy goes to lock down a heavy deal he wears those ties and those ties have never failed him. Mom and Dad are so proud of you! Mom has listened to the tape we made of you at the McCormick Center many times over. She just sits and laughs and cries and laughs again. She won't get off my ass with her constant, "Have you heard anything yet? Call them and tell those studio people that either they do it or I will drain my piggy bank and produce the movie myself!" Mom thinks that you should be the lead actor and not just the final chapter actor. She says Sylvester Stallone wrote the screen play for "Rocky" in just three days. He was so broke that he was sleeping in parks and ally-ways. A studio gave him a disgustingly low-ball offer for the script, he was willing to take it but only if he could be the lead actor. The studio said no, he said, than no deal and went back to sleeping in the park. He was so broke that he had to sell his beloved best buddy, his dog. He didn't have the money to feed it. The studio made several offers, each time he said only if he gets to be the lead, each time they said no. The studio finally relented and he was the leading actor in his own movie, "Rocky." It cost under $1,000,000 to make and it grossed over $200,000,000!

Mom thinks that you are the new 'Rocky Balboa!' I don't know who your #1 fan is but they are now a distant #2! Mother goes to the Cathedral and lights a candle for you twice a day now. I would kill to be left alone for just one hour without hearing your name, hell I'll settle for just half an hour. Hell maybe I will just kill you myself!"

I remained silent. Amanda paused and asked "Are you still there" I said "Yes, I am silently blowing you kisses, you better be nice to me or I'm telling *our* mom!" She started to laugh and hung up.

I was about to re-enter my normal life. Even if I were to consider myself an accomplished writer there is just no way I could write about that last four days of experiences. It was so far beyond of whatever normal is, it was like stepping into fantasy land and dropping down the rabbit hole, it was Willy Wonka and Disney all in one.

CHAPTER 22   STEPPING OUT OF THE DREAM

The following morning the Quinn's seemed to have worked through there, "Less Living Challenge." Maddie gave me a hug good morning, Woody a hand on forearm hand shake. I glanced around the room and asked "Where the hell is the box of donuts from Larson's Bakery?" Maddie gave me that sweet motherly smile with, "You know darling, you have gotten a bit thick around the middle, and people look ten pounds heavier on camera, you don't want to disappoint your public. This will be the first time they actually will get to see you. Everyone will be looking for that dashingly handsome lad with the lean waist and thick chest on the first page of chapter one! Perhaps we should be jogging as we talk?" I gave her my best scowling 'disappointed parent' look as I said, "Alcohol shall never cross your lips again in this fine establishment. Mimosa's are apparently not your friends!"

Me: OK you two little Darlin's, I just have to put this out and we can get to the guts of the book. I'm just a guy that had a story to tell. I knew that by my telling my story, others may become empowered to look at their own lives, repair the damage of their past and create their own story to tell. So yeah I guess if you need to call me any one thing, I'm an emotional avenging angel and I'm here to tell you that forgiveness is the key to all well-being. Forgiveness at no point means acceptance or approval, it means that I'm ready to move on with my life and enjoy the fruits of good living. Now who's first?

Maddie: I had an epiphany the other morning while we were on the tour boat. It was the first cruse of the day, it was misty and the wind was sharp. I went out to the bow of the boat and was all alone. A fog bank rolled in and I finally saw it! The answer came to a question that I had the first time I saw you the night of the Mayor's reception. I was puzzled with the people in the white tuxedos. Puzzling but not anything that was worth pursuing. I bought your statement the next morning of the people in the white tuxedos as their being representatives of the book store. That reception was semi-formal, if that. The tuxedos didn't fit, not at all. Then on Saturday and Sunday too? We even asked the white tux wearers about their outfits and they didn't know. The only consistent answer was, "Mr. Brown told us we had to wear them."

As we were in that fog bank it struck me! We didn't know at the time that the five tuxedo clad people were in such great peril. Then I remembered you telling us that every good book has a great backstory. The backstory was of five very nice people who were miserably failing. This was their swan song with only a very slight ray of hope. They were all hanging on with a hope and a prayer. You put them in those white tuxedos as a new skin for a new life! You wanted them to feel reborn, you wanted them to feel clean from their soiled past. You did the same thing with Missy. You put her in those gowns to revitalize her. You even told her that the scared little girl had left her forever the very moment she slipped into her gown. You put the four photographers in matching sport coats, slacks with matching shirts, ties and shoes. You dressed everyone to win. To win for themselves and to win for you. You believed in them and you empowered them to believe in themselves. Everyone was tireless without any signs of the dread they all started with. You sir are a genius, you read fear and sorrow like others read traffic signs! Not only do you see beyond the smiles of hidden pain but you actually know how to motivate people to want to change. You carry a power beyond that of mortal man.

Me: Sorry babe but it's not that deep. I am not capable of changing hearts or minds. I can only make suggestions, I can't make anyone do anything. None of those five wanted to fail, they just didn't know how to win.
Keep in mind the gifts bestowed them by yourselves and the Roberts family. We all got to witness the 'perfect storm' of hope and the rewards of believing.

Woody: I am damn glad that you insisted we each use a tape recorder. I will listen to this exchange between you two for a longtime to come. I am overwhelmed.

Me: Yup, me too, I'm going for a smoke.

Maddie: What is your greatest regret?

Me: Never experiencing the joy of being a parent. No child comes to me for comfort when sick or has a boo-boo or is scared, no child to bring something for me to fix. No child that reaches for me to pick them up, no child to walk with me and hold hands, no child that needs me. I can't feel the void as I never had the experience. I have never looked into a child's trusting eyes as a parent who tucks their babies in for the night.
Thanks for gutting me before 7:15 am. I'm going for a smoke.
No apologies or teary eye crap when I return.

Maddie: Who is your hero, who do you idolize or look up to, you know, in a special way more than you would anyone else?

Me: Well here is my hero, my definition of a hero is someone who goes to work every day, pays their bills, raises their children and lives a respectable and respectful life. If you want to talk about phony heroes it's this professional sports bullshit that pisses me off to no end. This protest kneeling crap with the National Anthem and all the support they get from society's dregs sickens me. Kaepernick kneels in protest and he is some kind of

205

fucking hero. Two years earlier Tim Tebow of the Denver Broncos kneels on the sidelines in prayer before each game and he is criticized and fined by the team. Sports announcers have their own clown-show going on before, during and after each game. The false praise that these phonies throw down to excite the fans and impress their bosses and the networks sponsors make me want to puke! The players catch a ball or score a touchdown and the player does some kind of dumb ass dance and the fans and announcers lose their fucking minds. Well guess what pal? You are paid millions of dollars to do that shit, try some humility and please don't do any TV interviews. These guys can't speak a full sentence that makes any sense and yet they somehow have a college degree? Bullshit!

My definition of a hero is somebody who is a common person that does uncommon things. Often times they wear a uniform and please don't confuse a uniform with a costume! First Responders wear uniforms to be identifiable. Professional athletes wear costumes to be identifiable. There is a world of difference. I'm just not into hero worship, I never have been.
I once again have to go back to my early learning years where I discovered that everyone poops and we are all going into the same size hole.

Woody: David for the life of us, neither of us can understand why you don't have a number one best-selling book. We just don't get why you are not on the late night talk shows. Why not Doctor Phil and Oprah's book club or those type of things. Kirk Meyer was absolutely right about you hitting a Grand Slam, you absolutely did that. Why doesn't anyone know about it?

Me: That must be a question you wrote last week. Prior to last week it's all back to the money, to find an agent to represent you cost money, to travel cost money, and that is if in fact they found anything about me interesting. Chances are there won't, I'm pretty much just a common guy. I don't want a fan club, I don't blog, tweet or twerk. I'm just a regular Joe, so there is low interest in me. I just do what I can do each and every day to get the word out about the book. Hopefully all that will change in the very near future. We just have to let life take its course."

Maddie: Have you ever thought that because of your deeply textured voice, of running your own radio program? You're a good looking guy, you could do a television program just as easily. Your voice is so seductively melodic and comforting that when I hear your sound, that soft soothing resonance of your voice, I hear the story before you even tell it. You have such a unique gift. I would like to see you put it to better use.

Me: I am 70 years old. I'm certainly not worn out but I'm getting tired, all of these things that are happening are overwhelming to me. This kind of stuff is a young person's game. My book is not a top seller because I don't have somebody promoted it is a top seller. Let's remember that 'The New York Times' has been bought and paid for. The big five publishing houses own the list. I have seen countless numbers of books go on the best seller list and the top 10 best seller list, before they have been printed and the publisher is doing pre-sales. The big publishing houses are self-promoting their next author who they've already paid a ton of money to. The big five are trying to recover their investment, so they slip a few bucks in somebody's pocket and it becomes a top selling book before it's ever gone to press. Often times these books have yet to leave the author's desk. Then I wonder of course, about how so many of these books, especially some of these supposed self-written books by professional athletes, politicians, business leaders and of course entertainers ever pass the smell test. Everyone's writing a book but few of the aforementioned can tell you what is in a particular chapter because they never wrote it! In most cases the celebrities hire a writer or the writer approaches them. Either way the celeb takes full credit for writing the book and the true author slinks away with an oath of silence and a very fat pocket of money and the scam continues like the sands of time. The entire publishing industry is dirty. Its

207

fuck you, fuck you and fuck you, some more. Since I'm on a roll let me expound with the fuckieness of being a published author. Many of the Vanity publishers have a laundry list of a la carte items. One of their biggest cons is offering the innocent first time author a "Celebrity Review" for a ridiculous fee. You buy a package of five supposed top book reviewers, they won't tell you who they are until you pay the, 'absolutely no refund' fee before you get the list. You only get to pick one of the five celeb reviewers. I doubt those top reviewers ever read any book. They too pay some school kid to read it, write a review and the celeb attaches their name to it as it's their work. The best hustle I experienced was from a book store in Colorado. This book store is in a large college town that loudly broadcasts their population has more college graduates, more master and PHD degrees per capita than anywhere in the nation. This particular book store follows suit with the brag of having only the top literary studies student's on their staff. This book store is full-on with social media marketing. Supports several reading and discussion groups and offers a weekly new book review by their staff. So you have these pimple farmers not old enough to drink in public, reviewing the NYT's top ten books. I paid a week's pay for a three hour book signing with their promise to broadcast my signing event on all of their social media channels along with newspaper tags and window show cards. I had to supply two laminated 11x17 posters for their windows advertising my appearance two weeks prior to my event. There was no social media entries of my book or my appearance. I had a card table and one free cup of coffee. I had to bring my own books and had to pay them 40% of any sale. All sales would be run thru their cash registers and I would be paid 90 days after any sales for that day. The only thing they did to promote my event was to place a four foot tall, chalk sandwich board on the sidewalk at curb side. I did not have a sale in those three hours.

Woody: Will there be a Trilogy, a third book?

Me: Thank you Woody, I know what Trilogy means. We live in northern Minnesota, we don't call anything a 'third something'. We are in hockey country, we call it a 'Hat Trick.' But to answer your question no I don't see a third book. Again, I'm 70 years old and I just no longer have the desire. I certainly don't have any aspirations of becoming a top selling author. Everything I've written has come from my head my heart and mostly from my guts. I am satisfied with my two books, it's all out there. I have left nothing on the table. I have accomplished my goals. I hope in the future to see other people, find the hope to their own goals. Maddie you have published a few books for your classes and you know it's exhausting and you knew how to write before you started your first book. It's a tremendous amount of work. If I were to be paid minimum wage for the hours I put into writing and thinking about writing, I could buy us all new pick-up trucks! But that's not the case, I just don't ever see me flourishing let's say financially.

I think we've run to the end of the line with this current events stuff. So I think now is the time we have to go back to the book, 'Daddy Had to Say Goodbye' and as you asked earlier, we will take it chapter to chapter to chapter. If you two don't have any other questions. We will start chapter #1 as soon as I get back from a smoke.

Maddie: I just want to say I agree. I think it is time we move on. We can see that you are a bit weary, we as well as many other people are still sitting in amazement as to what you did for that three day event for all of those people. You have bonded people together who had little or no hope. Somehow through your magic and no one else's, they're all bright faced succeeding individuals today. How did you do that, how does anyone do that? What I want to know is how did you recruit a man like Mr. Roberts who is very powerful, whose very wealthy, who has little or no time for everyday stuff. How did you turn him into being such a kind and loving former hard ass? How did you do that?

Me: Look you guys, I didn't do anything that's something Mr. Roberts did. I think he has always wanted to be a part of people's lives and make friends. In part he has an image and corporation to protect. As you both know, money people are at great financial risk anytime you engage with people. There is always someone looking for an easy buck. Some shithead can simply send a complaint letter threating lawsuit for the most ridiculous bullshit but it is cheaper to settle rather than defend. If you do defend and win, you win nothing. You've spent a fortune and that jerkoff has nothing so you can't recover your losses and judgments mean nothing because they have nothing.

Back to Mr. Roberts, and yes I call him Mr. Roberts when he is not in my company, it is a matter of respect. I have had the opportunity to get to know the man in the last month. He as most people, has a personal fear that has kept him from showing his own humanism and heart. When I tell you he has a heart larger than the entire City of Chicago you now know what I mean. He's just never had an outlet to where he felt he could be himself, so again it's the people that draw-out the trust of other good people. You two openly showed your cards, you earned his trust so he showed his. It is really just that simple. There are some heroes in this world who don't wear a badge or uniform. They are just regular folks with the kindest of hearts and dreams. I have two of them sitting directly across from me now! As I signed your personal copies of my book I wrote:

Dreams are worth Dreaming
Dare to Dream my Friend
And
Dream BIG!

Before we get all sappy I do know that you guys help people develop their own dreams and you help them work towards their accomplishing their dreams. You guys aren't as slick as you may think you are, I know about your charities and I know about your financial support to other charities. I do have to call you out for your calms of being weary of world travel and wanting to sleep in your own bed, you guys are fibbing about that. You want to dedicate more time to volunteering and supporting your charities. That is one fib that I can get behind. You both make me proud to call you friends. Let's call it a day, tomorrow morning we go to chapter #1, see you guys in the morning.

The following morning the Quinn's had a gift wrapped box on the table in front of my chair. Woody smiled as he said, it's from the both of us. I opened it, it was a 120 count, two-pack of, 'Over 50 Vitamins.' Maddie smiled and said, "We have a lot of time and heart invested in you. I want to protect my investment!"

Woody: I feel like we are about to board a not well cared for vintage aircraft. I can suspect some turbulence and flying blind into some thick cloud banks. I guess we have no choice but to trust our pilot and hope that we make it to our destination.

Me: Your pilot washed out of flight school. He is self-taught and doesn't care much for the rules of flying. I at times enjoy my lack of education. I'm not married to the rules of what successful writers must follow. I don't have to have a stable of researchers and editors telling me that my structure is not balanced, word and sentence flow is off and all that happy horseshit that the "Factory" writers have to follow. Or the poor bastards that take an advance from the big publishing houses, and if they miss a deadline they have to pay a penalty or worse yet, don't make sales predictions and have to pay the advance back. I don't want any of that bullshit. My worst problem is when I murder the spelling of a word so bad that spell check can't even give me a suggestion. Thank God for Google! If you are done dicking around, let's get to it!

CHAPTER 23   THE NEW BEGINNING

I smiled as I said to Maddie, "This is your day, this day. Your day has finally come. Ever since we met I have watched you coil like a rattle snake ready to strike. Perhaps more like a starving mountain lion with saliva dripping from your fangs as you wait for the newborn fawn to come within striking distance. The PhD in you is now on the hunt. I'm going to let you feed, no holding back, bring it, bring it hard, fast and dirty. Woody, I will need you to help me pull her off the kill from time to time and remind her to breathe. This is your time Maddie, no rules, no nice, no fear. Start with your first observation, not of me but of the book. This time is about the book, this time is about your experience with the book and where it took you. Well before the time we first met. Start with the cover we are of course talking about the 2nd edition of the book. Maddie I'm waving a green flag, bring it!"

Maddie: I like the additions with the subtitle, 'A Story of Hope.' It softens the title, the title and cover is confusing as hell. The moment I first saw the book I was shocked with my thoughts about the title, the child's wagon, the police line tape, the badge the patches and the firefighter's helmet. It threw me into instant mental overload. Was daddy killed, was he ill and dying, did he kill his child, did he kill his family in a house fire and is he now in prison? I think what hit me perhaps the hardest was the firefighter's helmet. I never considered that first responders, especially volunteer first responders had or could get PTSD. I was under the impression that only military service people got PTSD.

212

I am embarrassed with my lack of understanding. As a clinician, I can only see my unforgivable failures in this critical area of mental health.

Me: I don't have an opinion on your observations. What about the back cover?

Maddie: The picture of the ambulance on the back cover looks almost fluid, like it's already moving. Was that what you're ambulance looked like?

Me: It is a picture of the actual ambulance I worked out of, the only thing missing is the 'Federal Q' clutch driven electromagnetic mechanical siren. Also known as a 'coast down.' You could press the steering wheel horn ring or a foot pedal switch on the floor next to the headlight dimmer switch. The longer you pushed on the horn ring or foot switch, the louder the siren got. There was a siren break button on the dashboard that would slow down and stop the siren using the identical braking system that is on your car. The 'Federal Q' siren was mounted on the right front fender.

Maddie: The first sentence of the first paragraph, "My name is depression" made my throat swell, the last sentence of the end of that paragraph brought me to the tears that had been building in just seven lines. The second paragraph, I call the promise paragraph. It is only four lines but it made me feel like I was sitting all curled up on my daddy's lap with mummy sitting next to us, petting my hair and giving me kisses on my head. How in the fuck are you able to take me down so deep and completely fix me, in just eleven short lines of a book? I honestly resented you for doing that to me. I am a mature, educated, stable, confident, self-sufficient woman and you just took over every part of my being. I never realized that I could hate and love so quickly. What the back cover told me, was that I was finally ready to look at myself. I also noticed that the 'About the Author' section you did

213

not have the city in which you live or your relationship status, as you did in the first edition. Knowing you as I do, I know there is a distinct reason, what is it?

Me: I just copied the way other authors did, I realized that, that information was unimportant, at least to me. How about you Woody, what's that grin about?

Woody: You are the first and only man that I ever watched seduce my wife with your words and I have thoroughly enjoyed it! Our marriage and our relationship has become more honest and more fulfilling. I am impressed with the very bottom line of your back cover, below the barcode. You went from using (or should I say, being used) by an independent publisher or 'vanity press' as you like this say, to becoming your own publisher. I find that remarkable!

Me: I'm not going near that 'seducing your wife part', but what is the value of writing or even reading, if it doesn't invoke some emotional and mental realization. Remember that my core reason to write is to, "Stir your soul, not with a mixing spoon but with a Canoe paddle." Let's move on. Maddie, you got the ball.

Maddie: I love the very first page, I like the open page that you created where you allowed yourself a place to both sign and leave a personal message to your readers. That was very respectful. I also like the power you show with your name on the "Published by David J. Brown Books LLC." It says, 'I did this, I own this. This belongs to me.' I love your strength. The note from the author on page iii cracked me up, that is you. That is all of you! You take no shit from anyone and no one gets to tell you what to do. You really are a Viking at heart aren't you?
   I counted fourteen reader reviews. Each reader speaks of what you personally did for them and how you changed their lives. Authors write to entertain. But you in fact, write to change people's lives. This is God's grace, to gift you with such a rare talent.

Woody: I very much liked that you thanked Ms. Lombardo and Ms. Simpson on page viii. That was classy and kind. Your humility was glowing.

Maddie: You flung the door open with your dedication to your son. You made it abundantly clear that this book is not for or about you. It is for your readers. In your acknowledgments you used the words honor, remembrance, respect, admiration, reverence and humble gratitude. Your blood truly is red, white and blue, you are a lover of all mankind. Page X brought me up short when I read, 'With thanks to the women that loved me'...speaks of your loss and sorrow. 'For as long as they could'....speaks of your understanding and forgiveness. That is very powerful, I think that is where it began for me. You took my heart. In the next line you spoke of your gratitude for those who continue to stay with you. That again is remarkably humble.

Me: I thought we were taking this chapter by chapter not page by page. Jesus Christ we will be here forever. I know what you are both doing, your angling for a third book or as Woody was so kind to call to my attention, a 'trilogy.' That is not going to happen! Next please. They looked at each other as to say oh shit, we just got caught, again!

Woody: We need to discuss the introduction on page Xi. We knew how it affected us, we watched how it affected several hundred people in just three short days. David, we and all of them saw how it affected you as you read it. You were so raw and so gut honest and god honest, that you captured every mind and heart of each of us in that room!

Me: Thank you, let's just speak of chapters rather than each page. Do I need to send Vicki out for shock collars for you two? Reset your focus, you guys make me feel like a woman sitting at a bar having to listen to some loose lipped lounge lizard, telling me how pretty I am. So before you make me puke, I'm going out for a smoke and for you two to screw your heads on straight. This time isn't about me it's about you, it's about your experience how it made you look at yourselves and the effects in your lives today. I'm done with your amateur 'Best author Best Book reviews'. Get into your guts and stay there.

I went to Vickie's office, I didn't knock, tap or announce myself. I just opened the door and barged in. Vicki was at her computer, she looked up with a smile but sucked it back when she saw my face. I looked at the tape dispenser on her credenza as I asked, "You have more tape?" She nodded her head, I said get it and load your copy machine, as I took a legal pad from her desk. I looked at her still sitting at her desk and with a frown I asked, "You still here?" Vicki jumped from her chair and went to the supply closet next to the copy machine. She came out with a full roll of tape and a ream of copy paper. She had a fearful look as she was loading the paper into the copier. I took a pen from her desk caddie and wrote on the notepad. "It's about me, not him" and tore it from the notepad. I wrote another page, "It's about how it made me feel." I tore that page off and on a third page, I wrote "Don't poke the Bear." I turned to Vicki who was now standing stock still with a look of confused dread. I told her to use her computer to make signs of the three pages I just handed her. "I want 50 of each page, in 24 point type, all caps. When I come back from my smoke I will tap on your door, wait until I get into the conference room and close the door. One minute after I close that door you come in, don't knock or announce yourself. Come in without a look or word to anyone, just start taping these sheets as high as you can reach all the way down to the floor. I want them side-by-side. I want the entire wall to be covered with those sheets like its wallpaper."

Vicki gave me a shocked look. I knew what she was thinking as I said, "Don't worry about the tape ruining the paint, I will repaint the son-of-a-bitch myself. When you are done don't look at anyone, just step out and slam the door hard enough to wake the dead."

I finished my smoke and tapped on Vicky's door and I went into the conference room and closed the door behind me. It had to have been exactly 60 seconds and probably not a second on either side, as I instructed her, when she came in the door. The Quinn's sat statue still and stared with a look of shock as Vicki went to wallpaper the entire wall behind me.

I spent that time looking down at my shoes as if I didn't notice that she was even in the room. Except for when she was done, she went to the door and looked at the Quinn's and said, "I think you guys pissed him off."

She did a little kid finger hand wave as she said in a little kids voice, bye- bye, as she softly closed the door and laughed like a drunken sailor all the way down the hall and into her office. I could tell that they were taking their spanking seriously but were doing their very best not to burst out in laughter. I looked at the wall for a moment then looked back at them and said, "You may now laugh" and they did!

Me: We are done for the day. Enjoy your weekend we start with chapter #1 on Monday.

CHAPTER 24   FLESHING IT OUT

Revisit of Chapter 1 *'TIME FOR THE TRUTH'*
Monday 7:00 am

    Woody: David, I've been looking forward to this day for a very long time. To actually start looking into the book itself and into the character Clinton Flanagan is breathtaking. I do however have reason to pause with admitting my reluctance to risk opening any old wounds and yet that's all part of our process. Are you ok with that?

    Me: Kids, I lived this life. I wrote this entire book about this life. I relived this life as I wrote it. Your concerns are appreciated but are not necessary. Let's get to it.

    Maddie: In reading the first paragraph with the physical description of Clinton Flanagan and to see that it is an identical match to the man we are sitting across from at this moment, is startling. Startling that I would never have guessed in a million years, that Clinton Flanagan was such a greatly battered and damaged child. It does not fit with the physical description not at all, yet it is true and real. The title of your second book, 'Flesh of a Fraud,' is however very fitting. Flanagan's will to survive is astounding. The level of understanding and forgiveness testifies to his human spirit. The way Flanagan give his mother a voice as to where all this came from, I think is remarkable. To say he is grateful for Gods mercy in his mother's passing is again perplexing to most people. If there is such a thing as warranted or justified hatred, most would understand it, if not applaud it in this case.

David do you understand or have you heard of the, "Stockholm Syndrome?"

Me: Yes Maddie, I'm well versed on it. I had heard of it prior to my being taught of it in the police academy. In short, my understanding of the 'Stockholm Syndrome' is when a hostage develops a kinship, a fondness of sorts with the hostage taker when police have the suspect cornered in a standoff. There have been situations where the hostage has taken-up arms to protect the suspect from the police. There is a developed sympathy, even an empathy to the point where the hostage could possibly be willing to take a bullet intended for the suspect. They see the perpetrator as a victim and the police as the perpetrator. There have been times when hostages have formed a human ring around their captor to provide him a shield. Sweetheart, I get what you're driving at and its fun to show off my knowledge and life experience. But at no time did I ever believe I deserved to be beaten or starved. It took me many years to practice forgiveness. Yes I understood the why but I will not ever allow myself to give approval.

I also get the other thing what you're driving at, you think I was protecting my mother because all of us as humans want to believe that we have been loved by our parents. Parents are supposed to be the protectors, the providers of safety, shelter and food. Neither of my parents provided anything other than four walls and a roof and that was only because they needed them too. I was just baggage, nothing more than a financial liability.

The reason I'm coming so hard with this is I want you to understand just how insidious alcoholism and drug addiction is! I don't believe any two people would get together just to have kids with the sole purpose to fuck them up as some kind of sport or entertainment. My parents were sick. Their sickness made them evil but they were not evil, they were sick. They became well and the evil left them, but it stayed with me. I am still haunted by those early years, the memories still make me sad. Sixty years later and I still cry over those times.

219

Woody: David, are you aware that you just spoke of yourself in Clinton Flanagan's character?

Me: Good catch Woody. Yes, the back cover clearly speaks of my life running close parallels to that of my main character. Admittedly there are times when the two blend to the point where we become one. We are each other, a second self, perhaps my alter ego. I carry no shame about my being out of balance with the rules of writing. I don't write for anyone's approval, I write for your, mine and my reader's wellness.
My coping skills are extreme because my life's conditions were extreme. I have no problem with telling the literary police to go fuck themselves.
I follow the laws of God, country and decency. Beyond that nobody tells me how or what to write.

Maddie: David, I love your toughness and more than that I adore your ability to set your own boundaries. But isn't it self-defeating to resist the 'status quo' of the literary world?

Me: No, they need my truths because they have none. They hide behind college degrees and the many rules of writing that make them believe they are superior. They speak of their craft but not of their heart.
They write of others, real or imagined because their own shadows are so poorly blurred. I will hold up my writing to any author (past or present) and dare them to challenge me.

Maddie: I love it when your nostrils flare as they just did. It's a sign of the purest of passion and conviction. That is what makes you so believable as an author and a person. You speak of your earliest memories of being hungry, cold and scared and of the police coming to stop your dad from beating up mommy too bad. I am hung up on that statement, "To bad" when it came to your mother being beaten. How does a six year old child develop an ability to measure a person's injuries during an ongoing assault?

Me: My mom screaming was common when he was beating her, her screams had different tones and pitches as to the severity of her injuries. If she was gurgling from my dad choking her or if he was hitting her with a closed fist I would jump on his back and try to strangle him.

Maddie: How big was your father?

Me: He was 5' 11" and about 230 pounds. To answer the question before you ask it, my fear became rage and I lost my fear. I would kill him to save my mom. His size against my 60 pounds had no bearing on my rage. I would have killed him.

Maddie: What is your take on children who kill their parent's?

Me: That is like asking why water is wet. Kids kill for any number of reasons. I can only answer for abused children. For me, I stood over my dad with a butcher knife and the bathroom ice braking baseball bat in my hand several times when he was straddling her and smashing her head on the floor. Before you ask what kept me from stabbing him I can tell you it was God's grace. God had bigger plans for me. One of his plans was for me to tell my truths in my books. God also put you two sitting here across from me at this very moment.

Woody: I am now just starting to understand rage. All these years I thought it was just a description and definition of an emotion. Thank you for opening my eyes to that truth. Rage is an energy from within the body that transfers into boundless courage and strengths. Your rage never took you beyond that point of no return. I couldn't agree with you more, it could not be anything else, other than God's loving grace!

Maddie: With all the violence in your home and the many severe beatings you suffered, it would be understandable if you ran away. You did not run away or ask for help from the authorities. Why not?

Me: I had to stay to protect my mom. Besides, if I went to the authorities my dad would beat my ass even more. Child Services did not deal with battered children issues.

CHAPTER 25   THE BIG GULP

Maddie: I need to take a huge risk with you. I am willing to risk it all because it is that important to me. This is the most important question I could ever ask you or any other human being. I need the truth so I can begin to understand. With this truth from you I can teach all of the world of this incredible phenomena.

David there is a quiet rumor that we picked up on the first morning that you spoke and introduced yourself to us. It relates to your loyalty to your mother and to the understanding you developed and the forgiveness you favored your parents with. Fuck, I hate asking this but I must. David are you an illegitimate child or were you adopted by one parent?

I got up from my chair and said, "I'm going for a smoke, I will come back." And I left the room. I knew this game of patty-cake had to end at some point. Maddie is nobody's dummy. She has an intuition that is far beyond what a PhD could be taught. Maddie has a gut and a very compassionate and old soul. I can't lie to her, she deserves the truth. Well it's the truth as far as I know it.

Me: Maddie, I am proud of you, I applaud your courage. It speaks well of your character. So babe here it is:

I got a phone call on Christmas day of 2015. My first book, "Daddy Had to Say Goodbye," came out in August of that year. The caller was an elderly woman who had been a family friend

223

before I was born. She told me that she read my book and felt that I should be told the truth.

She told me that my dad had an affair with a woman who became pregnant. My parents were Catholic so abortion was out of the question. Because of my brother, Donnie's hereditary blood cancer my parents feared having another child. My dad had his girlfriend sign into the hospital as my mom and used her name. My dad's insurance covered the costs. I was born and my parents took me home. The woman caller wished me a Merry Christmas and hung up.

I was in my bedroom/office when I received that Christmas morning call. I sat for less than fifteen minutes and found a peace with that information. Was it true? Did this woman have a hidden agenda? Is she a crazy ole' thing with nothing better to do but to cause discourse and disharmony. I don't know, it isn't important enough to ponder beyond a possibility. Is she a frustrated wanna-be suspense writer who needed attention? Well it sure as shit would explain a lot of things however! Was that why my mother hated me? Was I a constant reminder of my dad's infidelities? Was that why my dad knocked me around? Was I the cause of his shame which brought their marriage such discourse? It is quite possible because women rarely had a driver's license in 1948.

A two car family was unheard of back in the day and there was no such thing as a photo ID. So it is quite possible that a person could assume another's identity. I don't need any of that dancing in my head. For me it is just another story. None of it will help pay the rent. So it is a non-issue.

Take it easy Maddie, you did not destroy me, not even so much as a paper cut. You were very clever to first introduce the 'Stockholm Syndrome' as a 'walk thru door,' before you got to the big double doors and kicking those fuckers off their hinges. Let's move on.

Woody: I wish the bar was open now, I could use a drink, several drinks actually. You will never know how much we labored to design the perfect line of questioning to bring you to the big question. Thank you for trusting us with your answers.

Me: You just thanked me for my trusting you but it is abundantly clear that you don't trust me. Do I need to remind you guys that the word fear is an acronym? I can see why you two can't even prepare a grocery shopping list or run simple errands without becoming frustrated. Your constant second guessing brings you back to the starting line without ever going anywhere. You guys should get that shit fixed!

Maddie: I wish I would have brought a bottle with us this morning. I am really ok with the idea of a vodka smoothie for breakfast, a long, long breakfast. You again amaze me, you don't allow any feathers to be ruffled. Your self-control is stellar, but my professional experiences tell me that if that caged beast was to ever escape that the destruction would be biblical.

Me: I gave Maddie the open palm to stop her, as I told her that asking me would be a waste of time, "Why don't you tell me why I'm not a full-blown psychopathic, serial killer?"

Maddie: Damn you David. You just killed another perfectly scripted line of questioning. I have been working on my strategies for weeks. Do you ever tire of always having to be on guard? You look at moves so far ahead of everything and everyone that I am sure that you could be a world class chess champion.

Me: Sweetheart you are stroking me again, I don't need that. I am not that slick or bright. It is just a coping skill that I had to develop to survive and nothing more. Forewarned is forearmed. I had to learn to develop a way to see people's intentions and motivation prior to their actions. If you are going to fight, you damn well better be able to read their eyes and watch their shoulder rolls. All punches and kicks start at the shoulders. That information has served me well in police work. Watch the eyes,

225

move on the cues from the eyes, be first, and strike hard. It's no different with mind games. Read them and you will win. Some say to never underestimate your opponent. I think that is a foolish statement. I say to never underestimate myself! I like to win. Simple right? Balls in your court babe, tell me all about myself.

Maddie: Vicki is right, you are a prick! Why don't you just trundle your ass outside for a smoke and stay there for a while. I have to re-group. Get the hell out of my sight! When does that damn bar open?

I went out to my truck and slid an AA meeting schedule booklet out of the rubber band stack that I always carry. I enjoyed my smokes as I devised a brief plan to derail the Golden Blond Viking Princess.

When I entered the room I flipped the booklet across the table and sat down. Maddie had a 'Cheshire Cat' grin as she reached down into her briefcase that was next to her on the floor and pulled out a bottle of wine and sat it on the table. I noticed the bottle was frosty as she said, "My favorite bar manager came in early today to do inventory. Lucky for you, I only drink my wine at room temperature!" Woody stood up and pulled a bottle of beer from each of his suit coat pockets. With a grin to rival Maddie's he reached into his inside breast pocket and pulled out a third bottle. As he said, "Let's catch a drunks-R-us meeting, I'll drive!"

My turn to grin as I said, "Your theatrics are cute and I'm sure you both had leading rolls in all the high school plays, of course you're parent's probably paid for that too! What did they do, buy the school a couple of brand shiny new, gold plated yellow school busses? Woody came back with a matching grin as he said, "Let's go out for an early lunch, I will drive." I said, "Fine with me, I will ride in the back seat with this little cutie sitting next to you." Woody came back with, "You can't do that, I drove the Ferrari today, sorry pal, no back seat, you will have to follow us in your truck!" We went to lunch.

226

We had an enjoyable lunch without any conversation involving the book. When we returned I gave them one hour to finish with chapter #1.

Maddie: Did you ever receive medical treatment for your injuries when you were a child? The reason I ask is you describe your ears buzzing and having blurry vision. You also mention the inability to hear well or understand. Those are classic symptoms of multiple concussions.

Me: No, but I suspect the same as you.

Maddie: I don't believe that you suffer from any mental illness issues of any kind. When I first read your book I had you down for several social abnormalities and borderline mental illnesses, as most all clinicians would.
You are the first survivor I have ever meet that has not become a lifelong victim from your life's conditions as a child. Again, this is why I want to study how you were able to avoid becoming incarcerated or committed. What is so sad is that I get less than thirty-six hours to study, evaluate and publish a recommendation for the courts, for a person for sentencing or commitment. Few if any, know how to argue their case or can go deep enough to expose themselves for their own defense. Even those facing a life prison sentence will rarely speak of their deepest sorrows. Instead they are most often times belligerent as they scream about social injustice and how they are victims of the system and they never take responsibility for their own actions. I know that I am going far beyond Chapter #1 but my shame just takes me there.
I so much wish the courts would allow more time for a one-on-one with these people. I feel bullied by the courts and the laws time restraints. Please don't get me wrong, I want to put bad guys away as much as you do but some are circumstantial criminals rather than career criminals. This is why I find you so intriguing, you had every justification to go the wrong way but you never did. So do you want to tell me or do I tell you?

Me: Keep in mind that I cut the rope swing, I peed in the holy water and put dog poop in the confessional. I stole UNICEF money and hubcaps. I beat up a nun and assaulted a shit load of kids. As an adult I was a bar fighter and I broke promises and hearts. I am no saint. No I'm not crazy, I'm kind of like the guy whose neighbors would speak about being a nice, friendly guy who must have just snapped, on the eleven o'clock news.

Woody: People do see the danger in your eyes but still seem to trust you. You have an uncommon quality to draw people to you. Kind of like those that want to hug a caged gorilla. I think you are a defender of people that is too humble to outwardly show his own strengths. Your strength is to show other people their own strengths. That kind of ability is not learned, it comes from experience. You know what it is like to have nothing, no strength and no hope. You reinvented yourself, you created your own strength and hopes. You developed your strength and hope to bring to others. I believe you did this at a great personal cost. I have watched a few people avoid you. I think they are afraid of your truths, they are afraid that your truths might also be their truths. That is the power you carry.

Me: I agree with you Woody, some people do avoid me for those reasons. I gifted several dozen close friends and relatives copies of my book. Only a few found the courage to read it thru. Some have not even opened it, others have started to read it and put it down. Their reasons are their own. I did my job.

Maddie: I don't believe there is a professional mental health worker that could miss your genius of simplicity. I do however know of a few who would want to argue it because you diminish their depths of ego driven narcissistic chest pounding.

Me: You got it babe. Throw in a fairly large dollop of
social workers and teachers to complete the broth. Many of the
"treaters" are in need of treatment. "I heal you, so I can heal me,"
is the name of that popular tune.
I believe all people have the right to their feelings but not always
the right to their actions. With that in mind how's bout we take
action and call it a day?

CHAPTER 26   THE QUICK FLIGHT

I called the Quinn's the night before and changed our meeting from 7:00 am to 10:00 am. I just wanted a little time for myself and a meal at Mike's Western Café.

The Quinn's had a glum look on their faces as I entered the room at 10:00 am. My greeting was waved off by Maddie shaking her head.

Maddie: You did it to us again. Every time we leave you, we feel like we just swam the entire length of Lake Superior! We damn near didn't even make it home, I drove right thru a red light on Haines Road and a big, power company utility truck missed us by parts of an inch. You do this to us every time, you suck us dry with the simplest of realizations and we feel stupid. We get lost in our own wonderment of how we can be so unknowing. Vicki is right, you are a prick! We laid awake trying to put everything in order and had to finally get up and we took turns reading your first eight chapters again. You prick!

Now, there is a lovely lady with the most beautiful olive toned skin in Vickie's office waiting to see you. You prick! Poor Woody just sat there with his, 'Don't blame me' look as he said, "She is a free spirit, and I can't do anything with her!"

The olive skinned beauty could only be one of two women, Heather or Amanda. For the first time I realized that they did have a close resemblance, other than Amanda's raven black hair. Then it hit me. When I walked thru the lobby earlier there were three well-dressed gentlemen sitting in the lobby who looked somewhat familiar, it's, the Bills! I opened Vickie's office door and found Amanda and Vicki sipping coffee.

Amanda said, "Don't bother to sit, we have a flight to catch and I want you to know that I met the Quinn's a few minutes ago and the consensus is unanimous. You are a prick! Let's go and on the way I want you to explain to me why I am not allowed access to your office in a hotel that I fucking own, you prick!"

Vicki walked us out of the office. The Quinn's were in the hallway, they both had misty eyes. I looked at Amanda and asked, "Is there something I should know about before I tell you to go shit in your hat?"

Amanda said, "You are going to make my mother's dream come true if I have to kill you doing it! We are going to Hollywood for a photo shoot and a screen test and a reading. I even got you a date!" Amanda and Vicki each hooked my arms and walked me to the lobby.

There was a crowd of hotel workers, the Walker bookstore clan, a few photographers and in the very middle of the room stood Jane and Heather holding hands, each with a bouquet of roses.

Amanda said, "You have two dates on this trip and you better be nice to them," as she opened her suit coat to show her Kimber Micro 9mm in her waistband.

Jane rushed up to me with Heather in tow. Jane said, "I like this woman, I think I will keep her!" I gave Jane a hug as I said, "She will require a pod of dolphins, that's twelve or more but I'm still keeping her." Heather said, "I've never been to California, this is exciting, oh yah, congratulations on becoming a movie star, I'll ask for your autograph sometime later."

So we all loaded into one limo and off to the airport. As we pulled up to the aircraft, Edna was standing at the bottom of the staircase with two other females. As I said hello to Edna I glanced to the other two women and said, "Hello Bill, hello Bill." The women looked perplexed as Edna was roaring with laughter. I didn't hang around for an explanation as I hustled Jane and Heather up the stairway ahead of me.

231

We got comfortable in our white plush, kid leather seats. Heather had never been in a private luxury jet before. She was all eyes, just soaking everything in. I said a few things to her but she never heard me. It was cute but I was in a bit of wonderment myself. An hour ago the Quinn's were biting my ass for keeping them awake and now I'm going to Hollywood for a major studio screen-test and a bunch of other stuff. Shit I don't even know if I have any clean underwear. I turned to ask Heather, she assured me that she packed everything I will need without looking at me. Amanda came to me and held her hand out to me as if to stand up. She looked at Heather and said, "I need to borrow him for a few minutes for a video teleconference, we can't take off until after the call, we won't be long."

We went to Amanda's bubble. She said, "Mr. Robert's wants a word with you. Don't fuck around, he is in Dubai, those assholes listen in on everything, keep your conversation brief and professional. You two are not friends for the next few moments, you are business associates and his name is Mr. Roberts.
Amanda sat next to me as she pressed a remote controller. Part of the wall behind her desk slid open to a standard size, flat screen TV.

A British sounding voice came on and Introduced Paul and I to each other. I noticed a red flashing light on the screen so I didn't lean over to ask who and what the fuck is this shit? I had never done a video teleconference before. Hell I don't even know how to skype! Paul was very formal as he explained that the Hollywood trip may be a bit rocky because he bought studio time away from some big producers and directors in mid-project. "They are not happy about it, but the studio is. You have two of the top entertainment representatives in the business on board with you. Take and heed their council. They work for you and me. Don't allow anyone else try to befriend you. Don't let anyone separate you or Heather from your lawyers. They will try to steal your work thru bogus contracts. Enjoy your flight and trip Sir."

The screen went blank and the TV went back into the wall. I looked at Amanda and mouthed if it's ok to talk. She held up a finger as she picked up a flush mounted wall phone and asked if the line is secure and closed. I heard a voice say, 'affirmative, disconnect is complete all commutations are secured.'

I leaned back and took a cigarette out, Amanda snatched it from my fingers and said, "Get your own damn cigarette, this one is mine." Amanda reaffirmed what Paul said, about some pissed off people getting bumped off their schedule for a 'nobody' screen test. "Personally I think they are scared shitless that the studio might suspend their project and go right into yours. We're going to the big leagues Skippy, there ain't no turning back once we take off. Are you in?"

I looked at her and said, "I have never had this kind of a dream, yes I am ready but I will need your help to keep me centered. How long are we going to be there for?" Amanda said, "At least four days maybe six. I want you to be comfortable, I want you to have Heather and Mother with you every step of the way. Unless that will bother you. If it does we will entertain and take good care of Heather. That's your call to make. Time will go fast, there are a lot of people involved in this project and they are the best of the best. They will expect you to be at your best as well. None of them know anything about you or your book and they don't care. At least for now. Be patient with them, the two agents you called, 'Bills' will fill you in once we are airborne. Listen to them, they know the game. I am staying with you all for the duration. Mother is a bit under the weather so I'm going to look after her. Ignore us and please go along with the studio requests, they work crazy hours and will try to squeeze everything you got out of you. Keep it in the front of your mind that everyone you will be meeting wants the best out of you and the best for you. These are the people that want you to become an actor, they are on your side. Now let's go upfront so I can watch you squirm as you apologize to the two top entertainment lawyers in the world for you calling them, 'Bills' was it?"

CHAPTER 27   IN A HEARTBEAT

We left the Pod and walked to the main cabin. The door of the jet was closed and the engines were starting to whine to life. Just as we got to the two, "Best entertainment lawyers in the world," I glanced at Heather and Jane. I saw Jane's eyes suddenly flutter and her head fall on to her left shoulder with her tongue lulling and the left corner of her mouth droop. I grabbed Amanda's arm and whispered, "Go tell the pilot to call for an ambulance, Code 3, your mother is having a stroke." I told Edna to get an oxygen bottle with a mask from the medical cabinet. I lifted Jane from her seat to the floor with the help of several Bills. Janes face was losing color and she had a thready pulse. She was breathing slowly as if she was sleeping. Her eyes were open but vacant. The ambulance arrived in less than ten minutes, the paramedics were quick and fluid as they started an IV and administered Jane the drugs. The scope on their heart monitor indicated a slight A-fib from what I could see. As they were readying Jane to deplane via stretcher I looked over to the lawyers who I had yet to meet and said, "Call whoever my appointments are with and cancel, don't postpone, cancel." Amanda shot me a quizzical look, I smiled and said, "Family is more important!" I asked which Bill was driving and told him, "Do not follow the ambulance closer than 200 feet behind. You will stop for all traffic lights, you getting in a wreck will not help Jane or anyone else. These paramedics are top-flight, Jane is in excellent hands." The one medic gave me a wink of thanks, I gave him a wink of thanks back.

234

I stepped off the plane and turned the emergency scanner app on my cellphone and put in my ear buds. We all got into the limo with one of the Bills getting into the passenger side of the ambulance and headed to the hospital. I sat up front with the limo driver to keep him calm and to point out the short cuts to the best trauma and heart hospital in the city. I heard the paramedic's radio Saint Luke's Hospital with a 'stroke alert' and give Jane's vital signs and the drugs they put on-board with an ETA of fourteen minutes. Saint Luke's radioed back that the 'stroke team' was standing by for arrival. I then dialed 911 and asked for five uniformed police officers and the duty watch commander for a high risk security detail.

When we arrived at the hospital several police cars were pulling up as we walked into the Emergency Department. I told Heather to stay with the family as I lagged behind to make contact and brief the arriving police officers. The five Bills started to post at each door the moment we got out of the limo.

I was introduced to the watch commander who was agitated with my calling for him and five police officers and my 'goons' of the private security detail. I explained that the, "Goons" he was making reference to, are former or retired and still in good standing FBI and Secret Service agents, who all hold federal concealed carry permits. I told him that the patient is one of the wealthiest people in the country and the mother to the, "Agent-in-Charge" of the FBI Chicago office and unless he wanted to be giving bicycle safety classes to preschoolers, he would give me the curiosity due the patient and her family. I could almost see him gulp as he said, "Yes sir, it will be a privilege to accommodate any and all of your and the family's needs."

I requested he post off-duty uniformed officers for 24 hour coverage until the patient left the hospital. The patients company will pay the premium rate for his officer's overtime and other considerations.

The watch commander turned out to be a pretty good guy after he smoothed his feathers. He directed his officers to post alongside the Bills and extend the courtesies to them as they would

235

any other visiting law enforcement officer. I smiled as I said, "Captain, the men in the suits call the ball and your officers are there at the protection agent's pleasure." I walked alongside with the Captain and police officers as they paired off with the Bills. I was surprised to see Edna on a post. She gave me a slight grin to cover her fear as she said, "On post sir." I introduced her to the Police Captain as her being a former Secret Service agent who was with the Presidential Protection Detail. I went on to tell him that the patient is her mother-in-law and Edna's husband is the agent-in-charge that I had told him about. The police Caption became a bit taller and a bit more official, as he extended his condolences.

I put my arm around Edna as I said, "Stand down agent, your family needs you. She started to pull away with tears running down her face. I tightened my grip on her as I said, "And you need your family." The police Captain said, "Ma'am, it will be an honor to stand your post in the name of your family and the city of Duluth." I took Edna to the Trauma Unit waiting room to join the family.

Amanda asked me to call her dad. I said, "Yes, as soon as we talk to the attending physician's for your mom's condition and prognosis."

We were ushered into a family conference room to await our briefing. A nurse came into the room and said the attending Physican would be in for a consultation in thirty minutes. I gave Heather a head nod towards the door, she got up and walked outside with me for a smoke.

While I smoked I called the aircraft and asked the pilot to reopen the Dubai phone line and contact Paul and have him call me from a secured line immediately with a strong admonishment not to tell Paul about the incident on board the aircraft with Jane. I then called the Corker Hotel and told Vicki to close down her office for the day and to bring me twenty, $100 Corker Hotel gift cards to the hospital immediately.

Heather lit a second or third cigarette as she said, "You are pretty good at taking over when the shit hits, I'm proud of you. Do you think Jane will make it?" All I could do was shrug my shoulder as I told her of the many advances of stroke medicines and the fact that we caught it so soon, should be to her advantage.

We went back to the family consultation room. Everyone was quiet and subdued. It suddenly dawned on me that the Bills were as close to the Roberts family as anyone else. Perhaps closer than most. I got up and left the room. I went to the four posts and pulled them off, each post was still maned by a police officer. I brought the four Bills into the family consultation room. When they sat down Amanda mouthed the words, 'Thank you' to me. Vicki tapped on the door and entered with a look of dread on her face, I waved her to a chair next to me. I was about to give her the short version when the Cardiologist and a Neurologist came into the room. They announced that Jane was stable and they expect she had a TIA/mini-stroke. It was too soon to do the battery of tests necessary to be sure there are no other hidden damages. The brain scan showed no abnormalities or bleeds. She is week and unable to speak at the moment but thought she would regain her speech in a few days. They did not see any life threatening factors at the moment but she will need to be under constant medical facility care for the next two weeks. Amanda asked if she could travel by air ambulance. The doctor said they will discharge her in 72 hours if there are no further events during that period. Travel can only be by air ambulance and ground ambulance to the receiving hospital in Chicago.

It was hugs, smiling and crying faces all around. Those Bills aren't as tough as they look.

I gave Heather the ole head nod and we stood up to leave the room. Amanda sprung out of her chair and said, "Not without me, you don't!" Two of the Bills stood and said, 'count us in.' I opened my hand in front of Vicki and she placed the envelope in my hand. I told her that she was still on the clock and to remain with the family. We all went out for a smoke.

After some nervous chatter Amanda asked me, "What did you say to that hot-headed asshole police captain to turn him into such a sweet fellow?"

I answered with a grin as I said, "I just reminded him of his long ago sworn oath, "To serve and protect, also covered visitors from Chicago." Everyone laughed as Amanda looked to Heather and asked, "Is he always this charming and full of shit at the very same time?" Heather brightly smiled and said, "Mostly always full of shit, not always charming however and he rarely backs down to anyone. Seems he doesn't have a reverse gear."

I told Amanda I needed her to walk with me as I sent Heather back to the family room. I handed her the envelope and smiled as I said, "Here is $2,000 of your money in food and beverage gift cards, you and I are going to go thank some cops. I will need two of those cards so I can go find two paramedics that looked mighty hungry awhile back. Amanda smiled and shook her head as she said, "You do have style......when you're spending our money!"

We went to each police officer and thanked them with Amanda saying, "A small gift from your law enforcement family in Chicago. The Captain that took over Edna's post was still there. He politely tried to decline the gift card when Amanda asked, "Do I need, 'Knuckles' here to appeal to your sense of reason?" The Captain smiled as he said, "No ma'am, I don't like bicycle safety either!" He and I had a hardy laugh and a handshake.

We went outside for a smoke. My phone rang with a twelve digit number that read: U.S. Consulate General Dubai. I answered and it was Paul. He apologized for taking so long to return my call but the only secure phone lines are at the Embassy. I told Paul that I am giving my phone to Amanda. I handed her my phone, my pack of cigarettes and lighter. I went back into the hospital.

Early the next morning I went to the hospital. Jane was in CCU and awake. Amanda and Edna were sitting with her. Jane smiled and said good morning with a heavily slurred speech pattern. She said, "The girls told me you saved my life, I want to hug you." Edna said, "You saw in Mother what no one else saw. We could have been airborne for some time before anyone realized that Mother wasn't just sleeping." Amanda did a head nod and she and I left the room.

We went to the cafeteria, got a coffee and went outside for a smoke. Amanda said, "Mother does not remember what happened or why we are in Duluth. She also doesn't remember any part of why she was flying or the intended Hollywood trip. She can only remember meeting Heather and what a nice girl she is. We are not telling her where we were going. It would break her heart to know that you gave up your only shot to stardom. David we all believe in you. You are truly a natural and greatly gifted writer. Thank you for putting us first. I would have fucked up everything on the plane, the emergency room and probably shot that smart ass cop. You handled everything flawlessly and without any direction, you reminded me of my father yesterday. The day's before alcohol took over his life. Calm, collected and expedient. Thank you for who you are. I will make this up to you, my family will make this up to you."

CHAPTER 28   THE UNBROKEN PLEDGE

Jane was recovering rapidly. It was late afternoon of day two of her hospitalization. She still dragged her tongue a bit when talking. She was picking up speed in forming her words and speaking in mostly complete sentences. Her thoughts were coming together in small blocks but she was progressing. The doctors said she would need speech therapy and a program to recover her cognitive skills. Amanda repeatedly told Jane that they came to Duluth to meet Heather and the Papillion's and to see David's new office. Jane seamed to buy that story. Heather smuggled Brookie, our smallest (4 pounds) and calmest dog into the CCU. Brookie snuggled into Jane's neck like a neck gaiter. Jane glowed with the feel of Brookie's soft fur and kisses. They became instant buddies. The nursing staff came in and out of the room several times and never commented on the hospitals firm policy of no animals allowed in the CCU as they all petted her and got free hand kisses.

I went out for a smoke with one of the Bills. We now only had two police officers on watch and of course the four Bills. I turned on my cell phone and saw I had a missed call. It was Paul's cell number with a 911 message repeated several times. I excused myself and went to my truck for privacy to return Paul's call.

Paul's first words were, "Don't say my name, are you alone? I said, "Yes, I'm sitting alone in my truck in the parking lot at the hospital, what's up?"

Paul: I'm losing my fucking mind, I have been getting hourly updates on Jane from the girls, Bill and the doctors. But you tell me, how is she really doing, how does she look, is she going to be ok? I should be there at 2:00 am your time.

Me: Jane is coming along quickly, nobody is bull-shitting you, but this is not why you are calling, so you need to stop bull-shitting me.

Paul: You know me too well.

Me: Buddy Boy, I don't know you well at all, but I do know the alcoholic mind quite well. You thinking about drinking?

Paul: David, it is all I've been thinking about! I have read you're Chapter 16, several times since I got the first phone call. I am just like Flanagan! I feel so guilty for what I am thinking about but the obsession is overwhelming. My alcoholic brain keeps telling me that I need relief from all this stress and shame that I am not with Jane to comfort her. I keep thinking that a drink is the same as a sedative that any doctor would give me under these circumstances. I feel the same sickness like the first day I quit drinking. I'm nauseous, my head is fuzzy, I can't concentrate, I can't sit still, I feel like I'm going to fucking explode!

Me: Jesus Christ Paul, you sound just like a fucking alcoholic! Our response to stress and fear takes us back to thoughts of the bottle in early sobriety, it's all we know. Thinking about drinking is natural for us, even without all the stress, It's what we do Paul, we are alcoholics.
The real truth is that you are afraid of the future. You have the money and power to control the outcome in most any case. You have been the heavy hitter if not the bully in your world. You don't have control over Jane's healing or her future and that is what's driving you nuts.

241

There is an old Cowboy cautionary saying that goes something like this: *"Step down off that Mare ole' son, she can't be rode."* Jane's condition is in God's hands, not yours. It is time you pray and you get yourself right with God. There is nothing that will improve her condition with you drinking. There is another steaming pot of bullshit on the stove that's about to boil over, that you are not talking about.

Staying with the wise ole' Cowboy sayings; *'it's time we saddle-up and get to the nut cuttin. We are going to eat this here buffalo one bite at a time. Powder river and let her buck!'*

Buddy Boy, you can no longer be the swinging dick of the West Indies or wherever the hell else you go. The greatest fear of a person whose life has just changed forever is the fear of being alone and dying alone. They know they will never be the same again, they know life will never be the same again. Run your passport thru the shredder ole' son, you are done.

Jane needs you, she doesn't need you to do anything for her. She just needs you with her. She needs to feel safe. Jane trusts you. Think back to last month, when you told me you would do anything in the world to make it up to her. It's *"anything"* time ole' son, saddle-up! I don't know anything about your business and I don't want to know. Spend the rest of your travel time laying out your new organizational plan. If that's too much for you Mr. Wizard, take a fuckin nap. Call when your plane is a half hour out and I will pick you up. We never had this conversation, get some sleep.

I went back inside the hospital. Heather was sitting next to Jane's bed and they were both petting Brookie. Jane was sitting up with a smile as she asked, "Do you think I'm pretty? I am having some special guests arriving in a few minutes!" I could see that someone had put some make-up on her and brushed her hair. Jane pointed to a vase of flowers as she said, "That very nice policeman that helped us out so much yesterday when I was sleeping, brought me these flowers and this pretty doily, isn't it beautiful? Jane's pretty doily was a uniform shoulder patch from the Duluth Police Department. All I could do is smile. Amanda said, "Mother, tell

242

David who the two men are who are coming to see you in a few minutes. Jane started to blush as she said, "I have never meet these men before but my girls said they are very handsome and they do ambulance work like you used to do!"

Just a few minutes later, in walked the uniformed paramedics that tended to Jane. They complemented her on looking so well and on her beautiful airplane. Jane asked, "You saw my airplane? It's a jet airplane, would you like to go for a ride on my airplane?" They both said yes but they had to work but perhaps another time. Amanda nodded to the door as they left and we followed. She thanked them and gave them each, two of the $100 Gift Cards. Jane told them that the Corker Hotel was hosting their company's Christmas party free of charge. Dinner, drinks and gifts for the children with Santa Clause. Day care will also be provided. There will be a second party for the crew covering shifts for the first party. Nothing but smiles as we wished them well.

Amanda and I walked around the block. She said she was worried about her dad. She said he sounded weak, maybe defeated. She feared he would get drunk and stay that way. Stay that way, until he died. She started to cry.

Well, it's not the first time that I broke a sponsor/sponsee confidence.
I think God would approve even if Paul didn't.

Me: I talked to your dad for almost an hour a little bit ago. We talked about that very same thing. Think back to the first day you declared yourself to be a sober alcoholic. Did the people that knew you believe you? Better yet, did you believe you? The one thing we all lacked in the early days in the sobriety department was credibility. When did people believe you, when did you believe yourself? The chance of your dad catching a cold are far greater then him drinking again! Your dad gets to prove his dedication to your mom and to his sobriety. He gets to be the man he has always wanted to be. Being an honorable man is paramount to your dad. It is time you look at him as you once did when you were a little girl.

243

Let your daddy hang the stars in the sky as he once did. Your belief in him, will increase his belief in himself. Now young lady, where do you stand in your sobriety?

Amanda: You sure do know how to cut thru it. Maybe you should be a therapist! I'm doing ok now. I have become much closer in my understanding of my position in life. I am going to work on being a much better daughter to both my parents. Business success is highly over rated. I am going to focus more on my character, I want to be more and I am going to walk away from having more. I want to be a better person. Mother's illness has been a real wake-up call for me. I find it amazing that I could become so detached from the heartbeat of life. My goals were empty and foolish. It was all about winning and I did win but I got nothing other than the drive to win again. I think it's time to challenge my fear of intimacy. I have been running from my loneliness. I keep my mind busy to avoid having to listen to my heart. Do you think I could be a gal that some dashing fellow would find as marring material? How would I look with a baby bump?

Me: Why did you drink?

Amanda: To shut down my loneliness.

Me: To quit drinking, does nothing to change your emotions. You have been treading water for 22 years but you have learned very little about how to swim. For me, it's about finding balance. It's always about and can only be about balance. Sweetheart, maybe now you can understand when I say that, 'I am no less an alcoholic today than I was the last day I drank on August 7th 1991.' I still got it babe, I will always have it. Today I get to manage it, and that is where I derive my hope from. I suggest you change your verbiage.
Take it from, *"I have to do…… to…… I get to do."* That simplicity could start you on a whole new path. Perhaps that is what you have

244

always wanted? I got nothing on that romance stuff. As for your marketability you are a beautiful woman in any man's book. For me, I just like your butt! Amanda punched me on my shoulder and laughed. I smiled as I told her to lighten up on her posture and power walk. Learn how to stroll, stop marching like you are going to blast thru a fuckin brick wall. 'Wonder Woman' is not real. Get softer, become approachable. No guy wants to fuck a Mako Shark! You set up that persona to put you on the same plain as your male counterparts. You have taken it too far and you border bitchdome. Turn down the volume a few notches and you will like yourself as others do. Practice breathing, you have become a rigid gasper. I get you and I see thru your defense plan but most men don't have the balls to dance with Satins little sister. You do understand where this conversation is taking you don't you?

Amanda: I am not sure. Tell me?

Me: I will tell you the same as I told your dad less than an hour ago. You listen-up and listen hard. It's over, the band has stopped playing and they are packing up their instruments. You have nothing more to prove. You have won, you have enough money to retire a big assed hunk of the national debt. Walk away and walk into the life you want. I am done with the lecture. Do as you wish. Lastly, remember this: I still think you have a nice butt.

Amanda leaned over and kissed my cheek as she said, "I don't know anybody with more life and death experience than you. I don't know how you have stayed sober and survived all the loss you have had to deal with. I trust your opinion, I will do what you have suggested and hope to someday carry your level of strength and wisdom. God put you in our lives for a reason and I will always honor that. There will be a time for me and that romance stuff later, the only thing on my mind now is to take care of my mother. I'm sure my dad and I will find the right people to run the business. I will never forget your sacrifice in caring for my mom and us."

I got the call at 1:40 am as to Paul's ETA and headed for the airport. Paul came off the plane looking like sun dried dog shit. I gave him a hug and told the Bills to go to the hotel and that Paul is coming to my house to sleep. We got into the truck and before I could tell him that we were not going to talk on the way to the house, he was already fast asleep. I steered him into the guest room where he was snoring before he hit the bed. I removed his shoes and put a blanket over him.

I woke to Heather's and Paul's voices coming from the kitchen. I staggered to the kitchen and toward the smell of fresh coffee. I was shocked to see the stove clock showed 8:50 am. Heather read my eyes as she said, "You've been awake for more than sixty hours. Jane is having tests until noon. You needed the sleep. The Roberts women are sleeping in also, come join us. I took the day off to get to know this lovely man better."

Paul looked remarkably fresh. We just lightly chatted thru two additional pots of coffee before I grabbed a shower and fresh shave. Paul announced that the Bills insisted on picking him up to take him to the hospital. He went on to say that he needed some private time with his girl before everyone showed up.

CHAPTER 29   THE STRANGE NEW NORMAL

Paul called before we left the house to come to the hospital. He said that Janes doctors in Chicago reviewed her test results and told the Duluth doctors to keep her there for an additional two days, they didn't like some of the lab work and wanted to balance her oxygen levels before her flight home. Paul said, "Jane would like to visit in private with Heather. I guess us boys and girls will go for lunch."

I went into the hospital with Heather. Everyone was there. Jane almost jumped out of bed when she saw Heather. She opened her arms for Heather and held her close with several cheek kisses. The girls had a bit of a shocked look on their faces. We all excused ourselves and walked to the town-car for lunch. Edna said she wanted to go to that, 'Mike's Western Cafe' mom and pop restaurant in the Western Hotel. It was my turn to look shocked as my only mention of Mike's Place was in my new book that was not yet complete. Edna had a naughty little girl grin as she said, "I found a few pages of your draft in the recycle bin at the hotel."

I made a mental note to speak with hotel security when time allowed. We went to 'Mikes Western Cafe' for lunch.

I explained the significance of the Western Hotel which is also known as the "Tavern Bar and Hotel" in my book 'Daddy Had to Say Goodbye.'

Paul looked down at the floor and said, "These tiles look just like you described them in the book. I am glad they removed the filth that you so eloquently described."

I told them that the floor plan had been changed several times over the years. It had been several different bars and as of late, the main body was used as an auction house. The only thing left as it once was is the front doors and the rear side door. The restaurant was added several years after my final visit. Paul asked if I thought the bar was still there. I told him, "I have no idea, and I have no interest in seeing it if it was. I would like to see this fucker burned to the ground. I come here most every Saturday morning to meet my pal Bob Boynton for breakfast as my twisted way to make peace with my childhood and my dad. The family that owns this ten counter stool and twelve booth restaurant are very nice people. Mike does all the cooking six days a week, his wife and son both have jobs during the week and come in on Saturdays to wait tables."

I suddenly realized the girls both had somber looks on their faces. "Sorry ladies for that foolish comment about burning the place down. It wouldn't make a difference if they plowed it under and made it into a Unicorn petting zoo. Memories can't be erased and few scars if any, will disappear. It's just a part of my journey, it is a time that was. Today is a time that is. The question I often if not daily ask myself is, "Am I going to give this my power and is any of this central to my sobriety and joyful living today? The answer each day must be no. No, if I want to live free from the bondage of self. So again, it was just a time that was."

Edna reached over and patted my arm as she said, "If it ever gets to be too much for you, I will buy this fucker and supply you the matches." I had no doubt that she would.

We kept the conversation lite thru lunch. I finally had to ask of Jane's condition, her short and long term prognosis. I started to test their emotional stability's with, "Is there anything I need to avoid in conversation with Jane? Does she know where she is and what happened?

Paul and Edna glanced at Amanda. Amanda said, "Mother is still in and out with her memory, she still thinks she is in Duluth to visit Heather and you. She only knows that she is in a hospital but doesn't think she had a stroke because she is too young and active for that. She has everyone's names right, but yours. She calls you *'Green Eyes.'* When we remind her that your name is David she gets huffy and insists that your name is, *Green Eyes.* She doesn't remember what she had for lunch but she can tell you everything in her and dad's closets, left to right top to bottom. The doctors think that her memory loss will mostly clear up in time. She will need both physical and speech therapy. They have only tried twice to get her to walk, her blood pressure drops so quickly that the risk is greater than any reward. There is a lot they don't know yet. We will take her home on Friday by Air-Ambulance. Our doctors have a room ready for her and have scheduled all the tests they feel are necessary. We are confident that mother has received the best care here and that will continue back at home."

Edna said, "I know why mother insists on calling you *'Green Eyes.'* I did not understand it until just now. I never got a close look of your ring on your right hand. Mother told me yesterday that she had the 'Angel David' visit her in her sleep. He told her that she could not leave, he reminded her that the children at the grocery store still needed her. 'Angel David' said, 'You cannot speak with me again for several years, you must not call out my name. The children need you. Than a hand tenderly took hers, the hand had a gold ring with black onyx and a camel.' Oh my god, look at David's ring!"

I showed Amanda and Paul the ring on my right hand, as I explained. "I never take either of my rings off. Of course you all know of my gold and diamond 'Keeping Saundra Safe' ring. My camel ring came from my father. The camel has a 24 in the center of its body. My mother gave it to my dad for his 10th AA birthday. The camel must go to his knees to drink, the 24 is representative that a camel can go 24 hours without drinking. The correlation is, we should go to our knees before drinking and like the camel we too can go 24 hours without a drink. It also follows one of our

249

mottos 'A day at a time.' There is a second significance to my having this ring. My dad had been dead for 35 years when my mother died. My brother found the ring in my mom's jewelry box. My mother either kept it as a reminder of him or she didn't trust me to stay sober and was afraid I would sell or pawn it. I don't know. I wear the ring in honor of my dad and fellow alcoholics. It also keeps me right sized."

Amanda's cellphone rang with a 911. Amanda answered, her only words were, "Yes Father, yes Father, I understand Father, thank you Father, God bless you too Father." Amanda sat in shock and momentary silence. Everyone else had a look of dreaded apprehension.

Amanda cleared he throat as she said, "That was Father Martin. He is at the hospital with Heather and Mom. He said he is in private conference and they are not to be disturbed. He told me he did not want any of us to come to the hospital before three o'clock. Who told him that mother was in Duluth?"

Paul said, "I did, I called for his prayers for mother and our family. Father Martin is a trusted and dear friend to mother and us. But what is he doing in Duluth? Any of you request him?" All heads shook no.

Edna said, "Mother can hardly speak and we know she can't dial a phone. So who invited him? He must have come on his own, how wonderful!"

Paul said, "Well I guess that doesn't matter at the moment. We are banned from the hospital until three o'clock, naps or should we play tourist? Amanda said, "Every time I try to lay down, all I see is how helpless mother is and how we almost lost her. I shudder when I think of what would have happened if we were to have taken off. The doctor said that even thou the planes cabin is pressurized, with her condition we likely would have lost her. I vote tourist."

I took them to the Great Lakes Aquarium. The Aquarium is a private nonprofit owned in part by the city. Many of the city's population call it just another fish tank that the city is financially strapped with. Many suggest to hold a fundraiser to level the

250

building by cooking the fish inside. The fish are common to the area. There are no exotic or salt water fish.

As we were touring the aquarium Amanda's phone rang. It was a Bill calling. He told her that Father Martin needed to see David and only David, immediately. He also said that everyone else can come at six o'clock and no sooner. Amanda hung up and turned to me saying, "Well Skippy, sounds that your exorcism is a go, haul your ass to the hospital, do you need cab fare?"

CHAPTER 30   TOO DAMN DEEP FOR ME

Father Martin was beaming with warmth when I came into Jane's room. Jane was smiling and Heather looked exhausted. I could see her eyes pleading for me to take her home. I smiled and asked, "What did you two do with the love of my life, she looks like you guys beat her up?"

Father Martin said, "Please sit down, this will take a while, I assure you kind sir that this will be time well spent." My comeback was, "I'm taking my girl outside for a few kisses and a smoke first. We will be back in fifteen minutes."

I took Heathers hand and we left the hospital. Heather looked at me differently, she held my hand differently and she even spoke differently. I lit her cigarette and she smoked half of that cigarette before she said, "They think you might be a Guardian Angel and I think you just might be. I am freaked the fuck out but I want more. Please don't screw around, answer Father Martins questions truthfully, I need to know too!" The seriousness in her eyes and her voice told me that she was already convinced. I only could come back with, "Even if I am, are you still going to sleep with me?"

Father Martin said, "I would like to tape record our conversation with your permission. I smiled as I took out my cell phone and turned it to record. He told us that he was on a team of priests that investigated "Marian Apparitions," from around the world.

He said, "David the church does not recognize new Angels. An Angel is a pure spirit created by God. The English word

252

"Angel" comes from the Greek Angelo's, which means 'Messenger'. I am of the belief that you are a message carrier of and for an Angel. I need and want to identify your Angel. I believe that you have been tasked to bring words and deeds forward to our modern times. Let me present my observations of you and your presence. I first must inform you that the church does not believe in reincarnation, as to bringing a person from heaven back to earth, the church believes that the soul in heaven is delivered to a fresh body on earth. My interest is in the selection of who receives an old soul and why.

My interest in you first came to lite when Jane gave me a copy of your book to read. She would only tell me of a startling revelation that deeply moved her and brought her to a new level of consciousness. After I read the book, I too was moved of Janes questioned discovery. What brought me to sit with you now is Jane's report of her experience while she was unconscious on the aircraft. I will speak for Jane with her approval due to her difficultly with speaking. Jane told me that she saw a small boy glowing within a mature man as he was holding her down from rising. She kept trying to float skyward but the boy-man spoke to her softly and told her that it was not her time to go. She felt the cold, tiny Childs finger tips that were attached to a Man's warm palm, on her forehead. The hand, just as the bodies were blended into one but were distinctly different. David, did you place your palm on Jane's forehead when she was unconscious on the aircraft? Did you tell her that it was not her time to go? Did you remind her that the children needed her?"

I answered yes to all three questions.

"David, Janes startling revelation came from the afternoon you spoke at the community center. Your command of that roomful of people who give talk of support but do little of which they talk, transformed them from 'saying to doing.'

Jane phoned me an hour before the AA banquet. Jane told me to watch for the glow to build. She saw you start to glow before

253

you told the community center audience that Chicago was the city of death. She than saw you glow brighter when you spoke of giving the children their own sense of purpose. I was sitting next to her but I did not see you glow. I did however notice how your voice tone and texture changed. Your voice carried your words like an orchestra builds to a crescendo. It reminded me of last year's Fourth of July celebration where the Chicago Symphony Orchestra played the Star Spangled Banner and the fireworks were timed to the music. By the time you finished with those reformed 'talkers of nothing,' I believe everyone in that room would have clucked like a chicken if you told them to. You are not a hypnotist, you are not a charlatan, what you are is a 'heart talker.' Those were some of the wealthiest people in the greater Chicago area. Many of them are philanthropists in their own rights. Those people didn't want to just be like you, they wanted to be you! You being a man of meager means had more than they had or could ever afford to buy. You showed them the difference between the means of wealth and a pure heart. They saw you were wealthy in spirit. You had what they didn't even know what they longed for.

Now my friend this is the core of the, what and why we are talking. As you know, Jane and I do a lot of fund raising work for 'Boy's Town.' Are you familiar with 'Boy's Town' in Nebraska?

"Father, I do remember watching the movie 'Boy's Town' when I was a little boy, but I don't recall the body of the movie other than orphans and troubled boys went there to be safe. At the time I just thought it was a movie, I didn't know it was real."

David, Jane and I were both awarded a plaque from 'Boy's Town' for our many years of supportive fundraising. The plaque was a photograph of what is believed to be the first five orphans of 'Boy's Town,' taken on or near December 19th 1917.

The third boy from the left is a dead ringer for you. Heather brought me childhood pictures of you and I was all but convinced they matched your facial structure and eye set. I forwarded those pictures to a mutual friend of ours at a government office that is held in high esteem with their extremely accurate abilities in facial recognition, using multi-level scanners. Their scans showed a

254

remarkable resemblance between that boy and you in your youthful years. David, you spoke of your Grandfather on your father's side and how his life was shrouded in dark mystery. David, the year is right, the exam proved to be all but conclusive and your personality along with your book, convince me that your Grandfather was the third orphan from the left in the photo of five as the first orphan children of 'Boy's Town.' Tell me of how you came up with the name, Clinton Flanagan for the main character in your book?"

"Father, I don't know exactly, but I am half Irish. I wanted an Irish name for reasons I'm not even aware of. I just picked it. Why?"

"David, the founder's name of 'Boy's Town' is Father Edward J. Flanagan! Father Flanagan had a love for cast-offed and disadvantaged children. I believe your spirit and your soul is shared with the teachings given your Grandfather by Father Flanagan. I further sense you to carry a part of King David's persona. He was a poorly treated child and ostracized young man who became wild and unruly. He found his way thru faith and became a gentle and kind man who dedicated his later life to the betterment of mankind.

I cannot attest to the things I have concluded as to the origin of your spirit. It is however my studied opinion.

The reason why Jane and I have asked you and Heather here is that we are asking your permission to use your name, David. Jane and I are doing a dedication in two months at 'Boy's Town' for a new library. We would like to name the library, 'The David J. Brown Library of Knowledge and Faith.' There is also an attached large study area that we would like to name, 'The Clinton Flanagan Hall of Wisdom.'

Jane and I very much agree that what you did for those Jr. High school, 'At Risk Kids' in your Chapter 24, "Atonement," closely matches King David's deeds that he accomplished in his later days of life. King David suffered much like you did from his kind deeds. You further damaged your marriage and you lost your income due to your kind heart.

When Goliath, the Philistine giant, laid down the challenge to fight one person with the reward of the victor taking the people of the defeated as slaves, David never saw that as a reward. After the brief battle was over and David took the head of Goliath with using Goliath's own sword, David refused to take those people of Goliath's, as slaves.

You asked for nothing for your efforts and you lost everything. Yet your project made a vast difference in those children's lives. Further and much like my own brother, Father Joseph C. Martin, you met another type of Goliath, alcohol. You both fought the good fight and you both won. In each of your cases of victory, neither of you bragged of your conquest. You took the spoils of your victories and shared them with all to enjoy and prosper. You both humbly give the glory to God. I have witnessed first-hand your selfless gifts extended to the Roberts family and the joy you delivered into their lives. David, please accept our most humble request."

Jane started to clap and opened her arms to us. It was hugs all around with tearful smiles. I excused myself as I told them I needed a few minutes alone. I passed the Robert's crew in the waiting area, they saw my tears and started to approach me. I waved them off without a word and went for a power walk. I stayed away for several cigarettes and a mile of city blocks.

When I came back to Jane's room the Roberts crew were all present. The only words I could find to answer Father Martins and Janes request was, "Yes, in honor of your brother, Father. Your brother, 'Father Joseph C. Martin' who brought so very much, to so very many alcoholics who never even knew his name. I am deeply honored to accept your blessings."

Heather and I left the hospital. We talked little but held hands all the way home. I had no appetite so I went to bed. I slept for eleven continuous hours.

CHAPTER 31   FIGHTING TO COMEBACK

I called Paul to check on Jane. Paul said she was making great progress and she is looking forward to going home in the morning. Paul asked if I would pick him up for a noon AA meeting.

Heather said that she would like to sit with Jane for a bit. I brought Heather to the hospital, I visited with Jane for a few minutes and Paul and I were about to leave when Jane said, "Do either of you two, self-important charmers remember that we have a daughter who is also an alcoholic? Do I have to break-up your cute little boys club?" We were all astonished to hear Jane speak so clearly and to complete a full sentence without pause. To hear her humor brought full mouth smiles.

Neither of us had considered Amanda. I turned to Amanda who had her face in her laptop slapping the keys. She raised her head and said, "Mommy said that if you two big boys don't take me along that you can't go either!" So off we went. Amanda received a phone call as we were driving to the meeting.

She hung up from the phone call and said, "We are all having an early dinner tonight at Heathers 'Steak-Cheese-French' place. Heather has arraigned for mother to join us. With her doctor!"

Paul and I just smiled as he said, "Heather is sounding more and more like a '*Roberts Girl*' every day."

Father Martin was dining with Monsignor Popish from the Catholic college.

Jane was beaming with joy to be out of the hospital. She sat between Heather and Amanda and was speaking with good clarity and her thoughts were clear. I don't know how either of those women got to eat a bite.

Jane just kept patting and squeezing their hands all thru dinner. Jane said, "David, did you know that this doctor here said I almost died? I told him that you said that I couldn't because I have to go grocery shopping." Everyone kept a straight face. Jane than said, "David, do you know that Heather has a real pretty gun and that her name is, 'Muffy-Ann?'
Do you have any guns David?"

We all just sat and smiled. We have all been assured that Jane's recovery would be a bit slow but the doctors do expect a full recovery. We were sitting there watching Jane working thru her memories and piecing things together. I am sure that everyone offered up a prayer of thanks to God.

We all said goodnight and goodbye. The Roberts plane was going wheels-up at 04:00 in the morning to be ahead of the air-ambulance take off time at 05:00. They wanted to make sure of a smooth transfer from air to ground ambulance to the hospital.

CHAPTER 32   BACK TO THE WORLD

I had phoned the Quinn's yesterday morning to go back to our daily schedule. I had made two copies of my recorded conversation with Father Martin. I walked into the Corker before 7:00 am. The desk clerk waved me over and handed me two cartons. One with a return label from the "Haberdashery on the Magnificent Mile." The other package was a 5in x12in x 12in overnight carton with a gold, raised embossed return label. I thanked her and dropped them in my shoulder bag.

The Quinn's had a look of both relief and concern. It was warm hugs and smiles but I could feel the tension in their bellies.

Me: Let's have it, something ain't right in river city......
give!

Woody: We have been following Jane's condition and progress. We didn't want to impose or disturb anyone so we stayed away from you, the family and the hospital. Edna and Amanda gave us updates a few times each day. Can we talk about the Hollywood trip, we know that it was you who canceled it?

Me: This ain't my first time riding this choo-choo train. I am old school and I believe in the teachings of the old timers. One of those pearls of wisdom goes like this........'Ya dance with who brung ya!'

259

I am nobody's hero. I saw Jane was sick and I reacted like I have thousands of times before. It just so happened to be Jane this time.

As far as the Hollywood deal, without Jane there would have never been a Hollywood deal. It was her dream and her money that put this whole Hollywood thing together, not mine. I dare say that the money she had to put up would rival the cost of a new 15,000 sq. foot house. If it were my own money I would have been crushed with that aspect. I have never had the luxury of entertaining that kind of dream of having my book made into a movie or my starring in it. I am not going to trap myself in sorrow of what it could have been. I will always remember, that intentions and plans are often times the sweetest of all rewards.

I reached into my bag and took out a copy of the disk I recorded. I slid it over to Maddie and said, "Listen to this. I'm going for a walk when I come back you tell me if we need to go any further with any of this. If I'm gone for a while listen to it a second time. If I'm gone beyond that time do some coloring and try to stay in the fucking lines, for a change."

I went up to my office and placed the unopened overnight box from the desk clerk in the safe and took a nap.

I had the most restful twenty minute nap in many years. The mattress and pillow were some kind of foam that seemed to cuddle me. My first thought was to slip the hotel maintenance guys a few bucks and have them swap this bed with my bed at home. I had to shake my head at my foolish thought. "No Brown, it will stay where it is, quit screwing with things that are meant to be."

I rode down the elevator thinking of what the Quinn's take is on Father Martin's words. The ride wasn't long enough to complete my thoughts so it was outside for a few smokes.

I went to Vicki's office to say hello and hopefully get a hug. Her door was closed and I heard voices of two different women. I sucked in a lung full of air and went to join the Quinn's. I smiled as I said, I would like to see your art work. I was met with two sets of wide and smiling eyes. I said, "Ok you tell me if we have any more to discuss."

Maddie: You are a puzzlement. Every time we think we have you pinned down, you pop-up somewhere else. You are a human whack-a-mole!

Father Martin took us to a much deeper understanding of what that *"Special"* thing about you is. Our thoughts ran alongside of Father Martin's but he went far beyond any vision we had. We saw you praying to have your entire family die, so you could go to an orphanage as your safety. David, children don't pray for those things and no child sees an orphanage as a safe place. But you did, it speaks of the torture of your young mind. Is there a chance that you saw the movie "Boy's Town' with Spencer Tracy and Mickey Rooney before you prayed for your family's demise?
Beyond that you have an ability to see a damaged soul long before there are any spoken words. Your first two wives, along with Heather are all adopted! I don't think you placed a newspaper add looking for attractive females to marry who were adopted. You possess some kind of intuition if not a spiritual radar that takes you to them. You have known such deep pain and loss, that it has put you on a lifelong rescue mission. We have not lost sight of the fact that your parents met in an orphanage when they were children. Do you David, believe that you have been directed to save souls by a higher power?

Me: The short answer is yes, no, maybe. I don't know. I have had those very same questions. I am guilty of being a 'helper' perhaps but I am no longer a rescuer. I sure as hell don't run into burning buildings or break up bar fights anymore. I try to help people that want to stop drinking when they ask for it. I don't do interventions. If there was one single greatest lesson learned in my years as a paramedic and police officer it is this. "You can't save or protect a fool from themselves!" As a kid I was a protector because I knew what it felt like to be bullied and beaten. I beat bullies and then I became one. The only normal I ever knew was abnormality.

It's not worth my time to try to scoop out my brain like it's a Halloween pumpkin. It is dead history, it carries no value for me.

Of the three significant women in my life, I only knew that Heather was adopted when I met her. Please don't ask me if an adopted woman is different than a woman who was raised by her natural parents. I don't fucking know and again it doesn't fucking matter!

Look you guy's, I am feeling a bit raw today and these questions and the events of last week have thrown me into a place that unnerves me. I have to tell on myself. I need to admit, at least to myself, that I have become close in heart to the Roberts family. I enjoy the way that they care for each other and for me as well. Yet I feel resentful of the very same. I wished I had that kind of family.

Getting back to the ex-wives, I have and still do carry a deep shame for the way I treated them. My first two wives of course, had abandonment issues with being adopted. I should have been more understanding and supportive.

Two other wives had chronic alcoholic fathers and all I ever did was compound their sorrows and miseries of their pasts. I betrayed every woman that ever cared for me. It was never my intention to harm them but I did harm them. I denied them all a sense of feeling safe and loved. I can never change that. I can only atone by making living amends by being a kind and decent man today. But for me, it will never be enough.

So back to your question. It is still yes, no, maybe. I don't fucking know!

I am sorry guys, I am feeling a bit wounded. More than a bit. One of my character defects is that I try to be strong for far too many, for far too long. I lose my center and my focus. I am afraid that I am not fit to be in public today. The last thing I want to do is offend or hurt your feelings. I just need to catch my breath. Tomorrow morning is about how you felt, what you have always known but you may have forgotten. I want to push thru but for now, I need rest. I am going home.

CHAPTER 33   FRESH BREATH

I woke up a bit groggy but felt a lot more rested. The Quinn's looked their same healthy and eager selves as always. I thought it was time to take them to where my head and gut has taken me in the last week.

Me: I believe that I have told you guys in the past that a resentment is an acid that eats its own container, is that right? Good, I thought so. I want to tell you of my life-long resentments that at times take me over, even yet today. I developed my silent rage as a small child. I knew that my life was different and I was different than most every kid. I knew what normal should look like from watching TV. I knew I wasn't normal. My family was broken, I was broken. I got poor grades, so I believed my dad when he called me stupid. I hated fat kids because that meant they had extra food. I resented kids that never got beat up by their moms and dads. I carried that same shit forward as a teen and well into adulthood. When I was a teen I hated kids with nice teeth and I wanted to kill kids with braces because I could never smile because my front teeth were rotted.

I think my work ethic and the bit of larceny that I derived from my having to pay to get my teeth fixed when I was 14 years old, actually taught me how to set goals. After years of watching my sick brother, drug addicted mom and drunken dad I was ready to die. I had no hope for them or me. I watched my Grandma die, my baby, my brothers, my dad and my mom are all dead. I have no one left. I am it and it sucks.

I guess what triggered this tsunami of emotions came from my time with the Roberts family. Paul telling me that if I had the support and backing that he did throughout his life, that he feared that I would be his fiercest rival. Paul and Jane both still having their parents and grandparents alive and well. The whole thing with the Chicago community center and the many people in front of me with extreme wealth and me with very little cash and a thousand dollar limit credit card, all just hung around my neck like a boat anchor from an ocean liner. I couldn't get away from it. It is embarrassing to admit that even in Jane's sickness, I became jealous of her quick recovery when I had lost my entire family.

I can't and won't apologize for my mind and believe me when I tell you that I wish it were different but it is not. It is just my truth.

I hate the holidays, they are just a reminder of the joy I never had. I want to throat punch all the whiny assholes that complain about having to spend so much money on gifts and having to sit with relatives that they can't stand to be around. I always find ways to interject with, "Thank God all my family is dead. Look at all the money I save!" It usually shuts them up and it saves them from an ass whoopin. I guess I will always carry my rage as I do my weapon. Not visible but within a moments grasp.

My mental wellness is simply not acting on my mental illness.

So kid's where shall we start?

Maddie: David what I have found to be remarkable throughout your book and with the time we have spent with you is your raw resiliency. Most adults don't have your kind of mental and emotional toughness that you developed and used as a preschooler! Your ability to understand and forgive is more than just a bit uncommon, it is unparalleled by any measure. From my

264

experience with working with dysfunctional families and small children you were nowhere in the range of their behavioral models. Most small children who are beaten and starved, fail to thrive in most all aspects of life. Why are you so different?

Me: I learned how to duck and turn away to deflect the physical punches and kicks as a small child. I used those very same tactics to protect myself emotionally. Understanding their pain made my pain more tolerable. I could mentally remove myself as the target and the root cause of their hate. I somehow crafted a way to not internalize the many vicious assaults I survived. I used my mind to ward off my emotions. If I allowed all that fear and sadness into my mind, I would have killed myself before I was seven years old.

So let me ask you, my enlightened mental health professional friend. How many children who are injured or killed in traffic accidents had a plan? Did little Billy really mistakenly ride his bicycle into traffic? Did little Sally really forget to look both ways before crossing the street? Did little Tommy really think he could fly jumping off the roof with a bath towel? Did little David really drown or did he welcome it?

NEWS FLASH: Little kids commit suicide!

Do the social workers, the school workers, the cops, the medical examiners ever do an emotional and mental post-mortem? Well fuck no they don't!

It might upset their well protected sensitivity's. Instead, they hang around the water cooler touting their deep knowledge of football and brag of their kids dance recitals, school and church plays and sports involvement where they are awarded a trophy for bringing popsicles for everyone! Everyone hides from the messy truths of life.

I had two friends (had being the operative) in Colorado. One was a child advocate thru a state agency. She was very proud about her educational achievements and the programs she supposedly designed and implemented. She took great pleasure in posting pictures of herself on Facebook receiving awards from state dignitaries and association chairpersons. She and I had several conversations about child abuse and neglect. I gifted her a copy of my book. She was openly excited to read it, or so it seemed. It's been three years now, I have messaged her a few times but all I get is crickets. Phonies tend to go dark when they are found out.

The other ass-wagon works for the state department of corrections. He sits the top chair of the Governor's commission of rehabilitation for violent alcoholic inmates. We too had several conversations before I gifted him a copy of the book. He claimed that he read the book (which I know to be bullshit) and he was developing a program to coincide with the book and was going to make it the state model for all offenders prior to release dates. He claimed that he would take it national thru his many national and international associations and personal contacts. Do I really have to say, "Guess what?"

These kinds of fucks will let a kid spiral into the ground before they will admit that they don't know. They don't know and they don't fucking care! It's a paycheck with a lot of attention as they achieve unpresented greatness.

I can't believe that I pinned on a badge and swore an oath to protect them phony fuckers with my very life!

Now that I see I have you both blown back into your chairs, I will tell you the real reason I wrote my book.

Nobody wants to see the truth. If you did see the truth for exactly what it is, you would have to admit that you failed. Do you remember reading when Flanagan was a paramedic and how he avoided going to sleep? Flanagan would haunt himself with, "Did I miss something, did I screw up, did I let them die, was it my fault, did I just cost someone their life?"

If the supposed healers of our society asked themselves these same questions we might not have a nation of addicts and suicides! But that of course would be too uncomfortable.

I am a hunter and trapper, of the soul. I wrote my book as bait to lure in people like you two. You have admitted to being caught and you want to make a drastic change to avoid that dread in the future. The beauty in all this is, that you both not only want to change but you want to and are going to make a difference in people's lives from your experience.

Should I take a bow or go smoke a cigarette?

I took a bow and went out for a cigarette. When I came back in the room I sat down and waited. The silence was all but deafening. I smiled my best smart assed smile as I asked, "Mimosa's anyone?"

Maddie started to slowly uncoil, as she said, "I am starting to understand your rage, I got nothing. Neither of us can debate any of what you said.

We finally got to see that thousand mile stare and the chest heaving curse of your 800 pound Silverback gorilla. You can be one scary mother-fucker! I have never in my life seen that level of passionate rage. We are sure glad that you have yourself together. I find your rage to be a turn-on, it is a beautiful thing to witness. And yes, Mimosa's are a consideration but I don't want to break our momentum. Keep going with your rants."

Me: If you are talking about how a Silverback gorilla is the leader and protector of his band that will fight to the death, yup, that's me. I fight for those who can't or won't fight for themselves. I know what it is like to be without hope or help. No one ever came to fight for me so I had to develop my survival skills to continue living. The most powerful thing on earth, is a soul on fire and I was in flames!

Woody: I would like to ask you about loss. Throughout your book you write about people dying and you having to walk away from people and situations, without ever speaking of them. I believe that you are quite foreign to comfort. Where do you go for your healing? Are you ok with discussing your coming to terms

267

with your broken marriages? Have you ever gone for counseling beyond your AA meetings?

Me: That is one hell of a stack of questions. I have pretty much covered the broken marriages aspect other than the residual resentments. Yes, on one side I understood but on the flipside I did not. The emotional part of me would ask, "How about those wedding vows of 'for better, for worse'? How about, 'thru sickness and in health'? The logical part of me causes me to drop my head and weep. I failed them repeatedly they had to leave."

I have a dear friend in Colorado who called me several times when I returned broken hearted from Minnesota. He told me that we must not only mourn the loss of loved ones but we must also mourn the loss of what it could have been. That simple statement put me into a place of surrender. I have never mourned the loss of anyone or anything. I have lived my entire life waiting for the other shoe to drop. I can't risk being blindsided, I can't stop long enough to mourn. I must keep going. If I stop it will catch me, the weight of all the loss will overwhelm and crush me. I know it all lives in my guts and it will always be there, I just can't let it get to my brain. It is just too much. I use humor to combat it when in public, I tried napping during the day to block the pain but all it did was intensify it. My healing outlet today is my writing. I don't have to tell the entire story all at one time. I may write for twelve to fifteen hours a day for several weeks. I take breaks to eat, play with the dogs and visit with Heather. I have a few two hour breaks a week with my pals as well. The breaks help me to emotionally digest what I have written. You two are a great distraction and you help me to stay right sized. Lastly, I have an AA sponsor and I attend two meetings a week. AA writings speak of outside issues and seeking help beyond AA. I don't go for outside help. If I am willing to humble myself, I know that all the answers for me are within the AA principles. I don't have any special needs and there is nothing unique about me. I just have to get honest with myself and God.

Woody: Can you tell us of the last time you had a 'live-or-die,' coin toss thought?

Me: I guess it was the last breakup with Heather. It was a passing thought, it wasn't overwhelming like several years ago. Today I don't carry those thoughts. My life is too good to throw it away. I am finally now, after all those years enjoying myself. I never dreamed life can be this good.

I do my best work with structure. We are dancing all over the place. We covered chapter one Lets go to chapter two, there is a reason the chapters are in sequential order.

Review of Chapter 2   'CHRISTMAS COPS'.....and go!

Maddie: You developed a fondness for police officers at a young age. Most kids are taken by the uniform and the duty belt and of course the gun. But your fondness came from seeing what police officers do and say. But you didn't stand in awe of or fear the police, you experienced them. Is that what made you such a good police officer?

Me: It had a lasting impact to see their humanism, little kids play cops and robbers the same as I did. Even adults think that cops are just for writing traffic and parking tickets and chasing bad guys. I saw myself as a "Goodwill Ambassador" who was a social worker with a gun.

Woody: You beat-up a Nun. At first that is a scary if not a horrific deed. Understanding the back story of that deed tells me it had nothing to do with your being mean or even crazy. You were a warrior at a very young age. When you boys returned to public school did the school principle do right or wrong by isolating you from the rest of the children.

Me: Even at the time I understood the reasons but I felt like I was being unjustly treated. Given the story, who wouldn't

269

protect their gravely ill brother? The extra punches and kicks I gave her was nothing but rage and fear. As an adult today I can say yes, I overreacted and I should have stopped when Donnie was no longer in jeopardy of injury. But I enjoyed it, I was extracting my pound of flesh for my horseshit life. I will make a bet that that bitch never did that again and the Nuns got a firm briefing of consequences of child abuse!

Review of Chapter 3   'THROWN AWAY'

Maddie: You have been conflicted with good and bad all thru your developing years. In your case the definition of 'good' was well below the normal measure in children of your age group. In one 24 hour period you went from the elation of the start of summer vacation, going on to the next school grade, your birthday, to being abandoned, to being murdered or eaten by wolves!
That is when the bells went off for me. That is when I clearly saw a 'life in prison inmate' or at least a state hospital for the criminally insane.

Your ability to connect with those scary dogs and you empathizing with the big stud dog, 'Spec' along with your loyalty to 'Jim' with you not burning down 'Jiggles' house because you feared injuring Jim, told me that you somehow would not be that prison inmate. I believe your compassion for others was your saving grace. Most children do not see the consequences beyond the act.

David, I must admit that Woody and I have tried to secretly study your right hand to see the burn scars from your grandmother. When we first met, you were deeply tanned. Now that the tan has faded we can vaguely see the outline of your burns. I must admit that if I ever met your grandmother I would do a hundred times more to her, than what you did to the Nun!"

We all got a bit weepy and I escaped to the garden for a few smokes. I had not finished my first cigarette when Vicki came out with a cup of coffee. She said, "Maddie thought you might need this, would you like me to sit with you for a bit?" I was about to say no until I saw the softness in her eyes. We sat in silence for a while, Vicki reached out her hand and took mine. After a few minutes she said. I want to give to you what you have given to me and everyone else. I just want to hold you close like a kitten. I am sorry for your pain, I love you and I will always pray for you."

Review of Chapter 4 'GETTING EVEN'

Woody: I have to wonder how many students slipped by me with your similar story. You are right, I put my career before my students. I can't describe my shame. But both Maddie and I will work to change that. Thank you for trusting us. On the lighter side I am damn glad that we are not Catholic. You pissing in the holy water and putting dog shit in the confessional would be absolutely hilarious if not for knowing the pain that drove you do those things.

Review of Chapter 5 'The PUNISHER'

Maddie: The whole ice skating thing is interesting. You were a loaner in a crowd. Everything was a personal affront to you. I don't see you assaulting kids as much as I see you trying to establish your presence and your territory. Your friend Mac gave you everything you needed. Mac trusted you with a key for his business and his money. I can easily understand you roughing up the skates of the snobs and bullies. As a saving grace you did your best work on the poor kid's skates and you polishing the leather on the poor kid's skates was a class act. You having to say goodbye to Mac was understandably heart breaking. Besides having to say goodbye to your grandmother's dogs as she sold them off, Mac was the first person that you lost in a very long list of people that left you. I can see why you became and remained a loner.

I sat for a moment before I excused myself for a smoke break.

Maddie: Have we taken this too far or too deep?

Me: I am fine with your observations and questions. I just went out for a smoke, not to re-group. Keep in mind that I lived this story at the time and for almost fifty years before I relived it as I wrote it. I can't help but smile as the both of you have been understanding to the point of you giving me a pass for my bad behaviors. Can you say 'Stockholm Syndrome?' You give me a pass because you know me for who I am today. One more chapter and we will be done for the day. I'm taking that little cutie down the hall for lunch when we are finished. She is already hungry so we better get to it.

Review of Chapter 6   'SMELT FISHING AND DROWNING'

Woody: Any human would be greatly affected by witnessing a drowning. But for a nine year old kid to watch two men drown at the same time had to be life changing. To see your dad make an attempt to save his friend and to see your dad actually have a brief hold of the man is something that adults have nightmares over.

Maddie: Staying with the smelt fishing drownings, you gave me the first glimpse of how you perceived alcohol to be a comforting agent. I am of course referencing your dad changing clothes and leaving the house to go to the bar for relief and you laying in your bed wishing that (and I quote) "How he wished he could have some beers too, so he could not be so sad and he could feel better, just like his dad." So at nine years of age you had the mentality that not only did alcohol remove sadness and loss but it also helps you feel better.

I would not blame your dad directly for your developing alcoholism but you can clearly see (or at least I can) that you had developed a perception of alcohol being a feel good answer to emotional pain. A month later and you almost drowned, perhaps of your own desire. Either way I can see how you felt with your dad

272

mistreating you and his not trying to dry you off, warming you, or comfort you. Your mother not speaking to you or trying to render any kind of aid to you is heartbreaking for me to hear. For you having to experience that treatment, I am taken back to seeing a child killing his parents. But for the grace of God.

A few years later when you were in your early teens you lost a friend to drowning. You rode the bus with him and the other boys to go swimming. The next time you saw him was the following morning when the rescue divers pulled his body from the water. You didn't even tell your parents about it and you went to his funeral alone and never spoke of it.

I need to go home for a long cry and a bottle of wine. See you in the morning, give me a hug.

CHAPTER 34   SHOULD YOU BE DOING THIS?

I strolled into Vickie's office. She looked apprehensive as I said, "You either have gas or this is a set-up. Are you hungry or not? Vicki smiled a thin smile as she meekly asked, "Would you please close the door and have a seat?" I took a seat at the small meeting table and said, "Come sit across from me. I don't like you sitting behind your desk and talking to you. It makes me feel like I am about to be scolded or I'm on a job interview and I don't want a fucking job!

Vicki: David, I don't know what to do. I feel so much pressure from everyone. People call me and ask how you are doing, every day. They are very concerned about you. I even have to lie to Mr. Roberts about you. I feel like you and I took an oath together and I will never break your confidence. The Walkers call every day, they know about how you gave up the movie and TV deals. All the Robert's family members call every day. Amanda makes me call her every morning after you come in, to tell her how you look and act. Even the staff watches after you, a housekeeper came to my office and said you were sitting alone in the garden and you looked very sad. She was worried about you too! Please don't tell on me, but even Heather calls and asks about you every day at lunch time. She has asked me to never mention her calls. David, there are so many people that love you and worry about you. Now, you are with the Quinn's every day putting yourself thru all the past pains of your entire life. Should you be doing this? David, how much more can you take? Is this going to break you?

274

I can see that you are losing weight and your eyes are puffy. Vicki started to let her building tears, finally flow.

Me: I am lost too sweetheart. I don't know what to say to me either. Yes it's painful to relive those days of the past and to currently think of what almost was. Do you remember our lunch date at the Radisson? (Head nod) Do you remember asking me why I was doing all those things for everyone when there was nothing in it for me? (Head nod) Do you remember my answer? (Head nod) Baby, that answer is still the same. Lock up your purse, this is probably the last decent fall day before the freeze starts. We are going to walk along the beach of Park Point and chat with our toes in the sand. Sounds like you have been appointed to be my new Mommy.

We left the Corker Hotel and walked along the beach in silence for a while. Vicki still was having a few tears. I turned her to me and hugged her. I than said, "You are a precious young lady. You have a wonderful heart and I deeply appreciate your fierce loyalty to me. I don't see you as being just a young lady and I most certainly don't see myself as senior to you. I see you as my equal, you are my friend and I cherish that. So here is the deal. You said you remember my answer at lunch that day and as I said a while ago, that answer is the same. Here is what's going on and why I am doing it.

The Quinn's are wonderful people. They are deep feelers much like you in that respect. They want to make a difference and they are both in a position to make that difference. We are gutting my book, chapter by chapter. They want to use the book to educate the masses. Their work and connections will bring the book to the hands of the people that can directly use it, worldwide! Maddie wants to take it into the medical and humanities departments as part of the curriculum of every University in the nation. They and the Robert's family are combining their money and connections to make it happen. The movie and TV deals would just be entertainment for some and a very dangerous ego for me. Keep in mind that my answer to you in that restaurant of my making living amends, is the most important thing in my life and it will always be. If you are worried about me falling into depression, as I know you and everyone else is, my short and long answer is, I won't let that happen. Yes I'm tired, I haven't been sleeping much and I don't have much of an appetite. What you are looking at and everyone is not seeing is an author who is writing a book. It's that simple, I look tired because I am tired. I am writing every free moment I have, I stay up until 2:00 or 3:00 am every night. And I am fucking loving it. The true beauty of all this is that all the people worried about me are the very people that inspire me to keep going! Not with what they say or do but by who they are, and you young lady are a '*they.*' I am fine baby, weariness shows more on an older person. I am not depressed, I have a shit load of stuff coming up and a book to finish. I don't have time to be depressed. When the book is published and released, I am taking Heather to one of Mr. Robert's private islands.

We better get back, you are still on the clock. I do very much appreciate your loyalty and confidence. Do tell me this, what is your most memorable experience with me?

Vicki: Finally an easy question from you! Nobody thinks you know how to ask an easy question. The thing that made me love you the most will always be, you bringing Marge Kivi into the office and the way you talked with her. That was the most beautiful and purest act of love that I have ever seen. I don't think that there is another person on this earth that could have done for Marge what you did for her at that moment. That is the moment that you took my heart. Sometimes it feels more like a dream than a reality. I have a secret to tell you and I know it will stay with just us, right? Marge calls me every Monday morning and tells me about her and Axel and all the fun they are having. They are planning to go to Finland and visit their ancestral homes. She says she is going to have a honeymoon after just thirty short years of marriage. She asked me go shopping with her to Victoria's Secret for some 'naughty-girl' outfits. Her giggles are so cute.

Me: You have a sensitivity for people well beyond your years. I hope you always keep that, save that girl too.

Review of Chapter 7   'WHAT LOVE FELT LIKE'

Woody: This is the most mind blowing chapter in the entire book for me. The dynamics in play are deeply unsettling. It was your platform that you built your life values on. How you out foxed those people is stellar. You were smarter than they were. They brought the game and you took it to a level that they couldn't keep up with you. I don't know how to measure where that falls into the standards of child development. You are a study in not just basic survival but you cannot be taken off your game. You prospered in mental and emotional maturity beyond most any twenty something college grad. You taught yourself how to think, how to weigh and measure peoples motives and how to take charge in their game. You tell us that you are not educated, your education is on a far higher plain than most all. I can't condone what those people did to you but I see where your mental quickness developed.

Me: It started long before Mr. and Mrs. G. My parents taught me thru their actions how to survive. That wasn't pleasant but it made me tough.

Maddie: I hate this chapter. It makes me so sad. If there was any enjoyable part it would be when Mrs. G was bitching at you about the water stain on her husband's desk and you told her to shovel her own fucking snow and started to walk away. If that was a movie playing in a theater the entire audience would have broken out in applause with the way you took over and put her in her place. Then we realize it was a nine year old child saying that. Not a man but a young boy. So sad.

I would like to see those bastards in jail. I am sorry to say that about your parents but not Mr. and Mrs. G. Your read on them was spot on. You were a toy to them. I can't possibly began to

277

consider where life would have taken you to if you hadn't been so emotionally damaged. I think Mr. Roberts is right about you being a threat to his empire if you were his competitor.

Review of Chapter 8 'FINDING A NEW LIFE'

Woody: You covered a lot of territory in just nine short pages of this chapter. Getting candy bars from the AA men, "procuring" vegetables from a semi-truck to give to the old and poor people in your neighborhood. You taking a sick pleasure in hurting other kids, feeling empathy for them and wanting to destroy them all at the same time. Stealing from the candy vending machine, earning enough money from salt-water-taffy sales to pay for a new candy machine, going to summer camp, having to walk alone to the dentist to have an abscess tooth pulled, stealing hub caps to sell for cigarettes and paying on the family charge account at the neighborhood grocery store, selling Watkins products, buying your family Christmas gifts, the death of your grandmother Ellen, meeting your uncle Billy and meeting your cousins from California. You were a very busy young boy.

Maddie: I will stay on track with Woody's observations but my take is on the mental/emotional aspect of your maturing. You learned that there were nice, sober alcoholics. You found honor in being a thief, with your sharing your bounty of ill-gotten vegetables. Not quite the Robin Hood type act but close.

You looked after and protected the elderly people in your neighborhood. Then you roll into fighting with weapons and bullying kids. Yes the kids were all older and bigger than you but you had no business hurting them because you hurt. You show an incredible toughness while facing the dentist alone after suffering several day's pain from an abscess tooth. You're stealing hubcaps for both safety and profit is unnerving. I can kind of go along with the vegetable deal but I have to draw the line with the hubcaps. It's no different with the candy machine, if you were actually hungry I

278

could understand that, stealing because you simply had no money is a crime.

Me: If this is a lecture on morality I'm going fucking home. Someone steal your hubcaps or raid your garden? Are you done with this bullshit? Think it over, I'm going out for a smoke.

Woody came out to the garden. It pissed me off that he was invading my safe place. Up until now they had respected my privacy. He said, "Dave you hit a nerve deep inside of her and it has nothing to do with vegetables or hubcaps or stealing. She lives in her belly but rarely ever speaks of it. Maddie has an ability to visualize a story as it is being told. She feels the story, when we speak of things she feels those things and all the implications that go along with it. Maddie is overwhelmed with that little boy having to suffer and wait for his dads pay day to have his tooth pulled out. She knew the next thing to come up would be your grandmother Ellen. The love and tenderness you had for each other was just too much for her to face. 'E', Mac the ice-skate guy and Tom the Fuller Brush man all loved you and then left you. The one thing that tears her up the most is that your parents didn't even tell you that E died. You went to the hospital to see your best friend and had to be told by a stranger that the only woman you ever trusted was dead. Knowing Maddie, I am sure she was jumping forward and comparing the loss of your daughter and again you were all alone being told by a stranger that your baby is dead and your dreams are dead too. I am sorry we upset you, we all knew that this would come at some point. This is just so heavy, so deep and so life changing. We can't help but to live between the covers of your book. We don't know how to manage the emotions that you bring to us. Please understand?"

Me: Woody, you go inside and tell your wife to get her shit right. I will be inside in a few minutes. And don't ever come out here when I am on a break. This is my time and my space and it belongs to me!

279

I went inside to find Maddie to look properly scolded. But it wasn't enough for me. I am not going to let her off that easy. I sat down to let the bear feed.

Me: I don't want to hear any apologies or excuses. Look at Vicki's wallpaper job. I had those put there for a reason but you two obviously missed the message. I guess these statements aren't meant for you, are they to simple for your highly advanced minds and life experiences?
Maddie, suck it up, you both better nut-up if you want to run with this dog. Nobody gets to rewrite my life for your own comfort. I don't give a rat's ass about what you think of how things should have been. They were what they were and I apologize to no one!
There is currently an entire society that wants to rewrite history because it offends their sensitivities. Statues are being removed to accommodate a bunch of sniveling pussies and holidays are being renamed to again redirect our nation's history. We have a mayor in this city that has declared Columbus Day to be called, "Indigenous Peoples Day!" Believe me when I tell the both of you that I can walk away any time I want. I don't need either of you. You poked the bear, respect the bear or we are done! I expect to find a box of Larson's Bakery donuts in the morning. See you tomorrow. Remember that this is my show and my time.

CHAPTER 35   REGROUP OR BE GONE

I came in a bit early to visit my office and look at the Express Package I received the week before. I opened the safe and removed the package. I pulled my wheeled desk chair over to the floor to ceiling windows and sat down. I had a complete and unobstructed view of the bay of Lake Superior. I sat back deep into the chair with the package in my lap. I brushed my fingers over the gold foil embossed return address label. (Which few people will ever see in their lifetime). I concentrated on clearing my mind and slowing my heart rate. The view was a great aid to my coming to terms with myself. I shook my head in submission while saying, "No... this is not for me." I placed the unopened package back in the safe and went to meet with the Quinn's.

Maddie asked if she could go first. I said, "Only if you don't try to apologize or explain yourself." Maddie smiled as she said, "Lesson learned teacher, on to chapter 9 please?" I nodded my head with an approving smile.

Review of Chapter 9   'LEADING THE VIPERS'

Maddie: In your first paragraph you speak of kids in your school being of several different income groups. The hostility is obvious with the mixing of these income groups. Is that why you fought them?

Me: I fought everyone, I even fought guys in my own gang if they went against our basic rules or got mouthy with me. I was loyal to the gang but I was even more loyal to myself. Everyone knew that if they fucked with me that I would hurt them.

Maddie: We are back to the confusion of your temperament. The teacher catches you smoking in the school, he takes your cigarettes and starts to take you to the principal's office. You smash his nose and recover your cigarettes and tore his shirt pocket. Which of the events set you off with him.

Me: They all did. He fucked with me and I hurt him. He violated my first rule, 'Don't fuck with me!' If he would have said come with me, I would have gone with him. You try to strong arm me I'm coming back at you in spades. That first rule of sixty years ago still stands with me today.

Woody: My being a former high school principle, I can see both sides to that. The teacher showed his fear when he grabbed your arm, he was hoping to intimidate you. You had your rules, he lost. I agree with Maddie by her saying she is confused with your behaviors.
You could have severely injured those 'Heights kids' in protecting those two cheerleaders, you had a free pass but you didn't use it. Why not, but my greater question is why didn't you report to the school what you overheard and let them deal with it? You were protecting girls that you didn't even know. They were the rich kids you despised, why did you step in the middle of it?

Me: The school would not have done jack-shit and the Heights would have just done it somewhere else. I had to stop it from happening. The school was the best place, they thought they were safe and I had the element of surprise. Don't lose sight that there was a time in my life that no one came to help me. I know how that feels. Those girls were snotty bitches but they didn't deserve to be raped. No woman does.

282

Maddie: The way you rallied the vipers and shut down the Heights was masterful. When you made them take off their jackets in front of all those kids you broke their spirit. The cut up and pissed-on black jackets is pure poetry. Lurch had to be an absolute God-send to you.

Me: That was the first time that I felt my true power and it felt damn good! I would have dropped out of school if not for Lurch.

Review of Chapter 10 'HOTEL TRICKS'

Woody: From your first day at the hotel you didn't follow the status quo. You looked at how things were and found opportunities that have never been explored. The mixing of the evening's dregs of alcohol was nauseating to read. Sitting on the edge of the roof, dangling your feet sixteen stories above the ground while drinking, sounded like two young men that had little regard for life. How you were never found out as a stowaway or a bootlegger or your little enterprise of selling free ice and leftover banquet food, speaks of a very cunning child. Your friend, "Dickie" who killed the police sergeant, was he prosecuted?

Me: Yes the booze was nasty, we weren't social drinking as connoisseurs of fine libations. We were drunks, we drank for effect. Sitting on the ledge was, if I fall, I fall. I won't even know it, I will be dead before I finish screaming, so who cares? We are back to larceny being a lucrative way of supporting myself. As for Dickie, I think he did six years in prison. I had lunch with him the day after he got out of prison. We were at a restaurant where several cops kept coming in and walking up to our table and glaring at us. Dickie got the message and left town the following day. I never saw him again.

Review of Chapter 11 'DREAMS COMING TRUE'

Maddie: I very much like the way you described Paula. I could feel your love for her. I can still feel it now. I can also see her beauty, it sparkles in your eyes. A woman knows when a man is in love. I have a strong feeling that you still love her today. The part where you and your brother got drunk watching the 'Wizard of Oz' on your honeymoon is head shaking. I find it interesting that you wrote of your bitch Homeroom/English teacher and what she did to you and what you did to her and in the very next page you write or the wonderful summer school teacher that changed your life forever. The loss of your baby breaks my heart. It had to have been awful, there are parents that never recover from that kind of loss. In your case you lost everything. I believe you knew that you lost Paula the same night you lost your baby. I can see it in your eyes right now. I am so sorry David, I want to give you some time before you respond. Woody and I are going to the bar.

I went out to the garden for a smoke. A part of me wanted to go home or to the beach or anywhere else that no one would see me about to break. My heart was sobbing. I didn't want to comment on Maddie's observations. I just wanted to run away. The other part of me was telling me that I was with friends, friends that understand and care about me. Maybe it is time, this might be God's will.

I called Maddie's cell and told her I was going back to the room and for her and Woody to double-up on their drinks and to bring them back to the room.

They came in the room with their drinks. Maddie asked for a hug, I could see she had been crying. She asked if I would take off my ring so she could hold it for just a little while.

Maddie: I have to assume that this is the ring you wrote about that you have worn for more than fifty years? Your, 'Keeping Baby Saundra Safe' ring?

284

Me: Yes, I still somehow feel her with me. I only take it off when I do heavy work or garden planting. I wear it every day. It was only forty dollars but remember back then, minimum wage was $1.05. I have not lost any of the three diamond chips. I clean it with tooth paste and a kid's soft bristle tooth brush. I won't let a jeweler or anyone else touch it. Only you and Heather have ever held it without it being on my finger. Now, let me respond to your earlier statements.

I know very little about Paula's adventures after we divorced. I understand that she married and moved to Florida where her and her husband raised some children. I always thought that the less I knew, the less I would hurt. The final paragraph of that chapter pretty much tells of a broken man's future. I know you intentionally left that out of your observations. I don't think you did that because of your education, training or experience. You did that because of your heart. Thank you. Let's keep going.

Review of Chapter 12   'REDEMPTION'

Woody: Strange how you found your way into being a paramedic. Your second wife Liz sounds like she was a sweet woman but not a very good match for you. Why did you marry her?

Me: Liz was a sweet woman. She was a total babe also. Some people look for depth in a mate, I looked for surface. I was an image, not a person. I couldn't allow anyone to get too close to me. I could not let anyone know my pain, I could not allow my heart to leak. We have already talked about Ivan and Sandy. We have traveled a long way today, let's bag it for now. May I please have my ring back?

I had dinner the night before with my friend and managing editor of the newspaper, Leif Eriksson, who is also Missy's boss. We roughly worked out an assignment for Missy for next month. He asked me to brief her as I would be the sole contact for the project. I gave her a call at work and she answered. I invited her for an after work drink. She said that she had time now but had an evening assignment. We met for coffee in the lounge at the Corker Hotel. She apologized for not staying in touch as her new position was very demanding of both time and effort. Missy said that she talks a few times a week with Vicki but that is pretty much it for her social life. She did say that she was interviewed by Mr. and Mrs. Quinn a few Saturday's back. They wanted to know about how we met and if we were friends or just business associates. They told me about their interest in you. They said they were mostly interested in knowing if you did anything for me as a person. I smiled as I said, "He bullied my boss into giving me a pay raise and three evening gowns with matching hand bags and shoes! We had a laugh as they remembered me in my gowns as I said, "I wasn't kidding, David made my boss do those things! I told them I really couldn't say any more until I spoke with you for your consent." Missy said, My Grandmothers think you are a gorgeous man with the personality of a talk show host. They call you 'Hollywood' and they both giggle when they ask me about you. I ask Vicki about you but she is very protective with any information about you. She either says you are in conference, out of town or in your office. Do you have an office here somewhere?"

I smiled as I asked her, "Want to go for a ride?" We rode to the top floor. The elevator of course stopped at the top floor. I took out my keys and inserted it to take us to the real top floor. Missy was wide eyed with that little trick. I took her to the entry door and let her step in first. More wide eyes as she took in the reception/formal living room. I showed her the suite with the California King bed and the 'His & Hers' bathrooms with matching garden tubs and clear glass showers with eight shower heads. Next came the kitchen and dining area. When we went into the office and study area she froze. Her head was on a pivot as she took it all in. Missy said that all the oversized computer screens and the different stations made it look like a space launch center. I took her to the center of the living/study area and told her not to move. I went to the wall switch and opened all of the blinds at the same time. I heard her gasp as her eyes went to maximum

286

wideness. You could see the entire city just by turning in your own steps. Missy asked if she could sit down. She was emotional as she said that she had no idea that anything like this existed anywhere in the city. She described it as, a "private space needle." Missy said, "There are rumors that you own this hotel, and Walkers Books Store, do you?"

"No, I just own this top floor of the hotel, this is my office." Missy looked more confused than ever before. She then said, "My boss, Mr. Eriksson is sending me on an assignment to 'Boys Town,' Nebraska next month for what he says will perhaps be the biggest event in my entire carrier. He told me that if I asked you, that you might let me fly in your private jet!
David please, who the hell are you really? What the hell is going on? You guys are going to give me a heart attack!"

I could only smile as I said, "I am still that same ole' schmuck that you blew off a few months ago that still drives that twenty year old piece of shit pick-up truck. I just happen to know a few people that own hotels and private jets. This top floor of the hotel does belong to me, it was a gift."

"Did your boss, Mr. Eriksson tell you about your assignment in 'Boys Town?' Don't answer, I know he hasn't. That is why you are sitting here now. Back to the wider than wide eyes. Here it is in a coconut shell, because it is just that big. 'Boys Town' will be dedicating a new library and study hall. This is not your average size library or study hall, it is colossal in size and can compete with any university in the nation. These buildings were totally funded by donations from outside the area. There is no debt involved, these buildings and their contents are paid for and will be gifted to 'Boys Town.' Your assignment is to report on the principles of the funding and the gentleman who the Library is dedicated to. You may begin now."

I leaned back and lit a cigarette and watched the smoke disappear as poor Missy was trying to put the puzzle together. I got up and walked around the glass encased room, looking at the bay of Lake Superior and the Duluth Hillside.

OK, time is up. You will be flying with me to 'Boys Town,' Nebraska in Mr. Robert's corporate jet. You are the only authorized print reporter that will be let in for personal interviews. You have exclusive access to everything and everyone. There will be national and international news teams doing a wide coverage on the event. There are four story's that will be reported on.

1 The first and of course the most important story is of 'Boys Town.'
2 The library and study hall and there benefactors.
3 The guy who is talking to you now and who the library is named after.
4 The small town gal who every reporter wants to know how she got the exclusive. That small town girl is you sweetheart. Congratulations!

Your appointment for tonight is a ruse. You don't have an appointment tonight. You don't have any appointments but one, for the next six weeks. You will work for your boss, Mr. Eriksson and me only. Your boss has hired the top newspaper reporter in the country to help you develop your interview strategies. You will do all of your own research. I want you to start with the original founder of 'Boys Town.' His name is Father Edward J. Flanagan. Get that silly look off your face, no there is no correlation between my charictor Clinton Flanagan and Father Flanagan. I am not that slick to be able to build a story around something like this.
I want you to go home now and relax. Pet your kitty, call your Grandparents, sit down with your mom and dad and get ready for the challenge of a lifetime. When amateur and minor league athletes get called up to the pros they call it, *'Going to The Show.'* Missy, you are, *'Going to The Show!'*

CHAPTER 36   GOING TO THE SHOW

Three days later

The Quinn's were all in their places with bright smiling faces. I thought I would have a little fun with them. I started with, "I understand that you two like to gang-up on little girls? Asking questions about me that made her so uncomfortable that she has talked with the newspapers attorneys and is considering filing for a restraining order against you two!" I couldn't hold back for the desired time of impact. I started laughing as I saw the puzzlement and panic on their faces.

The young lady that you guys were grilling will become a large source of information for you two in the very near future. She will carry the real story of how shattered children become whole and prosper. Enough of that for now. Time to get to chapter 13.

Review of Chapter 13   'THEIR TRUTHS HIS LIES'

Woody: Seams like chapters 13, 14, 15, and 16 could have been one chapter. Knowing you, I have to guess that it was not a sloppy oversite. Tell us about your strategy?

Me: Not a strategy at all. Each of those people deserve their own chapter, no different than the three of us. Would you like your major life event to be shared with an ad for Pork & Beans two for 97cents?

289

Woody: Chapter 15, 'Daddy's Little Buddy' ripped our guts out. There are so many levels of pain in so many people. The pain in 'Daddy's' life could be stacked several stories high! The real tragedy in this story is that we know it is a true story. We also know that you were the paramedic who sat on the ground and rocked 'Daddy' like two little kids on a sled with his dead baby in his arms. I understand your nightmares, we wish we could take them from you. We all know that we can't un-see what our eyes saw.

Me: When we put ourselves in the game of rescue, we quickly come to the understanding that sometimes and even oftentimes we can't change the outcome. All we can do is make the effort, the outcome is in God's hands. We face life's cruel unpleasantries that the public wants to deny exists. Remember that I was just the observer to his loss. We all know where his pain took him.

Ready for some freak-out? Ever wonder of where or how our efforts are received? Well get this. One of the principles that I had daily interactions with at the brewery is named, Rod Hixon. Rod is the logistics distribution coordinator. I would check in with him in the morning each day for the game plan. If there was a problem during the day I would seek his council. We had a lot of mutual respect for each other and we became friends. When I had the book published I gifted him a copy. Rod would read a chapter or two each night when he was able to. Being a Daddy to a two and a half year old and an eleven year old took a lot of his time.

He was crazy in love with his kids. He would tell me every morning about something cute, funny or sweet, one of them did the night before. We would also discuss where he was in his readings and what his take was on it. One morning I came into his office and he looked up with misty eyes. I stood in silence until he was ready to talk. Rod told me that he read last night about 'Daddy's Little Buddy.' He said, "I have the identical children's toy bubble mower that you described. My boy walks alongside me when I

290

mow, but never again! We just don't know what could happen. Thank you for writing the book and especially that story." Rod and I are still Pals and when I travel back to Colorado I always make it a point to drop in for a visit with him.

There was a tap on the door. It was Vicki. She said Mr. Eriksson was in her office to see me. I suggested the Quinn's go for an early lunch and I went to tend to Lief.

I knew that I put his ass on the line with asking him to let me have Missy for the 'Boys Town' story. I dangled an AFP, AP and Reuter's coverage carrot. Lief knew that his paper could be in line for a Pulitzer as Missy had all the exclusives to the principles of 'Boys Town' and their historical library which is vaulted and only opened to church scholars.

Lief was looking edgy. I shook his hand and walked him to the elevator, he too took a step back when I slid my key into the elevator control panel and we went up another floor. We went into my office. After the brief tour he grinned as he said, "Who the fuck are you? I don't go for smoke-N-mirrors. What is all this really about?"

Me: For now I am asking the questions. I have a pretty good idea why you are here. How long have you been in the newspaper business? What was your first job there? And yes I know what little Missy has been doing.

Lief: I have been with the paper for eighteen years. It's the only job I have had since college. I was a 'printer's devil,' I worked in the job shop. I set type by hand for small jobs. I melted led for the linotype machines, I ran the platen presses and the AB Dick 360 offset presses. I also had to clean all the newspaper press rollers, press plates and file them. I worked in production for six years. Then two years in layout, one year in reporting, eighteen months in special sections, three years as managing editor and since then I have been the general manager.

Me: Well good for you. And now you are scared shitless that you are about to get caned. I know the owners jumped your ass for the bar tab when you hosted the, 'Authors Reception.' Then we have the hair styling make-over, three gowns with matching hand bags and shoes and now you have to hire a replacement for Missy and for the last three days Missy has been disturbing the entire office with her out of control excitement. The twenty something, owners prick kid hates your guts, want's your job and is pissed that you are spending his inheritance and you can feel the walls closing in? Do you earn more of less than $90,000 a year?

Lief: How do you know all this shit? I am embarrassed to admit it but I only get $53,000. Some of the ad sales reps make more than I do.

Me: Give me your bank card. I'm serious, give me your fucking bank card!

I took his bank card and his check book into the hallway to make a phone call. I came back in and found him staring out the windows at the ships moving in the bay.

Me: Like the view? It's none of your business of who the fuck I am. There will be an additional $90,000 post tax, in your bank account before you sit down for dinner with your family tonight. The money is yours as a cushion if your boss bounces you. The same corporation that owns this hotel will buy the newspaper or start their own. The owners will be talked to in the next hour. How much fun would it be to fire that little butt-munch, owner's kid? Feel better now?

I called Vicki to bring up a note pad and menus for six. "Bring along the lovely Quinn couple. They will need their briefcases. Take the smallest unoccupied guest room and show it as occupied for an undetermined period of time and bring me the key. " Turning to Lief (who was still in vapor-lock over the $90,000) I said, "Call Missy, tell her to drop everything and to get down here, now!"

292

I was waiting for Vickie and the Quinn's in the formal reception area when they came in. The Quinn's looked like they had just seen Bigfoot. I sent Vicki to go sit with Lief while the Quinn's and I had a brief chat.

I told the Quinn's that if they asked me 'Who the fuck are you' that they would see Bigfoot! They agreed with my request. We went and joined Lief and Vicki. In a few minutes the front desk called Vicki to tell her that Missy was at the desk. I told Vicki to go down and to tell Missy to give her cell phone to the desk clerk and to bring her up.

CHAPTER 37   THE HUDDLE

I stood in the middle of the room and the five game players sat on the couches in front of me. I said, "We have a few problems and I have a few solutions. I don't need anyone's input, I want everyone's cooperation. We are going to do this fast, hard and dirty. Please don't interrupt me with any questions until I open the floor for discussion.

Me: Everything I say must be held in the strictest of confidence. Here is what none of you know and none of you are to speak of to anyone outside of this room. We all know why Missy is traveling to 'Boys Town' next month. Or so you think you do.

Mrs. Roberts had a great deal to do with building the new student library and study hall. Mrs. Roberts spearheaded and sponsored the first five girls to live in 'Boys Town' back in 1979. Missy, you would know that by now if you weren't so busy fluttering around the office with being the next top reporter in the world. You are done fluttering, I have just clipped your wings. You are disruptive to the newspaper staff and you are getting nothing done. Between ordering lunch and eating our meal Mr. Eriksson is having your desk and the entire cubical moved into a guest room here. Vicki, give her the room key. Vicki you are to have hotel maintenance remove all furnishings from that room. They will also set up the cubical and cover the windows with black plastic tarps. Missy, I'm sure you did not like having to surrender your cell phone to the desk clerk. You can have it at lunch but you must turn it in when you return. You can take it home at the end of each day.

That's how it's going to be. You are on furlough and this is your office (as I nodded at the key in her hand) until further notice. Now that we have all that cleared up, and I am most certain that there are no questions (as I locked my eyes on Missy) we can move on.

Missy, I know you are acquainted with the Quinn's. The Quinn's are both highly educated and have a lifetime of child development experience. They will be your mentors and chaperones during your visits to 'Boys Town.' I say visits because you will be going there on Monday for three days to get the lay of the land before next month's assignments. Here is what must never leave this room. Missy you are going there to do newspaper interviews. You are going to return to submit your work to Mr. Eriksson.

What we must guard is that you are going to write a book on your observations and personal experiences. That book will be written into a screen play and then a movie. Mrs. Roberts chose you because she wants young girls to know that dreams are worth dreaming.

Currently the student resident body of 'Boys Town' is almost 50% female. Six days ago the name of 'Boys Town' was changed to, 'Girls and Boys Town' by the vote of the nine hundred facility and student residents.
The movie, "Boys Town" was originally made in 1938, there was a movie for TV that aired in 1986.

Mrs. Roberts believes that it is time to bring the story forward. Do you have any problems with that young lady?

The Quinn's will be available to you each day in this hotel from 11:00 am to 1:00 pm. Let's order lunch and get an office built for our budding novelist."

Trying to eat lunch with those to young ladies was a feat in itself. Missy was acting like a kid in a bouncy castle. Lief was still grinning with the additional income and his fantasy of firing the owners, 'pimple rancher' kid. The Quinn's were soaking in the glow that they, 'Had Arrived.'

I looked over at Vicki and asked her if she was feeling left out. She was trying to be a good sport and she was genuinely happy for Missy but I could see that she was a bit wounded.

"Vicki, when these three go for their week long assignment you will be with me in Chicago for two days with Mrs. Roberts and Ms. Amanda Christopher who is Mr. Robert's personal assistant. I believe you met her last week? We will be visiting a grocery store construction site and the ladies will be taking you to the Magnificent Mile for lunch and a few new outfits. Then it will be off to the christening of the new library and study building at the now newly named, "Girls and Boys Town." I lit a cigarette and went to the restroom. When I came back they were all standing side by side looking out the window, they turned to face me as a unit and all said in perfect unison, "Who the fuck are you?"

Maddie said she had just looked up the event schedule for the christening event for 'Girls and Boys Town' and found a familiar name in the program along with an equally familiar name of a supposed fictional character. "You must have won the lottery or are hiding from the mob?"

I ushered everyone out with telling the Quinn's that we would resume in twenty minutes and sent the girls to go play in the street.

I opened the safe, removed the overnighted package and put it in my lap as I stared out the windows with a fresh lit cigarette and softly stroked the gold embossed return label. I put my cigarette out and returned the unopened overnight package to the safe. I went to play with the Quinn's.

Woody: Are there really people like you and the Robert's family in the real world?

Me: I think so, let's get to work. If you didn't hear me right, I just shortened our daily schedule by two hours. Now here is my plan for the two of you, you can accept or pass but I want to know now.

You two will be co-authoring a book on the children's history who currently live at 'Girls and Boys Town.' You will be assisted by their medical and mental health staff. Do you think that might be a worthy study to pick up your PhD Woody?

Woody: Sure, as soon as the rockets stop going off behind my eyeballs. I don't know how you do it, but we are exhausted with all these things going on today. We are going home to sleep until the alarm goes off in the morning.

I went to the lounge for a cup of coffee and called the hotel managers office. Alana answered and I invited her to the lounge. She came in acting a bit reluctant and apprehensive. I told her to order a drink and we would have a chat. She said, "I am still on duty and employees are not allowed to drink alcohol on the property." I smiled and said, "I think that this one time it will be ok, you have Mr. Roberts blessing." She ordered her drink and we sat in the rear of the lounge.

Alana looked like she was going to faint as she asked if she could say something. I nodded, she began with, "I know what a terrible thing I did to you those many years ago. I still regret it to this very day. I wonder how things would have been. When I saw you with Mr. Roberts and you two went into my office, I was sure I would be fired. When I was told I was going to corporate for training I was most certain of it. David, I know that you can fire me and I wouldn't blame you but I need this job. My husband has had cancer for three years and he can't work. Our daughter died eight years ago from a heroin overdose. She had infant twin girls. We are raising our granddaughters as our own children. If I lose my job I don't know what we will do. I work my ass off, both here and at home. I also do the books for the hotel since our auditor got fired for theft, five months ago."

I told her to sit where she was while I went out for a smoke. I went by the bar and asked the bartender (who I had never seen before) to bring the lady another drink. He paused as he knows the employee drinking rules, I smiled as I said, "It will be ok, I am the boss." He looked over at the bar manager who smiled at me as he said, "Yes, Mr. Brown is the boss."

I went out to the garden and I phoned Amanda, told her the deal and she approved my request without hesitation. I went back to the lounge.

Alana had not touched her first drink or second drink. She still looked queasy. I told her, "Look, we all make mistakes, I have made plenty of my own. I have been avoiding talking to you because I don't want my prejudice of the past to harm you. It was a time that was, besides, I turned out to be a real asshole. I have found the answer to life and that answer is, 'heartfelt forgiveness.' We are ok. You will have this job for as long as you want it. The company did not realize that you were doing the auditors job as well as your own. They will start an immediate search for an auditor. You will receive the annual pay for the auditor's position as a bonus. It should be in your bank account by morning. I saw the car that you drive, it does not look safe. The company will lease any kind of car you want. I suggest you pick out a SUV for you and your family. Our past will remain between us. Any questions?" Alana started to cry. After a few minutes she asked, "Can I tell you something?" Sure go ahead. "I have been following you for several years. I knew where you lived, your marriages, your police work and then I lost track of you about ten years ago. Did something bad happen to you?

Me: No, nothing bad happened.

Alana: Do you know that some people think that you are actually the owner of the corporation and you are using Mr. Roberts as a fake to keep people away from you? I sat in all of your book talks last month and I was amazed that at one time I knew that man and I loved him. I am amazed that you wrote a book, I had no idea. Thank you for not using my real name. You are such a good writer. Would you sign a copy for me? I read my copy so many times that it looks like it went to war and back. I was too ashamed to ask you to sign it, during your book signings and I didn't want to upset you. This one I will put on my mantel. You look the same as when we were together. You have become a man that the whole world is in love with. I will always regret what I did and how I hurt you. Please forgive me?

Me: First, do a Dun and Bradstreet on me, that should remove your or anyone else's suspicions as to who owns this joint. Yes, I know that you loved me. I have no ill will against you. It was just life and life is not always fair and we rarely get, 'do-overs.' My life today is a 'do-over' that is why I wrote the book. I wish I could take your pain and fear but I'm not capable of that. Let's shake hands and be Pals. We will keep our past in the past. Deal?

CHAPTER 38   BIG BRASS ONES

I woke up well rested. I am glad that I finally found the courage to sit with Alana. I held that pain and resentment for far too long. It felt good to be able to help her out. It was a cleansing for the both of us. I was dreading going to the Corker this morning to sit with the Quinn's and have to see Missy and Vicki. I just want to move on and do the book review with the Quinn's. We agreed on a 9:00 am start for today. When I arrived at the Corker I stopped at the front desk and asked the desk clerk if he was given a cell phone. He smiled as he held it up and said, "She said you would ask."

Me: Good morning my favorite two people at the moment. I want to focus only on the book today. Thanks for getting on board with the trip. Your air travel, lodging and credentials are being taken care of. We will hammer out the details a bit later, but for now, its back to the book. Agreed?

Woody: Those are some damn fine digs you have upstairs. Thank you for your sharing your private lair with us. We are honored to be included with the christening and the opportunity to pen your suggested writings. Tell us how you keep all these balls in the air. That in itself is fascinating and you act so cavalier about it all? The way you laid out everything and commanded action was like being in the war room of some kind of army general. Your power to demand cooperation is exemplary. Best of all, everyone was nodding their heads with smiles. Nobody had a grimace or questionable look or did they challenge the logistics of anything.

They just trust and know you will make it happen. You would be one hell of a strategist and commander.

Me: I like that 'Lair' comment but I'm not a wolf or lion but it is a safe place. I plan to spend more time there in the near future. It is a great place to just let my mind wander and to of course write. I have just gone there to meditate and reflect. I have never felt the comfort of a safe place before. As for my leadership and handing out directives, that is just second nature to me. When you are a paramedic you have the ball, there is no one to assist or guide you. It's just you and your patient, you don't have time to query a panel of experts. Often times, in multiple patient scenarios you don't even see or speak to your partner. You are the expert at that moment and you damn sure better be right. Police work is not all that different either. At times you only have parts of a second to react to take a life or risk losing yours. Cops don't get to back out or away from danger, we set and hold the line and at some point we go hands-on and face to face. You either lead or allow yourself to be led. I don't follow well, that is why I am not financially sound or some kind of bigshot. I know you guys and several others wonder why I not some kind of a big deal. Well, there is your answer.

Maddie: You have such a fluid way about you. You never seem to get trapped with finding an answer. You don't do that "I'll get back to you later bullshit." Better yet, you don't hedge or pretend you have the answers. You have the answers. I wish I had that level of confidence with the brain power to back it up. I love watching you in action. I would trade my academic skills for your life skills any day!

Me: Thank you both, but Maddie you would have to give it all up. Life skills don't pay the rent and nobody gives a fuck about whose life you saved yesterday. I can't send out bills like a doctor for tens of thousands of dollars for a hip replacement and be some kind of hero to the patient and their family. I save a human life and I'm just doing my job. The Doctors gardener and pool man get paid more than most any paramedic. Now we are moving forward, now!

Review of Chapter 16 'BECOMING A SON AND FINALLY A MAN'

Maddie: We know you call us, 'Boris and Natasha,' but for the record I was not born in December. We do kind of act like spies' but only for the good. We have meet with the three book clubs twice a week since you gave us the books. You do remember that the combined book clubs meeting with you is next Saturday? Well it seems that Chapter 16 is the most actively discussed chapter so far. Why is that?

Me: As soon as I can stop my inward laughter I will tell you. Chapter 16 is easy to talk about because it is safe. We can all relate to friends and family who are shiftless, asshole drunks. The more we criticize them the better we can deflect our own troubles. We stand on their chests to make ourselves appear taller. That kind of bullshit has gone on since 'Moby Dick' was a minnow.

Maddie: The part where you bought a new suit and shoes to go visit your father (that you couldn't afford to do) was sweet and heartbreaking all at the same time. I could feel your heart ache and the shame you carried, everyone in the book club could. You have an incredible way of putting people in your shoes. The lady newspaper editor in California absolutely nailed it, you do make us cry, and at some point we do realize that we are crying for ourselves! Your writing is as powerful as anyone's that we and the book clubs have ever read. Everyone askes who you are and where you came from? No one can understand why your book has not been on the NYT best seller list since the day it came out. Some think you are a famous author from another genre who is using a pen name. You are just too damn good to be a rookie writer.

Me: Do I need to stand and take another bow?

Woody: Maddie is right. Everything you write is so completely believable that everyone wonders why your book is classified as fiction. That deal with you telling your mother that it was your intention to stay with her until your father was released from the hospital is classic David! That is exactly how you operate today! You never break stride, you don't choke. Where did you develop that? That is a big part of your believability and why people trust you so much. Us being like the 'Boris and Natasha' (you so affectionately call us) we also know about Mrs. Kivi. The girls would not tell us so we asked Mrs. Kivi the next evening when she was there with her husband. What you told her could not have been scripted or brought forward from another past experience. You keep everything fresh and in real time. You just don't listen or look at people. You actually feel them.

The way you admitted your weakness both with alcohol and you character defects is purely refreshing to everyone who reads your work. You go on in the same chapter, to your mother once again abusing you with her crude and harsh words. You ignore those heart crushing words with your only thoughts of being to help her. You never gave up on your mom. Some people, maybe even most people, given those same circumstances would have walked away many years ago. Why not you?

Me: We are talking about alcoholism. Mine and hers and millions of other peoples. What if we gave up on cancer research, what if we gave up on heart disease? Today, heart and lung transplants are a common practice. That my friends, is why we, as a people never give up and we don't shoot our wounded! The power of practicing understanding and forgiveness carries lifetimes of rewards.

I need a smoke and we only have an hour or so left for this session. Missy needs you more than I do, I expect you guys to report any hedging or negative attitudes from her. She does have a propensity to being a bit full of herself. I'm sure you both know that it is just fear. But we must snap her ass with a wet towel like we did when we were kids. She is still just a kid. She has to know that she is safe with us having her back.

Woody: We will stay with her every step of the way. You and God have our word.

Maddie: I lost sight of how alone you were in your marriage to Liz. Until I got to Chapter 17 it shocked me that I somehow didn't pick that up. There was so much heavy drama with the constant shifting of situations and emotions that it all just took me away. Your mother's overused soggy tea bag and her eating a half of a peanut butter sandwich for breakfast and the other half for supper showed the depth of her love of your father. It somehow brought me to an understanding and a forgiveness of her. I am not the only one who hated your parents for the way you were treated.

Review of Chapter 17   'ANOTHER FRESH START'

Maddie: I find it remarkable that the first page of this chapter painted Sandy so clearly. She sounds like the perfect woman for any man. You never speak of any of the woman in your life in any disparagingly ways. How do you avoid that?

Me: Casting blame is an easy out. Taking personal responsibility is freeing. When you blame, it owns you forever. When someone tries to blame their mate for a broken relationship they only speak of the mate's failings. For me I hear them say that they failed, weather they speak of it or not. I don't like blamers, I find them to be weak or even void of character. That kind of negativity has no place in my world.

Review of Chapter 18   *'LOVING WHAT YOU HATE'*

Woody: I have only been on 14 medical calls with our volunteer ambulance service. Three of those calls we were canceled before arrival. Three other calls the patient refused transport after we arrived and attempted to treat them. It takes me a few hours to emotionally detox and for the adrenaline to burn off. I can't imagine running a dozen or more calls a shift and then being able to sleep. Sleep avoidance to stave off nightmares has to be exhausting. Is that the beginning of depression and PTSD?

Me: I have no idea. Now we are nearing the chicken and the egg question. Sorry, I can't help you with that. Don Prince is your man.

Maddie: Jack sounds like he was a quality man, it sounds like you two had a lot of fun together. Was it that way for all the crews?

Me: We all got along, gallows humor and pranking were the norm. It was our de-briefing back in the 'good ole days.' If a newbie was too serious we just ignored him until he got his head right. No, we never hugged it out.

Maddie: The prank with the TV crews and Jack, with you guys brushing your hair was hilarious! The story of 'Ole' Ass Face' was eye opening. I find it sad that people have to be that way. It sounds that your two partners, Scotty and Kenny were good men. Do you ever speak with them?

Me: I speak with Scotty via Facebook weekly. He and his wife even attended my Step-Pops funeral and sat with Heather and me. I have no idea where Kenny might be. Like most things in my life I just smile as I say, 'it is a time that was.'

I have never saved anything from the past. I don't hold on to the past, it's self-defeating. My past was always dark and muggy. I am done with this chapter, let's move on.

Woody: I have a few more questions, there is a lot I want to understand. This chapter is very reveling.

Me: Palm in the air. Woody that is a 'PASS'. We are moving on.

Review of Chapter 19 'THE HEALING MOVE'

Woody: Sorry, I understand the need for the safe word, 'PASS.' We had no idea what a medical responder or a police officer actually goes thru. That would be a sad and lonely life to live. I understand why you don't want to take it any further.

Maddie: I loved the warm side of you. Calling woman 'Ma'am was important to you. You wanted to show the same respect that the police officers showed your mother. I can easily see you giving drunks rides home and carrying their groceries. I never heard of cop's un-arresting people.
The whole thing about not seeking help from mental health workers out of fear of being fired still goes on today. I have treated a few police officers and they say the same, the very same thing about the rubber bullet room. They don't give their real names and I don't ask or charge them.
You running into the girl from your hometown whose father was the murdered police sergeant had to be haunting. Did your wife, Sandy know about your friend and you in that matter?

Me: No. I was not involved in the burglary or the shooting. I am ready to call it a day. See you guys in the morning.

CHAPTER 39   NEED TO PUSH THROUGH

Me: Good morning gang. I have to tell you guys that we are getting seriously bogged down. It's becoming boring as we hack thru each chapter. I decided that we are going to move thru a cluster of chapters each day. Today we will do Chapters 20-23. Let's start.

Review of Chapter 20   'I KNOW WHAT I KNOW.'

Woody: We have noticed that you are under a heavy load of pressure. I apologize for trying to push you. Please understand that what you may call mundane is fascinating to us. You lived it and you have had some of those things bouncing around in your memory for many years. Then you dissected all of it to author your book. But it is still fresh to us, even though we have both read the entire book three times and several chapters many more times. Chapter 20 is only a page and a half. Yet the twists are worthy of several pages. You have a unique way of cutting right to the core of it. There is no explanation as to how you knew to pack a suit, and a dress coat for that trip. We checked into the number of sworn police officers and found there were more than 150 sworn officers at the time of the killing. How could you possibly have known that the murdered officer was Detective Sergeant Watson?

Me: Remember that the name of the chapter is 'I Know What I Know.' To finish that statement I have to add...'but I don't know why.' I still don't know why I know these things. It got so spooky for me that I stopped telling people of these pre-event visions. I have had two other significant situations that I have never told anyone about. One took place on another Duluth visit. I was at my parent's house and we were watching the ten o'clock news. The first story of the broadcast was about a major four lane highway north of the city was shut down in all directions for the last half hour due to a two car accident with two fatality's. The newscaster said a news crew was enroute to file a live report. There were no pictures, no vehicle descriptions, no sex or names of the victims. I turned to my mom and said, "Those two fatalities are Liz's (my second wife) parents (who I haven't seen in thirty years). My mother was upset with me thinking I was wishing them dead. I said, "No mom, I liked them, I would never wish them harm. Something just told me that it was them." The morning TV news reported that it in fact was them. From that day on, my mom and step-dad never looked at me quite the same. The other recent premonition I have yet to work thru. I have no desire to climb into the world of dark investigative science. I wouldn't mind having the winning lottery numbers the day before the drawing however.

Maddie: I would have to live 3 or 4 lifetimes to understand all of that. There are some people that claim to be channels from the dead to the living. Some of the data is quite compelling to recruit believers.
I try to stay with what I know and I'm oftentimes left with asking myself what I do know. The spirit world is not my cup of tea.

Me: I have seen some of those TV shows where they do séance stuff with a medium as the show host. Reminds me of the teen years when the girls had pajama parties and they used a Ouija Board and their parents had to pick them up in the middle of the night from their freaking out. It's not my cup of tea either and I don't even drink that shit. I am sure that some wizard wrote for and is studying with a federal grant about that kind of stuff. I would be more than happy to sit down with that lad or lass if they had a very fat checkbook. Reminds me of one of Dani Harper's quips of, "If you hear voices, you are a lunatic. If you write down what they say, you're an author." Yes I am an author, I even write fiction but my premonitions can all be supported by credible witnesses.

Do you guys realize that we just covered twice the area (in pages) than the chapter actually did? On to chapter 21.

Review of Chapter 21 'MY VERY OWN FAMILY'

Maddie: I adore the way you speak of your wife, Karen. I can't and I doubt anyone I have ever known could fathom living with the fear of losing your second child and having to keep it to yourself. You could not even tell your wife! Your alcoholism is understandable.

Me: Nope. My alcoholism was well established many years prior to that. Some people drink heavily over life conditions, I drank heavily over life itself, all of my life.

Review of Chapter 22 'EMBRACING THE END'

Woody: I am overwhelmed with the torment you have carried all of your life. I have not been able to push through this chapter without having tears of my own and having to walk away. Hell, most every chapter does that to me. I am no sissy but this entire book takes me to a place of humility that I have never known. To simply read the chapter is unnerving in itself. Clinton Flanagan is a character in a novel. Yet I am sitting directly across from him. I look into your eyes and I know why I weep. It restores my faith in God to know that he carried you thru for a reason. A man who had all the earmarks of a suicide victim or some kind of madman killer sits and smiles thru his heart ache because he has a mission far greater than himself.

Maddie: Do you know what guts me? You don't fuck around with all that cutesy writer crap in describing each setting like you are sitting on a stage in a play. You don't describe the air quality, the temperature, a flickering campfire or the sounds of the night. I think it is a gift you carry to not belittle your readers as most wordy authors do to fill the page and add to their page and word count. Thanks for not insulting your readers by describing the color of leafs, seven ways till sundown. A lot of authors could learn from you.

Me: Maddie, you remind me of a post I saw on Facebook last year from FunnyMemes.com It goes something like this; What the author meant. What the English teacher thinks: the author meant. For instance: the author, "The curtains were blue." What your teacher thinks: "The curtains represent his immense depression and his lack of will to carry on." What the author meant: "The curtains were fucking blue."

That gives me the giggles. It's like when some ass-bonnet tries to correct my spelling on my Facebook posts or criticizes my writing skills. I enjoy saying, "Tell me of the many books you have written and published. Go ahead, I will wait." I have used that in a few book signings when a reader has a suggestion as to how the book should have really been written. I have had to put up with dorks who are content writers that wouldn't know an emotion if it bit em on the ass. They try to connect to my book in order to build search engine optimization (SEO) using manufactured dialog to gain a better ranking on Google. I avoid "Liking requests" and Linkedin stuff. Get your own damn pony, you aint riding mine! I call supposed content writers, 'factory writers' with no quality control, go sell your shit elsewhere

That was a fun trip. We couldn't be anymore lost from our path but thanks for giving me a platform to vent. Let's get back on task.

Maddie: I hope this question will not disturb you but I feel that I have to ask. Please forgive me if this takes you too deep. Do you think your son will ever understand the sacrifice you made for his wellbeing?

Me: Let's remember that he has a loving and supportive step-dad who adopted him. He is a well-adjusted and successful adult. I gave him a copy of the book. It is his choice to read it or not. I did all I could do and that is all I can do. He doesn't need my approval nor do I need his. This thing called life is what it is and nothing more. On to Chapter 23.

Review of Chapter 23 'FREAK DREAMS'

Woody: I found myself in awe of your vision and was memorized further with your letter to the editor. You spoke of the hidden thoughts that we as a civilization dare not admit or speak of. The police chief was right in asking who you wrote for. You wrote as a highly seasoned beat reporter. You are gifted beyond even your knowledge. You offering your article to support the 'Widow and Orphans Fund' defines your heart and your humanity. I am honored to sit with you and call you friend.

Maddie: It's a blessing to witness the tenderness of a man who has every right to hate the world, but only has a desire to help people. I can't even comment on your dream that three days later became a real life drama. The clarity of your vision compared to the actuality of the situation is so uncanny that I think your experience should be studied. I think you do have a direct link to both the spirit world and time travel. I am totally freaked out that someone hasn't approached you for an in-depth study. Like the many other things you have done so quietly for others, I am most certain that your efforts were far reaching. I honestly do believe Father Martin is on to something.

Me: Again, anyone other than Father Martin couldn't afford my time. I am nobody's lab rat. And honestly I don't believe I have any of that mystic power crap. Thank you both for your kind words. Let's move on to chapter 24.

Review of Chapter 24 'ATONEMENT'

Maddie: You are one fearless beast. For you or anyone else to firstly develop a viable concept and then to conquer it is nothing short of a miracle. But all this makes me crazy. How do you stay under the radar? You should have been recruited by several universities or think tank originations by now. Why haven't you?

Me: Guess I never knew who to send my resume to.

Maddie: Thanks smart-ass. You trusted something inside of you, it had to be a lot more than just desire. You carry a fire deep inside you. Few if any would take on a project of that depth unless there was profit or notoriety.

Woody: With my being a school principle for those many years I never once witnessed a teacher or lay-person who could, or perhaps who wanted to inspire and rally the, 'forgotten ones.' It would be interesting to study and follow those 'at risk' kids life's paths. Do you ever wonder about how their lives turned out?

Me: My hope is that they all went on to peace and prosperity. I further hope the teachers and the community learned some lessons from it. Don't lose sight that my only goal at the time was to supply children with proper fitting warm winter, outer clothing. The entire 'at risk' kid's deal was an unforeseen bonus. I think if anyone uses damaged children for financial or political gain they are doing it for the wrong reason. No, I don't have any need or desire to follow-up on the students or the clothing recipients. I will leave the 'chest pounding' and rooster strutting to the politicians. I do think there was a certain amount of embarrassment amongst the city leaders and 'shaker's and mover's' that an unheard of nobody bested their feeble attempts to grandstand through their many service club memberships. That year the black tie events weren't as sparkly as years past. Rowdy uncouth teenagers and little poor kids stole the headlines and their positions of prominence and stature. I recruited a city council member who is also a banker, onto our board of directors and had him set-up our bank account to dispel any potential claims of fund fraud or theft. I don't trust suits and their agendas. Let's move on. Better yet, let's call it a day. Chapter 25 'Peter' tomorrow.

CHAPTER 40   A VISON FOR YOU

I had been avoiding any further conversations of my vision problems with the Quinn's. I don't like (or maybe trust, would be a more accurate statement) when concern is shown to me. It has nothing to do with the Quinn's, it is just the way I am. I had an eye surgeon appointment after I left the Quinn's hanging on chapter 25.

I have had a lot of different exams and tests from ultrasound to brain scans trying to locate the problem, all to no avail. I was told of a pediatric eye surgeon who comes to Duluth only twice a month and does some kind of eye stabilization procedure to retrain the brain to process images more clearly. I do have a wondering left eye that parks itself in the lower far corner of my eye socket. I made an appointment with him and had to wait three months for the appointment.

As I was waiting for his surgical assistant, Terry to do the initial patient intake, I was taking notes from my first book, 'Daddy Had to Say Goodbye.' When the tech came in I set down the book. She glanced at the cover as she sat down to her keyboard. She asked, "Do you like to read about police and fire/medical?" I said, "No, I like to write about police and fire/medical."

She started to ask but caught herself and gasped with, "Oh my god, I see that it is your name on the cover! I am so sorry, no one ever expects to meet an author. What is your book about?" I

314

gave the short answer; depression, anxiety, alcoholism and suicide and what it takes to win over it. Her reaction was like she was about to fold up. I knew I struck a deep cord. I asked, "Do you have a troubled family member who is or was a first responder?" She nodded her head as she was reaching for a tissue. She dabbed her eyes as she said, "My husband was a county deputy sheriff. He had to leave the job after fourteen years. He watched his partner shoot himself in the head. His partner died instantly, my husband never recovered from that. He has PTSD. He has night sweats, night terroirs and wakes up screaming almost every night. He has only been off the job for four months but the dreams are every night. He is drinking heavily, daily. He won't go for help. He is driving a dump truck for four hours a day for my brothers gravel pit. He comes home and sits in the garage for hours drinking and carving fishing lures. He eats very little and is losing weight. I don't know what to do."

She again caught herself as she realized she had yet to start the intake. She said, "I am so sorry, I am usually not this unprofessional. I guess I just got caught-up in my own misery."

I smiled as I said, "I know you and I know your husband, although we have never met. It is obvious that you think you are protecting him by not discussing his condition with anyone. In the meantime he is getting worse and you are starting to stumble emotionally. You are both standing on the roof of a house of cards and the wind is starting to pick-up. There is help, I can give you some phone numbers of people much like yourselves who are working their way out of the dark and freighting forest. I think we better get the intake done first.

As she was playing three hundred questions I reached for my briefcase and pulled out a copy of my book. I always carry four copies of my book in my briefcase and another eight books in my pick-up truck in the seat pouches. For reasons only God knows, I run into people like Terry on a very regular basis. It's a pain in the ass to drag my briefcase around but I can't allow myself to miss an opportunity to reach someone. I of course will not take any money from those chance meetings. My old pal Carl Bergl taught me how

315

to fib with, "I am working off of a grant from some very generous people." That is one fib that I can live with.

I signed a copy for her and her husband. She thanked me and took her book and left the exam room.

All during the intake process I could faintly hear an adult male voice and children's voices. The adult voice was very soothing, I liked his comforting voice and soft words.

As I was waiting for the doctor I went back to my note taking from my book. The doctor came in and introduced himself with a kind smile and a firm handshake. He said, "You sure had a powerful impact on Terry. She was smiling through her tears as she showed me your book and the message that you wrote her. I usually don't like to see my employees cry but I think she was having a cleansing. You sir, have some remarkable skills, now let us put my skills to work. Tell me about your eye problem."

I told him that I had been uncomfortable most all of my life with my hiding left eye. How people would bob their head with trying to figure out which eye I was looking at them with. I always felt bad for the people I was talking to, I could see their embarrassment and their discomfort. Oftentimes, the people that I was speaking to directly in front of me, would look over their right shoulder thinking I was looking at and talking to someone behind them, when I was looking directly at them. What do I tell them, "Oh it's OK, I was a beaten child and I have brain damage from those daily beatings which caused me to have a hiding eye?" I have always avoided telling people of my childhood beatings because I felt that I somehow deserved it. I was afraid that they may have thought the same.

I gave him my recent, past medical history of the many exams and consultations. He asked where I think I came to have this situation. I told him of my many childhood beatings and suffered hearing and vision problems. How I was held back in the first and second grades and was thought to be retarded by teachers and the school district. I told him I strongly suspected (along with my eye doctor) that I had suffered countless concussions, along with starvation and malnutrition. He went on to ask about my

316

educational background. When I told him I never earned a passing grade and only drove by the college but never stopped in he shook his head and thinly smiled as he asked if that was what my book was about. I answered, yes impart. He seemed a lot more interested in my book than my vision. He asked, what was the motivation and deciding factor that led me to write the book. I told him of my spiritual experience off of Interstate 90 in Gillette, Wyoming.

His comment was "So that is how you were able to write a book with such a low level of education? You made a promise to God and that was it?" I nodded my head yes.

When I told him I didn't know how to use a computer or how to type so I was forced to write the entire book in longhand on 68 legal pads he did something that I never expected. He started to cry.

The surgeon gathered himself. He reached over to his desk and picked up his business card and handed me the card. He said, "Read the back of it." The back of his business read, "But for the grace of God go eye."

As he squared his shoulders he said, "My mother died when I was born, I always felt that my dad blamed me for him losing his wife. My dad left me with his sister and went to work on the Alcan Highway in Alaska. From there he went to work on the ocean going cargo ships that traveled the world. I only saw him a few times when I was growing up. He was always drunk and seemed angry with me. My Aunt didn't like me, she told me that if it wasn't for my dad's monthly checks that she would have put me in a children's home. I failed the second grade. I had buggy eyes and I wore thick lens glasses with big heavy black frames. She always called me stupid and told me that I wasn't even smart enough to dig ditches. When I was fourteen I had to go to the eye doctor for a new prescription for my glasses. He was a very nice man who was gentle and kind. He talked to me like he cared about me. When I was picking out the frames for my new glasses I told him I wanted frames just like his. My aunt said no, they were too expensive. She pointed to the same type of poor people frames that I currently was wearing. The doctor winked at me and told my aunt

317

that his frames were the same price as the thick plastic black ones. That was the moment. That moment defined the pathway for the rest of my life. So here I am today, all because of one kind man and a wink."

The doctor did his exam and read the past notes from the tests and said, "I can bring your 'hiding eye' as you call it, to dead center. It won't improve your vision strength but you will be able to see more of what you are looking at. You will need two additional minor surgeries after that to clear up your cataracts and glaucoma. The risks of the procedures are very low as to my damaging your current vision. If you need some time to think it over, you can call my office in a few days with your decision." I smiled as I said, "Your warmth, your kindness, your firm handshake and your tears have me sold. Let's do this."

He stood up and said, "I will be right back." I reached into my briefcase and pulled out a copy of my book to sign for him. He came back in and said, "I see that you have Medicare and part B. My schedule clerk is out of the office today. She will call you on Monday with your surgery schedule. Don't worry about the costs. What Medicare doesn't pick up, I will. It seems to me that you have given an awful lot to a lot of people. I think it is time that you be given to. I would like to be that person."

I signed his copy of the book and went home for a nap. I spent the entire weekend smiling and writing. I felt an even greater urgency to finishing my new book, in the unlikely event that the surgery somehow went bad.

CHAPTER 41   DARE TO SLEEP

I have been insanely scribbling and typing for the last few months in the fear of the possibility losing my vision. Heather could not understand why I stayed up so late and was becoming a bit lethargic and impatient. She said, "You don't sleep, you don't watch TV or play with the dogs anymore. All you do is write, you don't leave the house and I even have to coax you to eat, what is going on with you?" I didn't want to tell her of my fear of going blind. I never told her of my walking through the house playing the blind game and memorizing what was in every cupboard and drawer.

All I could say was, "I can explain to you what I can see but I can't describe to you what I can't see because I can't see it. My vision loss is worse than I've been telling you. I guess I feel a drive to finish the book before the worst of the worst happens. I could not deal with having the book not finished. I know I always take it to the bitter end but that is where my alcoholic brain takes me. I can't live with the thought that my dream was just a dream. Do you remember the guy that almost did it? Well of course not and neither does anyone else. I will be damned if I will allow myself to be that guy. I tell the entire world that dreams are worth dreaming, it's how I sign my books with that statement. I am sorry for my recent transgressions but I must finish this book, please understand. I will make it up to you later but for now the book is and must be, my only priority."

Heather put her arms around me and we both had a few tears. She said she didn't realize how bad it was and how deep my fear ran. She smiled as she said, "You know how everyone says, 'See you later'? Well the next time you say that to me, I will take it as a promise and pray that you do.

CHAPTER 42   WARP SPEED

I was exhausted with my weekend writing marathon. It was refreshing to have Heathers understanding and blessing. It was now time to level with the Quinn's and a few others.

I sat with the Quinn's drinking orange juice as I gave them a brief overview of what I expected to accomplish before the week was out.

Me: We must kick this thing in the ass. We have eleven more chapters to go. I must finish my current book but I won't rush it, quality is my first priority, ever over completion. Saturday is the book clubs meeting and a two hour 'meet and greet' with Walkers book store fans. I am taking a few days with Heather before the surgery. Let's get to it.

Maddie: I understand your animosity toward Petey and Stevie, did you ever level with them of how you felt and how it once was for you?

Me: No, everyone has a right to their own perceptions and memories. No two of us know the very same person in the very same way. Each and every relationship is unique onto itself. There is a statement floating around in social media that pretty much sums it up and it goes something like this: "Not everyone gets the same version of me. One person might tell you I have an amazing beautiful soul. Another may tell you I'm a cold hearted asshole.

321

Believe them both. I don't treat people badly, I treat them accordingly."

With that in mind my brothers only knew what they knew. Everyone has a right to their own lives and their own heroes.

Do you guys know of one of baseball's greatest ball player 'Shoeless' Joe Jackson and the Chicago Black Sox scandal of the 1919 World Series Fix? It was actually the Chicago White Sox, eight players intentionally threw the game for cash from the bookmakers. When fans found out there was a huge backlash. Back in the day, baseball was the only American sport. Little kids were crushed with knowing that their baseball heroes were cheaters. Little kids throughout the country were heard saying, *"Say it ain't so Joe. Please Joe, say it ain't so!"* A lot of children threw away their bats, balls, and gloves. The game of baseball was greatly injured from that incident. That may be an extreme example of the heartbreak of finding the truth but no matter who you are, we all need someone to look up to.

Woody: That is an intriguing story, I will look it up. I love the way you use real life examples to your statements. Your broad knowledge of things is amazing. Where does that come from?

Me: Woody, I love your questions that I actually have the answers to! Remember you two, that I am a generalist. I know a little about a lot of stuff but I know very little about any one thing. I think it comes from my childhood learning disabilities. My memory retention was almost non-existent. I locked onto snippets rather than full stories. That way I wouldn't feel so stupid. I guess it was a survival tactic of sorts. What say you Maddie?

Maddie: You know better than I do. You are a constant reminder of how the educational system is broken and how it has failed children and adults. I can't believe that my college students have never challenged me on my data that I throw out and worse yet, they must believe all that crap to get a passing grade. But then again, I never challenged my professors either. It was only about passing the class and getting my degree. How shameful!

Me: Lighten up babe, check this crazy shit out. This last summer the 'Denver Post' did a story on Colorado Mesa University. The outgoing editor of the school newspaper found a typo on his diploma as he was checking to make sure his name was spelled correctly on his diploma. His name was spelled right but Instead of the header reading, the "Board of Trustees" it read the "Coard of Trustees." Here is the best part of that when we talk of supposed higher education. They had been using that same diploma header since 2012 and issued 9,200 diplomas with that error. I don't know how many college presidents and deans signed those but is the perfect example of arrogance on the part of the people who signed them and the sheep like students who just wanted their degree. So much for the hallowed halls of higher education! OK my bad, now back to Petey.

Woody: Point taken. How you read and took in all of your family dynamics are things we usually see in movies. Your power of observation is very keen. To read your brother as you did took a deep heart. Most see the struggle but few understand the pains of the struggle. I will say no to your question of using dirty tricks for your own comfort. That took a maturity and wisdom that few people possess.

Maddie: The close of this chapter showed me the unselfish side of love. Throughout this entire chapter, hell throughout this entire book you have never asked anything from anyone. Was there ever a time that you felt you had nothing more to give? You always went it alone, why?

Me: If I don't ask, I won't be disappointed when I don't get it. I again 'go it alone' to avoid being with someone when I'm in pain but still being lonely and lost. On to Chapter 26.

Review of Chapter 26   'WHERE SHAME TAKES US'

Maddie: I understand how you struggled with being the 'bad' survivor. PTSD has been around from the beginning of time. Why do you think it has just come to light and received a name in in just the last few years?

Me: I think you are baiting me sweetheart. You know as well as I do that it all has to do with money. Nobody gave a fuck when American soldiers that were too young to drink, were being killed in double and even triple numbers before lunch. When the survivors returned home they were told to get a job, get married and get over it. Today however it is much different. But not really, not really at all. The vets are still being ignored but the treatment specialists are cashing in like a winning night in Las Vegas.

Some asshole treatment specialist, likely a social worker, dug up a name and a loose definition and wrote a grant for federal funding. They just created a high paying job for themselves and their buddy's and the vets are truly of no or little concern to them. As it has always been in the past, the best remedy is Vet's helping Vet's. The problem is the program money rarely goes to the end user.

Woody: That part of seeing yourself in all of your dad's cars and your age progression before you walked in the bar was eerie as hell. Reminds me of watching the old, "Twilight Zone" shows on TV when I was a kid. Giving your mind set, I was sure that you were about to kill someone and I don't think it mattered who it was.

Maddie: I thought that too. Were you on the brink of madness?

Me: That's funny you guys. I have been on the brink of madness most all of my life.

Maddie: What keeps you from losing it?

Me: Another easy one, thanks Maddie. I like coffee, cigarettes, Larson's Bakery and sex too much to risk losing my freedom. I understand that you can't smoke or get special deliveries from donut shops while in prison. That is my testimony as to my sanity. Agreed?

Woody: The way you describe entering the bar, the floor, the bar surface, the brass footrests, the back bar, the mirror and the bar activity is like reading a movie script and then watching the cameras and actors. It was an experience of a lifetime. I felt like I was sitting a few stools down from you and watching you watching them. It made the hair on the back of my neck stand up. It made me wonder if I had ever been in a bar with a man like you. It gave me the shivers. I don't see you as a writer, being much more different than a movie director. You have some incredible talents. Where does that come from? Are you a movie buff?

Me: No to the movie buff question. I don't like going to theaters or being in crowds where I can't see what is going on around me. I have never had any interests in movie productions. Remember that I never had a desire to write a book at any time in my life. It was brought to me in a way that I never dreamed. Just lucky I guess.

Maddie: The last paragraph was so telling that it brought me to tears. I remember setting the book down and walking out the front door and down the driveway, hardly able to see with my tears blinding me.

Woody: The last sentence told the entire story. I wonder how many people have asked that same question just before they killed themselves.

You know more than most mortals, of peoples final thoughts, it's almost like you are going thru a revolving door between the here and now and the afterlife. What's your take on that?

Me: I have dealt a lot with dying people, but I don't think they left any doors open for me. Let's move on to Chapter 27.

Review of Chapter 27 'MY BOYS'

Maddie: The Mountain Lion story gives me the creeps. We live in a rural area with Mountain Lions and Wolves and Bears. I wonder how many of those animals were watching me when I go on my walks. Gives me the shivers. If that was me facing that Mountain Lion I would have a heart attack or just sit down and wait for them to kill me. You were going to fight the killer of all killers with a knife? Than you sit here and smile like it was no big deal! You sir are a scary two legged animal. I hope you always like us.

Me: Honey, don't fear me, fear the people that aren't afraid of me!

Woody: Your chance meeting with Oliver and Shaggy and the relationship you three developed is a wonderful story. How are they today?

Me: I have no idea. We no longer speak, for reasons I am not aware of. So that is a HARD PASS!

Review of Chapter 28 'THE DOORS'

Woody: That is very sad, but I will respect your privacy. Now this chapter is paralyzing with sadness. I can't imagen living with that level of rejection and sorrow. How did you make it through?

Me: My AA meetings and friends. I have to remember and I have to remind you that this was of my own making. I made mistakes, I failed her and ultimately I failed myself. I have no reason to blame her.

Maddie: Just as you said, the 'Door Story' was about terror. The terror of being left alone.

Me: It was the lowest point in my sobriety, yes but I had friends who kept me from sinking into the depths of depression. I was blessed with having them in my life. Let's go to Chapter 29 as soon as I get back from my smoke.

I had been in contact each day with the Roberts family. I spoke with Paul twice a day. With Paul one conversation was always about Jane and his adjustment to home life. The other conversation was always about his sobriety, his step work, his sponsor and of course his meetings attendance. Paul was doing well, I had great hopes for him.

I had been uncomfortable with the 'Boys Town' naming since it was first suggested. I had been lobbying the family (excluding Jane) to not use my name as I believe there were many people, past and present that better deserved that honor. I suggested, 'Wilson/Smith Library' who were the two co-founders of Alcoholics Anonymous. My thought was because damaged children who came from broken homes had a greater risk of developing drinking problems. Chances are the core of the broken home had to do with a drinking problem. In truth, I did not feel worthy of the honor. My contributions were minuscule in comparison to the many who devoted their entire lives' in service to others.

I called Amanda to see how she and the other family member's efforts to change the name were being received by Jane. Amanda said she was holding up the sign company for installation but mom won't budge on the name change. I asked her if she wanted to swing for the fence. Amanda started to laugh as she said, "You want Satins litter sister to go to war, who with?

Me: As much as I enjoyed my time with Father Martin I think we have to rough him up a bit. Your family throws a lot of money into the Chicago Archdiocese, call in a favor. Talk to Cardinal Cupich to give Father Martin a nudge to turn Jane around.

Amanda: You sir, have lost your fucking mind and you are going straight to hell! You are the one that told me to stop kicking down doors and to start to act like a lady. Now you want me to lean on the Catholic Church so you can have your way? You are some kind of fucked up!

Me: That's some cute shit babe, but if the church was sitting on a piece of property that you wanted to develop, you would go to the mats with them. You owe me a favor, I loaned you three cigarettes in the last month and I want to collect! You need a stronger name and personality to carry the library name.

Amanda: You do know that I could kick your ass in three different languages, correct?

Me: Baby, find a man to love so you can ruin his life. But be nice to me, I'm still your mom's favorite!

Review of Chapter 29   'THE CALL'

Maddie: Do you think the drive to Minnesota was cathartic or torturing?

Me: When I am faced with heartache I never look forward, I don't need to suffer the outcome prior to my arrival. I look into the past, because it is safe. I can always glean a bit of joy if I look deep enough. What you have just asked me is the number one question asked by readers and friends. There are times that the book goes too deep, even for me. I had to do that for me and my readers. How do you encourage emotional and situational honesty when you are lying to yourself? I had to hold myself to the highest of standards, even when I didn't want to.

There was a time in my life when I stacked lie upon lie, like cord wood. That is a punishing way to live. There is nothing pretty about your own truths rolling around in your guts. The beauty of personal honesty and personal growth starts, when the truth leaves your lips.

Maddie: Your character Toby is a real person, right? He sounds like a good man, can we ever meet him? We only got to see Heather just once, in the lobby with Jane on the day of your Hollywood flight but we never got to speak with her. Can we meet her? We would like to meet all of your characters. All travel expenses would be on us.

Me: You don't ask for much now do you sweetheart. I have a little surprise for you two and your book club people. The characters, Toby and Scotty will be at your book club 'Meet and Greet' to sign the book also. I know that is unusual as hell to have fictional characters come to life but I don't follow rules, I make them. You two and I are having breakfast at Mike's Western Café on Saturday morning before the book club meeting. Heather will be with me. You don't want to make the mistake of trying to interview or analyze Heather. She is her own person, her identity is her own. She goes head to head with corporate executives all week long. If she winds you trying to look into her, she will shut you down with a thin smile and silence. Her silence can be deafening. Her moto is; 'The last one to speak loses.' Just be your sweet selves and you will find her to be warm and sincere. I need a smoke. Color something pretty, see you in a few minutes.

I enjoyed a few smokes as I made some phone calls. When I went to the door to go into the building the glass door was covered with colored, coloring book pages. I found a kid-like giggle come from inside me. I shook my head much like Carl Bergl used to do as I said, "Silly Bastards!"

Review of Chapter 30   'FORBIDDEN LOVE'

Woody: This is my favorite 'smile' chapter of the entire book. That is a beautiful love story. I had to turn my head away and stare at the wall for a few minutes when I read, "Heather didn't just hug him, she held him." The arms around each other's waist and the hug with the kiss on his cheek followed by the whisper of happy birthday and tucking of the note in your shirt pocket are what movies and dreams are made of.

Maddie: I can't wait to meet her! Such a beautiful loving soul. Why didn't you go after her sooner in your life?

Me: I was a mess, I was a drunk and I lived in a dark place. To me, Heather was the, 'Virgin Mary.' There was nothing more pure and pristine then Heather. I was protecting her from me.

Woody: Perhaps you should move to do romance novels? You definitely have the skills. That or psycho thrillers. You take us down such bumpy and twisting roads that we almost welcome sailing off a hundred foot cliff for just a moment or two of peaceful breathing, like the movie 'Thelma and Louise.' You are an absolute master of putting me in your guts. I do have to admit that I don't always like it however. Do people ever get mad at you for doing that to them?

Me: You guys have been to tons of "Meet & Greets' I doubt if you will hear anything you haven't already seen or heard. You will get to witness that first hand on Saturday morning. I know that you two have been questioning your book club readers weekly. There are always a few readers at each event who are critical of the story line or structure. They are usually frustrated, 'almost published authors,' who just can't get out of their own way. Some just need recognition from others in the room. There are always a few who criticize my use of profanity or sexual content. Should be great fun with your church group. That is when

I like to remind the audience that the book, "Fifty Shades of Grey" sold ten million copies in the first month and 125 million copies in its first year in 2015.

The movie version sold thirty eight million dollars at the box office in its first weekend and over a billion dollars as of February of this year. Comcast is the primary producer of the movie. Anyone here cancel their internet or TV cable service because of this movie?"

If anyone gets to uppity or challenging I will nicely destroy them with one simple question. "Please tell us all of your published writings and where can we buy a copy of it today?"

Maddie: That would be fun to watch but I highly doubt anyone would dare to challenge you once they see you and the way you command an entire room with your words and your eyes. Your entire appearance says, "Hi, I am a nice fellow, don't fuck with me."

Woody: I want a front row seat to that one! I do know that your spiritual experience on I-90 in Gillette Wyoming, has brought a lot of conversation to the groups. Will you be speaking on that?

Me: Only if asked. This is a 'meet and greet' for the readers. I let them lead, they took their time to read the book now it is their time to ask questions. There will also be a lot of technical process questions along with cost and marketing questions and the standard questions like, "How did you begin......are you rich now?" The Walker's book store invitees will be a bit more sedate for the afternoon meeting.

Maddie: It was sad to read of Steph's reception when you returned home. Thank god for your friend Tim and those buddy passes. You just refused to give up, that spoke volumes of your heart.

331

CHAPTER 43   THE END IS IN SIGHT

Review of Chapter 31 'SICK'

Maddie: I could feel my own rage coursing thru my veins, how could anyone who takes the Hippocratic Oath act that way, especially when the clinic is tax-payer funded? I guess racism isn't just a white thing. The doctor's ignorance and his off-handed remark about you buying a bottle is unconscionable. I hated him enough for the both of us. It was wonderful that you got to see Oliver and Shaggy again and to finally meet Kevin. What a wonderful thing to get to see your son and have him ask for pictures of just you and him with his arm around you. I got to make peace with hating Steph, I could tell she still had a place in her heart for you. I understand her having to be guarded with her heart, you are charming.

Woody: I think Maddie pretty much covered it. You gifting your son your watch and speaking so kindly of his mother was total class. Perhaps my favorite part, beyond the love and warmth extended, has to be you telling the woman at the Social Services Office that you would crawl up her steps and die just to make it her problem, was priceless. You being escorted from the building by security was fucking hilarious.

Review of Chapter 32 'GETTING WELL OR DIE TRYING'

Maddie: I found myself cheering when the ER Doc and the rest of the medical staffs finally did for you what should have done for you all along. The Peoples Clinic Doctor and his Physician's Assistant sound like people I would want to care for

332

my family. What sweet people they were! Now I understand why you sign some of your emails, 'Keep Grinnin.'

Woody: I like the Peoples Clinic's policy of treating the whole person. That whole deal with a stack of prescriptions that you couldn't pay for and what they did, was very telling of the medical staff's commitment to patient recovery and wellness. Most medical centers would just tell you to figure it out somehow.

Me: I spent the bulk of my life caring for other people. Often-times I put myself in great peril, but for some reason I never thought of fighting for myself. I guess that might be a part of depression and having a low self- image. My mind told me that community clinics were for poor people, mostly children and the elderly. I never saw myself as deserving as I was relatively young and able to work as soon as I recovered. It was my false ego that I had to surrender to.

Review of Chapter 33   'HEATHER'

Maddie: I have been waiting to discuss this chapter ever since we had our very first breakfast meeting. This is when you became larger than life. This is a remarkable chapter. The descriptors are far too many.
Wow....just Wow.

Woody: The next three chapters are so full of love and sorrow and loss that I found myself to be an emotional yo-yo. The innocent trust of a child, a man searching for his lost child and yet so many people around the both of you, never saw the suffering. You did not simply write three beautifully connecting chapters. You lived them, beautifully. With your consent I would like to review them all together.

333

Me: You do know where my heart lives. Yes, I like your suggestion Woody, we will do a three-in-one. After I have a few smokes and brace myself.

I knew that these three next chapters were going to be the most difficult of all of the chapters to discuss. The range of emotions was as broad as the earth itself. I knew I was about to revisit my put-away and well-hidden broken heart.

Maddie: David, you paint your emotions so clearly that there is never a visible brush stroke. I can see Heather peering up at you with her fawn like adoring eyes. That is a beautiful picture of a child but you saw far beyond that. You saw a lost child wanting so desperately just to be seen. Hell, I am 46 years old and a world traveler with a PhD and have more money than I can spend and I also peer up at you and hope that you will notice me too! You have a way that I don't understand but I do greatly enjoy. Heather want's to emulate you and I find myself wanting to do the same. Tell us about your, *way*?

Me: It was easy with Heather. I lost my daughter and I lost my dreams. They both died at the same time. Heather gave me the things that I didn't even know how to dream of. Every parent wants their children to look at them as their trusted protectors. I never had that opportunity. I didn't even know what adoring fawn like eyes looked like, until I meet Heather.

I think she saw her dream daddy. She saw someone who might have special time for her without having to share him with her siblings. She didn't see the stress in the eyes of a man who has four children and a wife to support. She looked right into me, she saw a man who wanted so desperately to be a daddy. I think Heather should be answering your "*way*" question! You tell me how a nine year old child can read a twenty-seven year old adult. No one in her family knew of my lost child. But somehow she did. She ate what I ate because she wanted to be daddy's little girl because she intuitively knew that I needed her.

334

Maddie: I think the wrong person has the PhD in this room. I could not have ever reached that conclusion. Yet it is so clear, you look for the innocence in people when the rest of us mortals look for the bad in those same people. That is your draw, I can't fucking believe that I could be and have been so stupid, all of my life. People with love in their hearts seek you out because they know you are safe, you share the same heart!

People with fear in their hearts avoid you because they know you know their truths. That is your power, which is the entire '*why*' of you!

Maddie started to cry. It was much more than just a cry, it was a cleansing. It was a surrender. It was an awakening.

I came around to her side of the table and kissed both of her wet eyes and said, "I love you." I looked at Woody and smiled as I said, "Stay seated, I will have your drinks delivered in a few minutes, I'm going home for a nap."

I went to the bar and ordered three mimosas in glasses along with a filled pitcher. I walked into Vicki's office and told her she was off duty for the rest of the day. "Young lady, there is another young lady and a gentleman in the conference room that would like to buy you a drink. Grab the spare keys and take the Quinn's up to my office. They will be staying the night there. If you have two full drinks you are to spend the night also. Am I clear?" "Yes sir, crystal clear." I kissed Vicki's forehead and went home for that nap.

CHAPTER 44   THE CIRCUS COMES TO TOWN

The next morning I fully expected to find three severely hungover people. That was not the case. When I walked into the meeting room all three were there with bright smiling, fresh faces. They had two guests sitting with them. Who other than, Gregory and Edna Roberts!

I smiled as I said, "What did you three do last night to bring the Feds to town?" We had a laugh with handshakes and hugs.

Me: Edna, there is nothing quite like hugging a woman and feeling the hard steel of a 1911 in her bra. Condition one I would guess?

Edna: No other way my dear man. And oh yeah, Amanda said to say hello to, 'Skippy.'

Vicki squealed like a little kid as everyone broke out in laughter with that 'Skippy' name. Maddie said, oh I am so going to use that! I like the name Skippy, for you David, it is just so fittingly proper! More laughter as Edna said, "Gregory dear, would you be a love and show everyone the big gun under your coat? You see folks, Amanda doesn't like it when people play with her toys or her pets.

Gregory smiled as he said, "We are here for two days to do a private assessment of a possible business venture here in Duluth and the surrounding area." Enda smiled sweetly as she said, "I would like to meet your mayor and slap the living snot out of her!

336

How dare she snub the President of The United States of America? When he was here three months ago she was at a protest rally and couldn't bother to greet the man that holds the highest office in the land. You don't have to respect the person who holds that office but you damn well better respect the office. It is the very core of the free world. Your mayor lady needs a brief lesson on civic duty, respect of office and common decency. David I want you to come along and guard the door, while her and I have a bit of a chat."

Gregory smiled as he said, "Now dear, you remember the last time you had one of your little 'chats'?

Edna lovingly smiled as she said, "Yes dear, I pistol whipped him and broke his fuckin nose. He grabbed my ass!"

More laughter as Gregory said, "David we need a few moments of your time in your office. Please excuse us everyone."

We went to my office. They were taken back with the layout of the office and the view of the city and the bay of Lake Superior. Gregory started.

Gregory: Dad has retired from the company. Our family thanks you for that. I will retire from the FBI at the first of the year. Amanda, Edna and I will take over the company. Here is where you come in. Mother has all but recovered from her stroke. Our family thanks you for that too! Dad still needs to stay active and wants to start a non-profit business with you at the helm. Note the word '*helm*,' we will get back to that in a minute.

Seems that a fellow from Duluth, Minnesota carries a very big and long stick that reaches all the way to Chicago. Mother had two visitors at the house three days ago. Archbishop Cupich and Father Martin extended their greetings from the Catholic Diocese of Chicago and the Vatican City along with a gentleman named David J. Brown of Duluth, Minnesota. Nice play David, well done indeed! I don't want to know how you did it however. It's not nice to twist the arm of the Catholic Church.

Now mother is thrilled to christen the library as, "The Library of Child Innocence" and the study building as "The Center of Hope." I hope that satisfies you enough so we can all have our lives back?

Now for the non-profit and yes that is your fault too. Father was not aware that the 'sober fishing boat' was the only one of its kind until you raved about what a brilliant concept it was. Now dad wants to have a fleet of charter fishing vessels that uses only sober crews and captains for a floating sober half-way house.

He wants you to figure out the type of boats and equipment you will need to sleep four and a captains quarters. 'You' as in, he wants you to run the entire program. He wants a large fleet of charter fishing boats in all the great lakes, to start with. Every port will have four 'for hire' boats and one each for 'Gold Star' family's and returning vets. The other boat will be completely outfitted for special needs people.

We are here to find a suitable home for the half-way house boat people in the off season. I want to meet Heather and eat some kind of steak sandwich with cheese. I also have to go and buy you a new truck because dad says yours smells like stored-up dead farts from smoking. Don't worry about being bought off, the pickup will be leased in the company name. You and I will do that together, Edna will be looking at a few start-up manufacturing companies to employ the boat people in the off season. You game?

Me: That's a lot to chew. I have only been out on Lake Superior a dozen times or so, with friends. I still don't know how to properly rig up a fishing line and I know nothing about piloting a boat or all the Coast Guard rules and regulations. I would have to hire that talent. I am not interested in the day to day operations of the company. I have a job, I am a writer. One more thing, I will smoke in the new truck too!

Edna: David your answer has to be yes. Dad has turned a huge corner in his and mothers lives. Dad no longer cares about the big money deals, he now cares about the people that don't dare to dream. That's your fault too. Father has never been so calm and so happy. He waits on mother constantly, I think she could do a lot of the things he does for her but she enjoys watching him care for her. They both enjoy the payouts of their love for each other.

Dad has never taken to a man like he has taken to you. He understands that he can trust you like his own family. You saved fathers life. He will, as the rest of us, will always be grateful. Guess you are buying breakfast, we got you out-gunned Skippy!

We took the Quinn's along and enjoyed a spirited breakfast. Edna asked the Quinn's about their time with Missy and if she had settled down. Maddie said that she and Woody have been enjoying the experience. "Missy is taking her assignment very seriously. The only problem she is having is this bully sitting next to you, he took away her cellphone and moved her office and desk into a dungeon. I think this could be a federal case."

Edna looked at me and said, "Gregory, be a dear and please shoot David."

Of course that was the very moment the waitress was pouring coffee. She vanished with a look of horror. I smiled as I said, "You two better drag out your, *'From the Oval Office of the White House'* ID's and badges I'm thinkin' the 'Heat' is about to join us. The Duluth Police Department is not all that fond of you guys." Edna said, "I still want to know what you said to that police captain to make him stand like a wooden soldier. All I got was he didn't like something about bicycles." Gregory said, "I read the police incident report, it had something to do with a guy that drags around a big stick. I believe we are amongst royalty!"

Gregory showed me pictures of the recently poured concrete slabs for two 45,000 square foot grocery stores. On photo had a crane setting pre-cast walls. He thinks they will be operational in three months.

The ladies went house shopping, us boys went boat looking.

From the very moment that the 'sober boat' thing was mentioned, it didn't sit well with me. I didn't say anything at the time because I wanted to process it. I talked with Paul that evening but there was no mention of it. The next morning I had Gregory and Edna join me in my office, we ordered and ate breakfast. I

339

dialed up a video conference with Paul. It was time to dole out Paul's first public spanking. I was not cordial with him.

My first question was, "What the fuck are you doing? Don't answer, I know what the fuck you are doing! You are fragmenting Buddy Boy. You are restless and need to feel your power. Don't bring me your bullshit of rescuing the world. You can't buy sobriety by running a fishing charter operation. Let go of that nonsense and focus on your sobriety and caring for Jane. She needs you, the man. She needs your support with the grocery stores but she mostly needs you. Put away your feel good toys and settle down. Figure out who you really are and improve on that man.

You my friend have a great deal to offer but it won't and can't come from your wallet. Get in your gut and roll around in it like a puppy in mud. I fully realize you're fear behind all that. Stop bull-shitting your sponsor, your family and me. Get honest with yourself and do your forth-step. That is where your true power lies. You can't do right if you don't get right! Do you need more ass-kickin or will that suffice for today?

Paul started to cry, as he said, "No one shoots as straight as you do. You are right about my needing to feel power. I feel like I will never find the real me. I have been running from myself my entire life. I always tried to be what I looked like rather than how I felt like." I smiled as I said, "There can be no hope for you if you keep changing tires expecting the car to start without an engine. Buddy Boy, you know exactly what you need to do, crack open your "Big Book" put on your big boy saddle and get to riding. "Powder River and let her Buck!"

I pushed the stop button and hung-up without another word. I poured myself another cup of coffee and looked at two memorized people. I smiled as I said, "Well that went well.........don't ya think?"

Gregory shook his head and asked, "How in the hell did I miss that?" I gave Gregory my second best grin, "Pal, you were supposed to. He is your dad. Family gets a free pass, they call it 'blind love' for a reason. You have been riding a desk for far too long. Remember when you were a rookie and you were taught that the first thing you look for in a suspect is motive?

Alcoholics are not bad people, we are sick people trying to get well. Never lose sight of that. Your dad is sober but he is not fixed. The both of you and Satan's little sister, need to attend Al-Anon meetings on a regular basis. Not just to stay a step ahead of daddy but for you to come to terms with how his drinking has effected your lives. Alcoholism is a family disease and needs to be treated as such. You both should be smiling your asses off right now. Your dad just had a break-thru, he got caught, with witnesses he owned up to it and he now, once again has a clear path. This is as common as peanut butter on toast. Edna smiled as she said, "Good looking and smart, maybe I won't have my sweet Gregory shoot you after all."

We went to the AA club room and picked up identical Al-Anon books for each of them. We had dinner with Heather at Grandma's Saloon and Deli. Gregory absolutely loved Heathers favorite sandwich.

He smiled as he said, "Please, don't anyone tell dad about this 'Steak-Cheese-French' he will want to open a national chain of this restaurant.' It was good for a laugh as Heather said, "Too late, he loved it too."

The Roberts flew home that evening, humbled and much wiser.

CHAPTER 45   LET'S TRY THIS AGAIN

The next morning I was ready to finish the reviews. The Quinn's appeared to be of the same desire.

Maddie: You were amazing the other day. We were in awe of watching your 'ah-shucks' game with a women who actually protected the president of the United States and her husband who has arrested most of the Chicago mob and put hands on, in the John Gotti' arrest. You never broke stride, you were always in control.

Me: We are back to everyone poops and we all get to be lowered into the same size hole. They are good people and easy to be around. Let's get back to work. We were on Chapter 33 'Heather.'

Woody: That new blouse story was very touching. I could see her bouncing in the car on the way home with her charge account. I could also see your grinning on the way home with thoughts of her father feinting interest with the credit story. That precious little girl knew that you and Liz loved her. Your thinking that there was a slim possibility that Heather was your daughter was gut wrenching. I could feel your torment that had to be haunting. Is it still?

Me: No, I came to terms with that and today it is a non-issue.

342

Maddie: The hockey story with Heather was cute, your inability to enjoy your *'save'* of the hockey player tells me how deep you carried the loss of your patient's lives. Have you ever talked to a professional about it?

Me: Let me know if there is someone that can make me un-hear the moans, whimpers and screams of the dying. Is there someone that can make me un-see what my eyes have seen and now is burnt deep into my brain?
I would very much like to dare to sleep. I have no idea what a 'sweet dreams' would be like. And yes, I am angry about it. I would never encourage anyone to work or volunteer in any of the first responder positions.
There is no honor in destroying your life in the name of strangers who could give a fuck less. How the fuck do you justify paying a lube tech more than a cop who may be laying in the street watching his blood oozing out of his body? How about the firefighter that falls thru a roof and is pinned under timbers that he knows will become his tomb as the flames consume him? How about the paramedic that dies in a horrible crash responding to some junkie that has overdosed for the third time this week? Let's not forget the thousands of first responders that suffer career ending injuries and whose lives will be changed forever. What the fuck kind of counseling will undo that kind of rage? Now are my nostrils flaring? I'm going for a smoke!

I had a few smokes and let go of the tears that I needed to. I went back in to take care of the business at hand.

Me: Maybe now you are closer to understanding suicide in the first responder business. The only way to survive those shit jobs is to detach and unplug. I never had that ability.

Maddie: I don't know what to say. Nothing I've read or nobody I've ever met has ever put it that straight. Thank you. You have given me a lot to think about.

343

Woody: Can we three go for a walk and an ice-cream cone? I am sure we could all use some fresh air and decompress.

We walked to the 'Crabby Shack' for the Ice-cream cones next to the lake walk and watched the waves washing to shore. I could see Woody and Maddie were deep in thought and reflection as they stood in silence holding hands. I felt somewhat guilty for unloading on them but it was time they knew some of the real truths. We walked back to the Corker and got back to business.

Me: We are now on Chapter 34, let's get busy.

Woody: Another beautiful love story. My guts got knotted with you going into the empty house and her bedroom. The innocence of the bedroom scene was beautiful.

Maddie: When you admitted to Heather that you used her to fill the void of your lost daughter and she admitted to knowing of your lost daughter and her trying to be your lost daughter for you, gave me a moment to pause. I felt the purest of all love from the both of you. Incredible story, what is even more incredible is that the story is true!

Me: Yes it was pure. Now chapter 35.

Woody: Your description of looking out onto the bay and finding yourself afloat put me in that same boat, all alone. Packing your bags and leaving without saying goodbye to your love and your dreams was heartbreaking. I understand your attraction to ending it all with those bridge abutments.

Maddie: I echo what Woody said. The letter you tucked under her pillow was the most beautifully tragic and loving piece of prose I have ever read. Ever. That letter will not let me rest. I

344

read it often, it helps me to readjust my selfishness. Thank you for your beautiful gift to us all.

Me: The entire letter, hell the entire chapter were not my words. Yes, I wrote them, and much like my many premonitions it came from somewhere within me but I don't know how or why. I think it is God's way of letting me know that he is with me. Let's call it a day. Tomorrow we will finish. Chapter 36 should tie it all together.

Friday morning couldn't come soon enough for me. I needed to be done with this. Today and tomorrow's meet & greet will complete this book. The Quinn's were a veiled blessing, yes they were at times a pain in the ass but they helped me see things I had not seen before. I got to learn a bit more about myself and it brought a deeper understanding of Gods will for me.

Maddie: I don't want to sit here with you today. I am afraid that we won't ever see you again. I have this nagging fear that you will disappear the same way you appeared. I can't bare that thought of losing you. Please don't walk away from us.

Me: Sweetheart, I am not going anywhere. After tomorrow I will no longer write. It is time to live the life that I have struggled to have. My wounds have healed, I can now look at my scars and draw strength in knowing I have won before and I can and will win again. The two of you had much to do with that. Let's get to it shall we?

Woody: You have suffered a pained life that few could endure. I marvel at your strengths and God's blessings. You brought life back into your cousin Rolene. I will never forget your and hers agreed conversation about you both needed to suffer early in life to survive the pains in your later lives. That did not make any sense when I read that at the time. Today that makes perfectly good sense. I am sorry that your kinship had to grow from your helpless sufferings. I had to get that out, thanks for letting me do that.

Chapter 36 speaks to me of a humble man showing his love for mankind. You told your truths so others may dare to examine theirs. You lovingly separated those 'fresh faced youngsters' from their excuses. That wasn't only crafty, it was brilliant. You gave them permission to enjoy and celebrate their lives.

Maddie: God I hate this. I am so sad that this day has come. Woody and I are no different than those 'fresh faced youngsters.' We as they, had no idea at the time, of how desperately we needed to hear and experience the power in your words. That is what you do, you empower people and you set people free. The selfish part of me wants you to keep writing until the end of time. I can see how you have aged in just the last two months. We know that you sleep very little in your rush to finish the book before you suffer the loss of your vision. We pray that your surgery is a success.
We would like to send you and Heather on a world cruise. I think the rest would do you good and hopefully put a pen back into your hand.

Me: I am a writer and I am suddenly lost for words. Today is the last day of reliving the entire experience of this thing, called life.
There are times and there are days that writing it was every bit as painful as it was living it. Retelling the horrors and the heartache of my life so poorly lived have been revealing and cleansing. The difference today is that I no longer want to die. Today I have faith and my faith brings me hope. As my tag-line reads: *"Hope is all that you need, each day."*

CHAPTER 46   WHEN WILL IT ALL END?

It was hugs and kisses with tears of fear and joy. Maddie asked if I would allow one more favor.

Me: Ask away.

Maddie: I know the garden is your private sanctuary. Can we go out there with you and will you help us smoke one cigarette each? We would like to honor your cousin Rolene and the love you shared for each other. It will be like a prayer vigil for us. We would like to show our respects.

Me: The only time you ever intruded on my space was when you bullied your poor husband to risk a serious ass-kickin to apologize for you. This time it would be my honor to escort the two of you to my hallowed lair. Give me a few minutes and I will be right back for the ceremony.

When I came back into the room Missy and Vicki were standing and grinning like Cheshire Cats! Missy said, "We want to learn how to smoke too, but just one."

The five of us joined arms like the cast of, 'The Wizard of Oz' singing 'Follow the Yellow Brick Road.' When we entered the garden, the bartender was right on cue as he was pouring Mimosas into tulip glasses. He also had a carafe of fresh coffee for me. I looked at the four of my new and dear friends and felt a warmth in my belly. I set my coffee cup down and said, I will be right back.

347

I knocked on the closed door, a female voice answered, 'come in. I stepped into her office and said, "I owe you a drink that I should have bought you almost fifty years ago, would you please join me?"

Alana sprung from her chair and we went out to the garden to join the party.

I stayed up late and had a fitful night's sleep. Something wasn't quite right. It was not frightening but something was somehow out of balance. I kept telling myself that I need to sleep because I have that meeting with the book club people in the morning. I might have slept for two hours and woke up feeling like crap. That feeling of something being not quite right was still nagging at me in the shower. As I was shaving, Heather came into the bathroom and said, "I am meeting my mom for an early breakfast and a morning of shopping before the stores get too crowded." She kissed me and left. I thought that she looked more like she was dressed for an evening of dinner and drinks and dancing. "My god, I am a lucky guy to have such a sweet and beautiful woman."

I dressed in my usual crew neck sweater with a starched white shirt, fed the dogs and headed out for the book club meeting like I have done many of dozens of times before.

I arrived at the Corker Hotel an hour and a half early and parked in the rear like I normally do.

I took the elevator up to my office floor. I had decided last night to turn in my keys to the office after today. I did a 'memory lane' stroll down the hall and entered the office. I walked into each room and scanned every inch from floor to ceiling to lock in the memories of a time that was. I opened the drapes and took my final look at the city and the bay of Lake Superior. I sat at my desk and opened the safe. I took out my unopened five week old overnight package. I stared at the gold embossed return label. I lit a cigarette and leaned deep back into the chair with my head looking up at the ceiling, spinning slowly with the package in my lap. It was time to talk with God.

I knew this life that I have lived of late didn't belong to me. It's just not who I am. I had no business writing the first failed book and now I have just finished the second one. I am not a writer, I am just a guy that told a story on paper. Writers are highly skilled in the craft of prose. I am not that guy. My stories are about the things in life that are foreign to most if not all. I have come to the realization that the suffering victims of abuse along with first responders PTSD problems do not need my help. There are plenty of agencies and support groups to help them. I have been self-indulgent and pompous in believing that I somehow had the answers or at least some of them. I have come to my core truth. The only reason I wrote was to stave off my inevitable suicide. The charade must come to an end. Today must be that day. Is this real or is it the start of a trilogy? Even I don't know!

I left the unopened package on top of the desk so it would be found. I did not look back as I turned off the lights and closed the door.

I still had twenty-five minutes before the thirty-some book club members would be ready for me.

I feel like my best friend has just died, the sadness in my belly is heavy. The thought of a drink, of several drinks was in the forefront of my mind. I went out to the garden and said a quick prayer and asked God to allow me to die sober. I burnt a few more cigarettes and went to my final 'Meet & Greet' event, in this lifetime.

As I stepped into the hallway I saw my lifelong pal Bob Boynton leaning against the wall with his famous "Gotcha Grin," and wearing a suit and tie. Bob does not wear suits. He had a garment bag over his shoulder and said, "No time to explain, put this shit on and hurry." I have known Bobby forever and I trust him, I went to the conference room to change. In the garment bag was one of the vested suits that Paul Roberts bought me. The French cuffed white starched shirt had a set of cuff links in the pocket. I dressed quickly as I asked, 'what the fuck is this' over and over again?

349

As we approached the ballroom Bobby held up short and said, "Everyone is waiting for you and some guy named Paul told me to tell you to, "Shoot your cuffs," whatever the fuck that means. This is your reception, these people here are not here because they admire you. They are here because they respect you and so do I old friend."

Bobby nodded at the two doorman at the ballroom doors and they opened them as we approached. The room was filled well beyond the fire marshal's capacity permit. Standing in front of me was Paul, Gregory and Amanda Roberts. All three were wearing white tuxedos. The room exploded with applause. Amanda said, "I am your escort sir, please come with me." The Roberts men followed behind. Amanda walked me to each person in the front row to greet them. Most of the front row of seats were filled with people in white tuxedos. First it was Vicki, then Missy, Leif, Kirk, Angie, Woody, Maddie, Tami, Mary, and Seth. All in white Tuxedos.

When we reached the center of the row was when I saw Jane and Heather sitting together holding hands, both in white Tuxedos. I kissed Jane hello, Heather stood and hugged me saying, "Sorry that I had to fib you, I love you" and she kissed me. I was so greatly shocked with everything that it brought me to the point of feeling like I was slipping on ice and trying to regain my footing but full well knowing that I was going to land on my ass.

There was an open seat next to Heather that I assumed was mine. Next to that open seat was Mrs. Marge Kivi and next to her was her date, Mr. Axel Kivi, both in white Tuxedos. Marge stood to hug me, Axel also stood to shake hands. I asked him, "Where the hell is your John Deere cap? He gave me a toothy grin and opened his coat lapel to expose the green bill of his John Deere cap. I turned to Marge and said, "I see you made your boyfriend shave again, I can tell by his razor burns. This is my party Mrs. Kivi and it would be a great honor if my guest here would be allowed to wear his John Deere cap today." Marge gave me 'The look' and nodded to Axel. He drew his cap much like a proud ranking cavalryman would his sabre. I could hear Axel giggling as

I worked my way down the line of guests. Next was Mrs. Johnson in her mobility cart. She was holding a framed photograph of Mr. Johnson against her chest as she introduced me to him. I got a kiss on each cheek as she introduced her three sons. Next were her ten grandchildren who all rose in unison wearing their, Class 'A' Uniforms representing their departments and agencies.

At the end of the first row Amanda turned me to face the crowded room and said, "You don't just help people to win their battles, you also win their hearts!" Amanda then turned me to face the orchestra sized stage where I saw the hanging colossal sized banner. It was as long as the stage and four feet wide. It had a picture of me in the center and pictures of both of my book covers on each side of me.

The banner had the very same statement that I use when I personalize a gifted and signed copy of my books for First Responders:
"For all that you do, for the so very many, whose names you don't even know. With admiration and respect." It was signed, "You're Crew."

The banner was covered with sharpie pen signatures. Amanda took me back to Heather. I sat and put my arm around her and leaned into her shoulder. The words of my old friend Stephen came to mind: "Celebrate your blessings and speak of them often." That was the moment that told me, I will live with purpose and joy until the good Lord calls me home.

And I wept.

David J. Brown

To contact David J. Brown
djbrownbooks@gmail.com
To order signed copies of:
'Daddy Had to Say Goodbye'
OR
'Flesh of a Fraud'
Or to schedule David for a speaking engagement
Please visit David's website at davidjbrownbooks.com

God Bless America

43667945R00205

Made in the USA
Middletown, DE
27 April 2019